DIE
FOR
YOU

DIE FOR YOU

A RED THORNE NOVEL

LAUREN JACKSON

PENGUIN BOOKS

PENGUIN BOOKS

UK | USA | Canada | Ireland | Australia
India | New Zealand | South Africa | China

Penguin Books is part of the Penguin Random House group of companies
whose addresses can be found at global.penguinrandomhouse.com

Penguin
Random House
Australia

First published by Lauren Jackson in 2022
This edition published by Penguin Books in 2023

Copyright © Lauren Jackson 2022

The moral right of the author has been asserted.

Cover illustrations by akepong srichaichana/AdobeStock, Dejan Zakic/Unsplash,
GRB Renders/AdobeStock, Jon Butterworth/Unsplash, Jon Moore/Unsplash,
Pedro Lastra/Unsplash and thananya_k/AdobeStock
Original cover design by Ashley Marie
This cover design by Ben Fairclough © Penguin Random House Australia Pty Ltd
Author photograph by Lauren Jackson
Typeset in 10/14.5 pt Sabon by Midland Typesetters, Australia

Printed and bound in Australia by Griffin Press, an accredited
ISO AS/NZS 14001 Environmental Management Systems printer

A catalogue record for this
book is available from the
National Library of Australia

ISBN 978 1 76134 515 9

penguin.com.au

We at Penguin Random House Australia acknowledge that Aboriginal and Torres Strait Islander
peoples are the Traditional Custodians and the first storytellers of the lands on which we live
and work. We honour Aboriginal and Torres Strait Islander peoples' continuous connection to
Country, waters, skies and communities. We celebrate Aboriginal and Torres Strait Islander
stories, traditions and living cultures; and we pay our respects to Elders past and present.

To those who never grew out of their vampire era.

Thank you for choosing to read *Die For You*,
I really hope you enjoy it!

Some of the content may be triggering to some readers.
Content warnings include profanity, explicit sexual scenes,
and descriptive scenes of death, violence, and brutality.

PLAYLIST

'Shivers' – Ed Sheeran
'Never Say Never' – The Fray
'Die First' – Nessa Barrett
'Hold On' – Chord Overstreet
'Do It For Me' – Rosenfeld
'Closer' – Samuel Jack
'Die For You' – The Weeknd
'False God' – Taylor Swift
'Love In The Dark' – Adele
'Killer' – Valerie Broussard
'I'm Yours Sped Up' – Isabel LaRosa

PART I

1

RAYA

The Survivor

ON THE DEATH CERTIFICATE, it states my sister died a year ago. Who would have thought a single piece of paper could hold so much weight? There was a funeral, there is a gravestone. But there is no body.

With a sigh, I look around the small apartment that has been my home for as long as I can remember. Warm, light, and cosy. My happy place. The one space that is filled with all the things, and the people, I love most in the world. At least it was.

Once upon a time, the thought of leaving this place would have had me on the floor in tears, but that version of me feels like a lifetime ago. People have always told me how overly emotional I am, that I feel too much, that I'm too empathetic. Not anymore. While I was the only one to survive the accident, I know a piece of me died that day too.

My mind floods with memories; running around the apartment, getting into all kinds of mischief. From children, to teenagers, these walls watched us grow into adults.

Now, there is just me.

I turn around slowly, remembering how it once looked. Now, everything is gone. The paintings, the lounges, the cabinets we assembled as a family. Looking to my right, I trail my fingertips down several markings on the wall, each one a new milestone as we grew up.

Cora and me. My sister. My best friend.

There's a tightening in my chest at the thought of her, and I distract myself by gripping the strap of the bag, feeling the weight of the box inside it. When I was clearing out the apartment, I discovered my sister's journals. Thick notebooks filled with Cora's messy scrawl. I know I should never read my sister's journals, but she's gone, and I'm glad I read them – they changed everything. Now, I carry the box everywhere I go. A gift, a curse – I haven't decided which yet – but the moment I started reading them, I knew my life would never be the same.

Pulling the front door closed behind me, I take a deep breath in an attempt to prepare myself.

You can do this. You owe it to her. To yourself.

Forcing myself to walk, I stride down the dingy hallway, refusing to look back. Eager for a distraction, I let my eyes roam around, taking everything in, knowing this is the last time I will ever walk this path. It's an eerie feeling, though it's not until I enter the elevator, that it starts to sink in. This is the last time I'll take this elevator, listening to it whirr and clunk, wondering, like I always do, if today will be the day it breaks down, trapping me inside.

Despite the heartache, I allow myself to feel everything, just for a few moments. Years of memories spill forward to the forefront of my mind. All the good times, the bad, and everything in between. Just when the despair reaches an overwhelming level, the elevator doors stagger open. Releasing a shaky breath, I leave those painful memories inside the lift as I walk out with my chin held high, feeling strangely cleansed.

Alex is waiting for me outside, standing there, his back against the brick wall, dressed all in black – as usual. His hands are dug deep inside his pockets as he gazes across the road, oblivious to my arrival. His unruly, midnight-black hair is kept in check by the black beanie he has pulled down over it.

'Hey.' I say, walking towards him.

As he slowly turns and looks at me, I see sympathy sweep across his expression when he notices my watery eyes. I swallow thickly, clenching my teeth and trying to keep a grasp on the grief threatening to break through.

'You okay?' he asks, with a slight frown.

'Fine.' I reply, wishing I had a more convincing poker face.

He nods, keeping his thoughts to himself, though I can tell by the slight raise of his eyebrow that he doesn't believe me. Silently, he picks up his bag from where it rests at his feet, and together we begin the short trek to the train station. It's an unusually cold night tonight, and for a while I'm distracted by the puffs of mist that release as I breathe. I find it somehow comforting, like a reminder that I'm still here. I'm alive.

Don't look back. Don't look back. Don't look back.

'Are you sure you want to do this?' Alex asks as if he can hear my thoughts. 'This is the last chance to turn back.' Reaching into his pocket, he withdraws a packet of cigarettes and offers me one before taking one himself.

'I'm sure,' I nod firmly, waving off his outstretched hand. 'Are you?'

'Yeah.' He holds the lighter against the cigarette, puffing as he encourages the flame to take, the orange embers bright in the darkness of the night. I watch him from the corner of my eye as he inhales deeply, holding it in for a moment before blowing out a cloud of smoke. 'Life sucks for me here, it will probably suck for me there. Doesn't really matter where I go.'

'Inspirational,' I reply dryly.

He grins. 'I should put that on a bumper sticker.'

'Totally.'

I've only known Alex for a couple of months. I discovered an online forum – *They Walk Among Us* – dedicated to people seeking answers to the unusual and unexplainable things happening around them. Knowing that my sister's disappearance was unusual, I thought the forum could help me uncover the truth about what really happened. Yet what I discovered was beyond anything I could have imagined. I mean, these people talk about vampires and other creatures as though they're real. At first, I thought they were joking, but the more I read, the more I realised that maybe the things I'd believed only existed in movies are in fact real.

And that was where I met Alex.

Alex went on the forum after experiencing a bizarre situation when travelling a few months ago. He woke up in an isolated park with blood stains on his shirt, and no memory of how he got there. Reading about that made goosebumps scatter across my skin. Yet our actual friendship started with an argument after I reposted an article I had read discussing the origin of vampires. He disagreed with the information I shared and what sources I used to obtain it. Finally, we compromised and concluded that some of the articles were accurate, and some were not. The one thing we could both agree on was that arguing was pointless, and we quickly became friends as we dove deep into a bunch of theories we'd both read about. After talking every day for a few weeks, we decided to meet for coffee. That's when I finally explained to him what I thought was the truth behind my sister's disappearance – and that I'm using her journals as a guide to finding her.

I never intended to bring Alex – or anyone – with me, but as soon as he suggested it, I realised it would be so much easier having someone else there with me. Safety in numbers is always the smart way to go about things and having company wouldn't be so bad. The support Alex has given me since we met has really helped me to stop doubting my sanity. Not once has Alex ever called me crazy for the thoughts and theories I've shared with him. Maybe because we're both crazy.

Noticing my lower lip trembling, he wraps an arm around me, drawing me close to him. The scent of his aftershave drifts over me; the warm, spicy scents of cinnamon and sandalwood. Sure, I hadn't known Alex long, but his presence, and his signature scent, have become a comfort to me. I'm not stupid, I know that I'm attaching myself to him, because everyone else has left me, but I am powerless to resist it. And I don't want to. Considering Alex doesn't have many people in his life either, I think he feels much the same way.

Slowly, he drops his arm back to his side, and I offer him a tight-lipped smile of thanks, not quite trusting myself to speak yet without bursting into tears. He smiles back, a dimple appearing in his left cheek. As we walk, my mind runs back through everything that has led me to this point. After all this time, it's still hard to make sense of, and I am becoming increasingly frustrated. All I can recall was sitting in the car – me, mum, and Cora. The next memory was waking up inside the wreckage of our car; one of us conscious, one of us missing, one of us dead. I was the conscious one.

'The Survivor', the newspaper articles dubbed me as. I didn't feel like one, not when my mother was dead, and my sister seemed to have vanished into thin air.

Even if Cora was thrown from the car in the accident, she would have been found, injured. But no. Instead, she disappeared without a trace – and I am determined to find out what happened.

My thumb absently circles over the scar on my left arm. A half-moon-shaped indentation that almost looks like a small bite or a deep scratch. I figured it must have happened during the accident. I'm sure it is only in my head, but it tingles whenever I think of my sister.

Two months ago, I saw her. Some viral video showed a guy backflipping from a moving vehicle in a bustling street banked with traffic. Yet, it was the sight of a girl walking in the background of the video which caught my attention. Even though it was posted after my sister was formally announced dead – it was her. I know it was.

Because she has a distinctive birthmark on her face. A small line across the top of her cheek, looking like a straight-lined freckle. We were often mistaken for twins growing up and that was an easy way people could tell us apart. Tall, with long dark hair and soft green eyes, framed by dark, thick lashes. That's the reason I have a violet stripe in my hair, as we were both sick of people getting us mixed up all of the time.

As soon as I saw the video, I messaged the poster, who told me it was filmed in a town called Red Thorne, which is the first stop on my journey.

I'm pulled from my thoughts by the sound of the train approaching. Alex drops his cigarette to the ground, grinding it with his shoe before picking it up and tossing it into the bin. We walk onto the platform as the train pulls in, and exchange matching looks of foreboding as we step into the carriage.

The train isn't as busy as I thought it might be, given that it is early evening. We are later than the peak traffic time, but I still thought there would be more people out and about.

Weaving down the aisle, we find a pair of seats facing each other towards the back of the carriage. I drop down across from him, dumping my bag beside me before nervously turning the thin black ring on my finger. I don't remember when my sister gave it to me, but since she disappeared, I haven't taken it off.

Alex props his feet up on the edge of the seat beside me, pulling out a book from his bag. He leans back, half-turning his back against the window as he gets comfortable, since we will be

travelling for a few hours. In turn, I take out my laptop and place
it onto the small table between us. I bring up the forums on Red
Thorne, even though I've read through them all countless times.

Red Thorne. The place where people disappear.

Intrigued, I clicked on that one. Leaning forward, I rest my
chin in my hand as I drag my finger across the mouse pad, scrolling through all the comments.

SoulEater888: I can't believe people still say they don't believe
when these types of towns exist. Red Thorne isn't the only place
around. Wake up people, they walk among us.

Clicking on this, I read the comments.

ThatGirlSteph: What walk among us?

SoulEater888: The supernatural.

ThatGirlSteph: Like what?

SoulEater888: Vampires. Werewolves. Witches. God knows what
else.

SugarPlum71: I hope they're hot. Like in the books and shows.

SoulEater888: There's nothing 'hot' about people being murdered
in cold blood.

WhiteFox89: Proof, or it didn't happen.

SoulEater888: *Attachment*

Clicking on the attachment, I narrow my eyes, scanning over
the articles. It's a collection of newspaper articles reporting missing people, violent attacks, and mysterious deaths.

I don't know what any of this has to do with my sister, if

anything at all. What I do know is that she was the girl in the video, and if someone took her, I'm going to fight to get her back.

Then there is the other thought. The one I hate letting myself even consider. The fact that she may have willingly done this. A lump lodges in the back of my throat. It's honestly unthinkable. That she would *choose* to leave me . . . That my sister could be so cold as to force me to return to our apartment after losing her and our mother on the same day. I wouldn't wish that kind of pain and loneliness on my worst enemy – and I couldn't let myself believe Cora would have wished it on me, despite what her journals may say.

Swallowing thickly, I turn my attention back to the forum and continue reading.

ThatGirlSteph: Why would anyone willingly go there?

SoulEater888: To die.

ThatGirlSteph: Damn . . .

SoulEater888: Or to become one.

ThatGirlSteph: Become what, exactly?

SoulEater888: A monster.

The comments stick with me. More than I'd like to admit. My mind wanders to some dark places because of it. Between these comments and reading my sister's journals . . . I've wondered about *things*.

Things that I thought impossible.

Rummaging through my backpack, I grab one of Cora's journals. Flicking through it, I find the page I tabbed.

He is so handsome. The most handsome man I have ever laid my eyes on. And he noticed me!

I can't stop thinking about the way his mouth inched upward into a smirk as he beckoned me over. His hands were cold to touch. When they slid over my skin . . . I lost my mind.

He is alluring. Addictive. Intoxicatingly handsome.

Did I mention handsome?

Right there and then, I wanted to be his. More than anything I have ever wanted in my life.

They say it's evil. Wrong. Selling your soul to the devil.

I don't care.

My soul is his to claim.

An icy shiver runs down my spine as I read over her words. Shaking my head, I slam it shut and shove it back into the bag.

Alex raises an eyebrow but doesn't lift his gaze from his book.

I close the thread and find another one.

Number One Rule: Be Prepared

BlackHeart: If you do decide to visit, ALWAYS be on the lookout for a predator. Armour yourself. Be smart.

NateDawg11: With what?

BlackHeart: Pure silver. Have it in liquid form. Spray directly into their eyes. Blinding them is your best shot at getting away.

NateDawg11: How do you liquify silver?

BlackHeart: Here's a tutorial.

BlackHeart: *Attachment*

BlackHeart: Always remember, if you run, it's only encouraging them to fall into their natural instincts. To hunt.

NateDawg11: So . . . don't run?

BlackHeart: Weaken them, then get to a public place. The last thing you want to do is run and get your blood pumping. That will just make you more enticing to them.

NateDawg11: Never thought of it like that.

BlackHeart: Most don't. They're no longer here because of it.

Taking a deep breath, I settle back into my seat and distract myself by gazing out the window. It's too dark to see much of the countryside. A blur of passing trees, road signs, and the occasional petrol station.

Closing the laptop, I shift in my seat, trying to mimic Alex's position as I close my eyes, hoping that I can get a little sleep before we arrive. I drift in and out over the next few hours, spurring awake every time the train jolts.

My eyes are aching when we reach our stop; they feel dry and tired. I rub them with the heels of my palms as I get to my feet, a huge yawn escaping me. Alex picks up my bag, handing it to me.

'You've been reading those forums again?' Alex guesses.

'A little.'

'You'll never sleep again if you keep reading them.'

'I had nightmares long before I started reading them.' I exhale as I stretch, hearing a few bones crack. 'Exhaustion is a part of my personality at this point.'

Alex cracks a smile. 'Do you want to get a coffee before we get to the apartment?'

Shaking my head, I slide the bag strap further up my shoulder. 'I just want to get there and crash. Thanks though.'

Nodding, he leads the way off the train, along the platform and out onto the sidewalk, with me right behind him. Here we are. Red Thorne. It's unusually quiet. Swallowing, I let my eyes scan the streets, noticing that most of the streetlights are blown. My eyes move to the giant sign that looms over us.

'*Welcome to Red Thorne. A town you will never want to leave!*'

Alex booked us an Uber, but the wait for it has me feeling jittery. I don't like standing here in the dark, with no one else around. I feel like we're sitting targets.

'Imagine if a vampire swooped in and ate us right now. Before we even got to the apartment,' he whispers, so close to my ear that I startle, whipping my head around to glare at him.

I give him a deadpan stare. 'That is really *not* funny.' His grin tells me he thinks otherwise. 'You know vampires don't *eat* people. Not exactly.'

'Mmhmm,' he says as he strides ahead, not seeming as terrified or alert as I am.

'Besides, you're the one who booked the ride at this ridiculous hour!' I hiss.

'This was the only time there was. Same time, every day.'

My eyes dart to his. 'What? Really?'

'Yeah.'

'You never mentioned that before.'

'I didn't really think much of it,' he shrugs.

My heart thumps loudly in my ears. 'You're saying only one train comes into town and it is at this exact time, every night?' I repeat, my breathing coming out in short, sharp spurts, my eyes quickly scanning the area around us, as if something might jump out this very second.

'Yes . . .' Alex trails off, swinging his gaze to meet mine, suddenly losing the playful smirk he was wearing before.

A stick snaps somewhere in the dark off to our left, and with how quiet it is, it sounds as loud as a gunshot. I yelp, clutching Alex's arm. I open my mouth to say more, when I catch sight of the Uber cruising down the road toward us. I sigh with relief, much to Alex's amusement, though at least he tries to hide it. We climb into the car, and while the driver seems friendly enough, I hold on to my can of mace just to be on the safe side.

'You kids better be careful being out and about at night in a town like this,' the man says, giving me a side-eye look that makes me even more concerned than I was before. A long scar runs downward from the corner of his mouth. My eyes linger on it for a moment before I quickly look away.

'I came prepared,' I say, withdrawing a knife from the shoulder bag I have with me.

The driver doesn't seem as phased as I hoped. He gives me a wry smile. 'You know how to use that, sweetheart?'

'Yes,' I reply, narrowing my eyes. Pointing the end of it, I jab it through the air. 'Aim and stabby stab.'

Alex snorts in the backseat and the man's smile widens, insulting my confidence further.

'What?' I ask, looking over my shoulder at Alex who snickers at me.

'Nerves make you act weird,' he points out. Only his mouth and chin are visible in the dim lights, casting the rest of him in a dark shadow.

'Shut up.'

'Just sayin'.'

Frowning, I turn to face the front once more and silence settles in the car. As relaxed as the driver appears, I keep the knife clutched in my hand, feeling extremely stupid for doing so, but I don't want to make assumptions that may have me killed.

I peer over to double check that the right address is showing on his map before I lean back and stare out the window. The real estate agent mailed the keys to us last week after we'd paid our deposit and the first month's rent. I have no idea what the apartment looks like, but I don't care. I just want a bed and a place that has functioning utilities.

Through the window all I can see are tall, dark buildings that seem ominous and unwelcoming as we pass. A chill shivers within my bones, spreading throughout my body and growing colder the closer we get to the centre of town. When the driver pulls up along the curb, Alex and I exchange a glance before we climb out of the car.

Gathering our bags, we pause on the pavement, staring up at the building that is our new home. It's an old Victorian mansion that looks like it is about twenty years overdue for renovations. Most of the windows have curtains drawn over them, as if the building is closing itself away from the outside world.

Dark cobblestones cover the exterior. When the headlights of the car swing across the building, several bats fly from the roof.

'Is it just me or does this place have a really empty feel to it?' I whisper, trying to hide my apprehension, but the anxiety inside me rises to the point of nausea.

'It's late, Raya. Most people would be sleeping.'

I nod – it makes sense, and I try to let his words reassure me, even though I'm still holding my breath. And the knife.

It's eerily silent as we walk through the lobby – there's not a person in sight. I know Alex said people are likely sleeping, but it's the absence of any presence at all that I find alarming. I tell myself it's just my imagination working overtime, but our steps sound too loud as we walk across the foyer towards the single elevator. As soon as Alex presses the up button, the doors open, and we step inside. It silently carries us to the fourth floor.

I glance up and down the dimly lit corridor as Alex unlocks the door. I can't get inside fast enough, and I am surprised to find the apartment seems quite cosy as I casually walk through, inspecting it. It has two bedrooms at opposite ends, with a living room and kitchen separating them, and I already know I want the bedroom furthest from the front door. The place is dark and a little cramped, with long dark curtains blocking out any natural light that will enter during the day. The bathroom and laundry are set off to the back corner. Some of the tension leaves me when I hear the door shut and the lock click into place.

We're here. We made it.

After we eat dinner together – two-minute microwave meals that melted during the train ride – I shower and walk into my room. Swinging my bag onto the bed, I begin to unpack. I'm impressed that my wardrobe space is more generous than I expected.

The room feels a little less stark seeing my things spread around it. If I was planning to stay here for a while, I would love to put up wall hangings and have a few plants on the windowsill, and of course, my bookshelves. That will be one of the things I miss the most about my family's apartment, not that much of it would fit in here.

The last item I pull out is a small picture frame. Cora, mum, and I smile up from the faded photograph. Tears spring to my eyes as I trace their faces. Placing the frame onto the bedside table, I sniffle, wiping the tears that had spilled down my cheeks with the back of my hand.

Feeling drained, I collapse onto the bed, kicking the now-empty bag to the floor. It lands with a hollow thump. The mattress is a little hard, nothing like the one back home, but it will do. It's not like I sleep a lot anymore.

With a sigh, I roll onto my side and stare out at the black, misty sky. Nothing about this place feels anything like home. I guess that's because it isn't. This place holds secrets and things I can't even begin to understand, but I'm not leaving without answers.

It feels surreal to be here, like a dream I'm expecting to wake up from. I lightly touch the ring on my finger.

'I'll find you,' I whisper to myself, my sister's pretty eyes appearing in my mind. *Even if I die trying.*

2

HUNTER

The Protector

I STARE DOWN AT THE corpse as I step over it. Male, late twenties, his neck bearing a bloody wound, and his once-white shirt now soaked with blood.

It's late. Cold, dark, and eerily silent, with most of the streetlights blown out, casting the road into a deep shadow. Red Thorne is a quiet place. Not many people venture out when the sun disappears – for this very reason. A dead body has been dumped off to the side of a footpath, bordering on the edge of the woods.

'They're getting messy,' Theo growls, a furious flash darkening his stare. He shoots his gaze over at me, the frown deepening the shadow over his features as he appears to study my face carefully. He's a total pain in my ass – and he also happens to be my best friend. Someone I simultaneously love and hate, if that's even possible.

'What do you know about this?' he barks, gesturing toward the messy remains of the body at our feet.

'As much as you do,' I reply with a sigh. 'I'm sick of spending my nights cleaning up after them. I have better things to do with my time.'

'Oh yeah? Like what?' Theo raises an eyebrow, the corner of his mouth curving upward. 'Studying?'

I give him a flat look. 'Yeah, actually.'

'You're such a fucking bore, man,' he rolls his eyes. 'I give you eternal life and you waste it by going to university and actually *studying*.'

'You make it sound like I asked for it?'

The fury flashes once more in those stormy eyes of his. This is the constant battle between us. He thinks I owe him for this life. But he made the decision for me. It's not something I would have chosen. He took that right from me.

'Asshole,' he mutters.

'Besides, what's wrong with getting an education? Just because I'm not going to die any time soon, doesn't mean I should waste the time I do have. I've always wanted to do something with my life, only now I have longer to do it. Otherwise, we're just existing, and what's the point of that?'

'I'm not having this conversation with you again.'

'Then stop bitching about it.'

We stare at each other for a long moment, equally as stubborn. Theo clears his throat, which he always does when he's about to cave, and we both return our attention to the dead man at our feet.

'Next time I see one of those douchebags, I'm going to rip their heart from their chest and put it in a pie,' he says through gritted teeth.

'You don't like pie.'

'That's not the point I was trying to make.'

Crouching low, I survey the corpse more closely. I pick up a variance in scent as I carefully inhale. The strongest smell lingers over the neck wound, but there's another, more subtle scent and I trace it eagerly to its origin. Another wound. I yank up his shirt and reveal a second bite.

'Oh shit,' Theo groans, glaring down at it.

Flicking my gaze between the two wounds, I notice the difference in the holes that pierce the skin.

'Two vampires,' I say.

Theo crouches beside me and inspects the second wound, his gaze sharp. His messy blond hair looks dark with the lack of lighting, his body composed of tall, hard, lean muscle. Winding, thick lines that run over his pale skin, and tattoos decorate his long arms, similar to my own.

'He's made another.'

'It could be more than that.'

'Do you know something? Are you holding out on me?' Theo demands, rising.

I groan inwardly as I follow suit. 'No, I'm not holding out on you.' I glance around, making sure we are still alone. My heightened hearing always detects people beyond my line of sight, but I can't help ensuring we aren't being watched. 'I want answers just as much as you. And for this to stop.'

'You're not the one with a target on your back,' Theo points out, glaring up at me – he's a few inches shorter than me, much to his annoyance.

'It makes no difference to me whether the target's on you, or me – I would still approach this situation the same way.'

He grunts, which is his way of letting me know he's happy with my answer. 'Well, what should we do with this one?' he asks.

'Burn it.'

'Good idea.'

Theo bends at the knees and scoops the dead man up and over his shoulder effortlessly before shooting off into the protection of the dense woods. I follow him. I can't believe they'd so carelessly left the corpse on the footpath, out in the open for anyone to find. *Assholes*. Blood has dripped over the grass, and I drag my foot over it, flattening the grass until the blood blends in with the dirt.

Jetting forward, I stick closely behind Theo until we are far enough amongst the trees not to be seen or heard.

Withdrawing a lighter from my jeans, I watch Theo throw the body roughly to the ground. His movements are at lightning speed, scouring the trees to find the gasoline we'd stashed after the last body we had to dispose of.

He douses the body generously before cautiously backing away, his eyes on the lighter in my hand. I wait until he's in the safe zone before flicking it on and tossing it toward the body, while simultaneously hurtling myself backwards to a safe distance. The body erupts into flames, the strong stench of burning flesh filling my nose. My insides coil in repulsion, and yet a hunger gnaws at me so violently I stagger slightly. Theo's head whips towards me, his eyes narrowing.

'What was that?'

'Nothing.'

'When was the last time you fed?' He asks, and by his tone, I can tell he has already guessed what I'm about to say.

'Two days ago.'

'You're kidding?' he growls angrily, striding towards me while giving the burning body a wide berth. 'Do you have a bloody death wish?'

I shrug. 'We ran out of blood bags.'

Suddenly, Theo is right in my face, but I don't let it deter me. I stare down at him, unflinching. His marble skin glows in the pale moonlight, and his eyes are silver-grey, the same colour mine should be, but instead, mine are so dark that they're almost black since I'm way overdue for a feed.

'I don't think I need to remind you that there's plenty of food sources, you know, walking by you every second of the day.'

'My classmates?' I ask. 'Oh wait, no, my professors?'

'Don't be a brat,' he spits. 'Act like the fucking vampire you are. Stop being an embarrassment to your kind.'

'I don't tell *you* how to live, Theo.'

'Because I don't need to be told.'

I look away, and step around him, watching the flames dance across the remains of the corpse, consuming every inch of it. I feel the heat of his gaze as he stares at me, but I refuse to turn around. It's not until the fire begins to subside, when there's nothing left to feed it, that I turn and flee without a word, leaving him in my dust trail.

When I finally slow, I stumble, falling to my knees. I clutch at the dirt as I steady myself, needing a moment before I stand. When I do, I feel woozy and disorientated and I take a moment to right myself, to refocus. It's dangerous that I'm this weak and light-headed being this close to town – especially with everything that is going on.

The sound of loud music piques my interest as it weaves through trees towards me, coaxing me back to my feet. Laughing, talking, the sound of footsteps, of bodies moving.

A party.

Usually, I wouldn't have an issue walking by it and ignoring it completely. But I have been disorganised and lazy this week. Now I'm paying the consequences, because I need to feed, and having vulnerable targets this close is too much temptation.

I pause for a moment, weighing up the options. I don't want to be this kind of vampire. The stereotypical predator that hunts humans. Yet, the hunger rises, clogging my throat, burning my lungs, and I know I've left it too long.

I hate this. I hate myself, and every part of this. The feeding. Taking from people. Innocent people. I can't stand it.

My body moves effortlessly as I speed through the night, feeling the air rushing past me. Within seconds, I'm walking into the party, smoothing my hair and straightening my jacket. I'd seen this party advertised around campus but paid no mind to it. I don't go out much, and I'd rather be anywhere except here right now, but desperate times and all that.

The first couple of years after I turned, I partied a lot, but I quickly realised how out of control I could get, and each time I did, I felt less like myself.

I refuse to be like *them*.

As I step into the room, I feel overwhelmed by the sudden onslaught on my senses, feeling my head growing lighter by the second. Clenching my jaw, I try not to gag over the smell of sweat and alcohol that permeates the air when suddenly a high-pitched voice screeches over the noise towards me.

'Hey!'

I silently curse. I should never be startled by a human approaching. Ever.

'You came!'

Turning, I force a smile on my face as I come face to face with Adriana, a girl who has shamelessly flirted with me for weeks. Not that I haven't enjoyed the mild distraction, though her insistence on inviting me to every social event on the calendar is wearing thin.

I try to focus on her pale blonde hair and blue-grey eyes, but I'm instead drawn to the delicate skin of her long and graceful neck. Her skin is so fair, I can almost see the veins beneath, and I am momentarily hypnotised by the pulsation of her skin at the base of her neck, keeping time with her heartbeat. Despite my best efforts, I feel myself start to salivate, and I clench my hands into tight fists, welcoming the pain as my fingernails dig into my palms.

'Are you not even going to say hello?' she chides, fluttering her eyelashes at me, forcing my attention back to her face.

'Hey,' I force myself to say with what I'm hoping is a charming smile. Her eyes glaze slightly, and I release a breath, relieved my charm still has an effect, even in my weakened state.

'What brings you out tonight?' She beams happily, enjoying finally having my attention.

Why can't I enjoy this? Why can't I be normal?

'I wanted to see you,' I say, forcing a relaxed smile onto my face even though I'm talking through clenched teeth. 'I felt bad for not coming out those other times you asked.'

Her eyebrows fly up, though she quickly tries to hide her surprise. I've been nothing but closed off to her since we met. But hunger changes everything.

'Oh,' she grins, a slight blush colouring her cheeks. 'Can I get you something to drink?'

My gums are aching to let my fangs descend and I struggle to control their premature release. 'Yes. Please.'

I follow her as she sashays over to the bar and mixes us both drinks. I notice how strong she makes them, but I'm thankful for it. Alcohol is great to help curb the cravings, although it'll affect me more in this weakened state.

Adriana is talking, but there's a ringing in my ears that is making it impossible to pay attention. My fingers tap restlessly against the bench as she finishes making the drinks, totally oblivious to my internal struggles.

My mouth waters as I absently inch closer. My gums tingle as my fangs threaten to descend and I quickly swallow, pushing the thoughts back but I can feel myself losing the battle. With a quick shake of my head, I clear my throat, and try to focus on the girl in front of me.

Innocent. Kind. Pure.

You can walk away. It'll be hard, but you can do it. One voice whispers. Just do it. She won't die, nor will she remember anything ever happened to her.

Shaking my head, I try to fight the dark thoughts taking over my mind.

Again, my gaze drops to the smooth skin of her slender neck. Heaviness weighs on my chest, like someone standing on top of me, constricting my airway. Unable to contain myself any longer, I growl, reaching forward as I grab her wrist and drag her out into the backyard. The cold and windy night is the harsh slap back to reality that I need, although my bloodlust still roars through my veins.

'Is everything okay?' she asks breathlessly, stumbling to keep up with my long strides. I can hear the slight tremor in her voice, like she's unsure whether she should be thrilled or scared. As the alcohol sloshes over the side of the cups and onto her dress, she curses. 'Hunter, what the hell?'

I slap the drinks out of her hands, and she yelps, staggering back against the brick wall behind her and hitting her head. Generally, I'm much more subtle about it, but I can't help myself. Gripping her face, I lean in, gaining access to her neck.

My fangs release and sink deep into her flesh before she has the chance to protest. The warmth of her blood coats my tongue and I groan as a shudder of pleasure courses through me. Wedging my knees between hers, I drink deeply and hear her gasp against my ear, her fingers tightening around my shirt. A breathy moan escapes her and when I step back, her expression is one of blissful content as she stares over my shoulder, out into the night.

Rubbing my pointer finger on the edge of a fang, I nick open the skin on my finger and press it to her lips, forcing my blood into her mouth. Instantly, the wound heals, and the cloudy expression intensifies.

'Thanks,' I mutter, licking my lips, stepping back. 'That was fun.'

'Yeah,' she murmurs.

'See you around.' I leave her there and disappear into the shadows, feeling rejuvenated and not in the least bit remorseful after seeing how pleased she looked. Strolling through the trees, I glance up at the bright moon overhead. *Ah. Full moon.* No wonder I felt so much weaker than usual – I always have less control on these nights. I keep my ears trained for any movements as I walk, knowing the full moon always brings out the creatures of the night. And not just us vampires.

I jolt as a scream pierces the air and I turn towards the rustling of leaves, the groans of a struggle, and a final scream for help. I take off in a blur, hurtling through the trees before coming to a stop at the edge of the clearing.

Standing there is a darkly dressed figure, wrapped in shadows, leaning over a girl with volumes of dark hair cascading around her. The hairs on the back of my neck stand. Another vampire. One that isn't in control.

I shoot forward, knocking him back with an easy swipe of my hand, while simultaneously reaching for the falling girl. She screams again and I catch her before she hits the ground. Across her neck is a gaping wound and I appreciate the fact that I just fed.

A solid whack to the head pulls my focus back and I grunt, taking the hit. I gently lower the trembling girl before I spin around and face the vampire. With a hiss, he bears his fangs, still dripping with the blood – the smell is distracting.

'You're going to regret that, Hunter.'

He knows my name. Interesting.

'Am I?' I raise an eyebrow, holding his gaze, daring him to try and hit me again so I can drive him into the ground. His eyes scan over me, as though sizing me up. I notice the miniscule shift of his foot, and my eyes narrow as I brace myself. Instead of coming at me, he turns on his heel and flees into the night. I consider chasing him for a moment, but quickly dismiss it as the girl whimpers behind me.

Crouching down, I reach out my hand. She flinches, scampering backwards, crying out.

'Hey,' I say softly. 'Look at me.'

Timidly, she raises her head, her dark hair falling across her eyes.

'You went for a walk and got lost. You feel a little disorientated, but you're okay.' I tell her, pushing my coercion onto her as strongly as I can. Her stare softens and she blinks slowly and sleepily as she nods.

'Yeah.' She agrees, her voice soft before she yawns. 'I got lost.'

I heal her wound before helping her to her feet. I decide to lead her back to the party, and she's quiet as we walk. As soon as the other revellers are in sight, I gently push her forward and quickly leave, but not before I hear her friend cry out in relief as they reunite. She must have been missing for a while.

Within seconds I'm home, and music is drifting out the open window. I walk inside and stop, staring at my friend and his girlfriend, with their fangs sunk into the neck of the human girl between them as she stares straight through me, blissfully unaware.

Crimson ribbons run down her pale, slender neck. Theo's hand trails up the girl's thigh, as Lucy leans in closer, her raven-black hair running like a midnight river down her back. The smell of fresh blood is potent in the air, raising a tsunami-level hunger inside of me.

I say nothing as I pass through and head upstairs to my room, deciding to tell them about my encounter with the baby vamp once they're a little less preoccupied.

Sprawled across my bed, I'm lost in my own thoughts, watching the moon from the window. My bedroom is my safe place. Simple, dark, and quiet – for the most part. When people leave me alone, anyway. Laying on my bed, listening to the sounds of the night makes me feel at peace after the craziness of the evening. At least for a few moments.

The creak of a floorboard is the only giveaway of Theo's arrival. I glance over to find him leaning against the doorframe.

His arms are folded over his chest, and he still has a dab of blood on the corner of his mouth. It's distracting and I wonder how it tastes, before mentally scolding myself. I hate that I have this nagging thought all the time. The line always wants to be crossed. It's *begging* me to.

'Didn't want to join us for dinner?' he asks.

Scoffing, I stare back out the window. 'Stop acting like you're a monster, Theo.'

'We *are* monsters.'

'We don't have to be.'

'You wouldn't have said that five years ago.'

'Five years ago was different.' I sigh. I don't enjoy thinking about the first twelve months after I was turned. It's basically a blur anyway. A whirlwind of blood, drinking, and reigning havoc. 'What do you want?'

'Have you fed?'

'Yes.'

'Good.'

He turns to leave but stops when I speak again. 'I stopped one of the new vampires from killing a girl tonight.'

'Did he fight?'

'No,' I shake my head. 'He knew my name.'

Theo curses, rubbing his hands roughly over his face. 'They're getting closer to me.'

Since Theo has been turned, he has made questionable choices. Ones that have led to him having enemies. Theo carelessly fed on whoever, whenever, and one day, he chose the wrong girl, and he went too far.

Six months ago, Theo was doing what he always does; partying, feeding, and having the time of his life when he took too much blood, and was too out of his own mind to heal the woman he fed on, he left her to die.

Turns out, she belonged to a vampire – Adrian Black – who is now making it his life mission to torment Theo and reign chaos in his life. My efforts in telling Theo to pack up and get out of this town fall on deaf ears. He has always been stubborn. Painfully so, only becoming worse after being turned.

He likes it here. We all do. It's the perfect place for us. The weather is accommodating, the people here make it easier for us to be ourselves, and most of all, we get to meet other people just like us. I don't particularly enjoy meeting other vampires, since they are all much the same, but Theo thrives on finding more of us. He loves the thrill of partying with someone who can keep up with him, on every level. In all fairness, vampires *are* fun, if they're not out to get you.

There aren't a lot of towns like this one, but I still argue that Theo has endless time. He can always come back, when things cool down.

'We're stronger than they are,' I say, facing him. 'We can take them.'

'Unless there's an army.'

Exhaling, I nod. 'Right. Well. We could leave.'

'I'm not leaving,' Theo quickly argues, eyes darkening. 'I like it here.'

'You can go anywhere.' He raises an eyebrow dubiously at me. '*We* can go anywhere.' I amend, not wanting another argument to start. I attempted to bring up the possibility of us parting ways a few weeks ago, and got a punch so hard to the jaw that it dislodged my teeth. I didn't get a chance to say we would see each other all the time, we just wouldn't live together. I haven't broached the subject since.

'I like it here.' he reiterated. 'Vampires run this town. We won't get this kind of . . . environment, elsewhere.'

I frown at him. *That's not much of a reason.* 'There's plenty of places just like Red Thorne, Theo. Places that aren't swarming with other supernaturals.'

'I'm not leaving.'

Sighing, I rub my hand down my face. Theo's practically a brother to me, and as much as I love him, he is hard to tolerate at times. It's his way, or no way. Back when we were at school, one of the student's descriptions of him at graduation was, 'Theo's always right. Even when he's wrong, he's still right.' Sums him up perfectly.

'Why?' I ask in exasperation.

'I am the top of the food chain in this town,' Theo growls, face darkening as I – yet again – don't just simply nod and take whatever he is saying and roll with it. He hates when I argue back, and actually *have* an opinion. 'I've started over again and again. Lasting only a few months in some random place is not my idea of a good time.'

'I know,' I say, understanding exactly what he is saying. 'But this time is different. You have people hunting you. They're using you like a pawn in their game, and you're letting them.'

'No,' Theo disagrees, pinning me with his brutal stare. 'I'm playing the game. They just don't know it.'

'You know that's not what I mean. This *isn't* a game, Theo. It's real life, impacting real, *innocent* people.'

'Running away scared is allowing them to win, Hunter. I won't back down.' He steps forward, thrusting a finger at me. 'I won't give up.'

With a sigh, I give up. Theo would argue the sky was green if the mood struck him. It must infuriate him when I always ignore his jabs that thinly veil his attempts to start an argument.

'We need a plan,' he says, pushing off from the wall. 'Let's brainstorm tomorrow.'

'Sounds great,' I reply sarcastically.

The room falls quiet once more after he leaves. Rubbing the palms of my hands into my eyes, I feel exhausted, and drained.

The war inside me rages on each day. The constant battle between the need to feed, and the urge to protect people. I've always wanted to do *more*, to be *something*. Someone who people could rely on, and look up to.

I've always wanted to protect people. I never would have imagined that I'd have to protect them from myself.

When Theo turned me five years ago, I thought I was being offered endless freedom.

All I feel now is trapped.

3

RAYA

The Survivor

RED THORNE IS A DARK and gloomy place. The sky is constantly grey, and there is a persistent chill in the air that has me reaching to pull my jacket tighter around me as I walk down the street. I'm not sure if I would feel so paranoid or find the place so eerie if I didn't know all the rumours about it.

Tall, black, brick buildings loom over the sidewalks, casting dark shadows in all directions, making me feel like I need to constantly check over my shoulder in case someone is about to jump on us.

'This place gives me the heebie-jeebies,' Alex mutters, casting a frown to his right as a man wearing a long trench coat strides past us, almost knocking us onto the road with his large, hurried steps.

The man lifts his eyes. Alex scowls at him, turning up his nose in a way that is completely snobbish, and mutters something under his breath before hurrying down the street as if someone is chasing him, continuously looking over his shoulder. For a moment, I'm just relieved to see I'm not the only one.

'It's certainly creepy,' I agree, scowling at the man. Every shop in town looks like it is decorated for Halloween – and that they celebrate it all year round.

'Is that a real spider web?' Alex asks in a hushed tone, peering up at the building next to the bus shelter.

Squinting, I watch how it moves in the breeze. It's huge, spreading across the wall of the building, and swaying down low. If we were much taller, we would walk straight through it.

'I'm pretty sure it's real.' Alex shudders, his grip tightening on my arm. I roll my eyes.

'I don't think that is the main issue you should be concerned about in this town.'

'I hate spiders,' Alex mutters.

Smiling to myself, I follow him. Alex is such dork. He loves to notice the weirdest things – he gets a real kick out of it. We definitely view the world in completely different colours. Where something would set off my anxiety, he sees excitement. When I'm tense, he's relaxed. When I'm crying or stressed, he's laughing, not having a care in the world. We continue walking along the narrow pavement. A few people are out and about, strolling between shops, but overall, it's quiet.

When we get to the end of the street, we walk inside a small, dimly lit café. Our footsteps echo on the dark, hardwood floor as we make our way over to a booth in one of the front windows. It's busier than I expected, considering how quiet the streets are.

Sliding into the booth, I relax into the worn leather seat. We order coffee – a soy latte for Alex, and a flat white for me – with a carrot cake to share. We settle into a few minutes of people watching through the window, noting that other than the dark feel of the town, it all seems relatively normal. I suppose vampires aren't going to be roaming the streets, showing people what they are. At least, not during the day.

The drinks arrive with a tiny marshmallow sitting in a pink love heart on the edge of each plate. Alex pops his marshmallow onto his tongue, simultaneously swiping for mine, and tossing it into his mouth to join the other one. He always does this – since the first time we met – stealing my food more often than just eating his own, always claiming that what I order is better than what he did, even though I pick the same things over and over, meanwhile he tries something new at almost every restaurant we visit.

Shaking my head, I lean back into the seat, still bewildered that I'm seriously considering the possibility that vampires exist. It's totally insane.

Isn't it?

Even though I have made the trip here, rented a place, and have gone to all of these lengths, a part of me still thinks someone is going to turn around and tell me I've been punk'd, or something. If it weren't for Alex, I seriously would have questioned my sanity by now. I never planned to move here. I wanted to stay at a hotel, but not a single one has a vacancy. Even the leases on apartments were a minimum of three months to a year long, not enabling us the choice of a week-to-week lease, or even monthly. Not here in Red Thorne, or in any of the bordering towns. I'm starting to suspect that they don't want tourists coming and going. They want people to stay here for the long run. A shiver ripples through me at the thought. It's why we decided that we would stay for three months, posing as university students. We will also need to find jobs to pay the rent here. Both serve as good opportunities for us to meet new people and ask them questions without raising too much suspicion.

Someone here must know *something*.

'Are you excited for classes to start tomorrow?' Alex asks sarcastically, leaning onto his forearms, and wiggling his eyebrows.

'Totally,' I reply, matching his tone.

'Would you be studying for real, if we weren't here right now?'

'Yeah, probably. I always wanted to go to an art school. I love to draw, paint, and sketch.' I shrug, a small smile finding its way onto my face. 'I haven't decided what I want to do yet.'

'I saw some of your sketches. They're pretty cool.'

'You did?' I ask in surprise. 'When?'

'You left one of your sketching pads on the kitchen counter.
I thought it was one of Cora's journals.'

'Oh,' I say. 'I don't usually show them to anyone.'

'I didn't mean to pry,' he quickly says. 'They were great, by
the way.'

'Thanks,' I say, feeling a little tense.

My drawings are extremely dark and edgy, and also very personal to me. Alex and I are close now, and have shared a lot with
each other, so I don't really mind that he has seen them, but it still
makes me a little uncomfortable. I don't really know why.

'If you didn't join me on this mission, what would you be
doing?' I ask.

Alex sighs, turning the coffee mug in his hands. 'I don't know.
I guess that's the main reason why I tagged along. This past year
I've felt so lost. I don't enjoy hanging out with my friends, I hated
my job, never really spoke to my family . . .' he trails off with a
thoughtful, deep expression on his face. 'I needed a change.'

'Fair enough.'

'The self-defence training we did made me feel like I had a
purpose again,' he continues, colour rising in his cheeks at his
confession. 'Sounds stupid.'

'No, it doesn't,' I say softly. 'After I lost my family, having this
to do gave me a reason to get out of bed in the morning. So I get it.'

A small smile graces his lips and his shoulders relax a little
at my admission. It's always nice hearing that someone else feels
the same way you do. Since we met in-person for the first time,
we just *clicked*. No topic is too sensitive or taboo for us. We can
have effortless conversations about anything and everything.
That's why I knew this would work out. We are open and honest
about everything and promised to make sure we stayed that way
throughout this journey. Alex and I did a semester of self-defence

training in preparation for this trip. Of course, we will never outsmart or overpower a vampire, but if we at least know basic self-defence we can hopefully get ourselves out of a situation and have the stamina and endurance to run.

'Have I mentioned this place is seriously creepy,' Alex mutters as he side-eyes a group of teenagers dressed in all black who walk by the window, openly staring at us. One even stops and presses their face to the glass, which causes me to break into a light sweat of paranoia. 'If I were to direct a TV show about zombies, I would film it here.'

I let out an unladylike snort of laughter, appreciating the fact that he distracted me from the creepy guy looming over at us, looking like he stepped out of a Halloween poster. The group finally moves on, and I feel the tension seep from my body – just a little.

'Zombies freak me the hell out,' I admit. 'That's why I don't want to be buried when I die. I want to be cremated.'

'Me too,' Alex says. 'I would rather my ashes be spread somewhere nice. I want people to visit me somewhere nice like Paradise Bay, not a cemetery. They are creepy as fuck.'

'Agreed,' I nod, brushing my hair back from my face. I used to love my curtain bangs, the way they hung around my face, but now they seem to always be in the way. Especially when I was training. I only got them to do something different from Cora, since everyone used to always get us confused. 'I actually have been to Paradise Bay before. I went camping there with my school. It was really beautiful. I learnt to stand up paddle board there. I got so sunburnt that my lips blistered and I didn't leave the house for a week.'

Alex laughs. 'Sunburn is a killer. I used to go camping there, too. When I was a kid. It's sort of my happy place. A place I got to visit before life got shitty.' He takes a sip of his drink, finishing it in one long gulp, making me screw up my face. He practically just shot a large coffee. I would be bouncing off the walls if I did that. 'Although being buried does have its perks. I would love to rise from the dead and terrorise the people that bullied me in high school. I would definitely go after them if I was a zombie.'

Breathing a laugh, I shake my head. 'Count me in, too.'

We finish our coffee, and cake before continuing our self-directed tour of the town, spending the afternoon wandering in and out of shops, and the museum, before finishing up at the library.

'Check this out,' Alex says, jerking his head toward the section of books he is standing in front of. The library is way bigger than I expected. Massive floor-to-ceiling bookshelves with long, sliding ladders that take up most of the walls. I always wanted a bookshelf like that growing up, but since our apartment was the size of a shoebox, I wasn't able to collect many books, only enough to fill the small bookshelves I crammed into my room.

Alex hands me the book that's caught his interest. It's heavier than I expected and I almost drop it. Thick pieces of dust fall to the floor.

'Wow,' I murmur, trailing my fingers over the spine. 'This must be ancient.' The book cracks a little when I open it, and I wince at the sound. The yellowed pages are stiff as I gently flick through them. 'Look at the pages.' The book contains pages of extremely detailed illustrations, and a shiver rolls down my spine when I see soulless black eyes and fangs staring up at me. Alex nods, already having seen it. My eyes travel to the chapter title.

The Monsters of Red Thorne

The chapter doesn't provide much information. It speaks about disappearances, unsolved cases, mysterious deaths, about the people of the town thinking they were safe during the day, when in fact, that was just a myth.

'Huh,' I say, tracing my finger over the sentence. 'Vampires don't just come out at night.'

'What?' Alex asks, leaning so close, I can smell his aftershave.

'See this,' I say, shifting the book so that the dim light shines over the section of the page I am reading. 'It says that's how no one in this town knew about vampires for so long, because they were out both during the day *and* night. Everyone assumed they were safe.'

'Damn,' he mutters, glancing over his shoulder at the sound of someone walking across the end of the aisle. The girl glances our way and both Alex and I instinctively take a step closer to each other. Frowning, she gives us a weird look before moving on. We probably look like the suspicious ones, not the other way around.

We get so caught up in our reading that we quickly lose track of time, and as I look up, I notice the sky darkening outside. I nudge Alex with my elbow, pointing my chin toward the street beyond the window.

'We need to go,' I say in a hushed tone, drawing my jacket tighter around me.

Snapping the book shut, he returns it to its slot on the shelf, and we weave our way back towards the front entrance and out onto the pavement just as thunder rumbles across the sky. Rain dances around us as we hurry down the street. After reading that article, my paranoia intensifies, even though I honestly don't know what I believe – if any of it. Either way, I don't want to be out on the streets at night. I continuously scan our surroundings, making sure no one is following us, trying to ignore the pestering question at the back of my mind: *Would we really know if someone was, if they didn't want to be seen?*

When we get inside, we lock the door, lacing the handles and doorway with silver.

'Do you feel as ridiculous as I do?' Alex laughs as he strings up a silver chain above my head. To anyone else, it would look like we have a very bizarre way of decorating the apartment. Since silver only wounds and weakens vampires, I imagine it won't stop one entering, but at least it might buy us some time. We must have looked crazy when we bought all this silver. I'm glad we weren't bag-checked on the train – it would have looked like we had robbed a jewellery store.

'One hundred and ten percent.'

'Are we really brave for coming here or really stupid?' Alex raises an eyebrow.

'I'd like to say brave, but let's be real. It's probably stupid.'

Alex grins, a small dimple appearing in his left cheek. I stare at it for a moment. My sister was always a sucker for dimples. Now when I see one, it reminds me of her gushing about the guy she crushed on for *years* during school.

After dinner, we head off into our rooms. I lock my door, my window, and then cover my neck and wrists with silver as I climb into bed.

Laying back on the mattress, I stare up at the ceiling, twisting the ring on my finger around slowly. Bringing it to my lips, I softly kiss it.

'I'm here,' I whisper. 'I'll find you.'

'This campus is ginormous.'

I murmur in agreement as I look around the huge court-yard filled with people clustered in groups. Most are situated at tables, a laptop in front of them, a coffee in their hand, earphones jammed into their ears. Overall, it looks like any other university that I've visited.

'We are going to need a map,' Alex says with a huff, staring around. 'I have no idea where our intro class building is.'

'They sent us a map in our welcome email.'

He faces me. 'Bold of you to assume I check my emails.'

I roll my eyes, shoving my hands deep into my pockets. 'I thought you said you were actually going to try to take this seriously.'

'Who told you that?'

'You did.'

'Ah, well, that's not a reliable source,' he shrugs, pushing the sleeves of his shirt up to his elbows. The slight breeze ruffles his hair, causing him to run a hand through it.

Shivering a little, I reach for my phone to pull up my email. I manage to find the map and bring it up on the screen.

Neither of us had the intention of studying. It's a cover and a good opportunity to meet and spy on people. Our plan is to blend in and start networking.

Our goal: be invited *everywhere*.

'Okay, we need to go that way,' I point north-west. At least, I think it's north-west.

'Aye, aye captain,' Alex replies, always willing to follow me basically anywhere, even though I generally don't have a clue what I'm doing.

It's another dreary, dark day, and despite the multiple layers I'm wearing, I still feel cold. There's almost an unnatural chill in the air, making my paranoia ramp up even more.

Will I ever not feel like this here?

'I need food,' Alex announces, patting his stomach. 'Do we have time?'

I glance down at my watch. 'Yeah, okay. I'll grab coffee while you order.'

We part ways and I line up at the coffee cart. Just as a tall guy steps in front of me, reaching the end of the line a few seconds before me, the ring I'm wearing sends an electric pulse that makes me yelp in surprise.

The guy is dressed in dark chinos and a leather jacket. He glances back at me curiously. *Jesus, he is attractive.* The kind of attractiveness that makes me feel taken aback, like I've accidentally just bumped into a runway model, or some big celebrity. Someone different than just a regular person such as myself.

'Slingshot myself,' I say, pointing to my hair band that is snagged around my wrist. I grimace when I see a bundle of dark hair stuck to it. *Great.* That's a good look. 'Sorry.'

Dark shades cover his eyes, but I feel them burning right through me. Nodding once, he turns to face the front once more.

Swallowing, I look down at my ring, inspecting it. What the hell just happened? It felt like I had just stuck my finger into a power socket. Bringing it up so close to my face that I hit the end of my nose, I squint at it, inspecting it for some sign that I didn't imagine it.

Cora . . . my mind whispers. Did she do something to this ring? Is this linked to her? She is the one who gave it to me, after all.

'Hey!' A chirpy voice startles me. I look up, but the girl isn't talking to me. 'I saw you last night, right?'

'Yeah,' the guy replies in a cool, deep voice. Goosebumps scatter across my skin at the sound of it.

'I was so surprised you came!' she continues, a radiant smile on her face. Suddenly, she looks a little awkward. 'Did we . . . make out? I feel like I remember going somewhere with you, but it's super hazy.'

'No,' he replies in a blunt, clipped tone that makes me wince from second hand embarrassment on her behalf.

She blinks, looking a little surprised. Or confused. Perhaps both. 'Oh. Um. Are you sure?'

'I think I'd remember that,' he states, and I wince at his harsh tone again.

She lets out an awkward laugh, ducking her chin, her hair cascading across her face like a dark shadow. 'Right. Yes. Of course. Me too.'

Swallowing, she turns to face the front again. I narrow my eyes and watch her hand move to her neck for a moment before she suddenly turns and leaves the line. I watch her retreat with growing interest. When I glance back, the guy is watching her too, a stoic expression on his face. He collects his order, something in a tall black tumbler, and then walks to the bin, tipping out its contents. I stare in bewilderment as he empties it before tucking it under his arm. When the guy starts to turn and I fear he will notice me gawking at him, I face the front again.

I make a mental note of what that girl was wearing, hoping to track her down later. I quickly think of an excuse to talk to the guy after I've ordered, but when I turn, he's no longer there. Scanning the courtyard, I try to locate him, but it's as though he vanished into thin air. An unsettling feeling sinks in my stomach, and I feel a little breathless at the thought of possibly being so close to a vampire.

I feel totally ridiculous even thinking that.

My number is called, and I grab the two coffees. I meet Alex back where we were previously. Collapsing onto the seat, I place the drink tray down. Alex, who is on top of the table, swings his legs around, bumping his knee into my shoulder.

'Something weird just happened,' I say, moving my eyes around the courtyard one more time to confirm the guy really has disappeared. I fill him in on the brief encounter I just witnessed, leaving out my ring, not totally sure that I even felt anything.

'Cool,' Alex says, not seeming as intrigued as I thought he might have been. 'We have a lead, then.'

'Yeah,' I agree.

'This is so good,' he moans, taking another ginormous bite of his burger. 'Want some?'

'Sure.' He tilts it toward me and I push up off the seat, taking a bite.

'Fuck, leave me some,' he grumbles, sending me a sour expression.

Smiling, my mouth full, I ignore his complaint. 'Are you free one night this week?'

'Why?' He raises an eyebrow. 'Taking me on a hot date?'

Brushing off the comment, I don't react to it. I have noticed that Alex's eyes linger on me for a heartbeat longer than necessary at times, and sometimes his comments border on the line of flirting. We were both open about not looking for anything of the sort when we first met. He stressed to me that he can come across as flirting when he isn't, so I ignore the little moments here and there, assuming he doesn't even realise he's doing it.

'No,' I turn, finding the girl sitting down behind a laptop. 'You're taking her out.'

'I am?' He gives me a baffled look.

I nod. 'Yeah. She's the one that was talking to the guy.'

'Okay, sure.'

After I finish eating, Alex and I part ways. We thought we had planned it well enough to have most of our lectures and tutorials together, but the timetable had different ideas.

I'm surprised to find that most students are already seated when I walk inside the lecture hall. The place is huge, and there are way more students than I expected for some reason.

Glancing down at the time again, wondering if I'm somehow late, even though I'm here a few minutes early. Most of the seats are filled and I scan the room, trying to locate a seat that will allow me not to have a neighbour.

My gaze pauses on a familiar looking guy. The one who was in front of me in line. His jacket is slung on the back of his seat, and I stumble over my own feet when I take in the sight of him.

He has dark tattoos covering one side of his body. They begin on his bicep on the left side, disappearing underneath his shirt, and spreading like spilled ink down his arm. It's such a stark contrast having so many detailed tattoos on one side and nothing on the other.

Noticing that the seat beside him is vacant, I casually make my way up to the back of the room. I drop into the seat beside him. He briefly glances at me. Offering a tight-lipped smile, I look forward and slouch in my seat, trying not to look as nervous as I feel.

The lecturer strides up to the front, dressed impeccably in a dark designer suit. He swings his briefcase onto the table with a thud and flashes a smile up to us.

'Hello, everyone.' His voice is deep, resonating around the room as if he is wearing a microphone. After a brief introduction, he instructs us to begin taking notes.

Everybody pulls out a laptop and I curse under my breath, feeling like the odd one out. Quietly, I withdraw my notebook, placing it onto the desk. Much to my relief, the guy beside me does the same. At least I'm not the only one.

I rummage through my bag, pretending I can't find my pen, and I'm hoping to use that as an excuse to strike up a conversation with the attractive and mysterious person who may or may not be a vampire. Grumbling, I search furiously for it, already having missed the first few notes I was meant to have written down, realising I actually *have* forgotten to pack a pen.

A throat clears. Looking up, I see an extended arm and a black pen between his thumb and pointer finger. He has black leather bracelets on his wrist, as black as his hair and the tattoos on his arms. I'm growing more interested in him by the second. A thrill rushes through me from how easily my plan worked. The noise I was making probably annoyed him.

'Thank you,' I murmur quietly, taking it from him.

I begin scribbling down the notes, finding it hard to concentrate when there is possibly a gorgeous but deadly vampire seated right beside me. Swallowing, I push all those thoughts to the back of my mind and pretend I'm focused and paying attention. Last thing I need is for him to get suspicious.

My hand cramps, and when I glance down, I realise I have written almost ten pages of notes by the time the lecture wraps up. I stretch and flex it as I skim over my notes. I found myself growing more interested as the lesson went on, as if I was a normal student here actually trying to learn. I mentally shake myself.

Don't get side-tracked.

'I hope you found today enlightening. We will be covering a lot of information very quickly. If you're unwell, away, or unable to attend for any reason, it is up to *you* to catch up. Find a study buddy. Pick someone near you, pick a friend, I don't care. But that person will be in charge of sharing class notes with you. If you do not have one by next week, I will assign you one.' He switches off the screen behind him. 'Have a fantastic day. You're dismissed.'

Gathering my things, I push them into my bag and stand.

'So,' I say, wrapping my fingers around the strap of my bag, feeling nervous. This is my chance to get my plan rolling. To get closer to him, and hopefully find out some answers. 'Wanna be my buddy?'

Turning, he raises an eyebrow. Under the golden lights, his eyes are a soft, silver colour. They're beautiful. I attempt to force my gaze from them, wanting to seem totally unaffected by his appearance, but I . . . can't.

'What?' His voice is deep, rich, and warm, making me shift the weight from one foot to the other as I try desperately to look away from him, but find my eyes are scanning every inch of his handsome face.

His voice. There is something so alluring about it. Like I could lay down in bed and listen to him talk all day.

'You know,' I say, throwing my hand toward the lecturer who is striding from the room, looking at his watch, managing to blink myself back to reality. 'The thing he suggested.'

'Oh,' the guy says, his voice soft and rough, caressing my skin, making me feel a little . . . hot and bothered. Meanwhile, he looks totally unphased. In hindsight, this is a very normal conversation, I don't know why it is making me feel so antsy. 'Sure, I guess.'

'Great!' I exclaim, and release a breath of relief, my shoulders slumping slightly. I didn't realise how tense I had been for a moment there.

'Hunter,' he says when I keep staring, his expression completely unreadable. I've always been told everyone can know exactly how I'm feeling at all times, due to my expressions. I wish I could be as cool and collected as this dude. His face is so sculpted and chiselled, like it was carved from God himself. Or the Devil, rather, since vampires are ruthless creatures who enjoy torturing others. Or so the articles say.

Hunter. How fitting. A vampire, who hunts humans. *Named* Hunter. I wonder if he did that on purpose. Is it a game he plays with us naive, oblivious humans? Panicking, I fear my thoughts are exposed on my face, and I quickly shift into a neutral expression, hoping that I'm not appearing as weird as I think I am.

'Hunter, with the pretty eyes and the cool tattoos.'

I freeze, blood rushing to my cheeks, my heart tripping over its regular rhythm in my chest.

Fuck my life, did I really just say that?

Lips quirking, his eyes roam over me, making my insides tighten.

Inhale, exhale. Yep, you're doing great.

'And your name?' he asks, the weight of his gaze making my mind blank, as I focus on those silver-grey eyes.

My own narrow and I take a step closer, convinced I can *see* the colours shifting and swirling. He clears his throat and heat jumps from my neck to my cheeks when I realise I'm studying him like he is an ancient, rare artefact.

'Um,' I mutter, as if I have suddenly forgotten my own stupid name. 'Raya.'

'Raya, with the heart-shaped face and purple streak in her hair.'

I make a soft humming sound, not quite a laugh as I feel the heat rush up my neck and into my cheeks. Folding a loose wisp of hair back behind my ear, I nod, feeling uncharacteristically breathless for no valid reason.

Gah. Get me out of here and away from this guy.

'We should trade numbers.' I suggest. When he arches a brow, the corner of his mouth twitching, I blush a little. 'You know, just in case we want to send notes that way.'

When the silence stretches between us, I regret asking, realising I've pushed my luck, but much to my surprise, he nods. Pulling out his phone, he looks at me expectantly. I quickly prattle off my number.

'Text me, so I have yours?' I ask, trying not to look as eager as I feel.

'Sure.'

My phone buzzes, and when I glance down, a smile emoji is looking back at me. I quickly save his number into my contact list.

'Well, it was nice to meet you, Hunter. See you around,' I say politely, ignoring the fact that I sound like I've just run a marathon.

'Yeah,' he says, sliding his bag over his shoulder, not casting his eyes in my direction again. Bullets of sweat slide down my spine. My mouth is paper dry, I anxiously lick my lips to moisten them.

As he descends the stairs, I notice how muscled his back is under his tight black T-shirt. Damn. He is sexy. Why do bad boys always have to be sexy? I hope he isn't a blood-thirsty vampire. He's too pretty and seems normal . . . kind of.

They blend in though, right?

I have to remember that everything about these creatures is meant to invite us in. Trust them, make us weak, so they can move in for the kill.

A clicking sound echoes around the now empty room. I glance down, seeing my thumb pressing down onto the pen I borrowed. It is a sleek black pen, and is heavy to hold, with the letter 'H' engraved. I'm surprised he was willing to give me something that feels like it would be valuable. Hurrying down the steps, I make my way out into the busy hall, to try and catch Hunter.

With his tall, broad-shouldered frame and striking tattoos, he isn't hard to find. His back goes rigid as another guy approaches him. The guy has a dark smirk twisted on his lips as he walks toward him.

Slowly, I make my way to where they are in the courtyard, noticing that Hunter is scowling. It looks like they are in a heated discussion from how tense Hunter stands and the way his brows are pinched together. A rational, sane person would walk away.

My ring zaps me, and my hand jerks in response. I don't allow myself time to think about it since I'm now right where the guys are standing.

'Hi,' I say.

They turn at the same time and blink at me. It's intimidating having the weight of both their piercing stares directly on me. The guy next to him has a similar eye colour. Under the light of the gloomy sky, they're a pretty silver-grey, deep and round, with darkness bleeding into them.

'You have something on your face,' I say, my mouth seeming to have a complete mind of its own.

The guy drags his thumb across the corner of his mouth, sucking on it before grinning. His eyes bounce toward Hunter.

'Must have been my breakfast,' the guy says, and I grit my teeth at the sound of it. 'It was delicious.'

My heart splatters painfully into my stomach. The red smudge on his lips wasn't sauce as I had initially thought. For a moment, I forgot where I am and what kind of people I am dealing with.

With my heartbeat roaring in my ears, I realise I have two vampires standing right before me. They have to be. No one I have ever met has eyes like that. Their skin is flawless, an unnatural smoothness to it, and they both have an air about them that is just *something else*. It's hard to decipher what exactly.

They can hear my heart. Shit.

'Um,' I say, just to say something. 'Thanks. For the pen.' I thrust out my hand. Hunter eyes it for a moment. He looks at the man next to him before reaching out and taking it. His fingers brush mine and the coolness of his skin makes me jerk my hand back.

'Sure,' Hunter says, eyes briefly connecting with mine, before he glances down, pocketing the pen. There is an undeniable tension in the air, just as there was back in the auditorium. *Something isn't right.* 'No problem.'

'See you later,' I say lightly, forcing a smile onto my face.

'Bye bye,' the other guy says, waving at me. His tone makes my skin crawl. Shuddering, I rush toward the largest group of people I can see, and reach for my phone, dialling Alex's number.

The line connects. I sigh with relief as I look back to where the guys were standing. My breath hitches when there is now no one there. I whip my head around. There is no way they could have left that quickly.

With my heart thumping and my knees knocking together, I lean against the table next to me.

What the hell have I gotten myself into?

4

HUNTER

The Protector

LOUNGING AGAINST THE COUCH, I read over my notes from class earlier today.

'Come on,' Lucy says, moving to the end of the couch and leaning forward, placing her hands on my shins.

Lucy is all legs. Dark skin, raven black hair, and glittery silver eyes. She was a model before she turned, and she loves to remind every single person she ever meets of that fact. She tightens her hold on my legs, digging her nails in to get my attention.

Scowling, I shake my head, feeling the muscle in my jaw twitching in anger. No one can make me angry as quickly as Theo and his girlfriend. I don't know what it is about them that makes me so tense, like I'm wound up as tight as I can go, locking up every part of my body until I can barely see or breathe. 'For the fifth time, no.'

'He's in a mood,' Theo says, strolling out of his room. 'He doesn't like it when I go to his school.'

Lucy rolls her eyes and smiles playfully over her shoulder at Theo. He winks at her as he wanders around the room, shirtless, picking up the first item of clothing that he can find and inspecting it. He is a slob to live with. Something that hasn't altered since before or after his transition.

'Why?' she asks, tilting her head, eyes shimmering with curiosity. She loves to pry into my life. I fascinate her, or so I have overheard from her hushed whispers to Theo when she thinks I can't hear her. She has met a lot of vampires, and yet, she cannot figure me out, or compare me to another, which only makes her think about it more. The fact that I am not *normal*. A normal vampire is power-hungry, cruel, cunning, always wanting to test the boundaries. They love the thrill of being the most powerful person in the room, but I feel like I'm the opposite.

Sighing, I massage my temples. I just want to be left alone. By every person. Anywhere. All the time.

I hate that I can't sit in the living room in peace. I always lock myself away in my room, so I don't know why I risked sitting out here.

'He doesn't want people to know he is different,' Theo coos, pouting at me. His face may be playful, but those dark eyes are as sharp as blades. Constantly assessing me, evaluating my moods, studying me. 'Or for me to meet his pretty little human friend he lends pens to.'

Groaning, I slam my notebook onto my lap, the distinct clap of the pages echoing around the room. 'You are both annoying as fuck. I don't want to go out tonight.'

'You never want to go out,' she huffs, turning her nose up at me. 'I have never met a more boring vampire than you.'

I ignore her, like usual. It's easy enough to do, and I admittedly garner a little amusement in the knowledge that it pisses her off.

'Hush now,' Theo says, moving behind her, planting a kiss on the side of her head. His hands curl around her hips possessively, dragging her close so that her back hits his chest. 'He will grow bored of it and join us soon enough. You'll see.'

Tossing my notes onto the cushions, I push to my feet. Making a beeline for the fridge, I pull out a blood bag and slam the door shut. My patience is wearing thin, and the hunger gnawing at me is intensifying with each passing moment.

'Go on!' Theo shouts at my back, as I make my way to the door. 'Go for your moody boy walk. We'll be out having fun, thinking of you!'

I stick up my middle finger in response.

Zooming through the trees, I place a healthy distance between myself and them. I land softly on a tree branch and sit down, dangling my legs off it. I rip open the blood bag, immediately intoxicated by the scent as I take a long sip. The hunger that has screamed at me all day finally eases and the tenseness in my muscles ebbs away.

Leaning my head back against the bark, I watch as the cars drive by below. Soft, murmuring voices, laughter, heavy footsteps. I listen to it all as I watch and drink, trying to keep calm and relaxed. I don't know what it is about Theo that riles me up so much. Him and Lucy both do a good job of pissing me off. It's like sport to them. But then, most things are.

A part of me wants to pack my things and move on. Somewhere where no one knows me. Where I can truly blend in – or at least try to. Theo would hate me for it, he thinks I owe him my life now that he has given me this curse. *Gift*, he calls it, which is exactly what my brother always says.

But I know he would come after me and drag my ass back here. He was clingy before and it's even worse now. He is insistent I stay here. Honestly, I can't for the life of me figure out why he is so fixated with the place. The world is his oyster, and he loves to proclaim that. Yet, he sticks to this small, little-heard-of part of the world. It makes no sense.

Exhaling heavily, I drain the bag, and close my eyes. A heart-shaped face and emerald eyes flash through my mind. I startle at the image of Raya. I open my eyes and blink, wondering where the hell that came from as I give myself a mental shake.

I've been lonely for a while, that much I know. It's a hollow feeling that burns inside my chest. That must be it. It's the first time I've interacted with a human for a while, outside of situations of needing to be fed. That's all it is. I don't care for her, or for anyone. It's nothing.

Withdrawing my phone from my jacket pocket, I pull up the security cameras that are connected to an app I have installed. A breath of relief escapes me when I do a headcount of my family. They are living incognito. I need to protect them from *him*. Kian, my brother, who became a vampire. The *worst* human to have been given that kind of power. He is psychotic, off-the-rails, and has totally lost touch with reality. I'm positive he would slaughter them in spite of me. Compelling them into a new life was the only way they will remain safe. I like to check in on them most days, and I always feel relieved when I see them all come into view, going about their ordinary lives.

Kian and I have never gotten along. It started from the moment we were born, I'm sure of it. He hated that I existed, because in his eyes, I could do no wrong. I had the better grades, loyal friends, girls who threw themselves at me. He claims I had everything handed to me on a silver platter while he had to work hard for all that he has. Like I didn't work hard to get good grades, or for anything else for that matter. At times, our family did treat me more favourably, but that was because he never did himself any favours. Narcissists only care about one thing.

Slowly, I make my way back to the house. It's quiet. Theo and Lucy must have left already and knowing them, they won't be back for hours.

Good.

Kicking off my shoes, I go to my room. After showering, I collapse onto the bed, finally able to breathe a little more freely now that I'm alone.

Lucy's words whirl around inside my mind. I have never met a more boring vampire than you.

I know I'm different from most other vampires. Hell, I've never come across one like me. Sometimes I wonder if it was the severe depression I often dealt with as a human which was heightened when I turned, morphing me into this dull state of not quite vampire, but not human either. It's a weird feeling. Not feeling *anything*. It's like a part of my body is numb. Or maybe, I just hate what I am, and I'm lonely.

With a sigh, I close my eyes. Eventually I drift off.

Long, dark dreams invade my mind.

5

RAYA

The Survivor

I WAKE WITH A GASP. Sweat coats my skin. My shirt clings to me as I kick off the blankets and swing my legs over the edge. My feet touch the cool ground, causing a shiver to slither down my spine. Standing, I move toward the window and glance out of it. Another dark, dreary day. No surprises there. I'm starting to question whether this place ever sees sunlight.

Stretching, I feel the crack of a few bones along my spine realign, and feel better for it, though my skin is hot and clammy from the nightmares. They're always the same. Loud clashes of metal against metal. My mother's screams. Sweltering heat. Bruising pain all over my body. A vicious, burning sensation over the skin of my wrist. My fingers rub over the area, and I glance down, staring at the mark there. I have no idea what it is. Something must have burned or cut me – neither the doctors or the nurses at the hospital could tell me for sure. I think they thought I had more important things to worry about. I don't have any memory of its inception except intense pain.

I'm not sure there ever will be a time I don't relive the horrific car accident that altered my life forever. The moment I lost everyone I loved.

Reaching for my phone, I look down at the time. It's barely 6 am. The floorboards creak as I walk out into the living room.

Alex's soft snores travel through the tiny apartment. If I was back home, I would go for a walk or run to clear my mind. I'm too scared to do that here. I feel like if I leave this apartment by myself when it's dark outside, I won't make it back alive.

It's too early in the morning to be thinking about death. I need coffee.

Moving around the kitchen and preparing my usual flat white gives me the feeling of familiarity. Like I'm doing something from my old life, even though I've only been here for a few days, and the normalcy of it helps push away the lingering shadows of the nightmare.

Dropping down onto the lounge, I fold my legs beneath me, and go about my new 'normal' of researching vampires, looking up articles about this town, and scrolling through endless threads. I'm always on the lookout for something new, or something about my sister. It's become an obsession.

Feeling much more alert now, I head into the shower to wash away the evidence of my sleepless night. When I step out of the cubicle, I smear my hand across the fogged window. Lifeless eyes blink back at me, rimmed with dark circles. Sighing, I lean in close, inspecting them. I might need to start wearing makeup again to hide these. I don't want people thinking I look as tired as I feel, because that will lead to questions I don't intend on answering.

Soon after, I'm dressed in a long-sleeved top tucked into high-waist, ripped jeans. I step into my Converse and shake my hair over my shoulders. I'm ready to go by the time Alex staggers out of his room, his messy bed-hair sticking up in all different angles.

He yawns, peering over at me. 'Did I sleep in?'

I shake my head. 'No, I just got ready early. No rush.'

'Mmhmm,' he mumbles, rubbing his eyes.

'Go shower, I'll make you coffee.'

'Not all heroes wear capes,' he states, saluting me before disappearing back through the doorway.

I like making coffee. It keeps my hands busy while my mind races with a million different possibilities about anything and everything. It's exhausting. I wish I could wipe my memory clear of all of this and live a normal life. But I can't, and my sister deserves better. We all do.

The wind howls and rattles against the window. I push it open a little and a blast of cold, icy air rushes into the small space. Shivering, I yank it shut again.

Alex reappears dressed in skinny jeans and an oversized jumper. The sleeves are so long they swallow his hands. Rolling the sleeves so that they sit mid-forearm, he makes grabby hands at the mug of coffee. I hand it over and follow him to the lounge.

'So, when are you going to ask him?' Alex asks, blowing unnecessarily loudly over the top of the liquid, as if that somehow cools it down quicker.

'Hmm?' I ask, only half paying attention to him as I scroll on my phone.

'Your friend,' he replies. 'When are you going to ask him if he is a blood sucker?'

I laugh at his word choice. 'Maybe after class. Or maybe I should stand up in the middle of class and ask him in front of everyone. You know, make it a bit interesting.'

Alex flashes a grin that shows almost all his teeth. 'I double dare you.'

'I value my life, thank you very much.'

'Do you?' he asks mockingly.

I shrug. 'Well. To some extent.'

'Morbid. I like it.'

Smiling, I glance down at the time. 'Okay, I said no rush before, but I changed my mind. We gotta go.'

'Roger that,' he replies, standing and draining the remainder of his hot coffee into his mouth like a psycho.

'It is so weird that you do that,' I point out. He does that all the time. Coffee, water, juice, energy drinks – no matter how hot or how cold. 'I'm positive you are incapable of drinking normally.'

'I just enjoy the look on your face when I do it.' He smirks.

'Go on,' I say, shooing him with my hands. 'Hurry up.'

Within half an hour we arrive on campus. It seems busier than usual today. All the eateries have long lines and every table in the courtyard is filled. Rubbing my hands together, I try to circulate the warmth they're generating through to the rest of my body with little success. My fingertips feel so frosty they've gone numb. Noticing, Alex takes my hand, wrapping it up with his. I glance up in surprise, but he is looking ahead, like us holding hands is something that we always do.

'Alex! Hey!' a guy calls out, beckoning us over.

'Friend from class,' Alex explains quickly, his fingers tightening around mine, another reminder that we are *still* holding hands. 'He knows that girl you want to question.'

'Perfect,' I say through a smile, pulling my hand away from him and politely waving at the group. I don't want anyone thinking we are together because that will make our plan fall through.

We make our way over. There's four of them at the table. Plastering a warm, friendly smile on my face, I quickly assess their eyes, coming to the conclusion that there are no vampires amongst them. Or so I assume, since none of them have that silver glimmer in them. Or the creepy black.

'Hey,' Alex greets them, and it's weird seeing a big, goofy grin on his face instead of his usual sullen and sarcastic smirk.

'Hey,' the guy replies. 'Everyone this is Alex and . . .' he trails off, looking at me expectantly.

'Raya. I'm a friend of Alex's.'

'I'm Seth, this is Brax, Adriana, and Jed.'

Seth has long hair that's pulled back into a ponytail. He's nursing a thick textbook in his lap and an iced latte clutched in his hand. Brax waves at us, his eyes lingering on me just long enough for it to be considered awkward. Jed doesn't even look up from his phone, just nods his head, and the girl perks up when she notices Alex. I sit down beside Seth, and Alex moves around to the other side of the table, casually dropping into the empty space beside Adriana.

'Are you new here?' Seth asks, combing his fingers through the loose wisps of hair framing his face.

'We just moved here, yeah.'

'What do you think of the place?'

I shrug. 'It's fine. A little eerie sometimes.'

'You get used to it.' He smiles, almost taking me out with his elbow as he re-ties his hair. 'Are you planning on going to the party tonight?'

I give him a curious look. 'What party?'

'There's a thing tonight that one of the TA's is hosting. Sounds like it is going to be pretty good. You should come.' Seth moves his eyes to Alex. 'Both of you.'

'TA?' Alex frowns.

'Teacher's assistant.'

'Oh.' Alex nods, looking like he just realised he probably should have assumed that.

'We're in!' I smile, not giving Alex the chance to respond. 'Sounds fun.'

As the time for class draws nearer, we push to our feet, gathering our things. I didn't even have to try, and our plan was already in motion. Off to a good start.

'We will meet you there,' I say. 'What time are you meeting up?'

'About seven-ish,' Seth answers.

'Sounds good!'

Alex and I exchange a glance before parting ways.

It appears I'm one of the first to class today. I make my way to the same seat as yesterday and fall into it. Steadily, the lecture hall fills up. Glancing toward the empty seat beside me, I frown. I'm unsure why I feel disappointed that Hunter isn't here today.

Throughout the lecture, I make detailed notes so that I can photocopy them after and give them to Hunter. I get a nervous – definitely not excited – swooping sensation in my stomach at the thought of seeing him.

After class, I go straight to the library to photocopy my notes. I have them stacked in a neat pile when I see him. I freeze, my heart seems to beat sideways as he walks up to the book return slot and slides a few books inside.

'Hunter,' I call out, jogging over to him. As usual, he is dressed in all black, contrasting the dark patterns on his arm perfectly with his lightly tanned skin. As I reach him my ring pulses against my finger and I startle, glancing down at it quickly. There is definitely something going on with it. This is the third time it has shocked me, and every time has been when I'm near Hunter. 'Hey.'

Glancing up at me, he pushes his sunglasses into his hair. Since the sky is a dark grey, I don't see how sunglasses are necessary, but everyone seems to wear them outside regardless.

'Raya,' Hunter nods, those hypnotising eyes sending a thrill through me. Straightening my back, I attempt – and fail – to appear nonchalant.

'Hi. I got this for you,' I say, thrusting out my hand and waving the stack of papers under his nose, breathless again. I blame it on the fact that I rushed over to him. It certainly isn't being this close to him, and how attractive I find him. No connection there.

Nope. None.

'What is it?' he asks, a little sceptical.

'Notes from class,' I reply, my voice a little quiet as I take in his hesitation to take the papers.

'Oh,' he says, a small but genuine smile flashing across his handsome face as he takes it from me. 'That's nice of you. Thanks.'

'Well, you're my buddy,' I reply, and instantly cringe.

Why do I say stupid things when I'm around him?

'Right. Yeah.' He nods.

'How come you weren't in class?' I ask. It's not until I say this that I realise it seems super nosy. Hunter always waits a second too long to answer, like he mulls over every word I say carefully, inspecting them, before deciding on a response. I wish I had that ability, instead of just blurting out every random thing that enters my mind.

'I was thirsty,' he says, raising the tumbler he's holding.

I do my best to keep my expression blank as I nod, glancing at the tumbler as I wonder what it holds, considering he tipped out the contents last time.

I wonder if he fills it up with blood . . .

The colour drains from my face. I feel a little light-headed, and I see Hunter frown in what I hope is concern. Reaching out, he touches my shoulder, and I shiver, feeling his coolness through the material of my jumper. It's surprisingly comforting. 'Raya? Are you all right?'

'What? Oh . . . fine,' I stammer.

I don't think I'm cut out for this kind of work, considering the mere thought of this guy being a vampire makes me weak in the knees. And not the good kind.

'You look as white as a ghost,' he comments.

'Just tired. And hot,' I say, and then blanch when I feel the sharp coolness of the wind slap my cheeks, as if purposely reminding me that this town is anything but hot.

'Okay . . .' he trails off, looking puzzled.

My mouth is dry, and I fiddle with my ring. His eyes dart down to it and I quickly stop touching it, not wanting to draw attention to it.

'Have you got plans tonight?' I blurt, the words tumbling out before I can second-guess myself.

He raises an eyebrow and leans casually against the wall. The change in angle causes his shirt to pull taut over his chest, show-casing the defined muscles beneath it. 'Um, not particularly, no.'

'There's a party on. I think I'm going to go.'

'Oh, yeah. I heard about that.'

'Do you want to go?' I ask, twisting the bottom of my shirt. I tell myself I'm only asking because finding out more about him is a part of the plan, right? Since he may very well be a vampire. Therefore, inviting him to the party to spend time together makes perfect sense in a non-datey kind of way.

'We could . . . er . . . hang out. If you want to.' Swallowing, I look down at my feet. 'If you don't have plans, or whatever.'

When I glance back up, his eyes are narrowed slightly as he studies me.

'I don't really do parties,' he says wryly.

'Oh,' I say. 'Okay then. Cool, cool, cool.'

Cool, cool, cool? Get me away from this guy right now before I say something worse.

Making an awkward clicking sound with my tongue, I salute him and turn on my heel, hating how my cheeks flame, giving away just how embarrassed I'm feeling.

Did I just *salute* him?

'I might call in for a bit.'

My head jerks up. Turning back, I smile, circling my fingers around the straps of my bag, trying not to stare at him in shock and disbelief. 'I might see you there then.'

'Yeah,' he replies. He holds the papers up in the air. 'Thanks again for this. I appreciate it.'

He turns, jogging down the steps two at a time. The way he moves is so elegant. The more I study him, the more I can spot tiny differences between him and us. *Us* as in the general, non-vampire population.

He *has* to be a vampire. I'm determined to find out more, whether he wants me to, or not.

Pulling the poster off the wall with a distinct ripping sound, I stare at the details of a welcome party. The theme? Supernatural. I blink down at it.

Wow, go figure.

I'm sort of looking forward to tonight, even though I shouldn't be. I remind myself that this is purely to gather information, and to investigate what the hell is going on in this town. Someone here must know something that can help me.

We are meeting the others there. At least I'll have them to hang with while Alex will be busy getting information out of Adriana.

When we get back to the apartment later that afternoon, I head straight for my room. Flopping down onto the bed belly-first, I open one of the journals and begin reading again. It's all I ever do now – re-read the journals, look for clues and hints, and then move onto the online forums and articles.

Being around him feels like being high. High on . . . something that doesn't feel like it belongs in this world. It's hard to explain. The way he looks at me – like he owns me. In a way, he does. Or he will. Very soon.

Not long now . . .

I spend the rest of the afternoon preparing for the party, my sister's words bouncing around in my head. I've gone with a plain white dress with fake blood marks slashed across it. My long dark hair falls perfectly straight down my back, and I plait the purple streak, pinning it to the side. If the circumstances were different, I would have gone all out with a costume, but I can't stand out or draw attention to myself. Alex and I are flies on the walls of this creepy fucking town.

I will get the answers I'm looking for, one way or another.

We allow ourselves only two drinks while we get ready. This party isn't about having fun. After I spend forty-five minutes drawing snakeskin across Alex's face and neck, since he is going as a basilisk, I allow myself one more drink for good effort.

'Here,' Alex says, when I lean away from him. He passes me the canister of liquid silver that we made. I slide one inside my boot, the other in my bra.

'You have yours?' I ask.

He nods, showing it to me before pocketing it.

'You're freakishly good at that,' Alex says, assessing my artwork in the small mirror that's hanging up in the lounge room.

'Cora and I used to do a lot of dress up that required makeup and art,' I reply, sipping my drink.

'What was she like?' he asks. 'I never wanted to ask much about her, in case it was too hard for you.' Clearing his throat, he lowers his gaze. 'I didn't mean to use past tense.'

'It's fine. Everyone does,' I say, leaning back into the seat and propping my legs onto the coffee table. 'She's fun. The life of the party. Firm, strong, and stubborn.' I laugh, thinking back to a time when we were both teenagers. There was always someone she loved profusely, and someone she hated, and as her sister, I was obliged to feel exactly as she did – her words. 'If she likes you, she'll go to the ends of the earth for you.

But if she hates you . . .' I take a long sip. 'God have mercy on your soul.'

Alex grins. 'She sounds fun.'

'Yeah.' I run my palms across the fabric. 'The last few months she was different. Cold. Like a total mean girl suddenly. Which is weird because we were always so close. It was totally out of character. Then I read her journal and it started making a little sense.' I stand suddenly and go to my room. I reach for the journal and bring it back out. 'But look at this.' I open it up to the tabbed page and place it in front of him.

He leans forward, dragging it closer to him.

I hate the way I've been treating them. The hurt in their eyes will haunt me forever. But it's necessary. I need to do this. It's all a part of the plan.

Alex's eyes lift to meet mine. 'It's all a part of the plan,' he murmurs, furrowing his brow. 'What plan?'

Sighing, I shrug. 'That's what I'm here to find out.'

The party room is big, and very dark. Reaching for Alex, I grab his hand as we weave through the bodies. Red neon light strips line the edge of the ceiling. The air is stale with alcohol and body odour, and there are way too many people crammed into this space. It's hard to breathe. It's disorientating when the lights start flashing, though after a few minutes, my eyes adjust to the dimness. The music vibrates the floors and shakes the walls.

The idea of separating from Alex makes me nervous, but I know it's necessary. Scanning the room, we don't stop moving until we find the group of people we met earlier.

'Hi!' I smile at the group, dragging Alex behind me. My eyes continue to search the room, subconsciously looking for Hunter. I wonder if he will come, or if he said maybe just to be polite.

'Hey Raya!' Seth smiles at me. 'You look great.'

'Thanks! You too.'

'Hi there.' Adriana beams, glancing at me briefly before turning her attention to Alex. He turns his smile up a few watts, having her totally dazed within moments.

Damn, he's good.

'Shall we go get a drink?' he asks, his voice low and sultry. That tone, mixed with his look, even made *me* shiver. Looking a little in awe, she nods, linking her arm with his. He looks over her head at me and subtly winks as he leaves with her.

Well. That didn't take long.

For a moment, I forgot it was all a part of the plan. Someone calls out to Seth, and he yells something inaudible back as he makes his way over to them. Damn. One less person to question now.

'Where are you from?' the other boy asks, and I try my best to think of what his name is.

I curse myself for not being more prepared. Suddenly, a bulb lights inside my brain. *Brax*, that's it. I suck at being a detective so far.

'Here and there,' I shrug with a small smile. 'I moved around a lot growing up. Hard to really pick just one place.'

'Ah, okay,' he replies, not seeming particularly interested in what I have to say, anyway.

Slinging an arm around my shoulder, he guides me toward the kitchen. I carefully watch as he makes us both a drink. I take the one that he looks like he is about to drink, just to be on the safe side.

He laughs. 'I'm not going to poison you.'

'Good to know,' I say, attempting to sound light-hearted, but it comes out tense, and a little awkward.

'Best to keep your wits about you though,' he says with an ominous wink. 'You never know who or what is out to play in this town.'

Tilting my head, I narrow my eyes. 'What do you mean by that?'

'Oh, you know, the rumours.'

'What rumours?' I ask quickly, and then relax my shoulders, hoping that I look easygoing. I need to play the newbie card. Make them all think I'm completely oblivious to the rumours about the town I just moved to. I also notice he doesn't take a sip of the drink he prepared for me.

A wicked smile lights up his face. 'This place is filled with creatures of the night. Haven't you heard?'

Goosebumps prickle against my skin. It's all fun and games reading about this stuff on a screen. Now I'm here, listening to it in person. Swallowing, I force a curious smile onto my face.

'Creatures of the night?'

'Yeah. Witches . . . wolves . . .' He suddenly lunges toward me, and slams me back against the kitchen counter. He shoves his face into my neck roughly. 'And vampires!' He makes an over-the-top sound of biting and slurping. Laughing, he steps back. I'm as rigid as a rod as I attempt a laugh, trying not to seem as spooked as I look. He lightly pushes my arm. 'Lighten up, it's a joke.'

It's not a joke. None of this is a damn joke. Pushing the thoughts of Cora and all the confusion around her disappearance away, I step toward him. I need to do something. To take control. Mustering up the courage, I inch closer, forcing a flirty smile onto my face.

'You got any stories to tell me?' I murmur, leaning in close, staring up at him through my dark lashes.

Brax's eyes lower to my lips, before travelling back to my eyes. His smirk widens. 'I've got plenty.'

'I'd love to hear them,' I say, grazing my arm against his, unsure whether I'm laying it on a little thick. The way he looks at me makes me think I'm doing something right.

'Maybe we should go somewhere quieter,' he suggests. 'So, you can have my full attention.'

'Sure!' I say confidently, hoping he doesn't notice the slight tremor in my hands as I hold the cup a little too tightly.

He finishes the rest of his drink and pours another. The smirk on his face makes me inwardly cringe, but I remind myself this is necessary. With his hand on my back, we move through the swaying bodies and people making out across the dance floor. We step out through the sliding glass door.

The cool night air nips at my exposed skin. We head around to the side of the house. Casually, he leans against the wall, sliding his fingers through mine.

'What do you want to know?' he asks, taking another sip. His eyes are a little glassy. He's had too much already.

'Something real . . . something terrifying,' I whisper with an excited grin, toying with his fingers. He pulls me a little closer, enjoying my open display of affection. So close I can smell the stale beer on his breath.

'People disappear here,' he says quietly.

'What happens to them?' I whisper, eyes widening.

'They're dinner.'

'Dinner?' A nervous, high-pitched laugh escapes me before I can stop it.

'For the supernatural,' Brax answers, loving the fact that I'm hanging on his every word. 'Or so they reckon.'

My heartbeat thuds in my ears. 'What do the police say?'

Brax laughs, reeling back a little. It's a humourless laugh that sends a shiver down my spine. 'They don't care, because they don't want to be next.'

'I don't believe that.'

'It's true,' he argues. 'The vampires run this town.'

'It's not real,' I say, unsure who I am truly trying to convince here. 'These creatures . . . they don't exist.'

'Don't they?' He quirks an eyebrow.

'Have you ever seen one?' I push, trying to work out whether he knows anything concrete.

'I was at a party last year. One like this. I met a girl. We danced, made out a little . . . the next thing I remember, I wake up in the middle of the football field. Blood is all around the collar of my shirt. I'm woozy, disorientated – like I had been running a marathon without any water. There were no marks on me anywhere, but I know, I just *know* one of the bastards got me.'

Nauseous bubbles form in my stomach. An image flashes through my mind of the guy in front of me, blood everywhere. An icy chill seeps into my bones at the thought of it. It sounds like a similar story to what happened to Alex. It must happen all the time.

'That's so scary,' I whisper, leaning in close to him. 'Why are you still here?'

He eyes me for a moment. 'Simple. I want to become one.'

'You do?' I breathe, my eyes widening. 'Is that . . . is that possible?'

He nods. 'It is. You find a vampire. One that is willing to turn you. You find a sacrifice. Boom, you're a vampire.'

'A sacrifice?' I question.

'Turning someone into a vampire upsets the balance of nature,' he explains. It's quiet out here, and suddenly, I don't feel safe. I look over my shoulder, realising we are completely alone. The ring on my finger pulses and I gasp, yanking my hand out of his hold, clutching it to my chest. The music is faint from where we are standing. An uneasy feeling settles over me and I swallow, stepping back a few inches. 'A human must die – as a price – for you to turn.'

I open my mouth to question him more, when his hands shoot out, shoving me hard. I fly backwards, landing in a painful sprawl. Choking on my breath, I lay at an awkward angle, blinking up at the dark sky.

'I'm sorry,' I hear his low voice. 'But I need this.'

Pure, unrivalled panic shoots through my body, and a scream rises into my throat when a blur of motion suddenly appears to my right and jerks me to my feet. My heart flip flops inside my chest and my breath comes in shaky gasps as I reach into my pocket and withdraw a cylinder of liquified silver. I remember what the article said. My heartbeat is hammering so loud I can barely think.

'Better run, little girl,' Brax says from behind me, his voice taunting, nothing like the way he spoke to me before. 'You're about to be dinner.'

A man appears in front of me. Tall, partly hidden in shadows. Two silver eyes glow in the darkness. My knees knock together as I tremble. Adrenaline courses through me like a torrent, holding me upright. I lift my chin, staring back at the thing in front of me. I don't look into its eyes, instead, I look at its mouth, which is twisted into a menacing snarl.

Everything inside me is screaming at me to run, but I don't. I didn't come all this way only to die my first week.

'What are you waiting for?' Brax shouts impatiently. 'Get her!'

Swallowing down the building panic, I force myself to focus.

I must think clearly. For Cora.

Taking a moment to even out my breathing, I go through the information in my head. All the things I have read about. All the research.

Cora's face appears in my mind, and determination wells inside my chest.

Narrowing my eyes, I step to the right. He mirrors me. I step to the left. He does the same.

This is what he wants.

The game.

The chase.

The *hunt*.

With a shaky breath, I resist the urge to back up. I don't want to be any closer to the betrayer behind me. 'Are you going to kill me?' I ask, my voice steadier than I expected. I suspect he can hear me perfectly clear even if I whisper. 'Or just stand there thinking about it?'

His lips curve into a slow, sadistic smirk. 'Oh, I'll kill you. But I want to have fun while doing it.' He steps closer. 'I want the chase.'

Everything inside me threatens to collapse, as I try not to let my fear overcome me. These words being spoken to me have opened up pure terror inside me. I have never felt anything like it.

Breathe, Raya.

I go over my options. Brax is covering the main exit. The vampire is in front of me. There is nothing stopping me from going right, but it's further away from the party. Less likely I'll be heard or seen.

'Tick, tock,' the vampire smiles, revealing two, long fangs. My heart shudders to a stop. There's no doubt now . . . this shit is real. And it is fucking scary. 'Make your decision, or I'll make it for you.'

Fuck it.

I take off at a run in the direction I told myself not to go. If I'm going to die, I'm going to go out fighting. I race around the edge of the fence. Not so elegantly, I vault over it. He gets close, I feel the whoosh of air by me. Darting to my right, I slide underneath a branch, skidding across the hard dirt. Sticks and gravel scrape my skin, but I hardly feel it.

A deep laugh that penetrates straight into my soul echoes around the dark cluster of trees.

'You can't outrun a vampire, sweetheart,' he says in a sing-song voice that makes my skin crawl.

Sweat beads across my forehead, sliding down the back of my neck as I run. Skidding to a stop, I see that I've reached a spot I can't get through. Panic swells inside me, fogging my brain.

Think, think, think.

I'm small. Smaller than average. I can do this.

Launching headfirst, I break through a small window of branches and somersault down a short hill. I'm nearly blinded when the dirt flings into my eyes as I fall. Scrambling to my feet, I keep going, despite my legs shaking, and the fact that sticks and leaves are clinging to me, digging into my skin.

I can't believe that in a matter of minutes – seconds, potentially – there's a good chance I'm going to be killed. This can't be it. This can't be how it ends.

In my research, it talks extensively about their hunting instinct, their quick-thinking, their superhuman speed. There's no way I'm seriously outrunning him right now. He's toying with me. The panic eating at my chest is making it hard to breathe and swallow.

'You think you can win, little human?' the voice whispers and I swear I can feel his breath on the back of my neck.

I get to a fork in the route, and I fake a right. I dart to the left just as I hear a crash through the branches, exactly where I was heading. Nausea clamps down onto my stomach at the thought of how close he is.

This is too hard, a voice whispers. I can't beat him.

Yes, you can, Cora's voice whispers in my mind, urging my feet to keep moving.

If I can stay on this track, I might get close enough to the house to make a run for it. I push myself so hard that everything inside me burns. A dull light pierces through the gap of trees and I propel myself forward.

The vampire drops in front of me, his feet making no noise as he hits the dirt. Gasping, I don't have time to stop. I slam painfully against him, and it's like hitting a concrete wall. I go flying backward and he grabs me tight, stopping me from falling. I feel sick from the intense stop-and-go motion.

'Game over.' He flashes a leering smile of all teeth.

I fling my arm up and direct the liquid silver straight into his eyes. Alex and I made it ourselves, and I'm pleased to see we must have done it right. The scream that leaves his mouth makes my ears bleed. Blinking rapidly through the sweat and tears, I lunge forward, and run. His fingers wrap around the end of my hair and he yanks me back. I let out a cry as I collide harshly with the ground. He swoops down, snarling angrily.

'I'm going to make it hurt, bitch,' he spits, looking like a ferocious beast with those black eyes and long fangs. Terror seizes me in an iron fist, stunting the breath from my lungs.

Gripping my throat in a vice-like grip, he lifts me half-off the ground. His fangs plunge hard into my neck. My scream fills my ears as a pain like no other spreads like poison through my veins. I grip the ice-cold skin of his arm, desperately trying to get him to release me. I bang against his arm, feeling my vision darkening. I reach blindly for the canister of silver, but my fingers grasp empty air.

Every limb of my body goes limp and heavy. My head lolls to the side as he continues to drain everything out of me.

The man is suddenly jerked back. I sag against the ground, drawing in deep, ragged breaths.

Slowly blinking, my eyes heavy, I turn to see another tall fig-ure, dressed in all black. In the darkness, I only see their outlines. He's tall. Muscular, but lean. Dark, unruly hair, a sharp jawline, and intense silver eyes. Tattoos. Very distinct tattoos.

'Leave. Now.' His voice is deep, and laced with a calm author-ity that rings through the air.

'You're going to die, Hunter,' the vampire roughly growls, his voice hoarse, and harsh.

I'm not hallucinating. It's really him.

The vampire – my blood coating his mouth – flies toward him. Hunter snakes his hands out, twisting the vampire's neck quicker than my mind can comprehend. A strangled cry escapes his lips. Hunter pushes his lifeless body to the ground, it lands with a dull thud. Swiftly, Hunter slides a stake from his pocket, his finger wrapped around what looks like a rubber handle. The silver glints for a moment before he plunges it into the vampire's chest with a sickening squelching sound.

The dead vampire's unblinking gaze stares ahead, straight at me.

Hunter turns, his silver-grey eyes flick over me.

'Raya,' he murmurs. He peers down at me. My heartbeat is so slow, I know death isn't far.

In a blur of movement, he is crouched beside me, inspecting the gaping wound in my neck. As the adrenaline ebbs out of my body, the weight and pain from the vampire's attack slowly sinks through. Every part of me burns.

He freezes. Gripping my wrist, he holds it up and inspects it closer.

'How did you get this?' he whispers, eyeing the mark on my skin.

Blood spurts from my parted lips when I try to speak and I gurgle, drowning in it. He tenses, watching the blood oozing out.

As if shaking himself back into focus, he scoops me up so that I'm on his lap. His fangs slide out and he bites into his wrist. In one fluid movement, his wrist is against my mouth.

Screwing my face up, I rear back from him, shaking my head in repulsion at seeing his blood so close to my face. I want to scream, cry, yell at him, but I can't do anything.

'Raya!' he snaps, making my wild thoughts slow for a moment. 'We don't have time for this. *Drink*.'

The command in his forceful tone pulses through me, and this time when his wrist raises to my lips, I let the warm liquid spill across my tongue. Activating some primal response inside me, I grip him as I swallow deep mouthfuls of his blood. Each swallow, I feel the pain and agony slowly seeping away. I feel stronger with each passing moment.

For the first time in what feels like years, I feel safe. Warm and protected, like nothing could harm me at this moment. I melt into him, seeking his protection, and strength. His grip tightens around me, and the wind I hadn't noticed before washes over us, whipping my hair around my face.

A pleasant, delightful blend of sunshine and moonlight twists in my mind, ensnaring my senses as a powerful rush fills my body, stealing the breath from my lungs. Everything turns black for a few seconds before the world flickers back to life around me.

Securing my hold on him, I plunge my teeth into him, biting, and sucking with an animalistic severity, feeling greedy, wanting more of this insane high that is coursing through my body, causing me to tremble. Letting out a low hiss, his finger traces patterns up my arm. His hand moves up to the side of my face, where he gently pushes it back at the same time he removes his wrist from my lips.

We stare at each other, both breathing intensely.

My mouth waters at the thought of his blood, and I let out a little whimper, my eyes focusing on his lips. 'I need more,' I whisper, reaching for him, threading my fingers through his dark hair.

Closing his eyes, he breathes hard, as if trying not to give in to some sort of battle waging inside himself.

'Hunter,' I whisper. 'More.'

A low groan leaves him, and he drags me toward him. Biting down onto his arm, I drink once more, the flavour exploding through me. Pulling me close, he yanks me from his arm, diving toward my mouth. The kiss is deep and intense, like nothing I have ever experienced. I feel so desperate to be closer, even though there is no space left between us.

His lips drag across my jaw, down to my neck, where his fangs bite into me. I gasp, a pure, electrifying bliss zinging through me.

Our hands move and explore over each other desperately. I have no idea what is possessing me to do this – it's hardly the right time – but there is something unworldly that has taken over my body.

I grope at him, feeling highly turned on, and horrified at my own actions at the same time.

Reeling back, he slams his mouth to mine, and I grind myself against him. A clap of desire sizzles through me, erupting something inside my body I had no idea was even there. Dots dance across my vision.

'No!' Hunter chokes out, wrenching his mouth away, a violent tremor rolling through him, rustling me in his lap. 'I can't take blood from you . . . after what just happened.'

Feeling light-headed, I place a hand on him. 'It's okay.'

I have no idea what I'm even saying. I should be screaming, crying, trying to get away from him, but instead I am calm, and even a little relaxed. I feel totally safe and comfortable right now, here in his arms.

'No, it's not,' he says, sounding nothing like the Hunter I've met before. He looks out of his mind. His eyes are closed as he grapples with getting his breath under control. 'The blood, it made my judgement cloudy. I'm sorry.'

Breathlessly, I gaze up at him. His chest is rising and falling rapidly. We both sit in a stunned silence, unsure of what to do or say, the high still racing through us at an inhuman speed.

His wide eyes soften as he gazes down at me. Gently, he swipes his thumb across my lower lip. Warmth fills every part of my being. I feel whole. Content. Dreamy.

Hunter's eyes are a stunning, bright silver, with faint strips of smoky darkness swirling around the iris. A strand of his dark hair falls across his forehead.

Tenderly, he touches the side of my cheek, eyes curious as they roam over every inch of my face. It feels like tiny bolts of electricity are shooting through me with every touch.

'Who the hell are you?' he whispers, tilting his head.

'Nothing. No one.'

His brows crease. 'A normal human.'

'As far as I'm aware.'

'This,' he says, pointing to my scar. 'Where did you get this?'

'A car accident.'

His eyes bore into mine so intensely, I feel like he is trying to look into my soul. A few beats of silence pass as he stares down at it, his expression unreadable, once more.

'A car accident?' he repeats slowly.

'Yes,' I say breathlessly, still trying to fathom what he is talking about, and why he's bringing it up right now.

A frown tugs the corners of his mouth, which still has a red stain around it. 'This is not from a car accident.'

I frown. 'Yes . . . it is.'

Shifting so that I'm propped more into a seated position, he leans back, and I feel the heat of his gaze all over me.

'Raya,' he says, touching my hand. 'Who are you?'

'A regular, ordinary human.'

'So you say.'

'It's the truth.'

'I don't believe you.'

I blink at him. 'I'm telling the truth. Why do you think I'm lying?'

Hunter gestures between us. 'This isn't normal.'

'What?' I say, louder than I intended.

'I don't know how to explain it,' he mutters, shaking his head, his frown increasing. 'It must be because you were so close to death.'

'What are you talking about?' I demand.

Saying nothing, he stands, helping me up. He brings our joined hands toward his face as he stares at them for a moment. I'm not sure if his eyes are on the scar, or our interlocked fingers.

Wow, I feel incredible. Energy flows through my veins, filling me with a strange, surreal sensation that ripples through my body with cool, calm clarity. I quickly adjust my dress, my cheeks flaming at the memory of what we just did to each other. Then, I remember he is a *vampire*, and I stumble, throwing myself off-balance as my thoughts catch up to me, realising how insane these last few minutes have been. Hunter's hands are on me, steadying me faster than I can even comprehend.

'You're not going to eat me?' I raise an eyebrow.

'No,' he answers, looking baffled.

'Why not?'

He laughs. It's rich and velvety, wrapping around me like a warm embrace, brushing across my skin with the faintest of touches. 'Shouldn't you be thanking me? For saving your life?'

'Thanks, I guess,' I say a little hesitantly, trying to force myself to relax again.

He breathes a soft laugh through his nose. 'You're welcome, I guess.'

Blinking, I rub my head. 'Sorry. I feel super light-headed. I have no words to express how grateful I am for you saving me. Truly.'

'Why are you in the woods? Haven't you heard what they say about this place?' His dark eyebrow arches upward as the corners of his mouth twitches. 'What people say about us?'

Dusting off the leaves and dirt from my clothes, I inspect myself briefly. I feel good. Strong. Like I could climb a mountain without breaking a sweat.

'I was cornered.'

'So you ran for the woods?' he deadpans.

'It was the best decision at the time.' I say, narrowing my eyes, taking a hesitant step back from him. He has no idea what it's like. I can't outrun or outweigh a vampire. I had to make a quick decision. Either way, I would have died. If it weren't for him . . .

'Right.'

'Your blood. It's making me feel . . .' I trail off, holding out my arms in front of me, inspecting them as if they've changed somehow, but still keeping a wary eye trained on him for any movements, not that I would probably see him coming anyway.

He leans against a tree, his T-shirt clinging to his chest, showcasing the packed muscle underneath it. When I raise my eyes to meet him, his gaze is already fixed on me, his brows furrowed slightly, a thoughtful expression on his face.

'Good?' he supplies.

I nod, still unsure how to feel right now. Other than the warm, floaty feeling blossoming in my chest from his blood – I don't know whether I should hug the guy for saving my life or run as fast as I can away from him, hoping I make it out alive.

But why would he save you, only to kill you moments later?

'Yeah.'

'We aren't supposed to give humans blood because of this. It's a high that is very addictive. Especially the amount that you took.' Running a hand through his windswept hair, Hunter shifts his weight, resting his shoulder against the bark.

'I see.' I nod, seeing and feeling the truth of what he just said. I imagine people would do anything to feel like this, especially if their health isn't good.

'What were *you* doing out in the woods?' I retort, slight suspicion etched into my voice.

'Walking. I was way, way over there.' He points in the opposite direction of the party. 'I heard the commotion.'

'Were you coming to the party?' My face flames as I ask the question, unsure why there's a swelling feeling of hope inside me at the thought of him coming to see me. Coming to the party *for me*.

Swallowing, I mentally shake myself.

Maybe I really am crazy . . .

A ghost of a smile flickers over his lips. 'Maybe.'

'You were, weren't you?'

'Yes, Raya. I was coming to the party.'

Interesting. Very interesting.

I smile, looking away for a moment, afraid he can tell what I'm thinking.

'So, you're a good vampire?' I ask, dragging my tongue around the inside of my mouth, tasting his blood. Hunter is watching me, his eyes tracking the movement, and I straighten my spine a little at the intense tingles that ripple through my body.

What the hell? Why did the thought of him watching me make me feel . . . like that? Must be the blood.

'Is there such a thing?' he asks quietly.

'You'd know more than me.'

'Fair point,' he replies, a slight smirk tilting his lips.

'You live here?' I ask after a moment, not sure what to say right now.

He nods, jutting his chin in the direction behind me. 'Somewhere over there.'

'Do you sleep in a coffin?'

He looks alarmed. 'No.'

'Damn. That would have been cool.'

He laughs again and it's just as good as the first time. Hunter pauses, tilting his head. He is suddenly gone, disappearing into thin air. I look around for a moment. Then, he's back just as fast as he left.

'Yours?' he asks, holding out my phone, which is vibrating.

'Oh. Thanks,' I say with wide eyes, still trying to comprehend the way he can move that quick.

I take it from him and answer it.

'Hi, Alex.' I attempt to sound normal, even though I feel anything but.

'Where the hell are you?' he hisses. Music blares in the background, making it difficult to hear him. 'I've been looking everywhere, and you haven't been answering.'

'Long story . . .' I say, glancing at Hunter, realising he can hear every word. 'I'm coming back. Meet me near the pool.'

'Gotcha.'

It's silent after I hang up. We awkwardly stare at each other. There's a strange tug in my chest, urging me to go closer to him, but I refuse to. He takes a step toward me, as if feeling the same thing.

'Was that your boyfriend?' he asks in a clipped tone. My stomach does somersaults at the question.

'Boy who is a friend.'

'Friends shouldn't let friends be alone in a town like this.'

'We planned it to be that way. Now I'm realising what a dumb decision that was.'

He grunts in agreement. Half-turning, I go to head back to the house, but feel a weird sensation rip through me, making me stop. I don't want to leave him. It must be the blood. It's making me not think clearly.

'Hunter?' I ask, my voice quiet.

He looks at me, his eyes darkening to an inky black which looks creepy as hell but also kind of awesome. His eyes travel over me, making me feel hot all over. The way he stares at me . . . I really do feel like prey, and he is a predator sizing me up. Yet, I don't fear him. Not like I did with the vampire from earlier. If anything, when he looks at me like that, I feel a little . . . thrill.

'Why are you so curious about this?' I ask, holding out my wrist. 'What does it mean to you?'

He's silent for a few moments, looking down at the ground before his eyes swivel back to me. 'It's my brother's mark.'

6

HUNTER

The Protector

I NEED TO GET AWAY FROM HER.

I brush a hand through my hair and yank on it for a moment as I pace.

Seeing my brother's mark makes me feel uneasy. Does she really not know what this symbol is? That she has been branded? Why is she not dead? My brother doesn't leave his mark on someone without ending their life. It makes no sense.

'Tell me,' Raya demands, holding her pale wrist up, shaking it in the air to emphasise her point.

'It's nothing,' I say. 'Don't worry about it.'

Her mouth falls open once, then twice, but no words come out. Snapping her mouth shut once more, she takes a step back, looking torn between staying and asking me for more answers, or running for dear life.

'Nothing?' she questions. 'You just told me this was your brother's mark, and now you say it's nothing?'

'Yeah,' I reply, schooling my expression into a carefully calculated and unreadable look, that even the most well-trained lie detectors would have trouble deciphering.

'Don't do this,' she whispers, suddenly looking much more vulnerable, and fearful, then she did a moment ago when my blood was freshly coursing through her veins, giving her confidence a boost that has most definitely impacted her natural instincts. Even if I *did* just save her, she should be more scared of me, running, trying to escape, but she is still here, studying me with an open, calm curiosity. 'Please tell me what you know.'

'I made a mistake,' I say. 'It's nothing.'

Lips flattening into a line, she nods, seeing the switch inside me. I can't be the nice guy right now. I need to get the hell out of this situation.

'Fine. I'm leaving,' she says, but stays standing where she is, waiting for my response. Waiting for me to try to stop her.

'That's for the best.' I nod.

Scowling, she turns, her dark hair flipping around in an angry arc before cascading down her back and swaying with each furious step.

An ache spreads through my body the further she walks from me.

What the hell is this?

Groaning, I place a hand on my stomach, feeling worse as the distance between us grows. I've never experienced something like this after being turned. This makes me feel . . . human.

My eyes widen at the realisation and I let my mind explore the possibility. Has she somehow made me human? It's impossible, surely. After a quick self-assessment, I confirm that I still have my superhuman eyesight, quick reflexes, and of course, the ever-present hunger for blood.

'Argh,' I grind out, falling to my knees, and wrapping my arm around my torso as the intense ache continues.

The burning hole in the pit of my stomach seems to cease after a moment. Not completely going away, but eases enough that I can stand. Bile rises in my throat, and I spit it out onto the dirt at my feet, feeling like I might throw up.

This is not normal.

'Where have you been?' A voice asks in a hushed whisper, snapping me back to reality. Raya is back at the house now, and each step she takes causes another fierce ache inside my chest.

I lean back against the tree, my arms still clutched around my stomach as I listen. My mind is reeling.

Who is this girl? Why does she have the mark of my brother? Why is she here?

'The most terrifying thing happened to me, Alex. You have no idea . . .' she whispers back, her voice shaking. 'Let's get the hell out of here.'

I'm on my feet and gliding out of the woods within seconds. I teeter on the edge. My eyes focus on the friend for a moment. He casts a worried look in her direction as they anxiously wait for an Uber.

Her back is turned to me and I realise I long for her to turn around. She was so fragile in my arms. Weak, doll-like. Her slender arms sway as she paces, quietly recapping what happened to Alex. There's blood all over her dress. Some of it is fake, some of it hers. It's difficult to tell the difference unless you're someone like me.

Her friend wraps his long arms around her, and I tense, watching with narrowed eyes. Studying him closely, I make out his midnight black hair, but his face is hard to see with all the paint and makeup of his costume. He certainly isn't a threat to her. If anything, quite the opposite.

I step out from the shadows, basking in the moonlight. I love the moon. It makes me feel calm. It shines down on Raya's pale skin, making her look like she's illuminated from within, emphasising how small and precious she is. The urge to go to her and protect her almost sends me to my knees.

Alex and Raya get into the car the moment it pulls up in front of them. As she closes the door behind her, I'm struck by a sudden and violent ache as blood spews from my mouth. I groan as I empty my stomach onto the grass in front of me.

'Dude, are you okay?' a random party-goer asks, stumbling toward me, squinting.

'Get away,' I moan, clutching my stomach.

'You need some water?'

I'm flying toward him before I realise what I'm doing. Since I just emptied out my blood supply, I'm hungry. Really fucking hungry. My teeth sink into his neck. I'm not gentle and he howls in pain. I haven't bit anyone like this for years. Sobs wrack his chest as I take more than I should, as though I'm trying to punish him for something I don't understand.

My insides curl in repulsion. Yanking my teeth from his throat, I stagger back, looking down at my trembling hands and ghost-white skin. The blood rises in my throat and floods my mouth, tasting like poison. Gagging, it sprays from my mouth in an inky, black wall of darkness.

'What the fuck?' I moan, feeling pain everywhere.

What is happening to me?

Collapsing onto my back, I heave, the dark sky above me blurring. When all the blood is out of my system, I stumble to my feet. I heal the wounded drunk beside me and convince him he never saw me. It hurts to use the coercion when I'm this weak. I don't even know how well it will work because of it.

Rushing home, I stagger through the front door, a trembling, hot mess. Hot is a feeling vampires do not experience, and I'm growing increasingly concerned by the second.

'What the fuck?' Theo exclaims, a human girl half-naked on his lap, his girlfriend nowhere to be seen. He shoves her off him like she's nothing and she squeals as she thumps across the floor. He is by my side in an instant, helping me up.

'Something's wrong,' I whisper. 'Really fucking wrong.'

*

When I wake, it's dark. Blinking, I slowly peer around the room. Cold towels are draped over me. Theo is leaning against the wall, gazing out the window. His head snaps to me as though he knows I'm awake. Relief floods his face.

He's by my side in an instant. 'Hunter,' he breathes my name, shaking his head, looking like he hasn't slept for days. He reaches for my arm. 'You scared the shit out of me.'

'How long have I been out?'

'Two days.'

'Two days?' I exclaim, reeling to a sitting position which only causes my head to spin.

Flashes of memories bombard my mind. Staying up all night, trying different blood bags, different humans. Trying to get *any* blood to stay in my system.

'You don't look good,' Theo says, frowning down at me. 'I think you've been poisoned.'

'Surely it would be out of my system now, if I were?' I groan, voice still raspy.

Theo shrugs, looking clueless. 'I don't know. You're not looking any better and you can't feed. I'm at a loss.'

'I've never heard of this.' I shake my head.

'Talk me through it again,' he says, pulling up a chair and sitting on it. He leans forward, digging his elbows into his thighs, clasping his hands together. 'You were out walking. Your normal track?'

'Well, I change it up all the time, but a track I've walked plenty of times before.'

'Sure. And then what?'

'I heard running, screaming – a hunt taking place. When I got there, it was a vamp I've never seen before. He was sloppy and inexperienced. There was a near-dead girl in his arms. I gave him the opportunity to walk away. When he didn't take it, I killed him.'

'How?'

Holding my hands out, I mimic the twist motion before striking my hand forward. 'Neck snap, and stake.'

'And then you saved the girl,' he says slowly.

'Yeah. She drank from me.'

Theo rocks back and forth, a crease appearing between his brows. 'How much did she drink?'

'A lot,' I admit, rubbing my jaw. 'And . . .'

'And what?' he demands.

Swallowing, I look away from his piercing eyes. 'Things got heated. We . . .' I exhale loudly, sinking back against the pillow and cover my face with my hands. 'We drank from each other, and got a bit . . . touchy.'

Heavy silence stretches between us.

'She drank from you, and then you drank from her?' he asks.

I keep my face covered, not wanting to see his expression right now. 'Yes.'

'Fuck, Hunter,' Theo growls, and I peer through the cracks of my fingers, seeing his storm fury eyes. 'The old vamps always say to never bloodshare like that.'

'They do?' I question in surprise, never having heard such a thing.

Theo rolls his eyes. 'If you actually spoke to another vampire, you'd probably learn a thing or two.'

Sighing, I don't reply, not wanting this to escalate into an argument. I don't have the energy for it.

'You said you had some sort of reaction to her leaving?' he asks.

'That's when it started. I felt . . . motion sickness? Do you remember that feeling, from when you were human?'

Theo nods. 'You can't have felt that.'

'I'm just saying that's what it felt like.'

'None of it makes sense. Vampires giving a human blood isn't all that uncommon.'

'I know.' I sigh, feeling weary and exhausted, despite having slept for two fucking days. 'I tried to feed on someone, to replenish my strength. That's when the vomiting started. And the shakes. Like nothing I've ever felt.'

'I know a guy. An old vamp. He might have answers.'

I shrug. 'Worth a shot, I guess.'

'Do you want to try and feed?' Theo asks, looking concerned.

My stomach turns at the thought of consuming blood. Raya's face spears in my mind. That's the blood I crave. I jolt in surprise at the thought of her. I push the want – and need – away immediately.

'I don't want to go through that again,' I insist, trying to stand, but feeling too weak to do so.

'You know what happens when you don't feed.' Theo gives me a pointed look. 'I have seen vampires enter that crazy state of mind. It messes with you, and a lot of vampires don't recover from it. Mentally, I mean.'

'Speak to your friend first. I'll try later tonight. See how it goes,' I persist, resisting the urge to groan in pain.

Theo frowns again. 'Okay. Sure.'

Laying back, I place the towels back over me. Theo stands and draws the curtains closed.

'Don't die on me,' he warns, narrowing his gaze, and jabbing a finger in my direction. 'Also, I don't want you to go full loon. There is only room for one psycho in this bromance.'

Smiling weakly, I close my eyes. 'I'll try not to.'

7

RAYA

The Survivor

IF I THOUGHT I HAD BAD nightmares before, they're ten times worse now.

As good as I feel – thank you, Hunter – the vicious nightmares that plague me haunt me even when I'm awake. I jump and jerk at every minor sound or movement in the corner of my eye.

'You're so jumpy,' Alex comments, moving around me in the kitchen, his arm brushing against mine. We had a long discussion last night, mostly with me in tears and his arms wrapped around me as I made a mess of his shirt. I ended up falling asleep laying on his chest, both of us tangled on the lounge. It feels a little awkward now, like we crossed a line that I never intended to cross. 'You okay, after what happened?'

'I'm traumatised,' I bite back, a little snappier than I meant to. 'He hunted me down and almost killed me. I don't think I will forget that any time soon.'

I have never felt so conflicted about something in my life. If anything I despise vampires more now. The lack of power and control we have over basically any situation with them is terrifying, and infuriating. I have no idea what to think. One hunted me down and almost killed me, and another one saved me. I don't know how I can hate the creature, when I also immensely appreciate one at the same time.

Or maybe Hunter is just different . . .

'I'm going to fucking kill Brax.' Two spots of colour rise in his cheeks as his jaw clenches. Slamming his fist down onto the kitchen counter, he whirls to face me. 'I should stake him. If he wants to be a vampire that bad, he can die like one.'

Silently, I blink at Alex, a little shocked at his outburst.

'I can't believe he led me out there to die . . .' I trail off, wrapping my arms around myself, goosebumps splintering uncomfortably across my skin as I think back to the moment when I realised I had made a *very* big mistake.

In my head, I painted vampires as evil, ruthless creatures with no soul or sense of humanity. I forgot that they are just like humans. Some radical and extreme, meanwhile others are just . . . normal. In their case, perhaps the average vampire is more evil than not, but I can hardly assume every single one of them is like that. No more than I can safely assume that every human is good. Especially after last night. I wouldn't want them to assume that about us.

'I'm sorry that I wasn't there for you. Splitting up was a terrible idea.' Alex's soft voice draws me out of my head.

'I'm alive. That's the main thing.'

'I can't believe these things are walking around in plain sight and the general public know nothing about it,' Alex says.

'People are busy. Some people believe it. Others don't want to.' I take a long sip of water and lean my hip against the counter. 'And it's done now. We can't waste time regretting things.'

My mind wanders to Hunter. *What do vampires do when they aren't feeding? And stalking around in the middle of the night?* He seemed so normal. If I passed him in the street, sure, his striking appearance would have made me double take, but overall, I would never have guessed anything was peculiar about him.

'Can you handle this?'

My eyes snap toward Alex. He's watching me. 'Yes.' I nod. 'I'm a little shaken, but I'm fine. I can do this.'

He steps in front of me, placing his large hands on my shoulders. His long hair falls over his face, and I feel myself tensing even further at his proximity. 'This is all up to you. Say the word, we go back and move on with our lives.'

I'm shaking my head before he finishes speaking. 'I am not leaving without answers.'

He nods. 'Okay.'

'Okay,' I reply, sounding more confident than I feel.

Pulling me to him, he wraps an arm around me, pressing his lips to my forehead. Hugging him back, I hold on a little tighter than I normally would.

We lounge together for a while, watching a movie. I can't stop thinking about Hunter. The way his hands gripped me. How his lips felt on mine. How his tongue would feel lapping over my skin, and other places. I shiver at the thought. This must be some after-effect of the blood-sharing. It must be. I'm not attracted to a vampire.

I *hate* them. I hate them for what they did to me, and what they have done to my sister. It makes me sick that I can't stop thinking about him.

That I *want* him.

Alex is snoring softly when the credits start rolling across the screen. I switch it off and gently place a pillow underneath his head. He rolls toward the back of the lounge, burrowing into it. I pull the blanket over him and turn off the light.

When I sink into bed a few moments later, my eyes are heavy and sore, exhaustion seeping into my bones, making everything feel heavy.

Large, veiny arms snake around me. Tight, secure. Protecting me. Providing strength and warmth when I need it most.

'You're thinking about me,' he whispers against my ear, his breath spreading over the skin of my neck.

Slowly, he wraps my hair around his hand. He leaves hot, wet kisses down my neck, to my collarbone. He shifts so that we are facing. His eyes, black as coal, bore into mine with an intensity that hits me like a wave.

'I can't stop thinking about you either,' he whispers, voice like silk, curling around my body, drawing me closer to him.

Leaning forward, his arms cage me in. He is everywhere, invading my space. He is all I can see. All I can breathe.

'You're mine.'

With a gasp, I reel into a sitting position. The room is pitch black. I'm struggling to draw breath and my heart feels like it's lodged in my throat.

His voice. His touch. It felt so real.

On shaky legs, I get to my feet. The cold night air blows over me, but I welcome it. I need to cool down, my skin is a sweaty mess. I whip my head towards the window with a sudden, alarming, clarity. It was closed when I went to bed, now it is slightly ajar. The curtains flap against it. I hesitate for a moment, enjoying the wind kissing my skin, before I hastily slam it shut and peer down into the darkness.

My heart drops to my feet.

Black eyes blink up at me. A shadow falls across his pale skin as he steps back into the darkness, disappearing into the shadows.

8

HUNTER

The Protector

MY BODY SLIDES THROUGH the window with silent ease.

It's dark and eerily silent. My feet barely touch the floor as I move across the room and slip beneath the covers. I hardly had the strength to get out of bed earlier and yet, the urge to see her was so strong, it overcame everything else. I *needed* to see her. To be close.

I shouldn't have done that. Let myself in. Got close to her. She knows I was there. She saw me.

I wanted her to.

Sweat breaks out across my forehead. Vampires don't sweat. Or do they? Honestly, I'm feeling lost on what to believe at this point.

I must be going mad – like Theo warned me I might. This craving, desperate feeling to see her is making me feel panicked. It's not normal and it's not right.

The door obnoxiously bangs open. Light filters into the room and I glance up to see Theo striding in. With the expression on his face, I assume he knows I left. He drags the chair to the side of the bed and collapses down onto it.

'Did you try to feed?' he asks, and I feel a small moment of relief that he doesn't seem to know about my recent trip.

The urge to feed was so strong it was almost violent when

I visited Raya. It took every drop of self-control not to. It's her that I want. I know that now. Her blood has ruined everything. I have no idea why.

'No,' I answer. My voice is weak. My breathing is shallow and each breath comes out in an audible gasp. If I don't feed in the next twenty-four hours, I really will snap. And I might not come back from it. Maybe that's okay. Dying wouldn't be the worst thing. I've been bored and lonely for years. Maybe it's a better option than being here, hating who I am. *What* I am.

'I spoke with my friend,' Theo says, his frown starting to look like a permanent addition to his face.

'What did he say?' I ask curiously.

Theo runs a hand roughly over his face. 'I don't know what to think about it.'

'Tell me, Theo.'

'He said you might have formed a bond. With the girl,' he says a little reluctantly.

Alarmed, I jolt upright. 'What?'

He nods, wincing. 'It's rare. Almost unheard of. But it's possible.'

'A *bond*?' I exclaim, incredulous, waves of shock coursing through my body at the thought of it.

'He said it's because of the way you are,' Theo continues.

'The way I am?' I repeat with a slow blink, not understanding what he means.

'Blood-sharing isn't totally uncommon, but only older, stronger vampires tend to do it because the risks of killing the human or turning them is really high. Since you're inexperienced, and a relatively new vampire, you didn't have the skills required to not let things escalate.' Narrowing his eyes, scrutinising me, he tilts his head. 'He also said there has to be attraction or feelings there beforehand. Anything you care to tell me about that?'

Swallowing, I contemplate this. I have never had confidence in my skills with anything about being a vampire. I don't trust myself not to go too far – despite never having lost control before – but I've always had the worry in the back of my mind that I would accidentally take a life. That's why I always stick to blood bags.

Of course I knew I was attracted to her. I knew that from the moment I laid eyes on her. She intrigued me, and for the first time in what feels like forever, I had wanted to get to know someone. The moment I met her, she drew me in, although with the nature of being a vampire, it's supposed to be the other way around.

When I say nothing, Theo seems to drop it.

'The bond means you will do everything you can to protect her. She will consume your mind, body, and soul.' He cringes at his own words as if they physically repulse him. 'And it gets worse.'

'What?' I whisper, eyes widening.

'She's your one and only blood source. She dies, you die. That's why your need to protect her will be so strong. Because without her you can't feed.' He shakes his head, bewildered. 'Also, the answer as to why you can't stomach any other blood.'

'That's . . . insane.' Right now, my body is jittery, like I need to pace, but I feel so weak.

'I know.'

'Surely, it can't be.'

'It is true, Hunter. Look at you. You're shaking, sweating, feeling sick. Unable to feed.' He gestures toward my mess of a body. 'Have you thought about her since the other night?'

'Uncontrollably so.' I sigh, the ache inside me growing more urgent as the minutes pass.

Theo exhales, raking his hands through his hair. 'You should've left her to die. You knew she was beyond saving, but you brought her back from the dead, and even worse, took blood from her after bringing her back. Now you've formed this life and death bond, linking you to her.'

A bond. I haven't ever heard of one. I never knew such a thing was possible. As much as I don't want to admit it, it all makes sense. I knew she was on the brink of death. Once that line is crossed, it's dangerous to try and turn someone, or save them. Things can go wrong and get complicated quickly. Yet, I risked it. I didn't want her to die. I had only just met the girl, and yet, she had somehow gotten under my skin.

Theo curses. He stands, kicking the chair. It splinters into a hundred pieces on impact, skidding across the wooden floor-boards.

'Well. That's just great,' he snaps, throwing his hands up. 'You know what this means?'

'What?' I dare to ask, peering up at him.

'You now have a weakness,' he says with a huff, always having the ability to make everything about himself. 'Which is a huge fucking problem.'

Dressing and getting myself to campus takes three times longer than it should have. With these vampires attacking, and potentially coming after Theo, I need to be on my A-Game. I really shouldn't be out in the open like this. I'm asking to be attacked. Or worse.

I need blood. More specifically, I need *her* blood. But I can't just take it from her. It's not just the bond that makes me want to make it as comfortable as possible for her. I don't want to force her. This world is new to her, and after everything she went through, she most likely is terrified of vampires. Of me . . .

I would hate to scare her away. The thought of never seeing her again feels like my heart is being torn in two.

My skin prickles with awareness the moment she walks onto campus. I can feel her. Sense her. Listening, I hear the car doors close. Their soft footsteps as they walk up the stairs. The low murmur of conversation. Forcing myself to walk and appear human, I casually make my way through the small crowd that has also arrived a little earlier than necessary.

Forcing myself to relax, I take the long way, chanting over and over to keep it together and not lose control when I see her.

By the time I get to the courtyard, she's seated at a table with a small crowd of people I recognise from some of my classes. Alex is introducing her, explaining how he met a few of them at the party. The party from hell that changed my life forever.

A vicious ache threads through my veins as I approach the table. Silence falls as I draw near. My shadow casts over her. The small breeze blows her long hair over her shoulder. The scent of her makes every inch of me feel like someone has lit it on fire.

'Raya,' I say, my voice coming out hoarse and deep. 'Hi.'

A ripple of *something* shudders through her at the sound of my voice. She turns, looking up at me. I feel every pair of eyes ogling me, but I can't pull my gaze from hers. She looks stunning. Her bag strap slips from her shoulder. A little too quickly, I reach for it and put it back over her shoulder.

'Hi, Hunter,' she says slowly, her eyes analysing me just as intensely as mine are hers.

'How are you?'

'Fine,' she says a little curtly, looking like she is ready to bolt at any moment. 'And you?'

Like death if he was a person.

'Fine as well.'

'Good,' she replies, swallowing, the movement of her throat making me take a step closer.

'Walk with me?' I ask. 'To class?'

A slight reluctance is visible on her face as she glances at her friend. Everyone is unashamedly gaping at the two of us. It must seem weird, I never engage with any other students, no matter how desperately they try, and neither of us seem to be able to stop staring at the other. As awkward as it feels – and as it should, after what we went through together – there is still a strange sense of calmness between us.

Inevitably, the tug between us is too strong for her to resist. Getting to her feet, she stands, and I immediately collect her textbooks. My temper is threatening to rear its ugly head at how delicately I need to approach this. It's the lack of feeding. Being hungry always makes me the ugliest version of myself.

Her friend's eyes are wide as he glances between the two of us. A touch of pink warms her cheeks and my hand twitches to reach out to her.

'I'll catch up with you later,' she says to him before turning to the others with a pretty, warm smile on her face. 'It was nice to meet you all.'

As she walks beside me, her arm brushes mine. The hitch of her breath fills my ears and I clench my fist so hard I break a finger. Wincing, I feel it reset itself after a few seconds.

'Hi,' she breathes, letting herself give in to the thread that is growing stronger between us as the moments pass. I feel relief like it's a palpable thing.

'Hi.'

Chewing her lip, she stares down at her feet awkwardly, neither of us really knowing what to say.

'How can you walk during the day? Aren't vampires meant to be creatures of the night?' she asks, peering up at me. 'I read in a book that you can walk in the day, but I don't understand it.'

Lazily throwing a hand toward the dark sky, I shrug. 'We pick gloomy places like this to live in. We can be out in the sun for a while, but it makes us weak and will eventually kill us if we don't cover up. But this sort of day.' I point to the dark storm clouds. 'Perfect.'

'Oh.' She nods. 'Makes sense.'

'Look . . .' I say, directing the conversation to where I need it to go, the hunger rising inside me, making it difficult to breathe. 'Something has happened that I didn't think was possible.'

'Okay?' She tenses a little more, eyes narrowing slightly.

'When I healed you, I accidentally formed some sort of bond. Attachment, if you will.' I explain. 'It's uncommon and practically unheard of, but somehow it happened. I've been doing some research and . . . well . . . it seems like we will form a bodyguard type situation.' I fumble over my words, sounding like an idiot.

'What?' she frowns.

'We blood-shared and since I'm not great at the whole being a vampire thing, I accidentally bonded with you.'

She blinks at me.

'We are basically attached to each other. In tune with the other's feelings,' I try again, not really sure how to make her understand the severity of the situation, without freaking her out.

'Accidentally bonded . . .' She blinks, looking bewildered. 'How—what—?' She starts and stops her sentences a few times, trying to gather her thoughts. In the end, she blows out a breath, looking confused, and frustrated. 'Honestly, this shouldn't surprise me. Everything I've learnt has been wild so far.'

I don't know what to say. Rubbing the back of my neck, I try to focus on her, and not think about the gnawing hunger that is rapidly increasing by the moment.

She nods. 'I want to be around you. It's like a hardcore craving I can't kick. I think about you all the time. Dream about you . . .' She blushes intensely, and I chew the inside of my cheek, trying not to reveal to her that I also have dreamed about *her*. She probably thinks she hallucinated seeing me out her window. 'I thought it might have been some sort of after effect from drinking your blood.'

'It's not unusual for humans to get attached to vampires when blood is exchanged, because of the high and whatnot, but this is much more intense.'

She nods again. 'I see.'

'There's another thing.'

Swallowing, she peers up at me. 'What?'

'You're now my one and only blood source,' I say quietly, in fear she might run away screaming at any moment. 'Which means I haven't fed for days and if I don't soon, I might . . . snap . . . I guess you can say. And eventually, die.'

Her eyes widen and her hand flies to her chest, hovering over her heart, as if it hurt at the mention of my death. Looking down at her hand, she frowns, as if feeling conflicted and confused with her thoughts. I get how she's feeling, since I am experiencing a similar thing myself.

'Okay,' she breathes. 'The thought of you feeding on me scares me, but not as much as I thought it would.'

'Because of the bond,' I say.

'Right.' She jerks her chin a few times, trying to get a grip on everything I just dumped on her.

'It's keeping you calm.'

'Makes sense.'

'I'm sorry. I don't often feed from humans unless I'm desperate. This is uncomfortable for me, too.'

She lifts a shoulder. 'Okay. I'm guessing we need to do this now, then?'

Wincing, I nod. 'Sorry.'

'It's . . . fine.'

Ushering her into a secluded classroom, I pull down the blinds, and lock the door. She walks backward. Her bag slips from her shoulder as I advance on her, the air thickening around us as I draw nearer.

'Will it hurt?' she asks.

'No,' I murmur, standing so close, she has to tilt her head back to see me. Gently, I lift her onto the desk and stand between her legs. She gasps as I push her legs apart. I can't help myself, I need her close. I never do this. If I have to drink from someone, it's almost clinical, and I put as much distance between us as possible. But she isn't just *anyone*. Leaning forward, I flatten my hands on the desk. 'In fact, you will love it.'

Rolling her lips into her mouth, she gazes up at me in wonder.

Slowly, my hand travels up from her hip, tracing the delicate lines of her body. I twirl a dark piece of her hair around my finger before she shakes it behind her shoulders. I touch the violet streak. My mouth salivates at her proximity.

'Ready?' I whisper, pressing a soft kiss against her neck.

She shivers, her small fingers trailing down my chest, curling my shirt in her grasp.

'Yes.'

My fangs slide out and she recoils, scrambling back, knocking her bag off the desk. In my weakened state, I stumble back in surprise, almost falling over my own feet.

'No!' she chokes out, tears welling in her eyes. I flinch at the terror in them, quickly backing away from her, my heart sinking in my chest. 'I . . . can't do this. I'm sorry.' Trembling, she hastily gets to her feet, her face as white as paper.

Everything inside me burns. Every fibre of my being aches for her, and I clench my jaw, stepping further back.

'Okay,' I say slowly, hating how frail and fearful she looks. 'I understand. It's okay.'

'I'm sorry,' she whispers, the tears racing down her cheeks now, shaking to the point I fear she is going to topple over.

I want to go to her, to cup her face in my hands, and wipe them away. I want to comfort her, and assure her I could never hurt her, and that the last thing I want is for her to be afraid of me, but I don't. I can't.

Unable to even look at her, I turn, fleeing the classroom, feeling dizzy and weak.

The thought of heading home fills me with dread. I'm honestly not sure I can even make it. Peering up at the building my next class is in, I force my legs to carry me there. Finding my usual seat, I collapse onto it, feeling lethargic and on the verge of blacking out. I just need to sit for a little bit, then I'll be fine.

Leaning back in my seat, I sink down into it, trying to keep my eyes open as the lecture hall steadily fills. Biting my tongue, I feel the coppery taste of blood. I don't look at her as she walks toward the front, dropping down into a random seat.

She didn't sit beside me like she usually does.

She's everywhere – when I inhale, when my eyes are open, even when they aren't. Clenching my teeth, I try to focus on *anything* but her.

The class crawls by painfully slow. My vision is swimming each time I try to take notes. The professor's words go in one ear and out the other. The pen in my hand tips from my grasp, rolling across the table, falling to the floor. I don't even have the energy to pick it up.

When it is finished, I don't trust myself to stand, so I wait for everyone to leave. Raya glances up at me, a look of concern on her face.

When we are the last two left, she takes a hesitant step toward me. 'Are you okay?'

'Yeah,' I reply, my voice not sounding like my own.

With a great deal of effort, I push to my feet, and the world tips. Collapsing on the floor, I land with a heavy thud. Rolling onto my back, I try to gather my bearings, but blackness borders my vision.

'Hunter!' Her scent fills my nostrils. A warm, flowery sweetness that makes my mouth water. 'Oh my God.' Her small hands grip my arms as she tries to shake me. 'What can I do?'

My eyes are too heavy now. I can barely keep them open.

'If I do this,' she whispers, her face dipping in and out of focus as she looks down at me. 'Promise me you will help me find out answers and tell me what you know.'

I make a small sound of agreement.

'Promise me, Hunter,' she insists.

'Promise,' I reply, my voice barely a whisper.

Taking a deep breath, she nods. Laying on her side, she flicks her hair back behind her ear. She is shaking as she inches closer to me, her heartbeat hammering in my ears.

'Okay,' she says, more to herself than me. 'Let's do this.'

Slowly, I drag her toward me and sink into her soft flesh in one fluid movement. We both moan. Her grip on me tightens as the explosion of her taste fills my mouth. It is more pleasurable than anything I have experienced. Holding her tighter to me, I drink long and hard for a few moments, feeling drunk off the high of her. My fangs retract with a harsh snap, as if the bond has complete control over my willpower.

Her eyes flutter closed as she presses her forehead into my shoulder. Curling my arm around her, I hug her to myself, relishing in the closeness. Kissing her hair, I breathe her in, feeling warmth spread over me. I haven't felt warmth like this since before I was turned.

Leaning away from her, I drag the back of my hand across my mouth. Her blood is addictive and the need to keep drinking is overwhelming. Within seconds, I feel like my old self again. Fit, strong, healthy. My vision sharpens on her pretty heart-shaped face.

'Thank you for trusting me.' She watches me hesitantly. I don't want her to be scared of me. I lift the corners of my mouth into what I hope is a light-hearted smile. 'You taste divine.'

She laughs quietly, and my smile becomes more genuine at the sound of it.

'That wasn't nearly as scary as I thought it was going to be.'

Leaping to my feet, I offer her my hand, which she takes and stands. She sways for a moment, and I look at her in concern, lightly holding her shoulder with my free hand to keep her steady.

I nick the skin on my thumb and offer it to her. She stares at it, then at me, and back to it.

'A little bit won't be enough to make you high. It will make you feel better.'

Slowly, she leans in, keeping her eyes on mine. She slowly sucks my thumb and I groan at the feel of her lips on my skin. Blood rushes to my groin, and I press myself against her involuntarily. She sucks it harder and deeper than necessary, as if playing with me, having quickly lost her fear, the high replacing it with something much more teasing and light.

'More,' I moan, surprised when the word falls from my lips.

Circling her tongue around the end of my thumb, she steps back, her lips making a popping sound as she releases me.

She smiles up at me, her dark lashes framing those pretty eyes that invaded my dreams all night.

This girl will be the death of me.

9

RAYA

The Survivor

I'M LATE TO OUR NEXT CLASS and everybody glances up as I walk in. I look over my shoulder to see Hunter following me inside. He sends me a small smile, looking a lot better now, but his expression is clouded with . . . guilt?

Feeling an odd mixture of nauseous and a little giddy, I make my way over to where Alex is sitting and drop into the seat beside him.

The stare Alex is giving me is drilling holes into the side of my face.

'What the *hell* is going on?' he whispers, eyes narrowed to slits.

'I'll explain later,' I say.

'Now.'

'Later.' I give him a pointed look.

Reluctantly, he faces the front, not looking very impressed. I don't even know how I'm going to explain any of this to him. It sounds crazy. Delusional. It feels like I'm in a dream and I'm going to wake up at any moment and realise none of this is real.

The moment class is over, Alex drags me out of the classroom, and basically shoves me underneath a hidden staircase. He stares hard down at me. 'Spill.'

I rehash everything to him the best I can. He blinks at me,

speechless. I think this is the first time I've ever witnessed words failing him.

'Fucking hell,' he hisses, his face pale, looking disturbed. 'Now you're tied to that vampire?'

I nod. 'Yes.'

'He knew this would happen,' he growls, his cheeks reddening. 'He probably set this whole thing up so that he can have a personal blood donor whenever he needs it!'

His words feel like a slap in the face. 'Ouch, Alex.'

'Don't let his coercion persuade you into thinking this is anything but a blood exchange! This is what they do. They lure you in and eat you alive.'

'No,' I argue. 'He seems different.'

Alex scoffs. 'He is a vampire, Raya. Open your eyes.'

'They are open!' I snap in frustration. 'I know, Alex. I'm trying my best to ignore everything that is going on in here,' I say, pointing to my chest. 'But it's not as easy as you think. Besides, he can *help* us, and if what he says is true – which I believe it is – he *needs* me. We can use this to our advantage. We can't forget what the end goal is.'

'He's lying to you!' Alex insists, grabbing my shoulders and shaking me. 'And I'm not the one who needs a reminder about the end goal, Raya.'

There's a whoosh of air and suddenly Hunter is here. He has Alex's arms pinned painfully behind his back. Alex squawks in alarm, wriggling furiously to get Hunter to let him go.

'You don't touch her,' he speaks, his voice deep, shooting shivers of desire down my back at the sound of it. 'Ever.'

Alex gulps, looking frantically at me.

'What are you doing?' I exclaim in panic. 'Let him go!'

Immediately, Hunter releases his hold. Alex stumbles forward, wincing as he rubs his arm. He scowls up at Hunter, who looms over him like a . . . well . . . a dark creature of the night. Alex's face is completely white as he glances between us.

'Never again,' Hunter warns, those pretty silver eyes morphing into something darker and much more sinister.

'Fucking hell,' Alex mutters, sending me a furious look. 'He is a total psycho.'

A deep growl rumbles in Hunter's chest in warning. I step between them. For a brief moment, I wonder why my ring never alerted me to his presence. I thought for sure that's what it was doing. Warning me when one was near. Perhaps it no longer sees Hunter as a threat now that we are bonded.

'I swear, if this is all some sort of act to get her under your thumb and you're going to kill her . . .' Alex warns.

'Don't threaten a vampire,' Hunter sneers, flashing his fangs. Alex flinches, stepping back. In the dark shadow of the stairs, he looks incredibly menacing. 'It won't end well for you.'

Alex frowns at that but is smart enough not to retort. Hunter's shoulders finally relax, and he looks at me, his face completely changing.

'Raya,' he says, offering me a small smile. 'Can we meet later?'

'Fuck no!' Alex exclaims.

'Yes,' I agree at the same time, my need to know answers overpowering any rational part of my brain.

'I'll be at yours at seven.' He nods.

And then he is gone.

Alex's jaw is so low, I'm surprised his chin isn't on the ground. He opens and closes his mouth several times.

'He knows where we live?' Alex breathes.

My mind reels back to seeing him from the window in my room. I thought I was still dreaming, but what if he was really there?

'We're not going to make it out of here alive,' Alex whispers, glancing in the spot Hunter just was. 'I truly believe that.'

The time has barely turned seven when there's a knock at the door. A swooping sensation of fear – and a little excitement – fills my stomach. A part of me wants nothing to do with any of this. I don't want to get closer to a vampire, and yet, the other part of me craves to know more about him.

'Creepy motherfucker,' Alex mutters.

I slap his arm, pointing to my ear, indicating Hunter can hear every word he says. When I open the door, I feel an immense rush of relief at having him near me, despite a healthy dose of nerves bubbling in my stomach. He looks just as unsure as I feel, offering me a tight-lipped, awkward smile.

'Hi.'

My heart skips a beat. Drinking in the beauty that is Hunter, I force the breath in and out of my lungs, trying not to let him being so close totally overwhelm me. My thoughts and feelings are confusing the hell out of me.

'Hi,' I say, stepping back.

Hunter walks inside and puts a middle finger up to Alex. Alex makes an annoyed face and returns the gesture. I ignore them both and walk toward the table, taking a seat. Hunter does the same. Alex eyes the both of us, taking a long sip of his drink. My palms are sweating. I subtly wipe them down my thighs, hoping my nervousness isn't as obvious as I feel it is.

'Can I get you something to drink?' Alex asks sarcastically.

'Are you offering?' Hunter counters. The deep, sensual sound of his voice does things to me. I've never felt lust and desire course through me like it is now as I take in his tall, muscular frame. Every inch of his body is hard, muscled, and perfectly portioned.

Alex scoffs, looking away. Sighing, I lean forward. Getting straight to the point, I tap my finger against the mark on my arm.

'You told me this mark is the same mark your brother leaves on his victims. Correct?'

Hunter leans back in the chair, propping up onto his elbow. He nods.

'I never had this until the accident, so I'm assuming this could connect your brother to it. It isn't a coincidence that my sister's body is missing. No one vanishes like that from a car wreck. It doesn't make sense.'

Alex perks up at this piece of information, leaning forward.

'You think my brother took your sister?' Hunter questions, looking frustratingly unreadable. He makes it impossible to figure out what he is thinking. All that I can feel is a quiet calmness coming from him.

I nod, dread inching through me at the thought. 'Or knows something about it. I found journals of hers that talk about a guy. It sounds like he was a vampire. I'm guessing it's him.'

Hunter chews his lips as he considers this.

'Since you need me,' I say, drawing in an encouraging breath. 'I'm hoping we can come to a mutual arrangement.'

'Arrangement?' He arches an eyebrow.

'This,' I say, tapping my neck. 'For information. Like you promised.'

The corner of his lips twitch. 'Well, I have no room to argue, do I?'

Shrugging, I tighten the hold on my fingers. 'So that's a yes?'

'Yes,' he finally says, looking just as reluctant about the whole thing as I do.

'Do you know where your brother is?'

'No.' Hunter sighs. 'But I can find him.'

'You can't call him?' Alex asks sharply.

'No.' Hunter doesn't even look at him. 'We aren't in contact. When a vampire wants to disappear, it's very easy to. Especially Kian.'

'Will you help us?' I ask tentatively.

'I guess so,' he says. His gaze turns to me and I feel like he is looking straight through me. 'I don't want anything to do with my brother.' Hunter clenches his jaw and I can practically see his internal struggle. 'But I'll do it for you.'

Alex rolls his eyes so hard they almost disappear into the back of his head. In a way, I'm reluctant to have the very thing help me that I came to get my sister away from, but it might come in handy having someone like him around to help and now, with this bond, I feel safe with him near me. Like nothing can touch me if he is close by.

'Where do we start?' I ask, trying to sound confident and in charge, despite feeling the opposite.

Hunter pulls out his phone. 'He dropped by Red Thorne briefly a few months ago, then he disappeared again, but someone told me they think he might be up north, in the city. It'll take a few days of driving to get there.'

'Can't we fly?' Alex protests.

'Vampires don't do well at airports,' Hunter counters.

'We can fly and meet you there,' Alex snaps back.

'Alex!' I huff in exasperation. 'Stop being an asshole. He is helping us. This is why we are here, remember?'

Alex bites his tongue after that.

Once the plan is decided, Alex gets to his feet.

'You can go now,' he says.

'Alex,' I warn through gritted teeth.

'I need a minute alone with Raya,' Hunter replies.

'No.'

'Alex,' I hiss. 'It's fine. Please.'

Looking furious, he points a finger at Hunter. 'No funny business.'

Hunter rolls his eyes, looking incredibly boyish and human as he does. Alex stalks off to his room, leaving Hunter and I alone at the table.

Hunter's long fingers tap against the table, and I study them for a moment, my mind reeling back to when they touched me earlier today. Squeezing my thighs together, I squirm in my seat, waves of heat rolling through me, making it hard to focus on anything else.

'Thank you for doing this,' I say, a little curtly.

He nods, a jerk of his chin that is short, and sharp. 'Sure. Anything to help.'

'What do we do now?' I question, once more dragging my sweaty palms down the top of my thighs. 'With this bond? We are going to be linked forever now, aren't we?'

Hunter contemplates this. 'Yes, I believe so. Let's just take it one day at a time. No pressure, no expectancy of anything.'

I release a relieved breath. 'That sounds great.'

'You're sure you want to do this?' he asks, leaning forward onto his forearms. 'Find her?'

I look at him in confusion. 'Of course, she is my sister.'

'She might not be the sister you remember.'

Coldness spreads through my chest at the thought. I nod slowly, understanding what he is trying to say. My mind has gone there before. It's not a place I like to visit, but I can't be foolish and not explore that possibility.

'I have to do this,' I say firmly.

He studies me for a moment and then nods. 'Then we'll do it.'

'Will we leave tomorrow?'

Hunter shakes his head. 'Give me time to sort some things out. I'll let you know.'

'Okay.'

He stands. He moves gracefully around the table, touching my shoulder gently. Warmth slithers through me.

'Sleep well,' he says. 'Talk tomorrow.'

We stare at each other for a moment, unsure of what to do. Swallowing, I give him a small smile.

'Until tomorrow.'

10

HUNTER

The Protector

THE NEXT DAY, I have maps, notes, and articles spread across my desk. Chewing my pen, I browse through them, circling parts of articles that discuss attacks and disappearances. My brother has a dramatic and particular way he goes about things, it's easy to pick out which murders are his.

I have narrowed it down to one spot that Kian seems to have stayed for a few weeks. It's a bit of travel on our part, so I will need to constantly be monitoring the news updates to make sure he doesn't move on before we reach him.

Taunting his 'gift' over me was his greatest joy. The fact that he was turned. He thought it was something that I wanted and envied. He toyed with it in front of me, offering to turn me, only to promise he never would. After seeing how much worse he became, I didn't want it.

Then, he turned Theo, out of spite. In his game, he never played out the fact that Theo would inevitably change me anyway, even when I firmly denied the offer. I blame both of them equally for taking that right away from me.

The thumping of a headboard against the wall can be heard, and a moan. Sighing, I stand, searching for my AirPods. Just as I'm opening the case, I hear the front door open. I instantly recognise the sound of Lucy, Theo's girlfriend, who I thought was the one in the room with him.

Groaning, I realise there is a shit storm about to take place. Moving quickly down the stairs, I get to the living room just as she is yanking Theo's bedroom door off its hinges. She snarls, glowering down at the human who is on top of Theo.

'Lucy,' I warn, my tone low and laced with authority. 'Don't.'

Screaming, she lunges toward the girl. Just as her fangs are about to rip into the girl, I reel her back so violently I hear the bones in her neck crack. She cries out in alarm, slamming into the wall, splintering the plaster.

'Don't,' I snarl. 'Theo is in the wrong, not her.'

She breathes hard, her hair blowing back and forth in front of her face. She shoves against me, and I press harder. My fingers bite into her flesh, drawing blood. She hisses, snapping her teeth at me like she is a rabid wolf.

'Get off me,' she demands, a threat lacing every word.

'Theo,' I growl. 'Get the girl out of here. Now.'

Looking like he is enjoying the show far too much, Theo stands and pulls his jeans on. He leaves, holding the girl's hand, and Lucy spits at him. I don't release her hold just yet, knowing how fast and brutal she can be.

'Why do you always go back to him?' I demand, shaking my head at her. 'You're both so possessive and jealous of each other, and yet not loyal. Makes no sense.'

'I don't have to explain myself to you,' she hisses.

'I'm sick of dealing with the both of you,' I snap, suddenly letting her go and stepping back. She collapses on the floor, heaving as the oxygen rushes back into her lungs. Making a disgruntled sound, she uses the wall to support her as she clambers to her feet, her hair wild, eyes furious as she glowers at me. 'This is not my mess to deal with.'

'Leave, then,' she says.

'I am,' I tell her.

'What?"

We both look to the door. Theo walks into the room, shirtless, blood smeared in the corner of his mouth. I'm half-convinced he purposely does this, just to see Lucy's reaction. Then they have passionate hate-sex all night. It's rather annoying since I have perfect hearing.

'I'm leaving.' I sigh.

'Since the fuck when?' he growls, striding toward me, a muscle spasming in his cheek as his jaw clenches so hard, I wouldn't be surprised if he cracks a tooth.

'Since today.'

'Where?'

'That's what I'm trying to figure out. North, somewhere.'

Theo's face hardens. 'This better not have anything to do with your bonded blood bag.'

My fists ball at my sides, anger flaring inside me, as tension coils in my muscles. 'Don't.'

Lucy's eyes widen at the ferocity in my tone. I'm the calm, patient one. I never get angry and lose my cool, but when it comes to Raya, I'm out of control it seems.

'You aren't serious,' he snaps, upper lip curling angrily.

'She's leaving, and I need to go with her. She needs me.'

'Don't you remember that vampires are literally hunting me?' He throws his hands in the air. 'You can't leave now.'

'I don't have a choice!' I yell in frustration. 'Wherever she goes, I go. We're bonded.'

A vein pulses in his temple. 'Unless someone snaps her fucking neck.'

A tidal wave of anger courses through me and I screw my eyes shut as I try to calm myself, my chest rising rapidly as I breathe hard. My eyes fly back open and Lucy is studying me with an open-mouth, her eyes switching between me and Theo.

'She dies, I die,' I say slowly. 'And don't forget, she is my one and only source now.'

'This is fucked.' Theo shakes his head, looking at me like he doesn't even recognise me. 'It's meant to be me and you. Until the end.'

'It's not like this was my choice, Theo.' I expel a heavy breath, leaning back against the wall, suddenly feeling exhausted. 'And you can leave. It's the smart thing to do, given your situation.'

Ignoring my comment, as he always does, his lips flatten into a line barely visible on his face. 'If you go, consider us done,' Theo says, his eyes darkening.

I push off the wall. 'It doesn't need to be like this. A friend should be understanding that I don't have a say in this.'

He says nothing. Sighing, I walk around him and begin packing up my things. I can't stay anymore. With him. With them. The last thing I want to be doing is a wild goose chase after my asshole, psychotic brother. But I can't stay here, either.

It doesn't take long to pack my things. My chest feels heavy as I hover near the door, unsure what to do or say to make any of this better.

'If you walk out that door, you're basically signing my death wish.' Theo's voice is low and deep.

A whirlwind of emotions circle inside me. I'm angry at Theo – and confused as to why he refuses to leave. There must be another reason. Something he is hiding from me. Once, Theo and I were closer than I ever thought two people could be. Since we turned, there's been a chasm that is inching wider and wider with each passing day.

Whatever he's hiding from me, I can't stick around to find out what it is. Theo is too smart to stay here, in a place where people are out to get him. At this moment, I realise, neither of us have been truthful to the other.

My hand is on the door, my back to him. I close my eyes for a moment, feeling the weight and pain of his words. I know he needs me for protection. A second pair of eyes, ears, and the lend of strength he will need if they come. But I can't stay.

With my heart in my throat, I open the door, a low and threatening growl at my back, but I know Theo well enough to know there's also an undertone of hurt. Walking out into the night, I don't look back.

It is mid-morning by the time I arrive at Alex and Raya's house. I had a sleepless night in my truck. I can't get the argument with Theo off my mind. It's not the way I like to leave things. I feel terrible, but I wish he tried to understand that this is something beyond what I want. It's out of my control.

Raya emerges from the house. Her dark hair falls to her hips in natural waves. My eyes track her easy movements as she walks toward me. Pretty pale skin, soft, full lips, round green eyes that shine brightly under the cloudy sky. She is truly gorgeous.

'I'm just saying, I wish we didn't spend a bunch of our savings on this apartment, only to move on from it five minutes later,' Alex grumbles, sliding dark shades up his nose.

'Life isn't fair,' Raya replies.

'Don't I know it,' he mutters.

'I think the problems we are facing are a little bigger than this.'

Alex doesn't respond to that. Instead, he offers me a tight smile and a wave. 'Hello, grumpy vampire bodyguard.'

'Hello, annoying friend who is totally unnecessary.'

'Fuck you, asshole.'

Raya sighs in exasperation. 'This is going to be a long trip.'

As Alex heads around to the other side of the car, Raya and I subconsciously draw nearer to each other. Reaching out, I stroke a finger slowly down her arm, appeasing the gnawing sensation clawing through my chest. I hear the tiny puff of relief that leaves her lips, telling me she is feeling the same.

'Hello,' I say softly.

'Hi.'

'Are you okay?' I ask. 'This is a big thing. Going after her.'

'I'm fine. I need to do this.'

It pains me. Seeing the determination and hope etched onto her face. She has no idea what she is getting herself into. *Who* she is dealing with.

When my brother was in town last, he had a woman with him. After meeting Raya, I know who she is now. It's Cora. The sight of her with black eyes, blood smeared across her face and hands, flashes in my mind. She is not the girl Raya remembers her to be. But how can I break this news to her? Besides, if she is involved with Kian, I am sure there is more to the story. I imagine he has a hold over her, like he does with everyone. I'm not going to make judgments until I know the full story, and meet her myself.

'What about everything that happened the other day, with us?' I carefully ask, leaning against the doorframe.

'Fine,' she repeats, and I frown. Clearly, everything is not *fine*.

'Raya.' I sigh. 'You can tell me what you're feeling. If I repulse you, if the thought of me feeding terrifies you. I want to know.'

Tilting her head back, she offers me a small smile. 'You don't repulse me, Hunter. Not at all. That's what is so confusing, honestly.'

'I don't want to make you uncomfortable in any way.'

'You don't,' she insists, and the breeze blows her hair across her face. 'It's like . . . the way I think about vampires and my opinion of you are totally separate, even though you are a vampire, too. I don't know if that makes any sense.'

'I get it,' I say. 'The whole situation is confusing. For me, too.'

With those round eyes blinking up at me, the craving to be closer to her, to learn more, surges. I want to know everything there is to know about her. Shaking off the feeling, shoving it far, *far* back into my mind, I nod, pushing off from the car.

'Are you ready to go?' I ask, assessing her once more.

Nodding, she tucks the loose piece of hair behind her ear. 'I'm ready.'

Opening the door for her, she sends me a small smile as she climbs into my truck. I glance up at the darkening sky, the promise of rain lingering in the air. The engine rumbles to life and I throw my arm around the passenger seat as I look out the back window, reversing.

I'm relieved that things between Raya and I feel less tense and awkward. As much as we shouldn't strengthen this bond, I want her to warm up to me, and feel like she is safe. I can't imagine how terrified she was the night I found her practically dead in the woods and how traumatised it made her

'I need to pee,' Alex says only a few minutes later.

Exhaling, I glance at Raya who is shaking her head.

She was right, this *is* going to be a long trip.

11

THE PREDATOR

I'M CAREFUL TO KEEP a few cars back from them. Their truck is easy to track with its blacked-out windows and all-black exterior. My thumbs tap against the steering wheel as we both weave in and out of the heavy traffic lanes.

This is it, I can feel it.

I've been looking for a lead for a long time. Years. I've been watching, waiting, gathering information, stalking. I was so close, only a few months ago, but he was gone before I had the chance to pinpoint his location. He's like a ghost, ever-present but always out of reach.

Always watching, always listening, always waiting.

The time has finally come.

He will be mine.

12

RAYA

The Survivor

IF SOMEONE TOLD ME a year ago, I would be sitting in a car driven by a scowling vampire, with someone shouting Britney Spears lyrics from the back seat who until recently was a complete stranger, I would have laughed.

With one leg on the pedal, Hunter's other leg bounces up and down as we continue to cruise down the highway. His continuous glares through the rear-view mirror are enough evidence that Alex's one-man-karaoke show is grating on his nerves. Honestly, it's getting to me a little too.

'How long have you been a vampire?' I ask a little too loudly, trying to drown out Alex's increasingly off-key singing. I was starting to suspect he was doing it on purpose.

Hunter looks over at me for a moment before focusing back on the road. 'Five years.'

'Oh . . . random.'

A breathy laugh escapes his lips and I feel a flutter in my chest. He has one hand relaxed on the steering wheel, the other resting on the gear stick where my gaze falls. I swallow thickly, taking in the details of his hand – the veins running along the top of it, his long fingers, the faintest hint of a scar along the skin that must have been there long before he turned. I never thought a hand could be sexy, but, here I am, admiring his.

'Why do you say that?'

'Sorry?' I look up, blushing as he certainly noticed me staring.

'You said my response was random. How so?'

I take a deep breath before I answer. 'Well, in all the shows I've seen, and books I've read, the vampires are always over a hundred years old.'

He scoffs. 'If I was over a hundred, I don't think I would still be going to university.'

'They do,' I say, a little too enthusiastically.

'Who?'

'The vampires in the movies,' I reply, in a *duh* tone, throwing an annoyed look back at Alex who continues to sing and whistle, his eyes closed now, so I now know he's at least in part doing it to be annoying.

'You mean the vampires in fiction,' Hunter states.

I look from Alex back to Hunter. 'Huh?'

'You're basing your knowledge of vampires on fiction.'

I hate to admit it, but he has me stumped here. Damn it. But before I can say anything, he continues.

'I figure if you were over a hundred years old there's bound to be other things more fascinating than study. I guess if you wanted to brush up on recent findings or tech then it might be okay. Otherwise, I don't see the point spending all those extra years studying.'

'I think it would be pretty cool to know so much.' I shrug.

'Yeah,' he agrees quietly.

'Did you know about vampires before you were turned?' I ask, flipping Alex the bird over my shoulder, though I'm pretty sure he doesn't see it.

Hunter lifts his hand from the gearstick and scratches his jaw. I can't tell if he's irritated by my questions, Alex's singing – or both. 'Only because my brother was turned. That prick of a vampire tormented me and my friend for months. Made a game out of it.'

'A game?' I ask, raising a brow.

'Used to fuck with us simply because he could,' he says, dead-pan, his face suddenly void of expression. 'He loves to play games, and conduct "experiments" as he likes to call them. He views everyone as pawns, not people.'

'And then he turned you?'

'Not exactly. He wanted someone he could control, and to prove to me he could take anything – or anyone – from me. So, he turned my friend, Theo. Then it was Theo who ended up turning me, even though I begged him not to.' He pauses and looks at me and my breath catches in my throat. 'I didn't want this life.'

I'm not sure why, but his confession surprises me, and I twist in my seat so I can see him better. His dark hair is messy today. I run my eyes down his sharp jawline, down his neck, resting along the curve of his broad shoulders.

'You didn't want to become a vampire?' I ask.

Alex's bleating comes to a startling stop, and I glance back at him, but his eyes are on Hunter as though he's curious to hear the answer to my question, too.

'Hunter?' I prompt gently, hoping I'm not pushing my luck.

'Not after seeing what happened to them.'

'What happened to them?' I ask before I can stop myself. I can't help it, I'm desperate to know more.

'It's like they forgot what humanity is. They treat humans like they're nothing but food. Sport, even. They've conveniently for-gotten they used to be one.' His voice has a clipped, cold edge to it, like he is talking about some monstrous serial killer, instead of his friends and family.

'So you *are* a good vampire.' I smile. 'I knew it.'

His fingers tighten around the steering wheel, bleaching his knuckles white. 'There is no such thing, Raya.'

'I don't believe that.' I refuse to believe that.

Hunter gives me a tight look. 'Based on your extensive knowledge about the species?'

'No.' I roll my eyes. 'Not exactly. You're here helping two people you don't even know solve a mystery that has nothing to do with you. I'd say that makes you good – vampire or otherwise.'

'I'm being forced by the bond, Raya. I don't want to be here,' he snaps.

My lips part in shock at his blunt words. An uneasy feeling settles in my gut as they hit me harder than I expect. Maybe I had been delusional for a few moments there. I shift in my seat and turn back to face the front, feeling Alex's stare boring into me from the back seat. He's probably gloating.

Hunter sighs heavily and I feel his eyes on me as I stare straight ahead, doing my best to hold back the tears that sting my eyes. I think he might say something, but instead an uneasy silence stretches between us. Turning my head, I lean against the window and absently stare out of it, my decent mood having completely evaporated.

Seconds turn into minutes, and before I know it the minutes stretch into hours. My eyes grow heavy, and the sky has grown gradually darker for several hours now.

'I think we need to find a hotel,' Hunter finally murmurs, breaking the silence and jolting me out of my daydream.

'I can drive,' Alex pipes up from the back.

'Fuck no,' Hunter mutters.

'Why not?' Alex gasps in mock-horror, forehead crumpling in confusion, like he has never been told 'no' before.

'Because I said so.'

'Asshole,' Alex grumbles.

'Bite me, dickwad.'

A snort of laughter bursts from me in surprise at Hunter's remark. A ghost of a smirk appears on his lips before it's gone again. I quickly glance over my shoulder and offer Alex a small, sympathetic smile, which he moodily returns.

Rain lightly pitter-patters against the window and I feel oddly nervous as I watch the lightning sparking on the horizon as thunder rumbles off in the distance.

'Are we safe to stop?' I ask, finally looking at Hunter, since I've been looking anywhere but at him for the last few hours.

'Yes.'

'You can fight, right?'

He looks over at me, lips twitching. 'I can fight, *legata una*.'

'What?' I frown.

Ignoring me, Hunter pulls into a car park beneath a neon red sign that flashes 'vacancy' before he kills the engine and gets out of the car. The door slams, rocking the car momentarily.

'What language was that?' I question, turning in my seat to face Alex. He has his leg propped up beside him.

'Italian, I think.'

'What did he say again? I'm going to Google it.'

'I don't know. Who cares.' Alex dramatically flings open the door and disappears.

Sighing, I follow their lead. Hunter has both our bags slung over his shoulders as he stalks toward reception. Glancing around the dark car park, I see ours is the only vehicle there, and the smell of rain fills my lungs with each breath I take. Alex glances at Hunter wearily a few times, and my shoulders tense at the look of mistrust in his eyes.

A sudden bolt of lightning forks across the midnight sky and I flinch at the loud thunder that follows immediately after.

Perfect.

If I wasn't already on edge at the thought of staying in a

creepy, secluded hotel in a town I've never heard of with a hungry vampire capable of snapping and killing me – the storm definitely now has me teetering there. Not that I think Hunter could snap and kill me, with the bond and all. Well. He could snap – just not kill me. Hopefully. Right?

After a few minutes, Hunter returns with a card in his hand and without a word we follow him up a narrow flight of stairs to the top floor. He taps the key to the door and holds it open as we walk inside. Alex beelines toward the lounge and throws his bag onto it as I hover behind him, inspecting our room for the night. It's small, allowing no personal space for any of us. Considering I can barely breathe when Hunter is near me, or looks at me, this forced proximity is going to be a problem. I doubt I'll be able to rest, having him so close. And Alex snores like a freight train.

It's going to be a long night.

'Shotgun this bed,' Alex calls out. 'And dibs on the first shower.' He disappears into the bathroom, the door clicking shut behind him, leaving Hunter and I staring at the only other bed, while trying to avoid looking at each other.

'You take the bed, I'll be on watch,' he mutters.

'Do you need to, you know, sleep?' I ask with a huff, planting my hands on my hips.

'Yeah, but I'll manage.'

'We can take turns,' I say, swinging my bag onto the bed while kicking off my sandals.

'It's fine.'

'It's not fine.'

A phone vibrating interrupts our bickering. Hunter pulls it from his pocket, a pained look appearing on his face as he glances at the screen. It might be the most emotion I've ever seen him express, except for when he fed on me. But I try not to think about that. It makes my mind go down a dark . . . and dirty . . . route. Which is the last thing I need given our current living arrangements.

'Uh, are you hungry?' he asked.

'No, I'm fine,' I lie, just as my stomach betrays me and growls loudly.

'I'll go see if there is somewhere nearby to get you both some food,' he says, stomping toward the door. He pauses before leaving, turning back to me and touching his finger to his ear. 'You're safe. I'll hear if there is anyone coming, no matter where I am.'

The door slams shut behind him after that, rattling the thin wall. I stare after it for a few moments, my mouth agape and my mind racing. Edging toward the window, I peel back the faded curtain and peer out at the night as I crack it open. The smell of rain makes me smile a little, despite how anxious and nervous I'm feeling. I love the rain. Droplets of water bounce from the railing down onto the cement. I stare at it for a few moments, reminding myself of why it is so important to be here right now, on this trip, endangering my life. It will all be worth it.

A sudden movement down in the parking lot sends my heart catapulting into my stomach, and I clamp my hand to my mouth to stop from screaming as I pull back behind the curtain. I'm positive someone was just standing there, looking up at our hotel room. With my heart thundering in my chest, I take a quick peek through the curtains but all I can see is the neon lights reflected in the growing puddles below. Swallowing thickly, I draw the curtain firmly shut and step back.

It's probably Hunter keeping watch. Nothing to be afraid of.

'What are you doing?'

I startle once more and spin on my heel. Alex stares at me, an eyebrow raised.

'Nothing.'

'Where's the leech?'

'Don't call him that,' I snap. 'You could be a little less hateful since he is here *helping* us. Not to mention paying for this room. If it wasn't for him, we would still be searching for a lead.'

'Has it ever crossed your mind that he has set this entire thing up?' Alex hisses, striding toward me and flinging strings of silver around my wrists. 'He could have brought us to this very hotel room to leave us as dinner for his friends!'

'If I die, he dies, remember?'

'So he says.' Alex scoffs. 'Like, we just have to take his word for that, right?'

Sighing, I eye my wrists. The silver feels cold against my skin. 'It's my turn for the shower.' I duck out of his reach as he tries to loop a string of silver around my neck. 'And there'd better be some hot water left!'

'Leave that silver on at all times!' Alex continues, 'Shower or no shower. I know he's pretty and he's helping us, but don't forget everything we have learned – these are scary creatures we are dealing with. They can snap at any moment.'

I ignore him as I walk through to the bathroom, though his words echo in my mind. I know he's right, even if I don't want to give him the satisfaction of telling him.

I feel a hundred times better after a shower, especially with my soft oversized T-shirt and comfy slippers on, and my hair up in a bun, away from my face. I'm a little surprised to find Hunter still isn't back when I come out of the bathroom. Alex is sprawled across his bed with one arm propped underneath his head as he watches videos on his phone, like he hasn't got a care in the world.

I'm feeling desperate for a drink of water, but when I turn on the cold tap in the kitchenette, it appears to be broken. I try the hot tap, but the colour of the water spurting out doesn't look like something I'd want to put in my mouth.

'I'm going to go see if I can find a vending machine and get something to drink.'

'Don't be dumb,' Alex says, without looking away from his video.

'I'm wearing my silver and Hunter isn't far.'

Alex shakes his head, not replying.

Slipping out the door, I trot along the walkway. The wind has picked up with the coming storm and it slams into me, making me shiver. I wrap my arms around myself and increase my pace. Most of the lights are out overhead, making it difficult to see. I brighten when I see a vending machine. It's dingy looking with half the lights blown, and the plastic of its outer casing faded from the sun, but at least there is an array of water, juice and soft drinks jammed inside.

'Hey.'

I gasp and stumble over my own feet at the sudden sound. Whirling around, my eyes settle on two boys. One tall, towering over me, and the other one significantly shorter, but twice as wide.

'Hello,' I mumble, involuntarily stepping back as I grip the silver.

Alex was right. I am dumb. So fucking dumb sometimes.

'What are you up to?' the shorter guy asks, his voice raspy. His greasy, floppy blond locks fall over his forehead. I can't tell if he is just trying to be friendly or if his creepiness is intentional.

I point to the vending machine. 'Getting a drink.'

'You here alone?' the tall boy dressed in a peeling leather jacket asks. He has long chains that hang from his faded jeans.

Standing a little straighter, I shake my head, deciding to embellish the truth a little. 'I'm here with my boyfriend and his friends.'

The boys' glance at each other.

'I see.' Leather-jacket-guy nods, a slow smile inching across his lips. 'What room are you in?'

'What about you?' I ask instead. 'Are you here with girlfriends or are you together?'

The shorter one scoffs, creating a little distance from his friend. 'We're not together.'

'Right,' I say with a polite smile. My hand moves to my side, and I realise I don't have my knife. *Shit.*

'Why don't you come see our room?'

'Thanks, but I just need to grab one of these waters, and I'll be on my way.'

'I think you might want to come see it,' he urges, flashing a smile of warning, as if daring me to disagree. 'It'll be fun.'

Swallowing, I step back again. With the roaring wind and my heartbeat hammering in my ears, I can hardly focus on my thoughts.

The taller boy withdraws a cigarette from his jacket pocket and lights it, although it takes him a few attempts with how strong the wind is. He dangles it from his lips for a few seconds as he takes a step closer.

'Don't,' I growl. 'My boyfriend isn't a friendly guy. You don't want to see him angry.'

The boys chuckle, continuing to glance at each other like they're sharing a joke I'm not privy to.

'He ain't here, little girl.' The short one sneers and if the circumstance was any different, I would have laughed at the irony of him calling me little, when he is in fact a few inches shorter than me. Yet before I can do anything, a whoosh of air wisps my hair around my face. With his vampiric speed, Hunter suddenly stands between myself and the two creeps. I can't help myself, I peer around him as the two boys stumble back, clutching each other, their eyes wide and their mouths agape by his sudden appearance. Hunter towers over the pair, and as I place my hand on his back, I feel his muscles taut as though he's ready to pounce. I haven't asked, but I'm positive Hunter is well over six feet tall.

'She's right,' Hunter says in a deep, calm voice. 'You don't want to see me angry.'

'What are you planning to do, then?' The tall one sneers, bravely – or stupidly – releasing his mate and taking a step forward, his chin raised.

Hunter slowly cracks his knuckles with an ear-cringing *pop* in response.

'I'm going to make you regret threatening my girl,' he snarls, the anger evident in his tone. I'm completely side-tracked by the unravelling situation because all I can think about is the fact that he referred to me as *his* girl. As if realising what he said he quickly glances at me, looking a little embarrassed. '*Any* girl,' he adds.

My excitement dims.

The tall guy steps closer again. 'Oh yeah?'

A deep growl vibrates through Hunter's chest, and I suddenly find myself out from behind him and cast to the side, struggling to stay on my feet as I look over at the three of them. I can't take my eyes off Hunter, bewitched as the silver in his eyes darkens to an eerie black. His lips curl, revealing two, long fangs that even in the dim lighting look scary as hell. The tall guy jerks backward so quickly he almost topples over the wet railing before quickly righting himself. Both of the guys disappear pretty quickly after that.

'Bad ass,' I mutter, staring at the now empty hallway.

Hunter's dark eyes turn to me, his face still twisted in anger and I gulp, hastily backing up.

'I didn't think I had to tell you to stay inside.' He snarls, his fangs seeming sharper and longer than I remember.

'Sorry,' I whisper, barely sounding like myself.

'Get back to the room,' he snaps. Instead, I take a step towards the vending machine, and he growls again, making me pause. 'Leave it.'

Without looking at him, I turn on my heel and storm back to our room, grumbling beneath my breath, knowing he can likely still hear me. I wasn't sure who I was more annoyed with – Hunter for telling me what to do, or myself for risking my life only to never get the damn drink after all.

Alex looks up when I fling the door open.

'Took you long enough,' he says. His eyes move to my empty hands. 'Couldn't find any?'

I feel Hunter's presence before I hear him. I side-step out of his way as the door bangs shut so loudly it drowns out the rumbling thunder in the sky. Alex's eyes flick back and forth between us for a few seconds as he lets his phone fall onto the bed. I guess we are suddenly more interesting than his videos. I can feel Hunter's eyes on me and I force myself to meet his cunning, cold look as he assesses me.

'I'm sorry,' I force myself to say.

A vein pulses in his forehead. My gaze travels down towards his hands that curl into fists before flattening against his leg. Nodding once, he looks over to Alex, his anger gone as suddenly as it arrived.

'I understand that but be more careful next time. Who knows what those guys had planned for you.'

Alex quickly pushes into a seated position. 'What guys?'

'Doesn't matter now. Are you hungry?' Hunter asks.

Alex shakes his head, yawning. 'Too tired now.'

Hunter nods. 'Get some sleep, we will be on the road early tomorrow.'

'Aye, aye, captain!' Alex gives a thumbs up before collapsing back onto his bed.

Alex sleeps like the dead. If the dead snored. I swear he is in a coma-like state from the moment his head touches the pillow. After brushing my teeth, I climb into bed, conscious of Hunter's presence in the room. I pretend like I'm not watching him as he reaches inside his jacket and withdraws a bottle of water and a packet of pretzels. He tosses it onto the bed without a word. I stare at it, feeling a little warm at the thought of him thinking about me, as well as feeling stupid for not trusting he would make sure I had everything I needed.

'Thank you,' I say quietly.

He makes a quiet hum in response, but still doesn't look at me.

Alex's snores are the only sound in the room, and with a sigh, I lay back on the bed and pull the covers up under my chin. I hear Hunter sigh and the scratching of his hand against his stubble as he rubs his face roughly. I hear him lean heavily against the wall, as if he is struggling to keep himself standing.

'Sorry if I stressed you out,' I whisper.

'It's fine, Raya.' His voice is frosty, and I swear the temperature of the room drops a few degrees.

'What's wrong?' I ask.

'Nothing. Go to sleep.' He turns the light off.

Silence stretches between us like his lie, but I don't dare press my luck. My eyes drift closed for a few seconds before they pop open again. All I can see are his dark eyes watching me through the pale slither of moonlight across his face.

'You're hungry,' I whisper. 'Aren't you?'

'I'm fine.'

'You look like you might pass out again.'

'If it comes down to a fight right now, I can still fight fine, if that's what you're worried about.'

'That's not the point.'

'Sleep,' he orders.

'Eat,' I snap back.

To be honest, I'm craving his closeness. I know I shouldn't want this. It's wrong. He is a supernatural creature. Aching to have him close . . . to touch me . . . isn't normal, or healthy, but I can't help it. It's all I feel. Everywhere. All the time. Seeing him come to my defence just heightened it.

His jaw clenches as he turns sideways and glares out the window. Quietly, I remove the silver that Alex draped over me. Peeling back the cover, I pat the empty space beside me.

'Let me help you.'

Sighing, he pushes off the wall and walks toward the bed and I move over. The mattress dips when he sits on it, and he rolls onto his side so that we are facing each other.

'You are delicate, *legata una*. I can protect you, but you can't be putting yourself in danger like that.'

'What does that mean?' I ask. 'Those strange words. You said them earlier too.'

'Bonded one.'

I smile softly. 'I like it.'

'Do you?' he murmurs, his stare intense, sending my heart fluttering in my chest. I like this softer side of him; it's almost vulnerable. I understand why he acts the way he does, but it doesn't mean I don't appreciate it when he does let me in. Even if it's just a little bit.

'Mmhmm,' I nod. 'You have Italian heritage?'

'Yeah.'

'I wouldn't have guessed. You don't have an accent.'

'I didn't live in Italy long, but my parents only spoke Italian in the house. They wanted us to be fluent.'

'That's cool. I've always wanted to visit Italy,' I say warmly. 'It looks like a beautiful place.'

Reaching out, he tucks a tendril of hair behind my ear. 'I'll take you one day.'

'You would do that?' I ask in surprise, feeling a little star-struck at the tender look in his eyes as he gazes at me.

A deep sound of agreement rumbles in his throat. 'Yeah.'

'I'm getting whiplash from your moods, Hunter,' I whisper.

His face softens. 'It's nothing against you. I'm frustrated at this situation.'

'I get that.'

I shake my hair off my shoulder and arch my back, angling my neck toward him. His hand leaves a hot, burning trail down my side as he gently touches me, moving down my bare thigh and without thinking about what I'm doing, my leg hooks around his waist. With a soft groan he pushes his hard body against mine. He lowers his face to my neck, his breath on my skin sends shivers of pleasures along my throat.

Like last time, he kisses the skin softly before I feel the bite. I gasp momentarily before the feeling of bliss spreads like warm honey through my veins. I grip his shirt in my fingers as I shame-lessly rock my hips into him, the high of the bite trailblazing through my body. He traces a pattern against my thigh with his fingertips as he drinks, and I revel in the sensations. Before I know it, it's over and he gives a final flick of his tongue over my neck moments before he leans back, satiated. We stare at each other, both a little breathless and dazed.

'Is it always going to feel that good?' I murmur, my hands run-ning over the smoothness of his chest with a mind of their own. Hunter's hands appear to be on the same page as he slips his fin-gers underneath the band of my underwear.

'Yes. I think so.' His voice is deep, and a little rough, making my spine tingle deliciously.

Impulsively, I lean forward, kissing his cheek before trailing my lips across to the corner of his mouth before I suddenly find my lips meeting the cold night air as I fall forward, face-planting into the mattress.

Gasping, I sit up and scan the darkness for him, wondering what the hell had just happened. Then I see him standing at the door, jaw clenched, hands fisted at his sides.

'Sorry,' he mutters. 'We got carried away.'

Rejection stings every part of my body, yet I still crave his touch. I don't trust myself to speak without revealing how upset I am, so instead, I fall back and let myself sink deep into the mattress, wishing it would swallow me whole – wishing I could disappear completely.

Beneath the protection of the blankets I clench my fists – and my thighs – and try to convince myself that what I'm feeling is nothing more than the consequences of the bond. I mean, it's not like we have real feelings for each other. Right?

Without sparing me another glance, he moves to the door. 'Get some sleep. I'll see you in the morning.' Then in the blink of an eye, he disappears into the night.

13

HUNTER

The Protector

THE COOL WIND WHIPS against my face as I dart along the walkway. Dark, blinking eyes burn in my mind. The cement is faded and patchy, my footsteps echoing as I track, searching everywhere for signs that someone has come through here recently.

We're not alone. They have been watching us.

'You better run fast,' I growl, my voice low and dangerous, my eyes flitting around the dark space, taking in every detail. 'I'm in no mood to play nice.'

Pausing, I listen, but all I can hear are the soft humming of the lights, murmured conversations behind closed doors, and cars driving across the busy street.

After a moment I'm satisfied that whoever was there is gone now. I consider that maybe I'm being paranoid, but there is always the chance I'm not – and that's not a chance I'm willing to take.

Striding back to the room, I slip inside, closing the door silently behind me. Raya lays still, her chest rising and falling. Alex obnoxiously snores on the other side of the room. Removing my shoe, I launch it at him. He grunts, tossing me the middle finger before he rolls over and goes right back to sleep.

Sighing, I lean against the wall and resume my mindless counting of the bizarre-shaped patterns scattered across the faded floor. I soon tire of that and rest my head back, letting my eyes drift close. Darkness envelops me instantly.

Soft breathing fans across my earlobe.

'Give in to the bond,' *a voice whispers.* 'You'll feel so much better if you do.'

Tender, delicate hands slide down my chest, causing a shiver to run up my spine.

'Give in,' *the voice murmurs.* 'Take me. I'm yours.'

I wake with a jolt, blinking rapidly. Raya blinks back at me from where she sits upright, her legs over the edge of the bed.

'Sorry,' she whispers. 'I didn't mean to wake you.' Her voice is an extension of the whispering in my dream, and I feel myself ache with desire.

'It's fine. I shouldn't have fallen asleep.'

As she runs her fingers through her long dark hair, the streak of purple glimmers as it catches the golden morning light slipping through the blinds. She sweeps it back, re-tying it in a knot on the top of her head.

'We should go get coffee and breakfast,' she says. 'Wait . . . Do vampires drink coffee?'

'No.'

'Well, at least you will always have white fangs,' she jokes. I blink at her. She releases an awkward laugh. To be fair, vampires really do have bright, white teeth. 'Okay. Tough crowd.'

'Get dressed. We will leave shortly,' I say curtly, trying not to smile.

Kicking off my other shoe, I throw it at Alex. He grumbles, rolling over and sending a death glare in my direction. 'Dude, you're lucky you're a vamp.' This time I allow myself to smile as I watch as he stumbles out of bed, tangled in his blanket.

'I've got first dibs on the shower!' Raya shouts, seeing her advantage as she bolts towards the bathroom and slams the door shut behind her.

I fly across the room, collecting my shoes, and have them back on before I sit down casually on the narrow lounge.

'Christ,' he mutters, peering at me through half-closed lids, yawning. 'Too early for this shit.'

As the bathroom door swings open and Raya walks out, I feel my heart pick up the pace at the sight of her. Dressed in a simple, white dress that hugs her body, delicate spaghetti straps baring her shoulders, it leaves little to the imagination of the amazing body she has underneath. My hands clench at my sides as I take it all in. Licking my lips, I hungrily drink in all her features, noticing that she's gathered half of her hair up with a pearly white clip, leaving the rest to cascade over her shoulders in waves.

Desire pulses through my body like an electric current, and before I realise what I'm doing, I'm on my feet and edging toward her.

'Raya,' I murmur.

'Hmm?' she replies, glancing up at me with an eyebrow raised.

Alex scoffs, breaking the spell and I cast my glare towards him. He seems a little smug as he makes a song and dance of gathering his things. 'You're a weird dude,' Alex offers before he trots into the bathroom.

Shaking my head, I clear my throat and take a step back, grateful the surge of lust has faded. Not completely gone, no, that would be too much of a blessing. I'm left with the realisation that I am standing a little too close to Raya.

'You ready?' I scowl.

'Yes . . .' she trails off, a slight frown darkening her beautiful features.

I exhale sharply and turn my back to her as I move toward the window and lean against the frame. It's gloomy outside, the sky laden with ominous, dark grey clouds, threatening rain at any moment. The perfect day for me to be out and about.

A few moments later, we're packed up and filing out the front door, and I direct Raya and Alex to wait at the car while I check us out.

'Can I drive?' Alex asks, his voice hopeful as I reappear alongside the car.

'No.' I don't spare him a glance as I unlock the doors.

'What about me?' Raya asks.

Pausing, I survey her trying to get a read on how serious she is.

'Okay *legata una,* but no speeding,' I reply, tossing the keys to her.

The smile that sweeps across her face is a sudden, glorious brightness against the dreary day. I turn and shoot a smug look at Alex as he glowers at me. I'm honestly not keen on Raya driving any more than Alex, but I just can't seem to pass up on an opportunity to mess with him. He just rubs me the wrong way.

'Prick.' Alex scoffs, stomping around to the back of the car, dramatically flinging himself inside, and then slamming the door.

I take further joy in the fact that Raya appears completely oblivious to Alex's sulking as she slides in behind the wheel. 'Where to?' she asks excitedly.

'Depends. Can you manage to actually reach the steering wheel?' I tease. She sticks her tongue out adorably as she reaches underneath the seat for the lever. It jolts forward abruptly, and I reach out, throwing my arm across the steering wheel as her face heads straight for it. Her forehead smacks into my arm instead and she blinks, a little dazed.

'Ow.'

'Careful,' I warn.

'She's not made of glass, mate,' Alex pipes up from the back, and a retort is hot on my lips, but I swallow it down, not wanting to expend energy bickering with him.

'Where are we heading?' Raya asks, a quickness to her voice that makes me think she's trying to diffuse any potential bickering.

'Head out to the highway,' I reply. 'We are meeting up with a friend of mine.'

She raises an eyebrow. 'We are?'

'Mmhmm.' I nod. 'I could use the extra pair of eyes and ears on this quest.'

'Awesome,' Alex barks out sarcastically, sinking back into the seat. 'Another one of you.'

'How do you know them?' Raya asks as she starts the car and steers us out of the parking lot.

'We met a few years back. I ended up meeting him once I grew out of my out-of-control-new-vampire phase. We have been good friends ever since.'

'That's nice. What's his name?'

'Cas.'

'Tell me more about this villain era of yours,' Alex says, jostling forward, poking his head between the two front seats.

'No.'

'Why not?' I can feel him sulking without having to look at him.

'I don't enjoy reminiscing about such things,' I deadpan.

'So we're adding boring to your list of qualities,' Alex grumbles.

'Alex,' Raya hisses, her eyes narrowing into slits as she glares at him through the mirror. 'Enough.'

I'm almost overwhelmed by the temptation to knock him the fuck out, and I force myself to take a deep breath, stare ahead, and try to relax my shoulders.

'So, will he be travelling with us?' Raya asks.

'Yes.'

'I'm looking forward to meeting him,' she says brightly.

I quickly dismiss the smile trying to work its way onto my face. If I could feel warmth, I'm sure it would spread through my body, oozing through my veins as smoothly and slowly as a spilt pot of honey. Instead, I shift in my seat, and look out the window.

I don't like these feelings she ignites in me. I don't want to be attached to her. Or to anyone for that matter.

She should be living the normal life of a teenage girl – even if that meant hanging out with Alex. Getting involved with me – and vampires like Kian – will only end in disaster. The best thing for her to do is forget about all of this and move on with her life. I'm not selfish enough to let the bond ruin both of our lives. I may be tied to her forever, but I don't expect her to feel the same. A breath of laughter escapes me. *Hunter.* My name is literally the very creature that I have become, and yet, I am bound to protect this fragile, vulnerable, human girl. How can I be a hero and a villain wrapped up in one being?

The clouds open overhead and rain cascades all around us. The wiper blades squeak across the window, growing more irritating by the second. My phone vibrates against my leg and, thankful for the distraction, I inch it out to find Theo's name on the screen. Guilt grips my stomach. I hate that I left him behind and wish he would pack up and leave that godforsaken town. But I know he loves it – most vampires do – as it attracts a certain crowd of humans. Ones that are willing to go the extra mile with particular things, since they know, or at least suspect, our kind's existence.

I want to answer his call, but I don't know what to say. I'm all too aware of the two sets of human ears in my presence. Besides, I already know Theo's calling to demand I return home, but I can't. He doesn't understand what I'm going through. This damn bond. I am forever tied to this girl. This *mortal.* That's partly why I want to see Cas. He has been a vampire for a long time. Maybe he will know how to break the curse placed on us. Though *curse* doesn't feel like the right word to use, but in a way, I guess it is. Raya and I are bound to each other now. Her life is forever altered and it isn't fair on either of us.

A sudden clap of thunder rattles the car and squinting, I peer out the windows. The bad weather looks settled, and I figure it's going to continue for a few days at best. Stretching my legs in front of me, I clasp my hands together, growing more mind-numbingly bored with each passing moment. At least when I'm driving, it doesn't seem so bad. With a sigh, I unclasp my hands and reach down for my bag where I rummage for my book.

'Oh my God.' Raya giggles.

'What?' I turn, an eyebrow raised.

'You're reading *Dracula*.'

'And?' I try not to smile, but I can't help it. I love the sound of her laugh and being the reason for it.

'A vampire. Reading a book about vampires.'

I roll my eyes. 'Ha, ha.'

Alex lets out a snort from where he is sitting at the back but I don't acknowledge it. Raya briefly looks back at him with a grin before facing the front once more.

'Where are we meeting up with your friend?' she asks.

'At his place. We are about an hour away.'

'Okay,' she says.

'I don't like this,' Alex mouths to her through the rear-view mirror, clearly not realising that I can detect even the quietest of movements. Idiot.

'If I was going to kill you, believe me, I would have already,' I say coldly as I turn and look pointedly at him over my shoulder. I take some satisfaction in the way Alex gulps, his face paling a little.

He nods and remains silent for the remainder of the trip. I'm thankful for this. I really hate it when someone interrupts my reading.

Precisely an hour later, I'm forced to look up from the pages to direct Raya off the highway, and we make our way through Rose Hills. I have visited here a few times, and Cas's house is so close to the beach. If I was to move again, I would consider coming here, where I could spend every night floating atop the waves and gazing up at the moonlight. Since I don't need oxygen like a human does, I can actually spend a long time beneath the water. It's an amazing feeling. A quietness I often crave.

'Here,' I say, pointing to a dark grey house. It's double the size of any of the neighbouring houses with black curtains shielding the tall windows, seeming to cast a dark shadow onto the road in front of it.

'Creepy,' Alex mutters.

Raya turns the car into the driveway, cutting the engine.

'You trust me, right?' I ask her.

Those green eyes, appearing a soft emerald in the natural light and framed by long, dark lashes, swing to meet mine. Light freckles kiss the tops of her cheeks and for a moment I forget myself.

She is truly stunning.

'Yes,' she answers breathily. I can all but hear Alex roll his eyes.

'You will be safe here. I promise.'

'Okay.'

'And that obviously goes for me too, right?' Alex leans forward and pokes his head between our seats.

'Get out of the car,' I growl and push the door open.

The gloominess of the day matches the aesthetic of Cas's house. Vine-like plants twist and wrap around the porch, almost consuming the entire railing and looking like snakes slithering across the surface.

The wooden slats of the porch groan beneath our feet as we walk across the porch and I rap my knuckles three times on the matte black door before stepping back. My arm brushes against Raya's and a sudden spike of electricity surges through me. We both shiver, glancing at each other before looking quickly away. Thankfully, the door opens and Cas stares back at us.

'Hello, Hunter.' His lips tilt in a small show of a smile. 'Welcome, again.'

'Thank you,' I say.

He steps back and I gesture for Raya and Alex to walk through ahead of me. I watch as Alex tries to catch Raya's eye, but she is already inside. He scowls, stalking in after her, his eyes darting wildly around the room as if waiting for something to jump out and grab him. It's all I can do not to take the bait.

'Cas,' I say, holding my hand out. He shakes it. 'Are you well?'

'I am.' He nods, his white-blond hair stylishly messy, his skin smooth ivory, like he hasn't seen the sun in ... well, ever. I can't remember him looking this pale, but it has been a while since I've seen him. His cool eyes quickly assess me, and I hate the feeling like he's taking in every single detail. 'And you?'

Deciding not to reply, I place a hand on Raya's shoulder. 'This is Raya. The girl I was telling you about.'

'Hello, Raya,' he greets her in his deep voice which is perfectly designed to lure humans in. It doesn't seem to have the desired effect on her – the bond most likely hinders the effects of other vampires now – but the quick jerk of Alex's head as he stares at Cas makes me think he felt it. 'Nice to finally meet you.'

'This one,' I say, gesturing to Alex. 'I have no use for him. Do as you please.'

A sharp gasp escapes Raya as she whips her round eyes to me. Alex hastily steps back, yanking his knives out of his pockets. I admire his confidence in thinking he can take on two vampires with those measly blades.

'You brought me a snack, dear friend?' Cas drawls, a sadistic smirk stretching over his lips. 'You didn't need to do that.'

'My thanks to you,' I say.

'You're a fucking piece of shit,' Alex spits at me. 'I knew you were evil.'

'All vampires are evil, Alex,' I say. 'Don't kid yourself into thinking otherwise.'

'I didn't,' he snarls, continuing to back up, glancing toward Raya, his expression raging with how angry and betrayed he feels knowing she trusts me so easily. The slamming of his heart against his ribcage sends a shiver down my spine, causing the instinct to hunt to rise. The thrill to chase. To feed, even though I know his blood is no good to me.

'Hunter!' Raya whispers brokenly. 'No!'

Cas and I exchange a glance before we burst into laughter. Raya's eyes almost pop out of her skull, meanwhile Alex sags against the wall as if he was a balloon and someone popped a pin into him.

'Your faces.' Cas grins, eyes flash with wild excitement. 'Priceless.' Turning to me, he smirks, looking far too satisfied right now. 'Humans are so easy to toy with.'

'That's for being a dick.' I smirk, moving my eyes back to Alex.

'I hate you even more now,' Alex seethes, his face blotchy and red.

I snicker, ignoring the glare Raya is shooting at me. I turn to her and shrug. 'Sorry. Had to.'

'Not funny,' she says, turning to assess the room again.

'It was a little funny,' I quip back.

'It really wasn't.' She huffs, but she can't hide the hint of a smile tugging at the corners of her mouth.

'Watch your back.' Alex scowls, shooting daggers to me.

'I will, big boy,' I say, yanking him to his feet, and clapping my hand roughly down on his shoulder, making his legs buckle slightly. He furiously shrugs me off and stomps over to stand by Raya's side. She sighs, shaking her head.

'Well?' I say, turning to Cas. 'Shall we give them a tour?'

Cas turns to the two humans, winking. 'We shall.'

14

RAYA

The Survivor

MY HEART STILL HASN'T returned to its regular pace as I follow Cas through his house. For a moment there, I really had panicked that Alex was going to become someone's dinner. I can still feel the goosebumps across my skin as I shudder at the thought.

Every window is hidden behind dark velvet curtains, giving the place a cold and eerie aesthetic. Everything inside the house – walls, floors, furniture – are a black, a grey, or a deep violet.

I gasp as we enter the living room. Strange and ancient artefacts fill most of the surface space, and the walls are covered in silver weapons in place of normal decor. My eyes slowly travel over the daggers, swords, chains, and handcuffs. The weapons make me feel nauseous. I don't want to think about them being used on anyone. Considering silver is painful to vampires, it seems a little odd to have it displayed as a feature wall for someone to easily use against him. Maybe that is the whole point of it . . . that he is so strong that he can comfortably live amongst weapons that are supposed to weaken him.

Alex lets out a low whistle. 'Damn.'

The whole place sets me on edge as my stomach twists in knots. I know Hunter told me I had nothing to fear in this vampire's house, but I can't shake the unease that has settled into my bones like an icy chill. This entire house screams creepiness.

'This is awesome!' Alex says, plucking a giant crossbow from the wall.

There's a distinct snapping sound and suddenly Hunter is in front of me. My hair flies over my shoulders as though caught in a gust of wind. He scowls, lowering his hand from in front of my face, and it's then I notice he's clutching an arrow. If not for Hunter, it would have hit me dead between the eyes.

The crossbow clatters to the floor as Alex curses. 'Shit, my bad.'

Cas *tsks*, gliding across the room at a speed quicker than my eyes can track, his feet hovering above the floor. I see it, I know I do, and yet I can't wrap my head around it.

'Don't touch my things.'

'Got it.' Alex looks like a bobble-head as he rapidly nods.

'Seriously,' Cas's voice drops low. 'Don't.'

'I got it,' Alex snaps back.

Sighing, I shake my head. That smart mouth and attitude of his is going to get him in big trouble one day. I can feel it.

I'm suddenly distracted as Hunter turns and faces me, his eyes roaming over me, leaving me flustered.

'Are you all right?' he asks. He reaches out his hand, as if he might touch my face, but it awkwardly hovers mid-air before dropping back to his side.

'Yes,' I say. 'Thank you.'

With a nod, he steps away from me once more. I feel my face flush as I notice Cas staring at him before he glances back at me, his interest apparent.

'Shall we?' Cas turns on his heel without waiting for a response and swallowing thickly, I trail behind him, glad for the distraction.

As we walk up the stairs to the next floor, I take a moment to study Cas. Dressed in faded jeans and a white T-shirt, he looks completely normal from the back. It's those silver and almost-black eyes that make you pause. Of course most would assume they are a deep, dark brown, but I know better. The eyes. It's what I always need to look for when I'm out. It's a dead give-away, separating the vampires from the humans.

Cas has a piercing in his left eyebrow, his forearms are covered in dark swirling tattoos. His white, blond hair is spiky, sticking up at odd angles. Combined with his borderline black eyes, there is no doubt that he has an unnatural look about him.

'If you are to stay,' he says, barely glancing over his shoulder at me. 'You will be in here.' He looks at Hunter, tilting his head. 'Perhaps both of you.'

Hunter's cheek spasms. 'No, only Raya.'

'Mmhmm,' Cas replies in a disbelieving tone. 'And you, emo boy, you will be in this one.'

'Righto. Thanks ghost-dude.'

Cas arches an eyebrow, a look of amusement falling across his face. 'Ghost-dude?'

'Yeah. You look like the fucking walking dead.'

'Alex!' I squawk in horror.

Cas flashes a grin, revealing his fangs. I startle, stepping back, and grabbing a hold of Hunter's bicep before I realise what I've done.

Damn. That's a nice bicep.

'I'll show you how close you are to death, boy,' Cas snarls, his face darkening, contrasting starkly with his white-blond hair.

'Enough,' Hunter barks, his voice ringing with command. As Hunter's fingers discreetly brush against my hand, I relax. It's as if he clears any fear and worry from my mind with a single touch.

Cas smirks at Alex, who glowers back at him.

We finally finish the tour of his monstrously big home. Unnecessarily big for one person, but I suppose when you're a vampire, you really can do whatever you want.

When I get to the bottom of the stairs, my stomach lets out an awkwardly loud rumble, and I place my hand against it as though that would somehow silence it.

'You're hungry,' Hunter states the obvious. 'I will go get you dinner.'

'Why don't we go out for dinner?' Cas suggests, placing his hands behind his back as his eyes move between each of us.

'I thought you couldn't eat food,' I say.

'We can eat, but we don't need to. That's why we don't bother. But we enjoy drinking.'

'Finally, something we have in common,' says Alex with a wry smile.

'I'm keen for dinner. What about you, Hunter?' I ask.

He's quiet for a moment and I can almost see his thoughts ticking over, calculating any perceived risks. After a few long seconds, he shrugs. 'Why not?'

I spend the next hour unpacking and getting ready for dinner. It feels nice to do something so normal. My hair, my makeup; things I haven't done since I started this adventure. I always enjoyed dressing up and wearing a cute outfit. I used to love trying on my sister's clothes. Her outfits always seemed so much better than mine. She was effortlessly gorgeous and trendy. I always aspired to be like her.

A quiet knock on my door pulls me from my thoughts, and I turn to see Hunter stroll in, dressed in all black, looking mouth-wateringly handsome. So much so that I have to clench my thighs together.

Yikes. I'm in trouble.

'Hi,' I smile.

He doesn't answer, instead his dark eyes travel sensually down my body. I've read hundreds of books, seen a thousand movies. I always see it. *The look*. The look of total lust and adoration. Now I am seeing it directed at me. It feels pretty damn good.

I'm being forced by the bond, Raya. I don't want to be here.

Hunter's words ring inside my head. Does he truly feel this, or is it the bond convincing him he is attracted to me? Insecurity ripples up my spine like poison as my smile falters. Yet as I watch him, my mouth becomes bone dry as his eyes trace the most intimate curves of my body. Biting his lip, the corner of his mouth tilts, sending waves of desire through my body.

'*Legata una, sei molto bella.*' His Italian drawl makes me feel warm and fluttery on the inside. Digging his hands into his pockets, his heated gaze continues to feast on me like I'm a cool drink after a long trek through the desert.

'What does that mean?' I can hardly get the words out.

'You are very beautiful,' he says with a cute, boyish smile. One of those rare, genuine smiles seemingly reserved only for me.

A blush warms my cheeks, but as much as I love the compliment and attention, I bristle a little at it, his earlier words punching through me. 'Thanks, Hunter. You look very handsome yourself.' I say a little flatly, smiling sweetly up at him. 'But maybe that's just the bond influencing me.'

He stiffens, a muscle in his jaw pulses. His eyes swirl, wisping from a glittery silver, to something darker. Not quite black, but something just as menacing, and not before I see the hurt behind his gaze. Running his tongue across his teeth, he nods, taking a step back. I instantly feel guilty even though it's exactly how he made me feel earlier.

'Are you ready to go?' he asks tersely, looking down at the floor.

'Yeah,' I say. He turns to leave, and as I see his fists clenched at his sides it intensifies my guilt, and I suddenly can't stand it. 'Hunter . . .'

'Hmm?' He stops, turning to face me.

'I'm sorry.'

'For what?' he asks, his expression blank.

'This situation. You don't want to be here, I get that. I never meant to involve you in this suicide mission. I'm sorry you've had to uproot your entire life for something you don't care about.' I let out a shaky exhale, suddenly finding the floor fascinating, unable to meet his gaze. 'I know you don't really care for me. Any protective feelings are bond-induced.' The more I talk, the more pathetic and whinier I sound. Sighing, my shoulders slump. 'I guess, I'm just . . . sorry. For dragging you into my mess.'

In two long strides, he is before me. I gasp as he raises my chin with his finger, forcing me to meet his gaze as he searches my face.

'I'm sorry if I seem harsh sometimes. It's not you – I just want more for you. Being tied to a vampire isn't going to enable you to live a normal life. I shouldn't have said that I didn't care to be here. I do care about you, and that's why we're in this position.'

'What do you mean?' I ask, my voice barely more than a whisper.

'Theo told me there has to be attraction beforehand for a bond to form.'

'Oh.' I don't know what to say, and he sighs deeply, his thumb drawing a circular pattern onto my cheek. I lean into his hand, seeking his comfort.

'I guess what I'm saying is . . . I don't need to have the bond to know how I feel about you.'

My lips part as I absorb his words. I never suspected that the infatuation I felt toward him before the bond was possibly returned. I assumed it was because a vampire is designed to lure a human in. Of course I would think about him and want to be around him. But for him to feel the same way . . . not as intensely, I'm sure, but still . . .

'Um . . . I . . .' I mumble, half-smiling, half-attempting to bury my face into his palm so I don't endure this growing-more-heated-by-the-second stare between us. 'I don't know what to say.'

'We should be careful,' he says quietly. 'We can't . . . It will only make it . . .' He sighs.

'You mean, have a relationship? A romantic one?' I ask hesitantly, my mind having instantly taken a dirtier train of thought, but I was *not* going to be asking that.

'I mean sleep together.'

I stiffen as the words leave his mouth. If I was blushing before, it's nothing compared to what is happening to my body right now. The thought of having sex with him does all kinds of wild things to my body.

'Oh,' I say, trying to look anywhere but at his face.

'Yeah,' he breathes, pushing his hand through his hair.

'So. No sex.'

'No sex.' He nods, eyes fixing onto mine a little *too* intensely.

'It will make the bond stronger?'

'That's what I've been told.' He sighs. 'It might make it so strong that I turn you. Even if you didn't want me to because the thought of your human life ending will make me desperate and irrational. I could never live with myself if I took that choice away from you.'

'Wow,' I whisper. 'That's a lot to take in.'

'Mmhmm.'

'But we could do other things?' The words are out of my mouth before I can stop them. My face feels like it's on fire.

Okay. Turns out I *can* ask him that.

The corner of his mouth tilts, and he breathes a laugh, looking down at his feet before his gaze travels back up to meet my eyes.

'Yes. I suppose we could,' he murmurs, and my heartbeat thuds loudly in my ears. 'We can't let things get out of control, however.'

'How would that work?'

'What do you mean?'

'If you turned me. Aren't I supposed to be your only blood source?'

'The bond would still be present, but we both can drink human blood freely. It breaks that part of the bond. Unless you died of natural causes. Then, I die, too. Of starvation, if I don't end my own life because of the misery of losing my bonded.'

'This sounds like it's all made up,' I confess. 'Some crazy plot in a movie.'

He offers me a lopsided grin. 'Yeah. Well. I wish it wasn't our reality.'

'Still. I'm sorry.' I wince.

Capturing my hand, he brings it to his lips, kissing it softly. 'I'm sorry, too.'

'What's going to happen to us?' I ask. 'Where will this lead if we don't pursue a relationship? You will be my forever body-guard? That doesn't seem fair to you.'

'Let's worry about finding your sister. The rest we can figure out later.'

Nodding, I accept that. I have to. Though the thought of not taking things further just now leaves a hollow pit in my stomach. I remind myself that it is the bond trying to control me. He will never be far – even if he wanted to be. I consider it the silver lining of the curse. It will all work out as it should. I believe that.

The door to my room bangs open, and Alex strides inside. He stops abruptly when he notices the proximity of Hunter and I. Hunter ignores him completely, most likely having heard him coming long before he knocked on the door.

'Um,' he says, his expression hardening. 'It's time to leave.'

'Okay,' I reply, reluctantly letting go of Hunter as he excuses himself, and swiftly leaves the room.

Alex tries to catch my eye as I gather my things, but I refuse to look up. I don't want to hear whatever he wants to say. I know it will be negative. My head is spinning with the information Hunter gave me. Later, when I have the time, I will conduct my own research. See if this whole having-sex-will-strengthen-the-bond thing is true. Sure, it makes sense, but I want to explore that thoroughly. In case it doesn't need to be ruled out. Totally hypothetically, of course.

Cas is waiting for us by the door. He's dressed in leather pants, boots, and a leather jacket with studs on the shoulders. With thick eyeliner around his midnight eyes, he looks demonic – or maybe like he belongs in a heavy metal band.

'That's a vibe,' I say, grinning at him.

'Is that a good thing?' He frowns.

'Yeah.'

'Okay.' He shrugs. 'Thanks. Are you ready?'

I nod. Cas opens the door and we file out before he follows closely behind. We walk out to the garage where his Ferrari awaits. Alex's jaw drops at the sight of the sleek black car with its blacked-out windows and matching rims. The darkest of dark. Totally fitting for Cas.

'Like?' Cas smirks.

'Love,' Alex breathes, his face lit up like it's his first Christmas, reaching his hand out hesitantly, as if afraid to touch it.

'Can this fit all of us?' I ask, eyeing the subwoofer that takes up most of the space in the back, allowing legally only two passengers to fit other than the driver.

'Yeah,' Cas replies. 'You may need to sit on someone's lap though.'

Alex sneers at that, and I hide my smile as Hunter climbs in first. He shoots me an amused look as he pats his lap. I don't need to be asked twice. Considering our conversation five minutes ago, sitting in this proximity to him seems to go against what he said we shouldn't be doing. Although he didn't seem opposed to the *other things* I suggested . . .

Drawing in a breath, I slide across onto his lap. His large hands settle on my waist, securing me better than any seatbelt. At his touch, every inch of me feels like it's on fire. His grip tightens, his thumb sliding down the slit in my dress, touching my skin.

Jesus.

'Hold on.' Cas smirks moments before the car launches forward.

I let out a yelp, holding on for dear life as Cas flies through the streets, overtaking cars with the ease of a racecar driver. He never slows for an intersection and runs every red light. In the end, I close my eyes and grip Hunter's hands as we careen down the road. Cas inches the music up to a deafening volume. The bass vibrates the seats and the doors, the music pulsing up my body. Neon strips light up the dashboard and along the inside of the car, casting a deep purple light over the interior.

Hunter leans forward, pressing a kiss on my bare shoulder. Heat burns like an untamed fire through me. I wriggle against him. I stare down at his hands on me, realising that it has been a little while since he last fed. Considering how heated things get when he does feed on me, it seems risky to let him right now, but since the others are here, it can hardly get *too* out of hand.

Turning my head, I feel his breath against my cheek.

'Do it,' I whisper. 'Bite me.'

He kisses my shoulder again. With his grip tightening ever-so-slightly, his self-control snaps. I hear the lengthening of his fangs before I feel them sink into my shoulder. A moan leaves me, and I shamelessly grind on his lap. My eyes flash over to Cas who has his arm out the window, gazing out of it as we weave in and out of lanes that are clearly not designed for overtaking.

Alex is not paying any attention to what we're doing as he lets out a whoop, drowning out the sounds of me whimpering as Hunter takes what he needs from me.

The cool night air flows over me, my hair whips around my face, blanketing my expressions from anyone who may look our way.

Hunter's hand moves between my legs, and I almost stop breathing. His fingers walk up my thigh.

'I thought you said . . .' I whisper, trailing off, suddenly not wanting to finish that sentence in case he stops touching me like that.

'I know,' he murmurs, his deep voice making a shiver run down my spine. 'But you're right. We can do . . . other things. Even though I know we shouldn't.'

Electricity crackles between us and I lean back against him, loving the feel of his hard muscles against my back.

'Don't stop,' I whisper, squirming in his lap.

My chest is heaving as I look over to Cas, who is still looking out the window, and if I wasn't so caught up in Hunter's touch, I might have been more concerned that he hadn't looked at the road in minutes.

'I don't want to stop,' Hunter murmurs into my neck, lightly tracing patterns onto my thigh. 'But this . . . these moans . . . seeing you like this . . .' His hold on me tightens. 'This is only for me.'

He bites harder into my shoulder, and the desperate ache inside me grows.

I need more.

My heart is galloping inside my chest, threatening to burst free at any moment. I have never felt more alive than I do at this moment.

Cas yanks on the steering wheel, almost taking out the car next to us as he does a completely illegal park in front of a dimly lit restaurant that is packed to the brim full of people. The whole trip here seemed to be over in the blink of an eye. If Hunter didn't have such a firm grip on me, I certainly would have flown through the front window at Cas's hazardous driving.

Looping his arm over the steering wheel, Cas flashes his fangs at me. 'Here.'

Turning, I smile at Hunter. 'Thanks for being a great seatbelt.'

Smirking, he drags his tongue across his lower lip, collecting the blood from it.

'Sure. Anytime.'

Heat blossoms in my cheeks.

I want him so bad.

When we exit the car, I look at the others. Cas's wild blond hair is totally windblown and messy, but it makes him look even more handsome. He winks at me, and I feel a flush right down to the tips of my toes. He definitely knows what just happened.

I could die right here, right now.

'That was epic, man,' Alex breathes, fumbling his way out of the car, eyes wide, cheeks flushed. It's nice to see him coexisting with Cas and Hunter without the snarkiness. 'You gotta let me drive it one day.'

'We'll see,' Cas replies as he exits.

'He is so much cooler than you are,' Alex points out, directing a bitchy look to Hunter as he and Cas head off in the direction of the restaurant.

Well. I spoke too soon.

I turn to face Hunter, and for a brief moment, it's just the two of us. 'For the record, I think you're pretty cool.'

And I really do. Hunter is effortlessly magnetic in a way I've never experienced. I'm desperate to know more about him, and to spend more time with him.

'I think you're pretty cool, too,' Hunter replies, reaching out to tuck a strand of hair behind my ear.

'Thanks,' I say.

Slapping my butt, he inclines his head. 'Off we go.'

'Yes, sir.'

The street is loud and busy with chatter, laughter, and people loitering out the front of several bars and restaurants. Cas makes a beeline for the entrance, bypassing the huge line that goes most of the way down the street.

I'm delighted when Hunter reaches for my hand. I know my feelings for him are developing a little rapidly. I'm still in two minds about how genuine they are, and how much my feelings are impacted by the bond. I'm starting to believe it is a mixture of both. It's exhausting feeling tense and on edge all of the time. I just want to enjoy this moment without overthinking it. I know the closer we get to finding Kian and Cora, the more danger we'll all be in. Right here, right now, I want to just enjoy being with Hunter, and getting to know him and his friend.

'Cas,' he says to the girl behind the desk, almost completely hidden behind a display of menus. 'I have a reservation.'

Shouts of protest follow us, but I don't make eye contact with anyone. I'm running with the vampire crowd now, and I'm going to enjoy it.

The young girl frowns, skimming over the list. 'I'm sorry, sir. I don't see your name.'

'Look again.' His voice is deep and a little rough. Alex's head snaps to look over at Cas. He shakes his head, fidgeting, as if realising Cas has an effect on him. Ignoring Alex's scowl, I look back at the girl as her expression becomes dazed. She blinks once and looks down at the list. 'Oh. There you are.' She beckons over a young man. 'Anthony will direct you to your table. Have a lovely evening, sir.'

Nodding at her, he winks. 'I will, thank you.'

'That is freaking cool,' Alex mutters to me, seemingly unaware that his cheeks are flushed, and he can't seem to take his eyes off Cas. I wonder if Cas is laying the charm on a little thickly on purpose, or whether he is oblivious to the extent of his effect on mortals. I'm even more convinced I'm not affected because of my bond with Hunter.

It's the classiest restaurant I've ever seen – I've always wanted to come to a place like this. As we follow the waiter to our table, it seems like every pair of eyes we pass swivel in our direction as we weave through the bustling restaurant. With Hunter's striking tattoos on display, Cas's white hair and their identical inky black eyes, we must look like a strange, motley group. I hold my chin high trying to ignore that I feel a little inadequate in my *humanness*. Alex must feel the same because he is pulling the collar of his button up like it's choking him all of a sudden.

The waiter stops at a table in the centre of the room – somehow vacant despite how packed the restaurant is. Hunter pulls my chair out for me, and I drop into it, shooting him a grateful smile. I love this side of him. The more I see it, the more of it I want. Violin music plays softly from a small band located at the back end of the restaurant, playing covers of well-known classics.

'So,' Cas drops into the seat opposite me, and I'm a little surprised as Alex takes the one directly beside Cas. He eyes Alex for a moment, and then sends us a cat-like grin. 'What are we drinking tonight?'

His jibe misses the mark as Alex snarls and I look at him, my head tilted to the side before I realise what he's looking at.

'What the hell is that?' he hisses.

Stiffening, I lightly touch my fingers to my shoulder, and feel the wetness there. Hunter and I were so caught up in our stolen moment that we forgot to heal the bite. A smirk stretches across Cas's mouth as he leans back in the chair. I glance at Hunter, who has his eyes closed for a brief second, most likely berating himself for his mistake.

'Nothing,' I say quietly.

Cas smirks, glancing at Alex. 'What, you want one, too?'

Colour rises in Alex's cheeks, and his jaw tightens. Glaring down at the table, he refuses to meet my eyes. I sink into my seat, feeling like I was caught doing something wrong. Hunter's hand touches my arm and I feel all sense of shame and embarrassment evaporate.

Alex knows that I am Hunter's only source of blood. Why is he acting like feeding on me is a cardinal sin?

I'm oblivious to the slight debate Cas and Hunter have over the wine list before Cas waves his hand and declares he's ordering the restaurants 'finest' wine. I'm not sure if the compulsion is somehow lingering, or if it's just their presence, but all the staff bend over backwards making sure we have everything we could possibly desire.

'How is everything?' A man asks, looming over us, hovering so close to Cas that it looks like they're about to touch.

It seems like the staff are on thirty-second rotations to check in on us.

'Enough!' Cas snaps in irritation, shooing the man and causing him to stumble back in surprise. 'Leave us be. Tell everyone to leave us alone unless our glasses are empty.'

'Y-yes sir,' the man stammers before rushing away.

Alex and I share a brief truce as we exchange equally awkward glances over Cas's flip in temperament. The staff certainly wouldn't be treating *us* this way if it was just the two of us.

After one glass, the wine totally goes to my head, and I can't stop talking, and thankfully, everything seems back to normal between the group. As normal as it can be, anyway. Alex seems to have calmed down from earlier, and while I'm sure he isn't impressed with the situation, he must understand that neither Hunter nor myself can help it. When dinner arrives, it is mouth-wateringly delicious. Quite possibly the best food I've had in . . . well . . . ever. I haven't had a decent meal for what seems like a very long time. I inhale the food so quickly, I should probably be embarrassed by it. I get so caught up in eating, I barely pay attention to the idle chit-chat between Hunter and Cas until Cas directs a question to me.

'So, that's why you're here?' Cas asks. 'Your sister.'

Placing the glass down, I nod. 'Yeah. I'm trying to find her.'

'If she is out there, we will find her,' Cas assures me. 'Most vampires go overseas. Here in Australia, it is much less populated than a lot of other countries. It's easier to blend over there. If she's not here, we will just have to travel.'

'I've never been overseas before,' I admit. 'The thought of chasing her across different countries scares the hell out of me. I also don't have the money for that.'

Cas waves me off dismissively. 'Money is no problem, little human.'

'I am not little,' I huff.

He grins. 'You are tiny. You barely come up to my chest.'

'Maybe you're just a giant.' The wine gives me bravado.

Alex snickers and even Hunter smiles, taking a sip of his wine. He looks relaxed and carefree, which is so nice to see. It's like he can finally ease up a little, knowing he has another person to help make sure we aren't in danger.

'Besides, that's assuming my sister is out there,' I say sourly, returning to the previous conversation. 'What if this is all for nothing?'

'It won't be all for nothing. You met me. That's an incredible thing not everyone gets to experience,' Cas declares.

Alex scoffs, shaking his head, but the corners of his mouth twitch. Hunter chuckles and I join in, our laughs blending together almost musically.

'Sure,' I say.

'So, let me get this right,' Cas says, leaning forward onto his elbows, linking his fingers together and resting them against his chin. 'You two completely untrained and inexperienced humans travelled to a known-vampire-infested town with literally no clue where to start your quest of finding your missing sister.'

'Well. When you say it like that, it sounds pretty stupid,' Alex says.

'Because it is,' Hunter mutters, swirling the glass of wine in his hand.

'But charmingly brave, nonetheless,' Cas continues as he arrogantly taps on his glass, and a man appears to quickly refill it before scampering off.

'We have had training,' I interject. 'We did a bunch of self-defence courses and learnt ways to escape dire situations. We didn't walk into this with no thought.'

'Not completely,' Alex added.

'Right.' Cas nods, looking at the pair of us like we're simply children with unachievable ambitions. 'You're saying then that you are trained to outrun a hungry, crazed vampire?'

'I'm saying we did training to increase our chances of getting away.'

I ignore how uncomfortable Hunter looks about this conversation. I suppose he doesn't like the thought of me being *in* these situations that we are hypothetically speaking of. Or maybe it reminds him of when the danger isn't so hypothetical.

Cas runs his tongue across his teeth, a challenge lighting up those endlessly deep eyes. 'Let's prove your theory, then.'

'What?' Hunter growls, whipping his head to look at his friend.

'Let's see if they can escape us.'

'Fuck no,' Hunter splutters, gaping at him. 'Are you insane?'

'Insane as they come, my friend,' he says, turning his attention to Alex, then to me. 'What do you say? Are you up for a little game?'

Swallowing my last bite and washing it down with the last remaining wine in my glass, I set it back down and fix Cas with an intrigued stare. 'I'm listening.'

'We go out on the street; the hunt begins.'

'Don't say hunt.' Hunter winces.

'The game,' Cas amends. 'Let's see if you can escape us.'

I lean back into the chair, exchanging a glance with Alex. He doesn't look opposed to the idea, even though I'm feeling a little reluctant. Clearly, Hunter doesn't think it's a good idea, and I trust his judgement.

'Could be fun,' Alex says.

'It's not meant to be fun,' Hunter grumbles, his hand balling into a fist. 'It's supposed to show you whether you really are equipped for a life-or-death crisis.'

'Do we get a prize for winning?' Alex asks.

'Surviving is your prize.'

Alex rolls his eyes. 'This is a game, no?'

Cas considers this. 'All right then. If you somehow escape me, say, you get back to my car safely, I will give you anything you want.'

Alex nods. 'Sold.'

'And if I catch you,' he says, voice smooth like silk whilst simultaneously rough. 'I bite you.'

The colour drains from Alex's face.

'You will like it.' Cas smirks, looking like he is enjoying this far too much.

'Fuck no.' Alex recoils.

'Ah, come on.' Cas *tsks*, looking disappointed. 'I grant you anything you could desire, and you will not grant me one, measly bite? A bite, mind you, that will give you a high no drug can offer.'

Alex is silent for a few long moments. Cas leans forward, looking at him intensely. The flush on Alex's cheeks deepens. 'It will hurt, won't it?'

'Perhaps at first.' Cas shrugs. 'Depending on how I feel. But the pain will not last long.'

Alex's fingers drum against the table. His eyes move to each of our faces. I can see the gears of his mind ticking over. I don't dare say a word, unsure if I want the game to proceed or not.

'Okay. I'm guessing it isn't as easy as just walking out to the car?' he asks, and I'm a little surprised at how chilled he sounds about this. Perhaps it is Cas's influence that is persuading him.

'No. You must go somewhere else, and then make your way back to the car.'

'Okay,' Alex relents. 'Let's do it.' He faces me. 'Raya?'

As reluctant as I feel, a part of me wants to test this. We trained hard for this very thing, and since it is not a real hunt, it will show us what the limitations of our capabilities are. Besides, I know Hunter won't let anything bad happen to me.

'I'm in,' I say, looking at Alex.

'Me too,' he agrees.

Hunter exhales, downing the remains of his wine in one swallow.

Cas's gleam is wicked and an excited tension crackles around the table.

'Let the game begin.'

15

THE PREDATOR

LICKING MY LIPS, I adjust my position as I remain squatted low between two trees, cast completely in the shadows. The two humans and two vampire hosts spill out onto the street. I can hear the heartbeats of the mortals like a drum beating inside my skull.

It's not the humans I'm after, it's their company. One in particular.

Desperation almost gets the better of me. I want to rush out there and hold a blade to his neck, demanding he tells me the information I so achingly seek. But I know he doesn't know, otherwise we would not be here right now.

I shall watch.

I will wait.

The time is drawing nearer.

I will be ready for when it does.

16

HUNTER

The Protector

THE EXCITEMENT LACED WITH terror that fills the air around us is palpable. I can smell it on them. The thrill of the hunt races through me, igniting my entire body. My fangs tingle, and I rock on the balls of my feet, ready to take off at any moment. I remind myself this is not real. I don't condone hunting. It's too easy to get wrapped up in it.

'Tick tock,' Cas taunts them, licking his lips, the neon lights of the nightclubs' signs drenching his fangs in vivid colouring, bleaching his hair a magnificent neon green.

'Okay, let's plan,' Alex says, turning to Raya.

'Uh-uh,' I intervene, placing a firm hand on his arm as it reaches for her. 'In the real world, you don't have time for planning.'

Alex huffs, not even looking at me as he turns his back toward me.

'Ten . . . nine . . . eight . . .' Cas begins.

Alex and Raya take off at a sprint. Cas and I exchange amused grins. We move toward a bench off to the side of the pavement.

'Anyway,' Cas says, leaning casually against the tree beside him. 'Talk to me. What is going on with you and the girl?'

'Yeah, I wanted to talk to you about that,' I say as I drop into the seat and rest my elbows on my thighs. 'Have you ever heard of a human and vampire bond?'

Cas stills, his eyes slingshotting to me. 'What?'

Confirming his question, I nod. 'Yeah.'

'I've heard of it, sure. Never seen it happen.'

'I didn't know it was possible.'

'It's very rare,' he says, giving me a curious look.

'So they say.'

'You know how old I am, and I've never heard of it actually happening.'

I can only nod.

'How the hell did that happen?' he questions, pushing off the tree and coming to sit beside me. He half-turns, directing his entire focus on my face as he assesses me, as if something in my expression will tell him if I've left anything out.

I quickly brief him on how it occurred. He listens intently, nodding, and never interrupting my explanation.

'Well. That's pretty cool,' he says.

'Pretty cool?' I deadpan.

'You're walking, talking history!' Cas exclaims, shaking my shoulders, his cold fingers digging into my bones. 'Vampirism can be an incredibly lonely life. Now you have someone to share it with you. This is an amazing thing, Hunter.'

'Tying her life to mine is not fair on her,' I argue. 'Nor is it fair on me. You should read the articles describing the grief of losing your bonded. It leads you into ultimate darkness. Complete and utter insanity. Then, you starve and die.'

'So,' Cas says, leaning back, propping up on his elbow. 'Turn her.'

'What?' I jolt in surprise at his words.

'Turn her.'

I'm torn by the thought. A part of me wants to keep her protected and sheltered from the harshness that can come from being a vampire while the other half of me is desperate to have her as my equal – to never have to be without her. The thought of anything happening to her cleaves my chest in two.

'And place this curse on her?'

'Curse?' Cas scoffs. 'What? The ability to get whatever you want? Do whatever you want? Live to see the entire world, through all its changes. Gifted with beauty, strength, cunningness.' He shakes his head. 'Vampirism is no curse. It is a gift.'

That is exactly what my brother says. And Theo.

Worry and regret swirls in my gut at the thought of Theo. As much as he gets on my nerves, I miss him. I hope he's okay.

My head falls back, and I look at the dark sky, glittering with colourful, flickering stars. With my eyesight, I can see the details of them, as if I was a mortal peering through a telescope. Cas's words swirl around inside my head.

A gift, he says.

'I think they have had a much bigger head start than they should have,' Cas says, rising to his full height.

'Yeah.' I sigh, reluctantly standing.

I don't like the thought of scaring Raya, and further traumatising her. This is a terrifying thing – being hunted – and she still has nightmares from what happened to her when she first got to Red Thorne. Yet, I respect that she's chosen this, and it's up to me to show her what she's truly up against.

'Let's go get them.' Cas grins before he takes off, leaving fallen leaves circling in his wake.

17

RAYA

The Survivor

I RACE DOWN THE STREET, ducking and weaving through traffic and parked cars like a crazy person. Shouts of protest follow me as I barge not-so-gently into anyone who gets in my way. Adrenaline courses through my body, fuelling me to move faster than I thought I was capable of. I have no idea where Alex ended up. We both sprinted in different directions. I'm not sure if that was the best decision or a stupid one. Either way, I'm now at the mercy of a hunting vampire with no one around to support me. I briefly wonder if he has made it to the car, or if Cas has tracked him down. My heartbeat is deafening in my ears as I launch myself down the alley alongside a club. The door is propped open by a brick and an employee sits on the ground, a cigarette in one hand, and his phone in the other. He's so focused on his phone that he doesn't see me slip past him and through the door. I run down the hallway, the music thumping so loud the ground vibrates beneath my feet.

As a figure appears at the end of the hallway, I skid to a stop, and my heart plummets into my stomach when Hunter steps out of the shadow. His dark, menacing tattoos appear all the more so in the dim lighting. He tilts his head, a predatorial smirk inching across those perfect lips.

I step back. His sharp eyes track my movements.

'Catch me if you can,' I breathe, smiling despite the fear coursing through me. It's not real fear – I don't think – but it's hard to distinguish since my heartbeat is pulsing madly in my chest to the point it is painful.

Hunter bares his fangs at me. A warmth spreads through the pit of my stomach as I gaze at them longingly, loving how they feel when they're plunged inside my throat.

I wonder how they would feel in other places . . .

Hunter is standing unnaturally still as his cunning eyes assess me closely.

'Run, *legata una*. I am coming for you.'

His words break my trance, and I turn and dart through a door. I'm suddenly faced with a throng of people congregating on the dance floor, and I take a moment to try and see a way through them. Knowing I barely have seconds, I shoot forward, throwing myself into the centre of the crowded dance floor. Sweaty bodies bump and grind together, gyrating and thrusting to the sensual beat playing from the DJ at the front of the dance floor.

Turning, I scan the room, quickly finding Hunter as he drifts along the edge of the dance floor, smirking.

Hunter draws nearer, slipping between bodies as if he is gliding through the air. I back up slowly and steadily, trying to find the easiest way to get back out onto the street. A girl whoops loudly, flinging her bra at the DJ. Hunter's eyes quickly follow the movement and I take it as my chance to flee. Ducking as best I can, I rush toward the closest door, and shove through it, hoping it leads to the alley. The door bangs shut behind me and I swallow greedy gulps of untainted air. I peer around me, quickly realising I have just made a mistake that would have cost me my life if this was a real hunt.

Instead of ending up somewhere that will lead me back to the safety of the public, I have somehow detoured to an empty corridor, filled with bright signs reading, 'fire exit, use this door'.

'Shit,' I curse, spinning around and jiggling the handle.

'In case of an emergency, this door must remain locked.'

Growling, I shove at the door hopelessly, trying to get it to unlock. When it doesn't give, I kick at it angrily. I turn around, taking off at a jog, and head down the hallway, seeing various fire exit doors that are all locked.

A blur of motion hurtles past before stopping in front of me. I shriek, and trip over my own feet in my hurry to backpedal. Before I know what's happening, Hunter sweeps me into his arms, and slams me against the wall. I gasp, and he grins wickedly as his fangs slide out, giving me barely a second to prepare before he bites savagely into my neck. I scream again, but it morphs quickly into a moan. The adrenaline surges through my body like a tsunami as I cling to him, sliding my fingers through his hair. His hands roam over me, gripping and grabbing me in places I have dreamt of him touching. He palms my ass, and I love how tightly he holds me against him. As he continues to suck on my neck, I trail my fingers down his hard stomach, slipping them underneath his waistband.

'I want to touch you,' I plead.

He moans, grinding hard against me. 'We can't.'

'Hunter,' I whisper. 'I want you.' Brushing my fingertips over his skin, I lean closer. 'I need you.'

Hunter breathes hard, and I can feel that we're both rapidly losing the battle over our self-control as the adrenaline from the hunt and his feeding overwhelms us. Ignoring his feeble protests, I push my fingers further into his pants and circle them around his thick length. I feel like all the air escapes my lungs at the feel of it. Yanking his pants down, he growls as he withdraws his fangs and pushes his lips to mine as I pump my hand along his length.

Sinking to my knees, I look up at him, his dark eyes connect with mine, mirroring the desire I feel as I wrap my lips around him. Hissing, his hips meet my movements, making me feel all kinds of hot as his heavy breathing fills my ears, drowning out any other sound around us. I don't stop until I gag and my eyes prickle with tears, and I reel back, gasping for air. Hunter lifts me up and slams his mouth against mine possessively. In one fluid movement, Hunter tears the top of my dress, ripping the material straight down the centre, including my lacey bra underneath. My breasts spill forth, bouncing for a moment before he captures my nipple between his lips. He sucks it, running his rough tongue across it. Arching my back, I whimper, reaching down to his length, moving it at a furious pace. His fangs slide into the tender swell of my breast, and my core throbs from the feel of it. I'm so caught up in the feeling of his mouth, I forget that my hand is moving like crazy over him. Warm liquid spills across my hand and he lets out a roar against my skin as he comes. Both of us are almost out of breath as he continues to bite. I close my eyes, throwing my head back as I bring my hand to my mouth. Hunter retracts his fangs, watching me intently as I lick off his release, loving the taste of him on my tongue.

Hunter makes a deep sound at the back of his throat, hoisting me up high. I let out a cry, my eyes flying open. I barely have time to reach for the railing above me. I grip it tightly, as he throws my legs over his shoulders. I hold myself up as he tears the underwear from my body, opening my legs, and diving between my thighs. Feeling his tongue lick straight down the centre of me, I yelp as he buries his face into me. I wrap my legs around his neck, already quivering, knowing my own release is only moments away. His tongue ravishes against my swollen clit at an inhumane speed. I come undone with a scream, feeling the spurts of my desire leave me. He swallows it up shamelessly, his face now coated in a sheath of wetness. Completely spent, my grip on the rafter above me loosens and I collapse into his arms. He cradles me against his chest as the last of my energy evaporates from my body. My dress is in tatters around me, exposing every part of my body to him. He sinks to the ground, holding me in his lap.

'I'm so glad we can do these other things,' I whisper.

Hunter chuckles and softly kisses my forehead, then my nose, before lingering on my mouth. He pricks the pad of his fingertip with his fang and smears it over my lips. I lick it, feeling the energy from him rush into my body, like a light that was on the verge of blowing out, suddenly burning at full brightness.

'How am I going to get out of here?' I laugh, looking down at the strips of fabric around my feet. The only part of my outfit still intact are my high heels. Hunter gently places me on the ground beside him before he gets up and collects my things. Indents from the heels of my shoes are visible on his back, but they clear up before my eyes.

'I'll go steal something,' he says.

'What?' I exclaim.

'Be right back.'

After a few moments, he appears with a leather mini skirt and a crop top. He dresses me quickly. The shirt slips off my shoulder and he adjusts it.

'Might be a little big,' he says.

'I'm not even going to ask how the hell you got these.'

'That's probably best,' he agrees.

'Well. I lost the game,' I say as we walk back to the corridor, the pulse of the music still humming through the walls. I feel like I've just woken up from an epic massage followed by the most amazing night's sleep.

'Didn't seem so bad losing, did it?'

Smirking, I glance at him. 'Certainly not.'

18

HUNTER

The Protector

ALLOWING MYSELF A FEW more seconds of holding her hand, I drop it once we are outside on the street. My senses are on overload in a place like this. All the sounds of the bustling nightlife, the music, the bright lights . . . it's easy to get overwhelmed. Usually, I would zone it all out, but I need to be on high alert. It's a *fun* part of the bond, I've discovered – the constant fear that someone will leap out of the shadows and steal her from me.

I hear Cas and Alex arguing long before I see them. When we reach them, Alex is looking all kinds of smug while Cas looks extremely pissed off. Raya and I sigh at the same time. As we approach, Alex spins around to face us. His eyes flash in confusion – with a hint of anger – when he notices Raya's wardrobe change.

'What the hell happened to you?' he asks, narrowing his eyes suspiciously as they flick between the two of us. His hair is messy, and his clothes a little dishevelled.

'I got blood all over her clothes,' I say.

'Damn, he got you?'

'Cas didn't get you?' Raya exclaims.

'This is one sneaky bastard,' Cas mutters, scowling. 'Slipped his jacket off. I tracked in the wrong direction.'

Alex's smug smile only grows. 'I hid between a group of people and made a dash to the car.'

'Nice!' She grins, looking impressed as they bump knuckles. I can hear Cas grind his teeth together.

'You won't win round two,' he challenges.

'Game on.'

'Enough for tonight,' I say with a headshake. 'Let's go back to your place, Cas. Everyone could use a good night's sleep.'

'Tomorrow.' Cas points at Alex. 'It's on.'

'You bet it is.'

We pile once more into the small car. I expel a breath and try to grapple with my self-control as Raya sits on my lap. My hands move to her bare thighs. Heat ignites inside me, making me all kinds of worked up. I can hardly think straight when she is this close to me – especially not with our recent intimacies so fresh on my mind.

The taste of her is potent against my tongue. My new favourite taste. Even better than her blood, which should be impossible.

Shifting her so that she faces me, I hold her gaze as I lean in to brush my lips against her shoulder. A shiver rolls through her at my touch.

'So,' Alex says, leaning over and draping his arms over the back of the driver seat, obnoxiously ruining the moment. 'I guess it's time for me to get that favour, yeah?'

It's a quiet night. Most people are asleep. The faint volume of televisions nearby tune in and out of my head. I'm sitting on the front porch of Cas's house, flicking the lighter in my hand on and off every few seconds.

I love being out at night. Walking or running through the woods. Bathing in the moonlight. It's when I feel most calm and comfortable. When everything around me is still. Looking up at the starry sky, I close my eyes, hearing the slight whoosh of the world breathing around me. I hear Cas approaching, his soft footfalls padding along the floor. I exhale, not really wanting to discuss more about Raya and our predicament right now. I'm already overthinking everything, talking to Cas about it just makes it worse.

'Hey,' he says, digging his hands into his hoodie.

'Hey.'

'Can't sleep?' Cas asks, rocking on the balls of his feet, gazing out at the dark sky.

'Nah.'

'You should try to get a few hours.'

'Yeah. I will.'

'What's on your mind?' He drops beside me and plucks the lighter from my hand, using it to light the end of his cigarette. He tosses it back to me a moment later.

'What isn't on my mind?' I try to laugh but it sounds strained even to my ears.

'The girl?' he guesses.

'Yeah. Just thinking about this bond. It's easy to tell myself not to give in and let it grow stronger, but then when I'm with her . . .' I exhale sharply, my mind recalling every delicious moment of the hunt. I can't get it – or her – off my mind. The lack of control I have is frustrating. Doing what we did . . . it can easily get out of hand. Of course I loved every second of it, but I specifically told myself not to go there with her. The line between us continues to get blurrier every day. 'I can't control myself.'

'I say fuck it. Give in. Is it all that bad?'

'It will only make it more unbearable when we part.'

After the mission, when things come to an end, she will go back to her life, and I will be there, protecting her, from a distance. It is how it will have to be to ensure she is safe and able to live her normal, human life.

'Who says you have to be apart?' Cas frowns, tilting his head curiously.

'She doesn't want this life. She never asked for it.'

'Neither did you,' he says softly, threading his fingers together as he leans forward.

'And I'm full of regret over those choices that were taken from me,' I explain. 'I don't want this for her.'

'Have you actually asked her?' Cas questions, drawing in a long inhale. The smoke leaves his lips, disappearing in a cloudy fog.

'If she wants to be a vampire?'

'Yeah.'

'No.'

'Probably should before you make all these decisions on her behalf,' he points out with a smirk. 'I remember how you felt after you turned. We talked about it, and you got through it. Besides, your situation is very different to hers.'

Cas helped me immensely after I turned. He has always made me explore things that I never considered. He always thinks outside the box, which I like. He offers great advice. As much as we are different in regard to our personalities, Cas is one of the only people, other than Theo, that I would consider a true friend.

'I think it's a bit soon to be asking her that. She doesn't even know anything about us. Not as much as she needs to before making this kind of decision.'

'Then teach her.'

Picking at my nail bed, I scrape away the skin, watching the blood ooze out, only for it to heal up just as quick as it split open.

'You're already in this far, Hunter. The choice on both sides has already been taken away. Why not embrace it?'

Considering his words, I let my mind explore the possibility of giving in to the bond and letting our worlds totally and utterly collide. There would be no going back. But the question is, would we want to?

'I don't think our future will be all sunshine and rainbows, Cas.'

'Why do you say that?'

'If Kian finds out we are bonded,' I whisper, levelling Cas with a heavy gaze. 'He will do everything in his power to take her from me.'

'Your brother is a piece of work,' Cas agrees, looking away from me. 'But I will be there to protect her, too. He won't get the chance to touch her.'

Rubbing my face, I pinch the bridge of my nose. 'He is the most cunning vampire I've ever known. He is stronger and more powerful than the both of us. If he wants her, he will take her.'

'We won't let it happen, Hunter,' Cas assures me. 'And if this is really a concern of yours, you know what you have to do.'

'What's that?'

'Turn her,' he whispers. 'So she can defend herself.'

Tiny, droplets of ice slither through my veins at the thought of taking her innocence, her humanity, away from her. I don't know what that would mean for us and the bond. A part of me wants to cling to her. I don't want her to go on with her life, without me. The thought of being apart from her . . .

'Turn her,' Cas repeats. 'It's the only real guarantee you can have that you won't lose her.'

19

RAYA

The Survivor

THE SOUND OF MY FEET *pounding against the cement overtakes that of my rapid heartbeat. I push myself to go faster, my legs screaming in protest, the muscles burning as I propel forward. Light blinks at me from the end of the tunnel, taunting me. The harder I run, the farther it seems. Hands circle around my torso, yanking me back so violently I hear a few bones in my ribs crack and break upon impact. Teeth slam into my throat, tearing open my skin. My blood floods out of the open wound, spilling down the front of my dress, soaking it.*

I wake with a scream, wrapped in my sheets, drenched in my own sweat.

The crunch and twist of my own bones breaking is a sound I will never forget.

Cold hands touch my face and I whip my head around, meeting the silver eyes of Hunter. He hovers over me as I lay tangled in the bed. Wrapping his arm around me, he sits down, dragging me onto his lap. Pressing his palm against my racing heart, he pushes against it. Gradually, it slows, the adrenaline fading from me as he absorbs all of my fear and worry.

Slumping forward, I rest my forehead into his shoulder.

'Bad dreams again?' he whispers.

'I can't stop thinking about being hunted to my death.'

'We shouldn't have played that game tonight,' he says quietly. 'It was stupid and reckless.'

I stiffen. Does he only mean the hunt, or what happened between us? I definitely don't think it was stupid . . . 'No, it's good practice for the real thing. I just need to get used to it.'

'It is not something I wish for you to get used to,' he says firmly, tightening his hold on me.

'I chose this, Hunter. I sent myself on this quest knowing there was a high chance I would die before I found my sister. I accepted that long before I met you.'

I will do anything for my sister, including die for her. I've always felt this way. She has been the closest person to me in my life, and I miss her terribly. The need to find her, and learn what happened, only intensifies each day.

'You will not die under my watch, *legata una*. I promise you that. Go back to sleep.'

I want to ask him to lie with me, but he seems preoccupied, and I can almost hear his thoughts ticking over. We haven't seen each other since *it* happened. It was only earlier tonight, but the moment we got home, I went straight to bed. I don't know if he is regretting what happened, or how he feels about it – and us. Considering we are bonded, I still find him extremely difficult to read.

'Okay.' I lay down and close my eyes.

I feel the weight shift off the bed as Hunter stands and swiftly leaves the room. It feels extremely dark and quiet in here now that he's gone. Shivering, I bring the blanket up under my chin, and close my eyes. After half an hour, I still can't get to sleep, and with a sigh, I rub my eyes, and quietly get out of bed. I rummage through my bag and withdraw one of Cora's journals. Flicking through it, I start reading.

Sometimes I wish I was born into a different life.

Of course I love my family. They mean the world to me. But I wish things were different. If only I grew up with a wealthy family, in a nice neighbourhood, with good friends I can rely on, and parents who don't need me to help so much. It might be a selfish thing, but I wish I got to enjoy being a kid.

I don't like living here. In this small, cramped apartment. I want to see things. Explore the world. Meet new people.

We never have any money. Always living week to week.

I don't want this anymore.

Life has always been hard. Hard on my mum, hard on me. I tried to be the big sister Raya could rely on, but it's a heavy burden to have on my shoulders. I'm envious of her. She has been sheltered through so much because I was always there to protect her.

Life would be so much easier if I was born as someone else.

My heart aches for her. I never would have guessed she felt any of this. I suppose that's what she is saying. I was sheltered and protected from the harsh reality of everything. Of course I knew things were hard for my mum, but I never knew the extent of it like Cora did.

'Hey.'

I startle, the journal slipping from my hands and clattering to the floor. Alex hovers near the doorway, rubbing his eyes.

'Christ, Alex,' I exclaim, placing a hand on my chest. 'Where did you come from?'

'I didn't want to interrupt you while you were reading.'

'Can't sleep?' I ask.

He shakes his head. 'No.'

'I thought I was ready to do the hunt, but it triggered me from that other time. I know what we did tonight wasn't real, but it still brought all the other stuff up.' I exhale, flopping back onto my pillows. 'Ignore me. I'm just complaining.'

'You have every right to feel the way you do,' Alex says, strolling over and falling into the space beside me. 'It's pretty scary shit we have involved ourselves in.'

'How are you doing?' I ask, reaching for his hand, placing mine over it.

'Fine. I'm coming around to these guys. A little.' He shrugs. 'I still don't like them, but maybe they're not *all* bad.'

'I agree.'

'I don't like how close you and Hunter are becoming. It worries me that you're getting in a bit too deep.'

'I understand that, but it isn't like I just have a crush on some random guy. This bonded thing is more serious than I can express,' I say. 'It's stronger than anything. I can't control the way I feel. I know the bond has affected that, but my feelings toward Hunter are genuine.'

Alex chews his lip. 'Just be careful.'

'I will.'

'I love you,' he says.

It's the first time he has ever told me that. I can see it in the way he looks at me, and how close we have become.

Smiling, I pull him towards me and wrap my arms around him. 'I love you, too.'

When we break apart, Alex swings his legs over the side of the bed and gets to his feet, stretching.

'Night, loser. See you in the morning.'

Rolling my eyes, I shake my head. And there he is, the Alex I know all too well.

Leaning over the side of the bed, I close the journal and toss it onto my bag. I make my way to the bathroom. As I wash my hands, I look out the window. I miss going for night-time strolls. I used to do it all the time. Now, I sketch, or reread Cora's journals. I miss the simplicity of going for a night stroll and forgetting about everything that is going on, even if it is just for a few moments.

Deciding not to think too much about it – since rationality will surely win out if I think too hard about what I'm about to do – I step into my shoes, shrug on a jacket, and slip out the side door. When it softly clicks behind me, I hold my breath, waiting for one of the vampires to appear. After a few seconds, I keep moving. I trot down the porch steps and inhale a long, deep breath of the fresh night air. My shoulders slump a little in relief. This is exactly what I need right now. The snapping sound of a stick causes my head to whip around and I gasp when I see a shadow disappear behind a tree.

'Hello?' I call out, taking a tentative step closer.

'Raya?' Inhaling sharply, I spin on my heel, seeing Hunter standing on the porch behind me, scowling. 'What are you doing?'

My knees knock together, and my heart beats wildly in my chest. I glance back at the tree, but nothing is there. I'm sure I saw something move behind it, but whatever it was, is gone now. Shaking my head, I flick my hair back and walk towards Hunter.

'Just needed some air.' I sigh. 'I can't sleep.'

Hunter holds his hand out to me. I take it in mine, and he tugs me up the steps. Wrapping an arm around my shoulder, he kisses me on the temple.

'Are you still thinking about the hunt?' he questions.

'I'm thinking about a lot of things.'

Without a word, I allow him to lead me inside, and back up to my room. I kick off my shoes, and Hunter gently slides my jacket down my arms, hanging it up on the back of the door.

'Why don't you draw?' he suggests.

Glancing up at him, I raise my eyebrows. 'How do you know I draw?'

He nods at the black leather-bound sketch pad. 'I've sneaked a peak a few times.'

Blushing, I duck my chin. 'You've seen my drawings of you, then.'

'Only little bits. I would love you to show me. Whenever you're ready to.'

'I'll show you now,' I say, wandering over to the sketchpad and picking it up.

'Only if you're sure.'

'Positive,' I reply, sitting on the edge of the mattress. 'I used to be embarrassed about people seeing these because they're so dark and twisted. But I feel like out of anyone in the world, you would understand them the most.'

Smiling softly, he holds out his hands. Gently, he flicks through the pages. Swallowing, my eyes switch back between the pages, to his dark eyes, and back to the sketchpad again.

His hand pauses when he gets to one of my drawings of him. It's a pastime of mine when I can't sleep. Faint lines cover the pages, indicating the hotel room we stayed at when we first started the trip. Hunter is resting against the wall, looking out at the moon through the window. He has a sad, serious expression on his face. His fingertips trail down the sharp lines of his sketched jaw. 'You're incredibly talented, Raya,' he murmurs.

'Thank you,' I whisper.

'Would you want to do something with this?' He questions, shifting so that he is facing me. 'As in, a career with your art?'

I shrug. 'Yeah, I guess so. I don't really know what I would do with it.'

'You can do anything you want, Raya.'

I brighten under the seriousness of his tone. The faith he has in me fills my heart with joy. I have never felt like someone truly and whole-heartedly believed I could succeed. If anything, I was always made to think my art was a silly side-hobby that would never generate any income for me to live off.

As though reading my thoughts, Hunter shakes his head. 'You can do anything you want with this, Raya. You have the talent. The world is at your fingertips. Anything you want, you can achieve.'

Tears spring to my eyes, and I smile at him. 'Thank you, Hunter. I appreciate that.'

Leaning in, he softly kisses the tip of my nose, and I flush all the way down to my toes.

Crawling into bed, this time, I feel like I can sleep.

Again, I don't want him to leave.

'Will you lie with me?' I ask hesitantly.

Nodding, he lays back against the mattress. Curling his arm around me, he pulls me against him, allowing me to bury into his chest. My body feels relaxed and boneless being so close to him.

'I don't want tomorrow to come,' I whisper, the thought of Hunter going back to being closed-off and distant makes my heart hurt.

'Why's that?' he asks, stroking his fingers through my hair. I love the feel of it. It's soothing, almost lulling me to sleep. His hand moves to the back of my head, down to my neck. A shiver of desire rolls through me once more.

'I don't want you to regret what happened and push me away.'

His fingers, which are trailing up my back, pauses for a moment.

'I don't mean for you to feel this way. We just need to be careful,' he says regretfully, looking troubled.

'I understand,' I murmur.

Drawing me closer, he kisses my temple. I crave this. I crave *him*. The urge to have him close, and to know more about him surges within me. It makes me wonder about Hunter. What was he like growing up, what were his hopes and ambitions? Was he always this kind, logical, and level-headed? Did he get in trouble at school, or was he good? I'm desperate to know more.

'Where did you grow up?' I ask.

Keeping his lips on my skin, he presses a little harder into my back. I sigh at the touch, letting my eyes drift close.

'I was born in Italy, but we moved to a small town in South Australia when I was a baby.'

'What brought you to the East Coast?'

'My parents moved us when I was about eight or so. Dad got a new job opportunity.'

'Do you like it here?'

'Love it,' he says. 'We used to spend every day at the beach, surfing, swimming, diving, snorkelling. I love the water more than anything. I often go out into the ocean for hours and hours at a time. It's even better now. I can go so long without breathing and I can withstand any harsh conditions.'

'Maybe you were meant to be a mermaid.' I giggle. 'Merman, rather.'

He chuckles. 'Maybe.'

'I used to swim around in the pool at midnight underneath the full moon and wish that I would wake up the next morning and be a mermaid.'

I feel his lips spread into a smile. 'That's cute.'

'Little cringe, but cute, sure.'

He breathes a soft laugh. 'Was it always you three? You, your mum, and your sister?'

I deflate a little at the reminder of my family. Having two people with you, by your side through everything, suddenly taken from you . . . it is something I wouldn't wish on anyone.

'Yeah. My parents got divorced when I was two or so. My father has a new family now. I don't even know where he is.'

'Do you miss him?'

'No,' I reply honestly. 'Because I never had the chance to know him.'

'I'm sorry.'

'Don't be. I had a great life. We struggled a lot, sure. Mum was a single parent raising two girls on her own, but she did what she could to give us everything.'

'I get it,' he says, drawing me out of my thoughts.

'Get what?'

'This bond that runs so deep inside you when it comes to family. They're all you had and you lost them both so suddenly.'

The hole inside my chest that my family left behind burns inside me. The dark, empty feeling of nothingness that has burrowed deep inside aches for me to let out all the emotions I've tried so desperately to keep in.

'It's a pain I wouldn't wish on my worst enemy.'

'You have no other family?' he asks. 'Aunts, uncles, grandparents?'

'My mum was fostered. She never knew her family. We had aunts and uncles when my dad was around, but when he left, so did they.'

'Christ,' Hunter mumbles, and I feel him moving his face a little closer, rubbing comforting circles on my back. 'That's . . . rough.'

'Yeah,' I reply softly. 'And you? What about your family?'

'Oh, I have a huge family back home in Italy. Massive,' he replies, and I can hear in his voice how much he cares about his family, and how much he misses them. 'I have an amazing family here though. They did everything for us.'

'Did?'

'I've compelled them. They think Kian and I are travelling the world together, and that we call every Sunday to update them.

They're living life under my protection. I fear Kian will hunt them down and kill them.'

'Oh my God. He would do that?'

'There is nothing he wouldn't do.'

I shiver at his words. The thought of my sister possibly being tied up with him makes my stomach clench in terror.

'You don't ever get to see them?'

'Not really.' When he moves, I re-open my eyes. Reaching over for his phone, Hunter brightens the screen and clicks open one of the apps. He tilts it so that I can see. Squinting, blurry figures come into view and after a moment, the screen clears. A security camera, watching over a family. The screen is split into different views, and they're all in night mode as the people sleep. 'I check in on them constantly. Making sure they're all okay. But not in person, no.'

'You must miss them,' I say, wishing I could see their faces. I'd love to know who Hunter resembles.

'Terribly,' he admits. 'A heartache I never thought I could endure. But as the years go by, it seems easier letting everything I once knew go. It's just a part of it all.'

'I see. Have you been back to Italy since you turned?'

'I've been all around the world. The first year after I turned is a blur of travelling, partying . . .' He sighs. 'I let my vampire side take over. I'm not proud of the things I did.'

Pausing for a moment, I shift, wondering what he means by that, and whether I will be okay with whatever he may be about to admit to. I swallow thickly and gaze up at him. He truly is beautiful. Sharp jawline, smooth skin, dark hair that falls messily onto his forehead. Perfection.

'Did you kill people?' I manage to force out, terrified of the answer.

'I have only killed other vampires who have threatened me or someone else's life. But I would take blood and toss people aside like they were nothing but leftovers. It's disgusting.'

'At least you didn't murder people,' I say. 'I bet a lot of vampires can't say that.'

'I've always seemed to have a moral compass that prevented me from going too far. Even when I thought I was totally out of control.'

'See?' I say softly with a smile. 'You are a good vampire.'

A ghost of a smile flickers over his handsome face. 'If you say so.'

'I know so.'

'Get some sleep,' he says.

'Okay,' I mumble. 'Goodnight, Hunter.'

With a final kiss as soft as a feather, he tightens his hold on me. A sense of warmth and safety floods through me, and I feel totally and completely untouchable in his arms.

'Goodnight, *legata una*.'

20

HUNTER

The Protector

IT IS WELL AFTER 8 AM. when Raya appears downstairs, rubbing her eyes. We let them both sleep in today, thinking they could probably use it after the night's escapades.

Dressed in denim shorts with her shirt tucked in, she looks cute as a button. Her long hair is pulled up into a high ponytail which swishes between her shoulder blades with each step she takes. Her scent washes over me, soothing me in more ways than I care to admit. A delicious sweetness of jasmine, sunshine, and honey blended with the signature aroma of her blood.

'Good morning,' I say as she enters the kitchen. 'Hungry?'

'Starving,' she admits, staring around at the variety of food selections I have spread out on the benchtop.

I want this for us. Waking up in the morning, having a routine. I wish it was that easy. A big part of me wants to give in to the bond. Let it strengthen. Deal with the consequences of that later. But it isn't just me involved here, and I care too much about her and the life she deserves.

'I made toast, and eggs,' I say, pointing to one side. 'And then over here are croissants and fruit.'

'How much do you think humans eat?' She grins, flattening down a piece of her hair that's come loose. Tracking her movements, my eyes roam down her slender neck, taking in every beautiful part of her.

I shrug, wiping my hands on my jeans. 'I wasn't sure what you liked. We can keep the rest for tomorrow.'

'I can't believe you made all of this. You don't even eat.'

'I eat some things,' I say with a smirk, winking at her.

Blushing, she takes a seat at the kitchen bench, perching on one of the stools beside it.

'Water? Orange juice?' I ask.

'Juice, please.'

I fill the glass and slide it across to her. She loads up her plate, filling it more than I expected from a tiny girl like her. She moans as she takes a bite. Blood rushes to my groin at the sound and I clench my jaw, wrestling with the emotions threatening to take over.

'Why are you looking at me all serious like that?' She raises an eyebrow. 'Are *you* hungry?'

Considering I had a healthy dose of blood last night, I probably shouldn't be craving her blood as strongly as I am right now. Swallowing, I nod anyway.

'Is anyone awake?' she asks, glancing toward the ceiling.

I shake my head. 'No.'

Standing, she moves around to my side of the counter, pushing herself onto it, her legs dangling over the edge. She yanks her shirt over her head, exposing her smooth skin and a black bra that barely contains her breasts. My hands curl into fists as my fangs snap out, desire coursing through me.

It was probably a mistake saying we could do things and not go all the way. I don't want to rush into things with her, but it is so damn difficult trying to hang on to my self-control and not give in.

She consumes me. All of me.

Grinning, she leans back on her palms, tilting her head back. Moving toward her on the counter, I push between her legs, spreading her thighs. Slowly, my hand travels up from her hip, tracing the delicate lines of her body. I twirl a piece of her dark hair around my finger. I touch the violet streak and give it a slight tug. My mouth salivates at her proximity.

Kissing her skin softly, I sink my fangs into her, and we both moan. Pressing harder into her, I drink a little deeper, while my other hand moves between her legs, and I walk my fingers up her inner thigh. Her breath hitches as my finger slides against her entrance.

'Will Cas hear this?' she half moans, half whispers, eyes snapping open as she looks toward the door.

'Don't worry about him, *legata una*,' I say firmly. 'Eyes on me.'

When her lips part, I lean forward, taking her lower lip between my teeth, sucking on it. I groan into her mouth when my fingers become slick with her desire. Pushing one inside, I bite into her neck. Throwing her head back, she moans, simultaneously bucking her hips. Adding another finger, I move them quickly. With the way her legs tighten around my waist, I know I've hit the spot. Coming undone, she whimpers as her orgasm crashes through her. Her legs tremble as she rides it out, sagging back against the bench afterwards. Slowly inching out of her, I drag her close and kiss her again as I bring my hand to her mouth.

'Taste yourself, *legata una*.'

Her tongue snakes out, dragging up and down my fingers before sucking them, tasting every bit of the climax that I created. Removing my fingers from her mouth, I place my hands back onto her hips.

'The best breakfast,' I murmur, kissing the tip of her nose, as I step back.

Coldness washes over me at the sudden lack of contact, and as I increase the distance between us, the lust fades, and the anger

I so often feel towards myself rises. I hate the lack of control I have when it comes to her. It makes this so much more difficult.

Shaking my head, trying to clear my thoughts, I start tidying up the kitchen simply to keep my hands preoccupied.

'What is the plan for today?' she asks, pulling her shirt back over her head and combing her fingers through her hair, looking as flustered as I feel.

'I thought we might explore the town. And while doing so, I'm going to do some digging. Try to see what people know.'

'How are you going to do that?'

'You leave that to me,' I say, turning around and offering her a small smile. With the afterglow of what we just did evident on her face, she looks even more beautiful somehow.

She has almost finished eating when Alex staggers down, his hair standing up at odd angles. He yawns, rubbing his hands over his face roughly. He pauses, blinking down at the selection of food before him.

'Woah,' he says.

'Hunter cooked this for us.'

'You did?' Alex asks in surprise, looking over at me. 'Is it . . . edible?'

I roll my eyes. 'Yes. Eat up before it goes cold.'

As Alex picks at the food, I turn my back on them, gripping the counter, trying to reign in my control after what we just did. I glance outside a few times. I can't hear Cas at all, which makes me think he is out.

Alex and Raya are ready to go when Cas strolls through the door, barefoot. His hair is a mess from the wind. He grins and waves as he walks into the kitchen where we are all seated.

'Hello, hello,' he says, dressed head-to-toe in a skintight outfit that looks like a swimsuit, but different. Some sort of sun-resistant clothing, perhaps. 'Beautiful morning, isn't it?'

'Sure is.' Raya smiles, meeting my eyes briefly before blushing.

'Where have you been?' Alex asks, peering over at Cas with interest.

'Went for a 20km run, then a swim. Finished off the morning with a beautiful surfer lad's lips wrapped around my co – ' I clear my throat. Cas grins. 'Anyway, let's just say I have had a great start to the day.'

Me and you both, brother.

Raya wrinkles her nose while Alex looks a little more intrigued than I like the look of.

'We are ready to leave when you are,' I say.

Nodding, he disappears for a few moments, and returns dressed in his usual attire, ready to go. We follow him out the door. A black Porsche sits in his driveway with a shiny red bow placed on top of it.

'There you go,' Cas says, tossing the keys at Alex. 'Your wish is my command.'

Alex's jaw almost hits the ground as he gapes at the sleek black car in front of him.

'You really got me a car?' he splutters.

'You ask, I deliver.'

'No way . . .' he breathes, rushing over to it and sliding his hands along the side of it. 'This is mine?'

'Yep,' Cas says.

'I could kiss you right now,' Alex exclaims, racing around to the other side of the car and practically dives into it, his reservations about vampires seeming to be nonexistent right now.

'You'd enjoy it too much,' Cas says. 'You'd become obsessed with me. Then things would get awkward.'

Raya giggles, but Alex isn't listening to him. His eyes light up as he gazes in awe around the interior of the car. I've never seen the dude so happy.

'I installed a subwoofer, just like mine,' Cas explains, gesturing to the backseat of the car. 'It's worth it, trust me.'

Alex is speechless. I mentally note this, since it is a rare occasion.

'Thank you,' Raya mouths to Cas.

He smiles, nodding at her.

'I call shotgun,' he says.

I slide into the backseat and Raya sits on my lap, since yet again, the backseat is taken over by the giant sound system. Swallowing down everything raging inside me, I try my best not to touch her with my hands or even look at her. I've let my guard down too much. The temptation to go further with her is overwhelming. I need to cool it and remember what is most important right now – finding her sister.

The car lurches forward and she almost slams into the seat in front of her. I whip my hand out, stopping her from flying forward. Alex sends a sheepish look over his shoulder.

'Whoops.'

'Hold on,' I mutter.

Raya reaches out, touching my hand. A part of me wants to pull away from her, but I just can't force myself to do it.

'What's wrong?' she asks in concern.

Pressing my forehead to her shoulder, I sigh. 'I have a lot on my mind.'

The conversation I had last night with Cas plays in my mind.

I have no idea what the hell I am meant to do. Whatever decisions I make, there are pros and cons to both.

Exhaling heavily, I close my eyes, wishing all of this wasn't so damn difficult.

21

RAYA

The Survivor

THE DRIVE INTO TOWN IS SHORT, but I feel instantly car sick with Alex's jolty driving. As soon as he parks, I leap out of the car, and greedily gulp in the fresh air, waiting for my churning stomach to settle.

'You okay?' Hunter asks, materialising at my side in an instant.

'A little car sick, but I'm fine.'

'Do you want my help?' he asks, pointing at his wrist.

I shake my head, nauseas from the drive, but also a little bitter about everything that is going on between us. I hate how distant he feels right now, especially after what happened in the kitchen this morning. The fact that we can't give in easily and continue to grow our friendship. Relationship. Whatever it is. I understand that he knows it will quickly develop into something more, and he doesn't want to alter my life forever, but doesn't he realise it already is? The bond has already formed. There is no going back now. I don't understand why he wants to torture us both. Especially when we keep having these slip-ups . . .

'No,' I say sourly. His eyes scan my face, frowning. 'Thanks, though.'

As we walk downtown, I distract myself with our new surroundings. I've never visited this part of Australia, and though it was always on Mum's bucket list, it was never achievable.

I try to keep my mind off Hunter, but as usual, I fail. My blood warms at the thought of his mouth on me. I break out in a light sweat, thinking of how good he felt touching me, kissing me . . .

'I'm going to do some investigating,' Hunter says. He points to his ears. 'I'll be close by if you need me.'

'Roger that,' Alex says, even though Hunter isn't addressing him.

'Anyone keen for a beer?' Cas asks.

'No,' we all say simultaneously before Hunter peels away from the group, drifting toward a couple of teenage guys leaning against the wall of a barber shop. Cas doesn't seem to care, heading off in the opposite direction, hands in his pockets as he hums to himself.

'Let's go in here,' I say to Alex, nudging him with my shoulder, directing him toward a cosy boutique.

'No way,' Alex protests.

'Don't pretend you're not interested in this. You wear more rings and bracelets than I do.'

Alex rolls his eyes, but I ignore him as I make my way over to the table of rubies. It's my birthstone, so I've always worn ruby jewellery. I used to have a necklace with a ruby charm that I wore religiously. It meant so much to me. I had always been jewellery-obsessed, but never able to afford anything worth any value. My mum bought it for me on my sixteenth birthday, and I swore to never take it off, until I lost it one day at the beach, either buried in the sand or swept out with the waves, lost to me either way. I cried for three days.

Suddenly, I gasp when I notice one necklace almost identical to the one I lost. Leaning in so close that my nose grazes the display glass, I study it. It isn't the exact same, but close enough. My eyes move to the price, and I baulk, backing away from it.

'Damn,' I mutter.

'What?' Alex questions, frowning.

'Oh, nothing. I just love that necklace,' I say, gesturing to the one I was just looking at.

'Why don't you get it?'

I point at the ridiculous figure on the tag beside it, and Alex lets out a low whistle. 'Bloody hell, does it come with a diamond, too?'

Letting out a snort, I elbow him as the cashier shoots a glare in our direction. We keep looking through the store, but I quickly lose interest as the prices grow further and further beyond our budget.

Alex's phone pings, and I watch as he pulls it out of his pocket, and frowns down at the screen. Peering over at it, I see a selfie of Cas, holding up a beer.

'Very helpful of him,' I mutter. 'And since when did you exchange numbers?'

Alex shrugs, pocketing the phone, eyes on his feet. I'm still watching him from the corner of my eye as we exit the store when my shoulder roughly barges into someone. I stumble back, almost falling on my ass when two hands shoot out, steadying me.

'Oh my god,' the guy blurts, blinking at me. 'What are you doing back here?'

'Huh?'

'Who's this?'

Alex steps between me and the stranger.

The guy smiles. He's tall, with fair hair, and a five o'clock shadow on his face. His eyes are kind and crinkled at the corners as he grins at me like we have met before.

'Who are *you*?' Alex says rudely.

His friendly smile doesn't waver. 'An old friend of Cora's,' he answers. 'I didn't realise you were back in town.'

I feel the colour drain from my face as my heart jumps into my throat. I take a step back, short of breath. My head spins so violently, I feel like I'm about to pass out, and I reach out to Alex for support. The guy grabs my elbow in concern.

'Cora? What's wrong?'

'Cora?' Alex says slowly, looking at me. 'He thinks you're Cora . . .'

'You know my sister?' I whisper. 'You've met her?'

The guy looks taken back as he glances between us. 'Wait . . . You're not her?' His smile falters.

'No.' I shake my head. I step closer to him, grabbing his arms and shaking him. 'Where is she?'

'I don't know!' he exclaims, trying to shake off my tight grip on his arm. 'I thought you were her, so obviously I don't know where she is.'

'When did you meet her?' I demand.

'Uh . . .' His eyes drifted over my shoulder, suddenly looking dazed.

'Hello?' I say loudly.

His eyes snap back to me suddenly. 'What were we talking about?'

'Cora!' I reply, unable to contain my impatience. 'When did you last see her?'

'Uh . . .' he says again, the same thing happening, as if someone is dangling something behind my head that has captured his attention.

'He's been compelled,' Hunter says.

I yelp when Hunter appears out of nowhere, and I clutch my hand to my chest as I whirl around to face him.

'Don't do that!' I hiss.

'Sorry,' he says, not even glancing at me as he studies the guy standing in front of us, who is still looking dazed. 'He's not able to answer when he last saw her because he has been compelled to forget.'

The guy blinks at us. 'I've been what?'

'How do you know Cora?' I demand.

'Umm . . .' His eyes shift from mine, going misty once more.

'Answer me, God damn it!' I yell into his face, shaking him so drastically that his head bobbles back and forth. People walking by us glance over with curious expressions.

Hunter rests a hand on my arm and the panic and frustration I was feeling moments ago blends into a much calmer, rational feeling.

'He can't answer, Raya.'

Sighing, I throw my hands up. 'What does this mean?'

'It means your sister has been here. She's alive!' Alex says, spinning me around, fingers biting into my skin. 'She's alive, Raya.'

Tears well in my eyes, burning as they release in blurred lines down my cheeks. I sniffle and smile, letting the tears flow.

'She's alive,' I whisper.

'And she has been here,' Hunter says, touching his hand to my back, drawing me toward him. Tilting my head back, I gaze into his silver-grey eyes. 'We are one step closer to finding her.'

22

HUNTER

The Protector

THE COOL AIR BREEZES THROUGH the deck area, scattering the newspaper articles I have spread across the table. With my vampire speed, they are all placed back in the exact position I had them, my eyes scanning their headlines.

'Third Attack in Three Weeks'

'Teen Found Dead Inside Car'

'Twenty-Two-Year-Old Missing'

'Governor Locks Down Curfew Due to Spike in Crime Rates'

Articles and articles from towns from all around, all reporting the same thing. Whether it's Kian and whoever he is travelling with, I can't be certain, but not many vampires are as careless as him when it comes to human lives. Most vampires will enjoy themselves, but make a conscious effort to cover up their tracks. I'm positive my brother *wants* to be caught. He loves an opportunity to go at it with someone. He was bloodthirsty before he was even turned.

Scribbling down notes, I add to my board of information, trying to figure out where they may be heading next. Vampires are incredibly unpredictable creatures. They can be as difficult as finding a needle in a haystack, trying to figure out their next move.

The human who ran into Raya confirms that Cora has been here. I'm just not certain of the exact time frame. Rubbing my jaw, I lean back in the chair.

The memory of seeing Cora, blood painted across her mouth, eyes blacker than coal as she drove her fangs into the neck of an innocent human that Kian had very obviously already had his fun with, plays in my mind. I feel nauseous and anxious thinking about it. My heart breaks for Raya, both in fear and concern that reuniting with her sister may not be as wholesome as she thinks.

I had only seen them briefly. My brother was back in town for 'business'. In and out within hours, but he always makes sure to pay me a special visit. To remind me he exists. Any excuse to torment me, even just a little bit.

Those cold eyes and cruel face. Cora. I don't think she is the sister that Raya remembers. At least, not anymore.

I drain the remainder of my whiskey and lean back in my chair. The secret of knowing my brother has Cora, and the fact that she is no longer human, is haunting me, weighing heavily on my mind. I don't have the heart to break it to Raya – especially when her hope of finding her is renewed. A part of me is convinced we could get through to Cora when we find her. That Cora seeing Raya again will awaken something inside of her. Make her remember who she used to be.

But if it doesn't, I don't know if Raya will survive it.

The afternoon sun casts strips of golden light streaming across the porch. The slight buzz of the whiskey has me feeling a little floaty as I lean my hip on the kitchen counter, observing Raya. She is seated on the lounge on the porch that wraps around the side of the house, legs tucked beneath her.

A frown creases her brow, and she absently chews on her lower lip as her hand furiously moves across the page.

'Hello, Alex,' I say, when I hear his light footsteps approach.

'S'up?' he mumbles, shuffling toward the fridge. He makes an exaggerated gagging sound as pushes a blood bag to the side to reach the water bottle on the top shelf. Ignoring him, I continue to watch Raya. The sun beam that nestled over her lap is shifting as the sun moves in the sky. Soon it will light up those gorgeous emerald eyes.

'You're being creepy,' Alex mutters.

'And you're being annoying.'

'How am I being annoying?' He scoffs.

I glance at him. 'Just hearing you breathe is annoying.'

Alex grins, looking pleased about that. 'Thank you.'

Sighing, I turn and lean back against the counter again.

'Look,' I say as Alex hunts through the pantry, looking for something to snack on. 'I understand your reservations about me and the relationship I have with Raya.'

Pausing, Alex's hand hovers over a packet of chips before he slowly reaches for them and turns to face me. Brushing his hair out of his eyes, he blinks. 'Oh, we're doing this then,' he states.

'I just want to be very clear that I have no intention in hurting her. In fact, my one purpose in this life is to *protect* her. I understand that has been your role since you met Raya, and I don't want to overstep.'

Alex's eyes soften and he nods. 'You promise me, right now, your intentions for her are completely pure?'

Pushing off the bench, I am in front of him in two long strides. Holding my hand out, I meet his eyes. 'I promise, *protettore*, my intentions are pure.'

His eyes scan my face for a moment before he takes my hand and offers me one firm shake. He nods. 'Okay.'

Nodding back, I step away, moving toward my spot once more. I enjoy watching Raya. I could sit here and stare at her all day.

'If I find out that means something rude in Italian, I'm going to kick your ass,' Alex mutters, splitting open the packet and popping one of the chips onto his tongue.

Side-eyeing him, I raise an eyebrow. 'I'd like to see you try, punk.'

A few hours later, I am sitting high up on a tree branch, my legs swinging over the edge. I've been watching the guy we met earlier. Trent, as I learnt his name is. I refrained from questioning him earlier in hopes he may lead me to others, or at least some sort of clue. He has finished his shift at the restaurant he works at and has been taking his time walking back home. He is sitting on a park bench, knee jiggling, as he smokes one cigarette, then another. Sighing impatiently, I shift my position so that my back is leaning against the tree. I wonder what Trent is up to – even a human must realise that sitting on a park bench on the edge of the woods at midnight isn't the smartest idea. I keep waiting for someone to turn up, but so far, no one has. After a few more minutes, I launch myself off the branch, landing in front of him.

Trent yelps and throws his arms up over his head, cowering away from me. Circling my fingers around his throat, I drag him to his feet, looking down my nose at him.

'You know Kian?'

His breathing comes out hard, blasting stale cigarette smoke into my face. I tighten my grip on his neck.

'If I have to repeat myself, I won't be so polite.'

'Yes!' he shouts, bits of spit flying from the corners of his mouth. 'Yes! I know him.'

'How do you know him?'

His body trembles beneath my grip.

'Answer me!' I roar into his face, my compulsion soaking into his pores, drowning him in it.

'Him and his girlfriend kept me in their apartment,' he whimpers, fighting against the compulsion that has already been placed on him. 'They fed on me and used me for errands.'

'When?'

Sweat beads across his forehead, and his eyes squeeze shut. I sink my nails into his skin, drops of blood oozing out of his flesh. He howls in pain.

'Open your eyes and answer me.' The command in my tone causes a ripple inside his body as his eyes snap back open.

'Three weeks ago.' Sweat races down the side of his face and the shaking grows more violent as I feel him wage with the war within himself. One half of him is trying to fulfil my compulsion while the other half is battling with the one already placed upon him.

'Where were they going next?' My eyes bore so strongly into his own I feel his knees buckle.

'A town up north,' he replies through gritted teeth, his breathing laboured. 'Harbour something . . .'

Releasing him, he falls in a heap on the ground, a shivering mess. Dropping to his level, I grip his chin, forcing his gaze to meet mine.

'Thank you, Trent. Forget me. Forget this conversation. Go home.'

Scrambling to his feet, he takes off at a run, tripping over his untied laces, and staggering to his knees. Waiting until he is out of sight, I sit on the bench, thinking over his words. After a while, I take the scenic route home, and formulate the next part of our trip. We will leave tomorrow for Harbourton. The town I believe Kian may be, if he has stayed that long.

A shiver of awareness pulses through me when I approach the edge of the driveway, and see Raya sitting on the porch steps. Her long, dark hair falls in a silky waterfall around her face. She's dressed in sleep shorts and a crop top. She stands when she sees me, revealing her stomach. My eyes focus on her nipples, which pebble as her eyes roam over me.

The desire that crackles between us as we gravitate to one another is palpable, and I half expect to see sparks surge between us in the darkness.

'What are you doing out here?' I ask.

'I felt that you were gone.'

'You did?' I question, pushing a loose strand of hair off her face and tucking it behind her ear.

'Yes. Where did you go?'

'I tracked Trent.'

'Who?'

'The guy from the boutique. Who knew your sister.'

Scanning her face, I watch closely as her brows pull together. It's overwhelming her, thinking about her sister being alive, and all the unknown questions that come with that.

'Oh?' she asks softly.

'I managed to extract some information from him. I'll fill you in on the plan tomorrow. Need to talk to Cas about a few things first.'

'Right,' she says, moving up a couple of steps, and then stopping to look down at me. 'I hate how you make me feel sometimes.' Clenching my jaw, I look somewhere over her shoulder, my heart sinking heavily as she continues. 'Pushing me away, only to show me the glimpse of what could truly be between us a few moments later, then going back to being stand-offish. I know you're living in denial about everything, but you need to accept the fact that the damage is done. Our lives are intertwined forever, no matter how much distance you try to place between us.'

Sighing, I lean forward, pressing my forehead against her arm, too exhausted to argue. She's right. She's always right.

'I know,' I reply softly. 'I'm sorry.'

She is silent for a few moments, before she runs a hand through my hair, forcing my chin up, levelling her gaze with mine.

'I mean it,' she murmurs.

I appreciate everything about this girl. Calm, reassuring, logical, and best of all? She knows how to communicate what she's feeling. At least one of us does.

'Anyway, it's late. I'm going to bed.' Stepping away, she looks back at me. 'Are you coming?'

When she holds out her hand, I don't refuse it. Letting her pull me along the stairs after her. We silently make our way to the second floor before I pause. 'One second,' I say.

I make a detour to my room – that I have yet to actually use – returning to find Raya waiting by the door of hers.

'This is for you,' I tell her.

Holding my hand out, she curiously takes the gift from my hand. She unwraps the tissue paper, and gasps when the ruby necklace glints up at her in the pale light peeking through the blinds.

'Oh my god,' she whispers. 'You got me the necklace.' Her face lights up as her eyes roam over it.

I saw the way she stared at it today. I want nothing but the best for her. She has had to bear too much heartache.

'You wanted it.'

'Thank you,' she whispers. 'Thank you so much, Hunter.'

The earnest smile on her face melts my insides. She offers it back to me before turning, pulling her hair to one side. I place it over her delicate skin and click the clasp shut.

'Thank you,' she murmurs. 'You have no idea what this means to me.'

Lightly touching her face, I nod. The tension between us is palpable, caressing each of us, drawing one to the other like magnets.

'You're welcome.'

'Stay with me?'

I nod. She walks over to the bed and picks up her sketch-pad. I gently take it from her, and flick through it. My eyes skim over the drawings, seeing my own features staring up at me amongst the pages. 'I still think you should do something with this. Have you thought any more about it?'

Raya gives me a soft smile. 'Well, I didn't say anything before, but I always wanted to go to a prestigious art school in London, but I never had the money for it.'

'London?' I murmur, closing the book, and placing it on the bedside table. 'I love London. I will take you there one day.'

'That sounds nice,' she says. Yawning, she crawls into bed first and then I join her. Rolling to my side, I face her.

'Was there ever a time you got along with your brother?' she asks, her tone soft and sleepy as she nestles into the pillows, inching closer to me.

A sigh escapes me. My brother is a subject that is exhausting and causes me a lot of tension and heartache. All I ever wanted was to be close to him. To have someone to look up to, to have a friend, to have someone I can rely on. I wanted all of that for us. I wanted to be that for him. He hated me before he ever got to know me, and it stayed that way. In his mind, everyone is a threat. It's just his nature.

'Not that I can remember.'

'Never?'

'We couldn't be more different,' I admit. 'He is extremely hot-headed, argumentative, sporadic . . .' I trail off.

'Sounds exhausting to be around.'

'It is. Now with everything basically on steroids, he is even more unbearable. Cruel and cunning.'

'What is going to happen if we find him?' she whispers, her voice barely audible as she opens her eyes, peering up at me. 'It's going to be dangerous. Isn't it?'

Nodding, I tangle my fingers in the ends of her hair. 'It will be. He is much more powerful than me, and I don't know how many vampires he is travelling with.'

'I wish there was something more I could do to help you. I'm so painfully fragile that it makes me want to scream.'

Cas's words hiss inside my mind. Swallowing, I twirl a dark piece of hair tightly around my finger. 'Don't ever think you're a burden.'

'I am. I can't help you with anything. I'm so *weak*.'

'Has the thought crossed your mind . . .' I swallow, averting my eyes, unsure how to word the question I have been so desperately wanting to ask.

'To turn?' she questions.

I nod, hardly daring to draw a breath. My eyes drift back to her face as she thinks. I know how she is feeling, and her opinion about vampires have certainly shifted since I first met her.

Like Cas said, the dynamic is different than usual since we are bonded. She still has a choice though, one I will never take from her. Ever.

'Well. Yeah. Of course it has.'

'Really?' I ask, studying her.

'Haven't you? We are tied forever, right? It will never work, me being a human, and you being a vampire. It's the classic story. I will continue to age, and you won't. I will eventually die and that will kill you. It makes sense to turn me. Right?' she asks, her voice so calm and matter-of-fact that it makes me feel a little . . . stupid . . . for thinking she may not fully comprehend this.

'It doesn't need to be that way. I accept that my fate is tied with yours. When your time is up, so is mine. That's just how it is.'

'You could have lived forever if it wasn't for me.'

'I would have died somehow, someday. We all do eventually.'

'Don't pretend that your lifespan hasn't shortened considerably since becoming tied to me,' she says, pursing her lips.

'I was miserable before I met you, Raya. I was miserable as a human, too. Why would I want to live eternity alone? If anything, this bond has granted me a favour. I didn't see it before, but now I have someone to share life with and when our time is up, I will go without regret or fight. I will not walk this earth too long.'

'But what if I was turned?' she presses. 'We could be together.'

'Is that what you want?' I question, searching her eyes. 'A decision like this cannot be made lightly.'

'I don't know.' She sighs. 'The thought of something like this never occurred to me until I met you and learnt that there are nice, humane vampires.'

I *tsk*, shaking my head. 'There you go again, painting me as a saint.'

'To me, you are.'

'Because of the bond.'

'*Not* because of the bond!' she snaps, startling me. 'Get that through your thick skull.'

'No need to yell, I have impeccable hearing, you know,' I grumble, wincing as I rub my ear.

Giggling, she leans back hiding her face behind her hands. 'Sorry.'

'Don't be,' I say.

'Hunter,' she murmurs after a moment. 'You say that you're miserable. What do you mean by that? Other than the obvious, of course . . .' She trails off.

'It's like . . . I am down in a dark pit, and the harder I try to climb out, the more I slide down the hole.' Chewing my lip, I continue to trace patterns over her skin. 'I had severe depression as a human, and when I turned, it got heightened. It has been very difficult to manage, and no one really understands the way I feel.'

I swallow. 'But . . . since meeting you . . . things aren't so bad anymore. I can see the light now, and I'm climbing my way out of the pit.'

'I'm so sorry you've experienced this.'

Leaning forward, I capture her lips in mine, kissing her tenderly. Pulling back, I feel her warm breath fan over my lips.

'You have no idea how much better I feel having you by my side. Someone to talk to, who I know respects me, and the way I am.' I smile. 'And I know you would go to the ends of the Earth for me, as I would for you. Even without having the bond as strong as it could be.'

'I'll always be here for you.'

Nodding, I kiss her once more. 'Get some sleep, sweet girl.'

'Stay,' she says. 'All night.'

'I will.'

'Promise?'

Leaning forward, I kiss her forehead tenderly. 'I promise, *legata una*.'

23

RAYA

The Survivor

THE SUN IS HOT AND unrelenting as it beats down on my bare back. Since we haven't felt sunshine in what feels like months, when we noticed this morning how bright and sunny it was outside, Alex and I decided to spend some time in the yard sunbathing.

Cas apparently had some errands to run before we travel to our next destination. It was hilarious seeing him completely covered head to toe, sporting an umbrella since the sun is out in full force. It sort of ruined his gothic vibe, considering it had a flower print on it. Hunter has locked himself in the office, madly trying to find patterns and clues to where his brother may be.

Therefore, Alex and I have a few hours to kill. The sun on my skin feels heavenly, like my battery is being recharged.

'I would miss this,' I murmur. 'How good the sun feels.'

'What do you mean?' Alex mumbles as he stretches his arms over his head.

'If I was to turn.'

Alex props himself onto his elbow, and yanks his sunglasses off his nose, his eyes narrowing with suspicion as he glares at me. 'You better not be thinking what I think you are.'

'I didn't mean anything by it,' I say dismissively.

'I'm serious,' he snarls. I can feel his sudden anger roll off him in waves.

'Calm down.'

'I see how much you're cosying up to Hunter. I don't like it.'

'You keep acting like this is something I have control over,' I say dryly, frustrated that he isn't more understanding about the lack of control that neither Hunter or myself have over any of this. 'You just don't get it.'

Alex's face falls for a moment, and I regret what I said. Sighing, I pull down my sunglasses, and rub my eyes.

'Look,' Alex says, his expression hardening. 'You're right. I don't understand it, not really. But I know enough to know I don't like it, Raya. We hate vampires. They *took* your sister.'

'We don't know what happened.'

He blinks at me. 'Right. Since when don't we think that happened?'

'I'm just saying we won't know exactly what happened until I find her,' I answer. 'And I think even *you* can admit that not all vampires are the same.'

'Raya,' Alex finally says after a heavy silence, leaning forward. 'I know Hunter is better than the average vampire, but make sure you don't lose yourself.'

Faces softening, I reach for his hand. 'I won't.'

Sighing deeply through my nose, I reach behind me, re-tie my bikini top, and roll onto my back. Alex lets out a huff of annoyance, but thankfully says no more on the subject.

Since my conversation with Hunter last night, I haven't been able to stop thinking about the possibility of turning. Would it be that bad? Aside from Alex, I have no friends or family to return to, and my life is bound to Hunter's now, anyway. Is there really even a choice?

If someone had asked me this when I first got to Red Thorne,

I would have been horrified by the idea of it. But things are different now . . .

After another twenty minutes revelling in the sun, I stretch and push to my feet, shaking off the small grass blades sticking to me. 'I'm going inside to cool off. Do you need anything?' I ask Alex.

'All good here.'

Throwing my towel over my shoulder, I walk inside, and drape it over the back of one of the dining chairs before making my way upstairs. Softly knocking on the office door, I wait a few beats before entering.

Hunter is surrounded by articles, pens, notebooks and sticky pads, looking a little like a mad man as he furiously scours over the pages, scribbling down anything he finds important.

'Hello,' he says and finally looks up, the pen that he'd held between his lips clatters to the table as his eyes hungrily scan over every inch of my skin. A low growl rumbles in his chest as his fists tighten. 'Sweet Jesus.'

'You like?' I smile, glancing down at the bright red bikini that is slightly too small for me. I may or may not have purposely picked this one out to wear for that exact reason. His Adam's apple bobs up and down as he swallows. And as he licks his lips, I feel myself alight beneath his molten stare. With two fingers, he beckons me over to him.

'Hungry?' I whisper, shifting my hair over my shoulder, exposing my neck to him.

'Hungry for more than just your blood, *legata una*.'

Battling the smirk threatening to show, I perch on the edge of the desk, between his legs. His fingers dance up my bare thighs, his eyes feasting over me once more, as if he can't get enough of what he is seeing.

'We need to be careful . . .' he says quietly. 'With what happened in the kitchen, I struggled to control myself.'

'Sure,' I say innocently.

Closing his eyes for a moment, he swallows. When they re-open, tantalisingly slow, they crawl over me. My insides turn to liquid under his eyes. He truly makes me feel like I am the only girl in the world with just one look.

Propping my foot up on his thigh, he leans forward, dragging his nose against the inside of my thigh. My breath hitches as his hot breath fans across the sensitive spot between my legs.

'I can smell the sunshine on your skin,' he whispers, inhaling long and deep.

'I bet it tastes even better.'

Eyes flashing, he smirks, running his tongue over my skin softly. I tilt my head back, moaning, unable to comprehend how good it feels when he isn't even near the area I'm aching for him to touch.

Not breaking eye contact, his fangs slide out, and slip into me in a single, fluid movement. A blissful gasp escapes me as I see a trickle of my blood spill out, running a crimson jagged line down my skin.

His fingers skitter across my entrance, and I grind into them impatiently. Sliding over my clit, he circles it teasingly, letting my frustration build before sliding his finger inside me. My legs tremble at the feel of him. As he inserts another finger, I buck my hips when he curls them into the exact position I need.

'Hunter,' I whisper.

'Yes, love?' he asks as he breaks from the bite for a moment. My blood smears across those raised lips, running down his chin.

'I want all of you.'

'And me you,' he groans, biting into the tender flesh of my thigh once more.

His thumb slides across my clit, applying just the right amount of pressure as his fingers move at an inhumane speed. A cry leaves my lips as I shatter, the orgasm detonating inside me like a bomb that released well before the timer went.

My legs shake as he releases me. His mouth moves to my centre, running his hot tongue down me, tasting all the desire he created. I whimper as the rough feel of his tongue grazes my most sensitive point.

'I thought we needed to be more careful,' I whisper.

'We do,' he says.

'Who says?'

'Me.'

'You don't seem to follow your own rules very well.' I point out with a breathless smile.

'I've never been good at that,' he replies as he stands between my thighs, pulling my legs open, and wrapping them around his waist, allowing me to feel his hard length stabbing into me, making me ache for him all over again, even though I'm still riding the aftermath of the orgasm he just gave me.

Leaning down, he kisses me. Long and hard, stealing the breath from my lungs. Looping my arms around his neck, I pull him tight against me, our tongues slipping and sliding against each other as he tries to claim dominance, and I'm the brat who fights him every step of the way.

'I want you,' I breathe, reaching for his pants. 'Now.'

'You have me.'

'*All* of you.'

'Raya,' he groans, but doesn't stop me unbuckling his pants. 'Don't.'

'Stop me, then.'

His chest is heaving as I not-so-gently yank him out of his pants. He feels perfect in my small palm. Rubbing my fingers tenderly over the head of him, he lets out a feral sound. I tighten my fingers around his length, moving it as fast as I can, keeping in time with the thrusting of his hips.

Shifting, I poise him at my entrance, running the head of him down my centre. He hisses, slamming his hands down either side of me, splintering the wood in the desk. I stop breathing for a moment, feeling him tremble.

'We can't,' he whispers. 'We can't, we can't, we can't.'

'We can,' I insist.

Slowly, I rub him over my slickness, and he growls, yanking back, and fisting himself. I gasp when his hand moves maniacally over mine.

'No,' he says firmly.

'Fine,' I growl angrily, hissing at him through gritted teeth. I fall to my knees, blinking up at him through my long lashes. 'Leave us both aching and wanting.'

He releases suddenly, spurting his load straight over my face in a hot burst. It splatters across my cheeks, threading through my eyelashes, and dripping down onto the carpet below. He slumps back into the office chair, looking as spent as I feel as I peer at him through barely-open lids.

Dragging my tongue over my lips, I taste every bit of him. Within a second, I'm no longer in the office, but in the bathroom as he wipes gently at my face. The tension between us is thicker than ever as the need to be together, all the way together, burns between us.

'It's never felt like this,' he whispers. 'If we take it to the next step, I don't know what it will do to us.'

'What do you mean?'

'We already crave each other. It will only make everything more heightened.'

'Worth the risk, I say.'

He chuckles softly, throwing the washcloth into the sink, and threading his fingers through my hair, pushing it back from my face.

'It's getting harder to resist you.'

'There's an easy solution to that,' I whisper. 'Don't.'

Pressing his forehead to mine, he is still breathing hard. 'Think this through, Raya,' he pleads, fingers tightly latching on to me. 'Please.'

Rational thoughts are slowly starting to creep into me. I nod, understanding what he is saying. He wants what is best for me. I need to remember that he knows a lot more than I do and has experienced the dark side of life in a different way than I have.

'I will,' I promise.

Pressing a hot, lingering kiss on my lips, he nods, stepping back. 'Good.'

24

HUNTER

The Protector

MY MIND, BODY, AND SOUL ache for her. Stopping us from going all the way earlier was a test to my self-control that I have no idea how I passed. After a sprint around the forest, two ice-cold showers, and a vicious session on a punching bag that now lays in tethers on the floor, I feel no relief of this desire.

I have felt true, gnawing hunger that consumes me to the point of insanity, but I can confidently say this is worse. So much fucking worse. It is killing me not knowing what it feels like to be inside her. The girl who barged into my life, took over it, and laid a claim on my heart. The girl, brave, loyal, and strong, with a kind heart and unwavering spirit. A girl destined to ruin me.

Because I'm in such a state, we have to push back the trip to tomorrow. I don't know what they think is going on with me. I hope they don't realise the real reasoning. I can't think or stand to be near her right now. If I see her, I'm afraid I won't be able to be so strong this time.

I just can't risk the bond strengthening – not now, when I don't know what our future looks like. We are already on a dangerous mission, and this could make things worse. I don't even know how I can be gentle when the severity of what I want to do to her is running thick and hot through my veins. I know my bond would stop me from breaching the line of safety, but it still concerns me that I could hurt her in some way. I have known humans to die because of this. It's an easy thing to do. Can I really trust myself not to, bond and all?

'Are you okay?'

My hands are splayed across the wall as I lean into it, chest heaving. 'Don't come any closer.'

Does she listen? Of course she fucking doesn't.

'Don't,' I warn her through a clenched jaw.

Slipping underneath my arm, she stands before me, the tiny, little thing she is. Her scent invades me, burning through me so intensely that it ignites a raging fire that lights up my entire body. Slamming my fist into the wall, the plaster shatters around it, raining down onto the floor.

'I respect your decision to not go further,' she laments, her tone indicating how highly she disagrees with it, not even flinching. 'And I have an idea to get your mind off of it.'

Swallowing the lump that has lodged inside my throat, I drag my gaze from the ground, to meet the stunning doe eyes that I've fallen in love with.

Fuck. I love her. I tried my hardest to stop this from happening, and I have epically failed.

'I want to know what it is like to be a vampire,' she says, placing her soft hand against my chest. 'Will you show me?'

Tingles erupt over me at her touch, and I battle to give in and kiss her senseless like I so desperately want to. Swallowing down the agony of denying myself, and with gritted teeth, I nod.

In one movement, I swing her onto my back and run. *Fast.* She squeals, clinging tightly onto me as I zoom out of the house faster than the blink of the eye. I'm flying through the air, over the tops of cars, traffic lights, so fast that the human eye cannot see me. Twisting my head, I watch her eyes light up, and the shocked mixed with delight expression on her face reminds me how much power us vampires really possess. I guess I sort of had forgotten the fun side of it all there for a while.

We land with a thud on the branch. I turn my head, watching her flushed cheeks and wide eyes. She grins at me.

Jetting forward as fast as I can, we spin and dive through the air. She squeals and laughs the entire time, filling my cold body with warmth I thought I'd never experience again.

I whoosh us up to the top of a building in town, having launched us effortlessly from the ground. Raya's eyes widen as the distance from the cement pavement to where we are now continues to increase. She stumbles off my back, hair crazy from the wind. She throws her head back, breathing up at the sky.

'That was insane,' she says breathlessly.

'You think that's insane?' I arch an eyebrow, yanking her up to the side of the building.

'Oh, *hell* no!'

Grinning wickedly, I swipe for her hand, and leap off the side of the building. She screams louder than I thought was possible for such a tiny person. I laugh wildly, feeling her adrenaline course through my own body like a tidal wave.

Landing swiftly on the sidewalk, I hold my arms out, catching her, and swinging her around. Pressing her up against the side of the building, I dive toward her mouth, kissing her passionately.

Kissing me just as ferociously back, our bodies tangle together as one. This time, as powerful as the urge is to claim her truly and completely as my own, it is somehow easier to break the kiss. I plant a tender kiss on her nose and lower her to the ground.

'That was so fucking scary,' she whispers. 'And the coolest thing I have ever experienced.'

'Yeah?'

'If you're trying to convince me *not* to be a vampire, you're doing a very poor job.' She laughs.

'Well,' I say with a shrug, 'maybe I've changed my mind.'

'Really?' she whispers.

'Maybe. Is it what you want?'

'I don't know,' she answers honestly. 'How do you feel?'

'I . . . can't keep doing this,' I admit.

Her chin jerks. 'Doing what?'

'Pretending I don't want to claim you as mine. Acting like I don't want this to go further.' Taking a deep breath, I stare into her eyes. 'Pretending I don't want you by my side, as my equal. My soulmate. My forever.'

We breathe hard as we gaze at each other.

'But you need to want this for *you*,' I say. 'Not for me, not for your sister, not for anyone. It must be what *you* want.'

Rolling her lips into her mouth, she releases a breath.

'Don't say anything back right now,' I murmur, twisting a bit of her hair between my fingers. 'About the things I said. Ignoring the bond for a moment, what else is on your mind? What are your thoughts?'

'My thoughts and feelings are all over the place. I need to focus on finding my sister.'

'That's right. That is what is important here.' I nod. 'The rest we can figure out when we need to.'

'Agreed,' she says, looking a mixture between concerned, thoughtful, and a little relieved.

'Ready to go again?' I ask.

'You bet.'

Throwing her onto my back once more, we race into the night.

25

THE PREDATOR

MY PATIENCE IS WEARING THIN.

Slinking back into the darkness of the night, I let the veil of shadows embrace me. Tracking Hunter and Raya all over town was not on my agenda for the night.

Movement in one of the upstairs windows captures my attention. Closely, my eyes survey Cas as he paces back and forth. Narrowing my eyes, I shift into a seated position, watching closely.

When Raya and Hunter appear in the driveway, Cas glances out the window at them. After a moment, he disappears from view, his room blanketing into darkness.

Moving for a better angle, I check in on the other human, who is sprawled on top of the bedspread in a deep sleep.

Raya and Hunter move into her room, acting like a pair of lovesick teenagers. My stomach roils. I can't think about that right now. I can't lose focus.

If they don't move this adventure along, I will have to do it for them.

I am not waiting around while they explore the exciting perks of 'being a vampire'. I might have all the time in the world, but I do not have time for *that*.

The clock is ticking.

They better get a move on before time runs out for his little human.

Tick, tock.

26

RAYA

The Survivor

THE DRIVE TO THE NEXT TOWN felt like it took twice as long as it really did. Every slight movement Hunter makes sends my nerves haywire. Despite him being in the front seat, I feel his breath hot against my skin with each exhale.

Shifting, I squirm in my seat, trying to get comfortable as I forcefully shove the ache between my legs to the back of my mind.

'Quit moving all over the place,' Alex complains, shooting me a glare.

'It's hot,' I snap back at him, even though it's only my temperature that is raised, considering it's raining outside and there's a sharp, briskness in the air that has everyone else wearing long pants and jumpers.

'It's really not.'

'Shut up and listen to your murder mystery podcasts.'

'I will.'

'Good.'

'Great.'

'How about you both shut up?' Cas suggests from the front.

Grumbling, Alex and I both glower out our windows, facing away from each other. Hunter's hand swings around the side of his seat, grazing my leg. A calming sensation washes through me, easing the throbbing my core is enduring being so close to him. I breathe a little easier, relaxing into my seat.

His silver eyes meet mine in the rearview mirror. I smile in thanks, and he dips his chin briefly in acknowledgment, gradually retracting his hand and pulling it back into his lap.

When we pull into the driveway of the house Cas has temporarily rented, Alex lets out a low whistle. And rightly so – the place is gigantic. My jaw drops when I see the water fountains and rainbow-coloured gardens that border the driveway, making it look more like a holiday resort rather than an Airbnb.

'Woah, this place is incredible,' I say.

'We travel in style around here,' Cas replies.

'Clearly.'

The vampires are out of the car and hoisting their bags over their shoulders before I even realise the car had come to a stop. Shaking my head, I climb out and follow them inside, my eyes roaming appreciatively over the gorgeous décor.

Alex and Cas disappear immediately to find their rooms. Hunter and I walk up the stairs, the tension sizzling between us to the point where it's uncomfortable to be around him. My skin feels like it's on fire each time he glances at me.

'I will have my own room,' he says.

Disappointment sinks in my chest. 'That makes sense.'

'It's getting too . . . difficult.'

'I understand.'

Pausing, he looks like he is going to say more, but in the end he turns and vanishes into thin air. Sighing, I resume my normal-paced walk down the hallway, and manage to find a free room. It's huge. The bed alone is double the size of mine when I was growing up. In fact, I could fit my room into this one twice and this is just the spare room. Natural light pours in through the blinds, highlighting the beige fluffy pillows and patterned comforter.

Throwing my bags down, I sit heavily on the bed, cradling my head, trying to get my emotions under control.

A zap on my finger makes me jump. My eyes briefly move to the delicate black band around it. I have gotten used to the electricity, since it always pulses whenever Cas is around. It doesn't warn me about Hunter anymore.

'Dinner tonight at seven,' Cas says as he breezily enters my room without announcing himself, making me startle. 'And round two of the hunt.'

I raise my eyebrow, trying not to look as affected as I am. I'm still having nightmares about the first time I got hunted, when all of this mess started.

'Round two, you say?' I question, cursing my heart for picking up pace, revealing to Cas how stressed I really am about it.

He nods, a smirk dancing on his lips, giving me a knowing look. 'Yeah, if you're game.'

'Sure.' I force a smile onto my face.

Winking, he slithers back through the door faster than I blink.

I spend the next two hours reading over Cora's journals.

I have never felt anything like this. The urge to know him, learn more about him, be closer . . . There is no one else like him. So beautiful, yet mysterious.

There's a tug in my chest when he's near me. Begging me to come closer. To give him whatever he wants.

He wants me.

I want him.

I will be his, and he will be mine.

Snapping it shut, I push it away, feeling ill. It's so similar to how Hunter makes me feel, but I know it's different. *We are* different. Hunter is nothing like his brother. He is kind, thoughtful, and good-natured. I am not repeating my sister's mistakes.

When I head downstairs, there is a bowl filled with fresh fruit waiting for me on the table. Picking up the note with my name on it, I read Hunter's neat scrawl.

I bought you some fruit, and there's a salad wrap in the fridge. Let me know if there is anything else you need.

Smiling, I fetch my lunch. Alex trots into the kitchen, peering over my shoulder. Reaching inside, I withdraw the small bag with Alex's name on it.

'Did Hunter get us food?' he questions, eyebrows raised.

'Yeah.'

Alex stares at it for a moment. 'Hard to hate the guy when he is so damn thoughtful all the time.'

I smile, handing it to him. 'So does that mean you *don't* hate him?'

'I guess I can say I *tolerate* him,' Alex replies.

'And me?' A voice asks at the same time my ring zaps me.

I wince, looking down at it. It only seems to do it when Hunter isn't in the room, but Cas is.

'Jesus!' Alex recoils, almost knocking me over as he leaps about a metre in the air. He glowers at Cas, who is smirking down at us. 'Don't do that.'

'Apologies,' Cas says, moving around us. 'I'm thirsty.'

Alex screws his face up, and touches his finger against the silver draped around his neck. Cas's smirk widens as he notices.

'I'll be tasting you tonight,' Cas purrs, and goose bumps prickle uncomfortably across my skin.

'I think the fuck not,' Alex grumbles, his cheeks dotted with pink.

I feel awkward, since they are looking at each other like they've forgotten I'm even here. Quietly, I step back, walking out of the kitchen, and into the living room. A movie is playing on the screen. Cas walks in behind me, collapsing onto the lounge.

'I'm just starting a movie. Wanna join?' he asks.

I blink at him. It seems so weird to see a vampire casually lounging around, watching a movie. It seems so . . . normal. I need to remember that a lot of vampires are just like this. I happened to have met a few bad ones, but I'm sure there are plenty of vampires out there living a totally normal life.

Alex walks in next, dropping onto the lounge, draping his legs over the armrest. As much as he sulks around the house, and drips himself in so much silver he looks like he is being sponsored by a jewellery store, Alex seems quite at ease around Cas and Hunter now. It's nice to see him acting more like himself.

As the movie plays, I continuously glance at the door, waiting for Hunter to come join us, but he doesn't. After I doze off to sleep for the second half of the movie, I wake when Alex and Cas start bickering about the plot of it. Stretching, I glance out the window, seeing the sky darkening. I get to my feet and wave at them as I exit, heading back up to my room, since we will be leaving for dinner soon.

I take my time showering and doing my routine of self-care that I have been neglecting since my life turned upside down. Once I'm dressed and ready to go, I drag the strap of the holster up my thigh, sliding in my knife and my canister of silver. My second canister, I stick in my bra and toss my hair over my shoulders, helping disguise the slight bulge it leaves.

Dressed in a sexy black dress with nearly see-through lingerie underneath, I feel bold and sultry as I descend the stairs, my heels distinctly clicking on the hardwood floor. A ripple of awareness slides down my spine as Hunter's eyes track my movements, his gaze hungrily roaming over every inch of my body. With a clenched jaw, he runs his hand through his hair, a pained expression springing onto his handsome face. Heat flares inside me as I greedily take in his tall frame clad in a white T-shirt, a leather jacket, and dark chinos. He looks edible.

Swaying my hips, I stroll up to him, tilting my head back and levelling him with a playful smile.

'Hello.'

'You're going to be the death of me,' he whispers, his hands gripping my hips as he tugs me close to him. 'Every part of my body is in pure agony.'

'Why?'

'Because I want to claim you as mine,' he growls, darkness swirling in his eyes. 'I want to fuck you into next week, and brand you in every single way possible.'

The oxygen leaves my lungs as our bodies draw closer, inch by inch.

'Claim me,' I whisper. 'I'm already yours.'

His fingers tighten on my hips so hard I fear it will leave bruises. The pain is delicious, and I crave more of his firm hand and dirty mouth.

'Alex!' Cas yells out, his deep voice echoing around the room, giving me a fright. I blush, realising he would have just heard everything that Hunter just said. 'We're leaving, with or without you!'

Alex appears with a scowl and trots down the stairs. 'Yeah, yeah, I'm coming.'

'You look good,' Cas says to him, his lips tilting. 'I bet you taste even better.'

'You won't get the chance to find out,' Alex hisses hotly, glowering at Cas's flirty remark.

'Sure, I won't.'

'You won't,' he says firmly.

'Let's go,' Hunter sighs, stepping back and tugging at his collar, as if he is struggling to draw in a breath.

Tingles erupt over me, craving to be close to him, and have skin on skin contact. My hand reaches for his and he swiftly dodges it, practically throwing himself into the front seat. Fisting my hand and biting down on the sting of rejection, I climb in beside Alex. The hole in my chest, the bond that ties us, glows unbearably, itching to connect with its other half.

To not draw attention, we take Hunter's truck, meaning it has much more space, but also means I don't have an excuse to be on Hunter's lap like I had before. Images of the night flash through my mind, making my core throb with need.

A low hiss sound escapes Hunter, and he slams his hand on the door and I freeze, wondering if he had felt the exact longing sensation that I just did.

'Who pissed in your cornflakes?' Alex side-eyes him.

Hunter says nothing as he continues glaring moodily out the window. Cas's eyes find mine in the reflection as he smirks to himself.

Cas takes us to a restaurant at the top of a tall building that overlooks the entire town. It is a breath-taking view and it distracts me from the fact that Hunter hasn't acknowledged me for the last half an hour.

Of course he is hurting. I am, too. I understand why he is resisting this thread that is drawing us closer and closer to the edge, but it doesn't stop me from wanting it any less.

I don't want to fight this. I don't want *him* to fight this. It's exhausting trying to resist the lust and longing we have for each other.

A steady drizzle rains down onto the window as we finish eating. I feel flushed from the wine, my cheeks warm and rosy. Pulling my hair over to one shoulder, I lean forward, feeling Hunter's eyes hovering over my face and then down my neck.

As Cas and Alex continue debating something about

conspiracy theories, the rain swiftly changes from a light shower to a heavy downpour. Suddenly, a loud crack of thunder erupts outside, and a streak of lightning brightens the sky, briefly turning night into day.

Cas leans forward on his elbows, a grin spreading across his face. 'Run along, little humans. Round two is about to commence.'

My bare feet slip and slide against the mud as I sprint as fast I can, my heels having long gone. My ring pulses against my finger and I'm momentarily distracted by it.

Cas drops in front of me, moving faster than I can comprehend. A scream gets trapped in my throat as I skid to a halt, chest heaving. Although he is meant to be hunting Alex, it doesn't mean he can't hunt me, too. I realise my mistake instantly. I was so focused on escaping Hunter, I forgot the number one rule – where there is one, there's a high chance there is another lurking nearby.

I've been aiming to get back to a public place for the past few minutes. I never meant to go this way but in my panicked state, I took a wrong turn and here we are, down a back alley somewhere, where my death would be looming if this was a real hunt.

The pale moonlight makes his fangs glow as he grins wickedly, taking a taunting step closer.

Since the canister is already in my hand, I throw my hand up, directing it straight into his eyes. He screeches, flying backwards, clawing at his face, not anticipating the attack.

Launching myself onto a bin, I throw myself over the fence, going straight into a forward somersault before I'm back on my feet again. A dog barks, running toward me, snapping at my ankles. It's then I realise I've jumped into someone's yard. Not stopping, I haul myself over their fence. I hiss when my skin scrapes against the wood, feeling the blood trickle down my leg. Running towards

the light where I can see people walking, I almost make it, when
Hunter steps out from the shadows. My heart pounds so loud,
I feel dizzy. Sweat slides down my back as we both breathe hard,
waiting for the other to make a move. Jesus Christ, he looks good.
His shirt clings to his chest, outlining the hard muscles beneath it.
The vicious, dark tattoos that line the right side of his body look
villainous under the dim light. Every fibre of my being throbs to
go to him and touch him. To soothe this growing pain inside me.

The corner of his mouth twitches. His head tilts to the side.

'Are you going to let me bite you, or will you make me work
for it?'

'You can work for it,' I hiss.

Darting to the right, I run down the hill. My foot catches on
the raised root of a tree, sending me tumbling down it. With the
adrenaline coursing through my veins, I barely feel it as I right
myself and keep moving.

A hand curls around my waist and the world tilts. I land hard
on my back, the air rushing out of my body as I slam to the ground.

I don't know if it's because I'm scared, or if our bond knows
this is all a game, but instinct has me spraying him in the eyes. He
roars a deafening tune in my ear, and I roll out from underneath
his heavy weight.

I've barely run two steps before his fingers circle around my
ankle, yanking me back. My cheek slams into the ground, dirt
spilling in through my parted lips, filling my mouth. Rolling onto
my back, I blindly reach for my knife as Hunter drags me across
the grass. Fury and anger swirls in my gut in a fit of fiery rage. I'm
furious at him, at our gnawing bond, this whole damn situation.

My hand flies into his thigh, the knife sinking into his flesh with
as much force as I can muster. He howls, his grip tightening to the
point that I yelp in pain. Dragging me harder, he rips the top of my
dress in one swift movement before his fangs plunge into my neck.

I scream as pain splinters through my body before twisting into the familiar warmth that I crave every moment of the day.

'You can never outrun me,' he snarls against my skin, sinking his fangs further inside my flesh. 'You're mine, Raya. *Mine*.'

'Prove it.'

Rearing back so that a part of his weight is lifted from my body, his eyes bore down into mine, our breaths mingling into one due to the proximity. My heart thunders against my ribcage as our stares melt into pure heat.

His hand trembles as it touches the side of my face, carving a firm yet tender line down my neck, his fangs still out, glittering red with my blood. Shivering despite the heat I'm feeling, I arch my back, craving more of him. Always needing *more*.

Drawing in a ragged breath, his fingers twist, tangling in my dark hair.

'This might change everything,' he whispers, eyes searching mine intently, the high of the game oozing out into a wispy cloud around us as the seriousness of our need for each other takes over. 'I tried not to. I tried to protect you from all of this. From me.' Blowing out a sharp breath, his lips inch closer. 'You're irresistible.' His gaze doesn't waiver from mine. 'Do you love me, like I love you?'

I stare at him, wide-eyed, processing his words.

'You consume me, mind, body, and soul.' I touch my hands to his face. 'I want this, Hunter. I want you.'

'I don't want to hurt you,' Hunter breathes, pressing his forehead to mine, the cool breeze washing over my flushed skin.

'I can handle it.'

Breathing a soft chuckle, he offers me the only-reserved-for-me smile that I've grown so fond of. 'My brave girl. I know. I know you can handle it, but I still worry.'

'Don't be afraid.'

'I'm very afraid,' he admits. 'What if I lose all control and turn you, even when you haven't given me your blessing? You would never forgive me.'

'Turn me, then. Take this as my blessing.'

His hand tightens. 'You're not thinking clearly.'

'I want you. That's all I care about right now.'

'No, it isn't,' he insists.

'Maybe this was all meant to happen for a reason. This adventure. Whether or not I find her, maybe this was fate pushing us together. Maybe we were always meant to meet.'

Hunter swallows. 'Can a human and a vampire be destined by fate?'

'Why not?'

'Vampires are supernatural, and they mess up the balance of nature. I don't believe fate would ever do us any favours.'

'Hunter,' I say, sliding my hands over his skin, interlocking my fingers behind his neck. 'I am meant for you. I believe that.'

'And I for you, *legata una*.'

Shifting, I tilt my head back, exposing my neck. 'Turn me, Hunter. I want you to.'

He is silent for a few moments. He lowers himself, kissing me tenderly over the bite wounds. My fingers twist his shirt as I grip onto him like my life depended on it. Like we are swinging over the edge of the cliff, and I am hanging on to him as my only lifeline.

'Not now,' he whispers, his lips a feather-light touch over my skin, 'when the bond isn't surging inside you, overwhelming your senses.'

'Okay,' I agree. 'But if it happens accidentally, I give you my blessing, Hunter.'

His face softens, the wall he has been so desperately trying to build between us crumbling right before my eyes, shattering around us. He swoops toward me, claiming my mouth with his with a fiery passion that consumes my body.

Thunder booms overhead, the rain belting down faster and harder over us. It's a cool, dark night, but I don't feel the cold, when every part of me burns where he touches. His lips are everywhere, kissing over my face, inching down my neck, sucking, and biting me deliciously in all the sensitive spots that have me whimpering and twisting in his grasp. I kiss him hard when his lips return to mine. So hard, they pulse under his touch. His mouth moves to my neck where he bites down once more. I choke on a sob, overwhelmed with the crushing sensation of needing more. The bond inside my chest sings as our bodies melt together, forming one. My legs wrap tightly around his waist, and he tears my underwear straight from my body, leaving me bare. The night air strokes my skin tenderly as he drinks greedily from me, his fingers grazing over my thigh, inching closer to my entrance.

Threading my fingers through his hair, I pull on them, desperate to feel him inside me. His finger slips across my sex, and he groans, feeling how much I want him. Impatiently, I yank his pants down his legs, shamelessly grinding and rolling my hips against him, kissing him desperately. As his finger slides inside me, I dive toward his shoulder, biting him so hard it draws blood. He moans, quickening his pace, biting down on my breast as we both drink from each other. When the lightning tears across the sky, I swear I feel it in every part of my body. I'm buzzing with fire, electricity, and everything in between. I feel light-headed as any bruises and battered parts of my body heal as his blood races through my veins, fixing any errors it finds in its path.

He tastes like heaven and sin wrapped up in one. With a breathless gasp, I tilt my head back, drawing in deep breaths as the stars in the night sky brighten. The night twists into a surreal purple as his vampire senses fade in and out over me, teasing with me the taste of what life is like through his eyes.

Feeling him between my legs, he jerks my chin, forcing my gaze to his as he thrusts inside me. A ground-rumbling clap of thunder detonates around us as I cry out.

The feeling of him inside me is better than I could possibly imagine, filling and stretching me perfectly as if I was moulded exactly for him. My heart, my bond, my soul, everything is aching and blossoming inside me, filling me with light, love, and pure happiness. Tears stream down my face as I sob, unable to control the overload of sensations filling me.

'You are mine, as I am yours,' he breathes into my ear. 'There is nothing I wouldn't do for you.'

I want to confess all of what I would do for him, but I am unable to form a sentence when feelings I never imagined feeling ripple through my body.

The air is filled with the sound of our bodies meeting and our heavy breathing. Digging my nails into his back, I let out a whimper.

'This,' he whispers. 'Me and you. This is it. We are forever.'

'Forever.'

His eyes melt my insides. He is gazing at me with utmost adoration, like he is only just seeing me clearly for the first time. Overcome with his feelings, as am I, he presses his forehead to mine as he drives inside of me, our skin slipping against the others as sweat and rain coats us. When he kisses me, I taste the salty tang of his skin and my own sweat.

Our limbs tangle, our breaths ragged as we move together as one.

'I'm going to spend the rest of our lives proving that I am worthy of you.'

My insides are simultaneously tightening and dripping for him. My hands skate across his back, feeling every tense of his strong muscles flexing as he drills into me hungrily and mercifully.

My orgasm stutters through me almost violently, barrelling through every limb. I cry out, a sensation I have never felt swelling inside me.

'Ah, fuck,' Hunter whispers, his voice dripping in sin as he lets out a guttural groan, melting every nerve inside my body.

As his own orgasm washes through him, his eyes shine bright, as pure silver rings glow around the edges of his eyes. He slams his hand down into the earth, sending dirt erupting around us as he spills inside of me.

Catching my hips, Hunter does a few slow, sensual strokes that has my body humming in delight before he slides out of me. Releasing a whine at the loss of contact, I collapse back onto the ground.

The aftermath continues to roll through my insides, and I can't stop quivering in response to it.

'Hunter,' I whisper. 'Your eyes.'

Deep, silver rings border his midnight eyes, a light swirling brightly, blending perfectly with the darkness. Drawing his dark brows together, his finger grazes close to my temple.

'Silver,' he whispers. 'Your eyes are black and silver.'

'So are yours,' I murmur, tracing the edge of his eyes with my fingertips. 'The bond . . . It's stronger now. Isn't it?'

His own widen in wonder as he draws closer to me, inspecting my eyes. Slowly, he nods. 'Yes. It is.'

My heart is still thundering in my chest, and I feel dizzy.

Wrapping me securely in his arms, he tucks me to his side. The rain pelts down on us, but it feels calming as it cascades over my skin like silk. I let out a shuddering breath, trying to tackle my emotions that continue to spiral out of control.

The thread between us is stronger and sturdier than ever.

Burying my face against his chest, I feel warm and safe in his strong arms.

'I'm sorry I wasn't strong enough to stop us strengthening the bond,' he whispers.

'I'm not.'

'Are you sure?'

'Yes,' I whisper. 'What happens now?'

'I don't know,' he replies. 'But we will figure it out. Together.'

27

HUNTER

The Protector

WHEN WE REACH THE meeting point, neither Alex nor Cas are in sight. Tightening Raya's hand in mine, I survey our surroundings. Considering the time we took in our hunt, I would have imagined they would have been here impatiently waiting, a retort hot on their tongues.

Instantly, panic swells inside me, and I draw Raya closer to my side. Pulling out my phone, I dial Cas's number. He answers on the second ring. I frown when I hear the music blaring through the speaker. 'Where are you?'

'With a friend.'

My jaw ticks. 'Where is Alex?'

'Licking his wounds somewhere.'

'You left him?' I snarl, gripping my phone so violently I hear a crack pop through the screen.

'He's fine.'

'Can you see him?' I demand, growing impatient and frustrated with Cas's cavalier tone.

'Yes.'

'What club are you in?'

'Sin City.'

Hanging up, I search the streets until I find the neon pink sign with a half-naked girl pouring a drink flashing brightly above a propped open door with a line so long it takes up most of the sidewalk.

Pulling Raya with me, we cross the street and skip the line. Ignoring the shouts of protest, one look at the security guard has him stepping back and allowing us to walk through.

As we head inside, I gently fix Raya's dress. It's torn, but still covers everything it needs to since we turned it around, making it look like the rip was intentional to show off her back. I should probably stop destroying all of her clothes, but I enjoy it too much. Memories of hearing the fabric shred, exposing her bareness to me makes me feel hot all over.

Cas is leaning on the bar, propped up on his elbow as he speaks to a tall guy with ash-blond hair. My spine involuntarily straightens when I realise he is also a vampire. Raya flinches, looking down at her hand. I follow her gaze, looking at the ring on her finger. I notice she often has a reaction whenever a vampire is near. I haven't been able to figure out what that ring is made out of.

'Hunter, my man,' Cas says with a grin. 'Want a drink?'

He holds his glass up, the dark liquid sloshing over the edge. I can smell that it's whiskey from here.

The guy looks lazily over at us, his eyes stopping on me for a moment before drifting to Raya. A low growl emits from my throat as I step in front of her.

'Cool it.' Cas rolls his eyes at me, placing his drink down. 'He's here with me.'

'Hi.' Raya smiles, peeking around me, her warmth and innocent nature only riling me up further. Sometimes she forgets how blood-thirsty and murderous vampires can be.

My eyes narrow when he gives her a charming smile, reaching forward to shake her hand.

Shifting so that she is forced behind me once more, I shake my head at him in warning. 'That's close enough.'

'Sorry, he's not usually this much of a prick,' Cas mutters. 'He gets weird about the girl.'

'This is not time for socialising, Cas,' I snap.

'I'm the one finding answers, not rolling around in the dirt with my girlfriend.'

Ignoring his remark, I raise my eyebrows. 'Answers?'

'Gabe here knows your brother.'

Stiffening, I level the other vampire with a look to spill what he knows.

'They were here only a week ago, maybe two,' Gabe says, taking a long swig of his drink. 'They kept going North. Something about visiting a friend.'

'A friend,' I repeat, mulling that over. 'Who?'

Gabe leans toward me, frowning. 'What's up with your eyes, dude?'

Cas's head snaps in my direction. He lets out a little exclamation of shock when he sees the rings. 'Holy shit,' he breathes. 'You solidified the bond.'

'Bond?' Gabe blinks, whipping his head to Cas, then back to me. 'What do you mean bond?'

'Cas,' I hiss, trying to silence him, but he ignores me.

'You know, linked. Connected. I don't know.' Cas shrugs dismissively, like this titbit of information isn't practically unheard of.

'Where's Alex?' Raya asks, her eyes moving around the room, trying to locate her friend.

Cas points to a surly looking Alex standing in the corner of the room, bordering on the edge of the dance floor. The top of his shirt is ripped, and blood has soaked through the material. Underneath the bright, flashing lights, it looks like it's a pattern on his shirt.

'So, about my brother,' I begin as Raya inclines her head toward her friend before she heads over to him. 'Tell me everything you know.'

Gabe stares a little too intently at my eyes as if trying to figure something out. He shakes his head after a moment, his face relaxing into a smile, leaning back against the edge of the bar. I don't like the way his eyes are constantly assessing me, like he is sizing me up.

'He's a wild one, that's for sure.'

'What were they doing here?'

Gabe shrugs. 'Drinking, partying, feeding.'

'You were with them?' I ask, narrowing my eyes.

'Yeah. For a bit.'

'What did you do?'

'This.' Gabe gestures around him.

'Was a girl with him?'

Gabe nods. 'Yeah. Looked a hell lot like your pretty little friend over there.'

My saliva feels thick as I clench my jaw, exchanging a curious look with Cas.

'Was she a vampire?' Cas asks.

'Yeah.'

Cas finishes his drink, placing it down onto the counter. He claps me on the shoulder as he passes, looking way too calm considering the information Gabe is so freely telling us. 'Enough serious talk. Let's dance.'

'Cas,' I snap, fury rolling off me in waves. 'This is important. This is the whole reason we are here.'

'I know,' he says, turning to face me. 'And I'm sorry.'

'Sorry?' I question, forehead crumpling as I stare at my friend. 'For what?'

The knife slides into my back with ease. I choke on my own breath as I feel the silver sizzle against my insides. Gabe's hand locks hard around mine as Cas moves to my other side, restraining me.

A knee-jerk reaction is to flee, but the knife digs deeper into my side, searing me with white-hot agony as it causes a ripple-effect through my body.

Blood floods my mouth, spilling through my lips as another knife drives into my side, piercing my flesh with vicious intent.

'Fuck,' I groan, gritting my teeth, fighting through the pain. 'What the hell, Cas?'

'Sorry,' his voice murmurs. 'It's not personal.'

'Feels pretty personal,' I snarl, my vision blurring.

Throwing my arms out, I try to knock them back, but both vampires are much stronger and older than I am, making me feel like I'm lodged between two brick walls.

'Raya,' I try to shout, but everything fades around me as I fall into complete darkness.

28

THE PREDATOR

THEY HAVE BEEN INSIDE the house for a day now.

When I saw Cas attack Hunter, my first instinct was to fly across the room and break every bone in his hand. Until I realised what was going on, and that this is what I have been waiting for.

Cas is the only one that has come and gone. A few humans have gone inside and not come back out. Wherever Hunter is being held must be soundproof, because if I hadn't seen him being dragged inside, I wouldn't be convinced he is even here.

A door to the side of the house bangs open, and I hunker lower in my position. Cas exits the house, one of the human girls I saw him take inside now limply flung over his shoulder. Her lifeless eyes stare ahead as he tosses her into the back of the car.

My stomach churns at the sight of it. These vampires are monsters. I should go inside right now and risk it all just to ensure there are no more deaths. But I can't. I've waited this long. I need to continue to be patient. I need to choose my entrance wisely. I will be outnumbered, so I must be smart about this.

The time is nearing.

I am ready.

29

RAYA

The Survivor

WHEN I OPEN MY EYES, I have no idea where I am. A throbbing sensation fills my head and I wince, regretting having woken up. My limbs feel heavy and slow.

Blinking, I peer around the pale room. I'm in a bed in a room I don't recognise. Bright light filters through the blinds, leaving lines across my legs from the sunlight. Rubbing my head, I sit up. The room is plain, very minimally designed.

'Hey.'

Looking over to the side of the room, I see Alex standing near the window. There is no colour in his face as he rests against the wall. He offers me a weary smile, looking nothing like the Alex I know.

Licking my lips, they feel cracked and dry, my throat screaming for water with each painful swallow.

'What happened?' I ask, feeling groggy.

'I have no idea.' Alex sighs, walking toward the bed, sitting down on the edge. 'I don't remember leaving the club.'

'Where's Hunter?' I whisper, panic making my heart race. 'And Cas?'

Alex shrugs. 'I don't know.'

'How long have you been awake? What time is it?'

Alex shrugs, again. 'Maybe, like, an hour. I have no idea what the time is, though.'

'Where the hell are we?'

'You're asking all the same things I thought to myself.' Alex exhales. 'I keep hearing footsteps.' He gestures to the door. 'But no one has come in.'

Dread fills me like poison, making my stomach clench painfully.

When I stand, my head spins, causing me to collapse heavily back onto the bed, gripping the sheets.

The door swings open, and the breath exits my body.

'Cora,' I whisper.

'Hey, little sis.'

Looking at Cora is like looking into a mirror. We have the same heart-shaped face, pale skin, and freckles dotting our cheeks and nose. She has her distinct birthmark, but her mossy green eyes are now an endless black, giving her a demonic look.

My heart slams inside my chest to an uneven tune, making me feel nauseous. She gives me a moment to stare at her, taking in all the similarities and differences. Familiar, yet unfamiliar.

'You figured it out,' she says eventually, her voice dry.

My mouth opens and closes several times before I can muster up a reply. My mind is reeling, too many sentences trying to form before they float away as a new thought overrides it.

'Hey,' Alex says, and both Cora and I glance at him. He waves. 'So. You're not dead. That's cool.'

Cora's face is icy as she gives him a brief once-over before she returns to ignoring him. I keep my focus on her, trying to make sense of the thousands of thoughts racing around inside my mind.

'You . . . you planned this.'

'I did.'

'You left me.' A sob tears from my throat as the emotions come flooding out. My hands and knees wobble as I try to stand, but I still feel too weak.

My sister drops down onto the chair at the end of the bed, folding one leg over the other, and fixes me with a stoic expression. One I have never seen her wear before. Warmth and sunshine no longer emanate from her. She's cold, dark, and empty.

Alex sinks to the ground, watching us, all remaining colour draining from his face, and I see the realisation on his face, certain I'm wearing the same expression. That Cora isn't here to save us.

'I did.'

'Why?' I whisper, choking on my breath.

'It wasn't enough,' she admits, her black-nailed fingers drawing invisible patterns on her leather pants. 'That life. It wasn't enough. I needed to escape.'

'So, you left me,' I whisper. 'With no one.'

'It wasn't supposed to go like that.'

'What?' I say, trying to understand. 'What do you mean?'

'I knew there was going to be a sacrifice. That's why I planned the accident. I didn't . . .' She trails off, and for a brief moment, I'm sure I see a flash of regret and despair crack through her cold exterior. It disappears just as quickly, making me question whether I truly saw anything, or if I'm a fool holding on to hope. 'It was meant to be a stranger who died. Someone who didn't matter to me.'

Her words cut into my skin, opening me up, tearing me from inside out. My stomach churns uneasily as her words whirl inside my brain.

'Mum,' I choke out. 'You killed her.'

'Well,' my sister says, leaning forward, clasping her long, slender fingers together. 'Yes. I did.'

My chest is rising and falling rapidly as I stare at someone who once was such a big part of my life. Someone who was so similar to me we could have been one person. Someone I shared everything with. My other half. Now, a stranger.

'Oh shit,' I hear Alex mutter.

'You're a monster,' I murmur, my words shaking.

'We are all monsters, Raya. Don't kid yourself.' Flinging herself to her feet, she strides over to me. Her fingers bite into my chin as she drags my gaze to meet hers. I flinch at the sudden jerk and the coldness of her skin. Her eyes narrow into slits as she inspects my eyes. 'Foolish girl,' she snaps, upper lip curling. 'You weren't meant to follow in my footsteps. I purposefully detached myself from you so that when I died, you would mourn and move on.'

'You're my sister,' I seethe, gripping her arms, holding on tight, wanting to convey the pain and betrayal that I feel ebbing through me so forcefully it threatens to knock me over.

'I *was*,' she growls. 'I am no longer.'

'Yes, you are!' I cry out. 'You're here, right now, flesh and blood.'

'I am not the girl you remember, Raya. I need you to understand that.'

'Yes, you are.'

'I'm not.'

'*You are.*'

Cora's eyes flash and her hands strike toward me, flattening me on my back. She presses harshly down onto my arms, hovering over me, her black eyes dark and menacing as they pour into mine.

Alex clambers to his feet, wide-eyed.

'I am not *her* anymore. The Cora you knew died the same night our mother did.'

I inhale sharply at her words, feeling all the wounds that never truly healed rip back open. 'I don't believe you.'

'I don't care what you believe.'

'If you're such a monster, then do it,' I snap at her, flinging my hair back, and tilting my chin toward the ceiling. 'Kill me.'

Cora freezes, her eyes piercing into mine as we breathe hard. The air crackles around us, heavy with tension that the two of us have never had before. A strong feeling of defiance carves through me, and if I had something close to me, I would slit my skin up and offer my blood to her on a silver platter. If she attacked me, only then would I believe her.

'And have your bonded mate avenge you?' she quips, raising a dark eyebrow. 'I don't think so.'

I let out a laugh. 'That's a convenient excuse.'

Releasing me suddenly, she is on her feet, and across the room in the blink of an eye. She peers out the window and winces as the direct sunlight penetrates through the glass. Spinning, she shuts the blinds, and walks to the end of the bed.

'I didn't want this life for you, Raya,' she says, suddenly looking a lot more like the girl I remember and not the monster she is pretending to be. 'I wish you had ... just ...' She exhales, not finishing her sentence.

'That's a lie.'

She doesn't look at me as she continues to pace the room, her dark hair cascading down her back in thick tumbles. 'A lie?'

'You left journals for a reason. You wanted me to find you.' Pushing to my feet, I stride toward her, stepping into her space, and ignoring the warning in her eyes. 'You couldn't let go, could you?'

'You're pathetic.' She sneers. 'You are trying to cling onto me and our old life, but it does not exist anymore.'

'You left me breadcrumbs, Cora. You ... oh my God ...' I step back, raking my fingers through my hair, everything piecing together one by one. 'You stood purposefully in that video. You made me see it. You ... you planned all of this.'

A muscle in her cheek jumps, her eyes flicking toward the door and back to me, as if she is worried we may be overheard.

'You were meant to leave your life and everyone in it,' I say slowly, shaking my head. 'But you couldn't let me go. You left me clues. You knew I would come.'

'That's absurd.'

'And now you're pretending you didn't do all of that. To what, protect me? Why? Why did you need to leave me behind?'

Yanking me forward, she stares down her nose at me, her cold fingers clawing into my skin. 'Because they will kill you, Raya. Don't you get it? They will kill you.'

'I can protect myself.'

She scoffs, a dry cackle escaping her as she pushes me from her, continuing her fervent pacing. 'You can't protect yourself from them.'

'But he can,' I say.

She stills, swinging those dark eyes to me.

'Hunter would die before he let anything happen to me.'

'That may be true,' she nods, coming to a standstill. 'But he will not be around to protect you once he is dead.'

30

HUNTER

The Protector

MY BLOOD DRIPS SLOWLY onto the floor. A soft thud fills my ears as each drop lands one after the other. Pain echoes inside me, pulsating in a rhythm that has me writhing.

She's out there, without me, and that thought terrifies me to my core. Because I can't protect her when my wrists are draped in chains, the silver burning me over and over as I heal only for the skin to blister instantly.

Thrashing against them, I let out a deafening roar, my body vibrating with unleashed fury as I tug and pull. Blood is oozing out of me from the multiple stab wounds and cuts the silver has caused since they so kindly left the blades they stabbed me with embedded in my skin to prevent any healing.

When the slab of cement the chains are attached to lifts a little, I use all my strength, savagely pulling until it lifts another inch. The metal door bangs open, slamming against the brick work so hard parts of it crumble on impact.

Icy dread fills my veins when Kian's stormy eyes latch onto me, a slow, wicked smile taking over his face.

'*Fratello.*' He smiles, holding his hands out wide as he enters the room, walking unhurriedly toward me. Kian and I are similar in many ways. Same height, same broad shoulders, and same long arms. Same dark hair and black eyes, but with the way he eyes me, a dangerous glint to his gaze, and a sadistic smirk on his lips, you can tell we are *very* different. 'I hear you've been looking for me.'

Spitting out the blood from my mouth, I glower at him.

'I didn't come for you.'

Pouting, he gives me a sad look, even though he is the definition of a sociopath. 'That hurts my feelings.'

'Where is she?' I ask through clenched teeth. 'Where is Raya?'

'Your little friend is fine,' my brother replies with a tilt of his lips. He points to the roof. 'Safe and sound, right up there.'

My chest is heaving as I stare up at the ceiling, wishing for it to crack open and show me a glimpse of her, to reassure me she is safe, even though I can feel that she is physically unharmed.

'Give us Cora, and we will be on our way. This doesn't need to turn into a big thing.'

'No can do.' Kian smiles, flashing his fangs, rubbing his hands together. 'Cora belongs to me.'

'No,' I growl. 'She doesn't.'

His gaze slides to mine. 'Oh, but she does. I own her.'

'You don't care for her. You don't care for anyone but yourself.'

'I said I own her, not that I care for her.'

Inhaling sharply, I swallow down the anger rising inside my chest, trying not to let it get the better of me. The way he cares so little about anyone but himself makes me sick to my stomach.

'Let me go,' I growl.

'But where's the fun in that?'

'What do you want with me?' I bark, yanking on the chains with savage brutality, watching in satisfaction as one of the bolts come undone, pinging across the room.

Kian's eyes follow it as it soars across the room.

'Can't I see my brother without having an agenda?' He arches a brow, a smirk curving his lips.

'Perhaps if you didn't have me beaten and chained.'

He smiles. The cold, cunning smile that makes him look dead on the inside. Perhaps, he is.

'You know I can't pass up the chance to ruffle your perfect little feathers.'

'Let. Raya. Go.' I demand, my voice thick with command.

His smile widens. 'You sound like Father when you speak like that.'

'I'm not joking, Kian. I will kill you if you touch a hair on her head.'

'I like my odds.' His lips tilt as he steps closer to me, assessing my eyes. 'I'm curious about these, though. Will this strengthen you if her life is in danger? Could you outweigh a more powerful opponent if put to the test?'

Baring my teeth at him, I growl furiously. He chuckles darkly, stepping back, his black hair falling over his eyes, cloaking them.

'We shall see,' he says before melting into the shadows, leaving me with nothing but my own angry screams.

31

RAYA

The Survivor

EVERY PART OF MY BODY aches for Hunter. The longer the time stretches out that we haven't seen each other, the worse it gets.

Swallowing, I swipe the back of my hand across my forehead. I have been sweating all day, and the cold shivers began about an hour ago. The hole inside my chest gnaws desperately, my bond seeking its other half.

I have no idea how much time has passed, but the sun has replaced the moon, blanketing me into darkness twice now. Since my sister visited me when I first woke up here, no one has come by, except for Cora who dragged Alex out of here, refusing to meet my eyes as she did.

My hands ache from the bruises on them from banging on the door, and my throat raw from screaming. I have no idea what has happened to Alex, or what is going on outside this room. It's eerily silent, which makes me even more anxious.

At some point during the night I must have passed out from sheer exhaustion, and when I wake, there is a small amount of food on a plate next to a glass of water on the bedside table. It concerns me that someone has been in here while I slept, but that seems to be the least of my worries right now. Laying on my side, my mind wanders to Hunter, replaying every word, every touch. When I close my eyes, I can convince myself he is right here, caressing my skin, kissing my hair. It makes the ache almost bearable. Key word: *Almost*.

Tears spill forth at the thought of anything happening to him. Not knowing is driving me insane.

The door bangs open, and I startle with a gasp, wiping the tears from my cheeks as I reel to a seated position. A shiver rolls down my spine when black eyes blink back at me. A sinister smirk curves his lips. Despite never having seen this man before, I know without a doubt that he is Hunter's brother. The resemblance is uncanny.

He is tall and thick with muscle. The same smooth, unblemished skin. The same midnight black hair and piercing eyes that seem to stare straight through me. His have a darker, menacing look to them, but similar, nonetheless. Dressed in all-black, he looks villainous. The way he stares down at me, like he is a predator, has my heart skyrocketing. Chills break out over me, and I grip the sheet to stop my hands shaking.

'Kian,' I say, my voice hoarse from not having spoken for so long.

'I see my reputation precedes me,' he says, strolling into the room with confident strides, the small space filling uncomfortably with his presence. 'You are Raya. The girl attached to my brother.'

I grimace at that. The words sound dirty from his mouth.

'I guess that's one way of saying it.'

Lowering to my level, his soulless eyes stare into mine. Trying my best to hold my chin high, I resist the urge to reel back in repulse – and fear – not wanting to give him the satisfaction of getting a reaction from me.

'Interesting,' he murmurs, assessing my eyes. My skin crawls having him this close to me. 'I'm very curious about this bond you have forced on him.'

'I didn't force anything,' I hiss through clenched teeth, glowering at him.

The corner of his mouth twitches. 'I see.'

'What do you want with me?'

'Well,' Kian replies, pushing back, thankfully increasing the distance between us. I take a deep, gasping breath, not realising I'd been holding it. 'It's simple, really. I am going to conduct a little experiment.'

Everything inside me hollows. 'What?'

'You see,' Kian continues, looking down at his hands as he twists the black rings he is wearing. It looks so similar to mine that I balk at the sight of it. 'I want to see if this bond can strengthen the power of a vampire beyond its usual capacity.'

Anger surges through my body at the thought of any sort of experiment happening to Hunter. Heat flares across my skin and I swallow the lump in my throat, forcing myself to exhale heavily through my nose and remain as calm as possible.

'How are you planning to do that?' I ask, my voice dropping lower than I intended, giving away the anger and fear coursing through me.

'I've starved him. He is weak now, and worse off, being parted from you,' Kian says, as if we are simply discussing the weather. 'When a vampire is older than another, the eldest one can overpower the younger. I'm curious to see if this bond can change that.'

Ice drips through my veins, making me feel nauseous. 'And if you are proven correct?'

'Then I will learn how to create more bonded vampires, of course.' He grins wickedly, clapping his hands together. 'It would be handy having bonded vampires at my disposal. To serve and protect me.'

'You're insane.'

'Insanely clever, cunning, and handsome.' He winks, and my stomach clenches. 'Come now, let's get this show on the road.'

Grinding my molars, I stay where I am. Kian's grin widens.

Moving faster than my mind can comprehend, he yanks me to my feet.

'When I ask you to do something, you do it,' he snarls, making my arm ache from his hold on it.

'I don't take orders from you,' I spit, fury reigning through me in an angry torrent.

Sinking his fingers so deeply into my flesh that he most definitely is leaving bruises, he drags me closer to him. So close that the tips of our noses graze, and I recoil back as far as he allows me to.

'I thought you were a smart girl.' He sneers, fangs sliding out in a quick, fluid snap. 'I guess not.'

My scream splinters the air when his fangs drive into my arm. Pain pulses through me, making my knees knock together. This is *nothing* like the tender bites exchanged between Hunter and I. This is a form of pain I have never endured, not even when that vampire almost killed me.

'Kian!' a voice snaps and I force my rolling eyes to focus on my sister's concerned, pale face.

Kian abruptly releases me, and I collapse to the ground. My sister's hand twitches, as if she is fighting against herself not to come to me.

Kian smiles, my blood smeared messily over his lips. 'I just wanted a taste.' Sliding his tongue around his mouth, he removes the remainder of my blood from his skin. 'This is the first part of the test. Let's see if he can get himself out of his cell. He would have felt that pain.'

My sister's eyes are wide as she stares down at me. Placing my hand over the gaping wound, I press hard into it, trying to ease the blood, already feeling a little woozy.

Kian squats to the ground. He reaches for my arm. Flinching, I crawl backward, but his punishing hold halts my movements.

'Do you remember this?' he asks, ignoring the mess he created on my arm, instead pointing to the soft half-crescent moon that scars my skin.

'No,' I force out, my voice loaded with the emotion I'm refusing to let release. I don't want him to see how much pain I'm in. Heat pulses around the bite, shooting bullets of throbbing aches through the rest of my body.

'After I killed your mother,' Kian says calmly, as if those words aren't picking at the stitches on my heart. They are already holding on by a thread, one harsh pull and I fear it will split open, crushing me when it does. 'I fed on you. I laid my mark on you – you were my intended victim – but a police officer arriving ruined the moment. Too many witnesses arrived too quickly. It's a shame, really. It was almost cinematic, the car wreck. So much chaos.' He smiles, a sick, twisted one that makes my insides roil. 'It was truly beautiful. The smell of death was . . .' he trails off. 'Heavenly.'

'You're a psycho,' I seethe, chest heaving, refusing to let myself indulge in the traumatic memories he is wanting me to relive.

'A psycho your sister traded you and your mother for.'

The silence is thick and heavy in the room. Cora's face crumples, her eyes pleading at me to understand. I can't think of that right now, not when every part of my body is screaming for Hunter.

Kian chuckles darkly. It's deep and harrowing, giving off the same feeling as when you listen to nails claw down a chalkboard.

'Get up,' Kian says, not even glancing at me as he moves toward the door.

Rushing over to me, Cora scoops me up in her arms since my legs fail to do as I command them to. She gets me to my feet, and I weakly push her away. It feels like pushing a cement wall, and she doesn't budge. Releasing me, she steps back, and I almost fall when she isn't there to hold me up.

'Don't let him get to you,' she whispers.

'I'm not stupid,' I snap at her.

Sighing, she brushes her dark hair back from her eyes. She gestures to the door. 'After you.'

Holding my arm securely to my chest, I walk out into the hallway and follow Kian, quickly realising there is no other way to go about things. He leads us out to a living room. My heart skips a beat when I see Cas sitting at the table, flicking through a magazine. He glances up at me, offering a wave.

'Cas?' I whisper. 'What are you doing here?'

'Didn't you know?' Kian smirks, smile lines flickering around his mouth, making him look so much like Hunter in that moment. 'We are old friends, Cas and I.'

'Oh my God . . .' My voice is barely audible. 'You sold us out.'

Cas's face is completely stoic as he nods, eyes moving back to the magazine in his hands. 'Guilty.'

'Where is Alex?' I ask in horror, staring around the room. I gasp when I see him, sitting in the corner, blood splattered across his shirt. He is pale and sweaty, leaning against the wall as if it is the only thing holding him upright. My hands fly over my mouth as tears blur my vision.

This is bad. *Really* fucking bad.

'He really is delicious.' Cas smiles, noticing my horrified expression.

Goosebumps pepper across my skin at the cruelty in his eyes. I don't recognise the man in front of me.

There's a loud clattering followed by a few grunts and thumps. Kian and Cas exchange a knowing glance.

'That answers that question,' Kian says.

Cas makes a hum of agreement just as a door I didn't even realise was there splinters open, pieces of wood scattering across the floor. My bond sings hot in my chest, showering me with strength and warmth, making me instantly forget about the pain radiating in my arm. Hunter's eyes lock onto mine. Chains hang from his wrists and his shirt is torn, hanging off him in strips of fabric, barely covering his chest.

He is in front of me as quickly as he entered the room. His hands cup my face and the immense rush of comfort and joy that tidal waves through my body is so overwhelming that my legs buckle.

Sweeping me up, he presses his forehead to mine, kissing my cheeks, my nose, my jaw, and finally, landing on my lips, eliciting a moan from me as the taste of him erupts in my mouth like an explosion. Warmth and home, wrapped up in one delicate taste. I don't care that anyone else is here right now, at this moment, it is only him.

'How strong was he to get out of that cell?' Cas asks in a low voice, and I reluctantly blink back to reality.

'Very strong,' Kian answers.

'How is it possible he broke through the barrier?'

'It's not,' he says, eyes locked on Hunter and I.

The high of having him so close to me runs strong through my veins, but my thoughts and head begin to clear as adrenaline courses through me, reminding me of the dire situation we have ourselves in.

'*Fratello*,' Kian greets him, and we look over to where he is hovering beside Cas. He flashes his fangs. 'Good to see you made it.'

Turning, Hunter inspects my arm with an eerie calm. His cool fingers shoot tingles through me. The wound heals over before I even realise that he had moved, and I taste his blood on my tongue. He has always been fast, but he has never moved with the speed and precision like he had just now. Turning, he faces the other vampires in the room.

'Who touched her?' His voice is deep and laced with a threat that is felt in the room like a palpable thing, completely unrecognisable from his usual voice. A low growl emits from him, making the air around us vibrate.

After a moment of silence, Hunter half-turns to me.

'Who did this to you?'

My eyes lift, meeting the endless pits of Kian's. For a moment, something flickers in his gaze, making me wonder if he feels afraid at this moment. Hunter has obviously outweighed incredible odds to be standing in front of me right now and the storm in his eyes indicates his wrath is about to be released.

'Kian,' I whisper.

Hunter is across the room before I realised he had moved. Blood spurts across the floor as he savagely takes a chunk out of his brother's arm in an attempt to mirror the mangled bite he left on my arm. The wall crumbles as Kian flies into it. Cas dives out of the way, rolling across the floor, ending up near a dazed Alex.

Kian fights back, sending horrific sounding punches against Hunter. The two fall to the ground in a blur of motion, swinging and growling as they bite, punch, kick, and spit at each other.

Backing up, my body trembles as I watch them fight hard, fast, and brutally, destroying furniture as they go.

Cas shoots forward, snaking his arms underneath Hunter's armpits, jerking him backwards. A snapping of bones crackles in the air and I scream when I see Hunter's rib tear through his skin, poking between the skimpy bits of fabric loosely hanging off him.

'Help him!' I scream at Cora, who is standing there in frozen shock.

Kian hammers his fists into Hunter, getting decent shots now that he has Cas restraining him.

A blur of motion catches my attention and someone I don't recognise materialises out of thin air, yanking Hunter out of Cas's hold, tossing him across the room. The vampire glances back at me for a moment before levelling his gaze on Kian.

'Who the fuck are you?' Kian hisses, black eyes narrowed into slits as he glares at the stranger.

'Dante,' the vampire growls, his jaw clenched. Dante's dark skin has the smooth, marble texture of all vampires and midnight hair and eyes, similar to Kian's. Dark tattoos run down his arms in lines that disappear underneath the sleeves of his shirt. 'You remember me?'

With startling clarity, I remember seeing his face ever-so-briefly at the hotel. Someone *was* watching us, and it was him.

'Should I?' Kian's dark brow arches.

'You murdered my wife and daughter.'

The room grows silent as every pair of eyes turn to Kian. He straightens, staring unflinchingly back to Dante, lifting his chin.

'I've killed a lot of people. You might need to be more specific.'

Goosebumps scatter across my skin at the coldness in his tone. The temperature in the room seems to have dropped a few degrees as Dante's fists curl at his sides, his chest starting to rise and fall at a rapid pace.

'St Kilda beach.'

The cocky smirk painted on Kian's face slips. He tilts his head, studying Dante for a moment. Closing his eyes briefly, he nods, a soft breath of laughter leaving him.

'Ah, yes. The family who decided to go for a midnight swim.' Kian's smile makes my insides curl. 'Your wife. She tasted divine. But you know who tasted even better?' Running his tongue across the tips of his fangs, he smirks wickedly. 'The blood of your virgin daughter.'

The hoarse scream that tears from Dante sends chills over me. He launches himself at Kian, their bodies connecting with the force of two trucks colliding. The house staggers and I stumble over my feet to stay upright.

'So, you turned?' Kian pants between throwing punches and ducking from Dante's wild swings. 'And you've been hunting me.'

'To beat a monster, you must become one,' Dante replies through gritted teeth, slamming Kian hard on the ground, the tiles beneath his head shattering.

Dante's fist dislodges Kian's jaw, blood spraying across the cracked tiles. Kian lets out a deep laugh as he rolls out from under him, jumping back to his feet.

'She tasted so good,' he whispers, licking his lips. 'So fucking good, Dante.'

The pain in Dante's eyes is unbearable to witness as he howls, throwing a punch so violently at Kian that his skin splits open, and his collar bone protrudes from his skin. My stomach roils when the bone resets itself and his head snaps back into his normal position.

Cas moves silently as he lifts the glass coffee table, swinging it at the back of Dante's head. The metal bangs into his head, the glass raining over him as he takes the hit with a grunt, collapsing to his knees.

Kian dismisses Dante the moment he sees him collapse, moving toward Hunter who is still trying to reset his ribs back into position. Blood streams down his skin as he shifts and twists, re-aligning his spine. It seems to be taking him longer to heal than normal as he is so weak, and desperate for a feed.

Cas and Kian move together as if in a choreographed dance. Cas's hands slither around Hunter, holding him in place, as Kian plunges his hand into his chest. I feel the moment his hands enclose around my bonded's heart because it feels like he has hold of my own. Like an iron fist has reached down my throat and clutched my own heart with the kind of pressure that has me shaking.

'You are meant to be his friend!' I scream at Cas, white-hot anger flowing through me mixed with a strong dose of panic. I'm so fucking *weak*. There is nothing I can do right now to help him.

'Cora!' I shout at her. 'Help me!'

'No,' Kian snaps at her when she takes a step toward them. Immediately, she stills. I can't even fucking looking at her right now.

Spinning, I sprint toward the kitchen and grab a handful of knives. Launching myself at Cas's back, I slam all three knives into his back. He grunts and hisses in pain, letting go of Hunter enough that he can shove Kian back, forcing him to release his hold.

Cas suddenly flings his arm out, backhanding me. The hit feels as brutal as a car. I fly backward, landing in a painful scrawl on the ground, the air leaving my lungs. Everything throbs in pain.

Suddenly, as if gaining an extra ounce of strength, Hunter spins, headbutting Cas so harshly, his nose crunches. Hunter dives for one of the knives I dropped, lashing out and splitting Cas's face from ear to ear. Cas shrieks, recoiling back, howling in pain as he grips his face, the knives still sunk deep into his flesh. Hunter's hand snakes out, and twists Cas's neck. Cas drops to the ground as if his body weighs nothing.

A hand wraps around my neck. I stare at those dark and soulless eyes – I never saw him move.

'Hello, Raya,' Kian says smoothly, smiling menacingly down at me. 'Goodbye, Raya.'

His fingers circle around my throat, crushing my windpipe with an abominable *snap*.

PART II

32

HUNTER

The Protector

I HEAR THE MOMENT HE crushes her windpipe. I see her collapse, and yet I cannot believe it. The pressure from Kian's knees crushes her chest, and I feel the agonising pain of it through every part of my body.

Blood gurgles from the corners of Raya's lips as she clutches at her throat, unable to swallow or breathe. Unable to do anything other than cough up blood. Drowning in it. Her heart pumps furiously. Too hard. Too fast. There's no time.

Cora is frozen in shock, trembling from head to toe as she watches everything take place before her.

The roar that escapes me rattles the house to its very foundations. Panic surges violently through me as though I've been electrocuted and I struggle to think straight.

Stumbling over to Raya, I fall to my knees.

Kian launches at me, knocking me to the ground. He grins maniacally as he leans over me, and a feral growl rips from my throat as I kick him with both feet, knocking him on his ass while simultaneously hurling myself back on my feet.

Slamming Kian onto the floor, white-hot fury flows through me to the point I lose all control. I hit him over and over, until streaks of his blood cover every surface and his face is unrecognisable. Yanking him to his feet by his throat, I hurl him towards the wall, which he strikes with a deafening crash. It cracks and crumbles on impact as he disappears through it.

Dante clambers to his feet and chases after Kian so quickly he is a mere blur as he races off into the night. I don't care what anyone else is doing right now. Raya is dying, and she needs me.

Cradling her to me, I pull her arm toward me and bite it, holding her so tightly I fear I might break a bone.

Nothing happens.

I'm too late.

'Raya!' I shout at her, feeling so desperate, I can barely think straight.

Her eyes are closed now and her breathing has slowed so much I can hardly hear it. As Cas gets to his feet, I whip my head up as he quietly moves toward the gaping hole in the wall while rubbing his neck.

'Cas,' I plead, my voice unrecognisable as I blink up at him, my vision blurry from the tears. 'Help me. Help Raya.' He glances at the wall, and then back to me. I see his hesitation, and right then, I decide to forgive him for everything if he helps us right now. I'm not sure if I imagine the shift in his foot in my direction, but with a shake of his head, Cas turns and leaves without a word, or so much as an apology.

I stare helplessly down at Raya. Dread seeps through every fibre of my being.

My bonded.

My love.

My soulmate.

She's dying.

'She can't turn unless there is a sacrifice,' Cora says quietly.

I hardly hear her as everything is dimming in and out of focus. My vision is hazy as I desperately bite Raya once more, begging her to return to me. I'm only vaguely aware of her walking towards Alex. I don't need to look up to know how weak he is. I can hear it in his heartbeat. He's barely conscious. It's only when Cora effortlessly pulls him to his feet that I force myself to look at them. Alex's head hangs loosely against his shoulder.

'No!' I shout at her in panic. Alex's eyes flicker open, darting about as he tries to orientate himself. His eyes widen as they meet mine, realisation dawning over his face. Shaking my head profusely, I look at Cora, who ignores me.

Gently placing Raya down, I'm by Cora's side in an instant.

'*Protettore*,' I whisper, reaching for Alex, but my hand clutches empty air.

I don't make it in time.

Placing her hands either side of his face, she twists, and just like that, Alex is dead.

I don't have any time to process what just happened because I *feel* my bite flaring on Raya's arm, sending a fire through my veins. I jerk back in shock before quickly darting back to her side, blinking down at her. My heart thunders against my chest as I clasp her hand in mine.

Her transition has begun.

33

HUNTER

The Protector

HER PAIN SPLINTERS THROUGH every fibre of my being. Raya convulses, soft groans escaping her as she writhes on the ground. Holding Raya's limp hand in mine, I desperately try to harness her pain into me, so that she doesn't feel a thing, but with the way tears flow down her cheeks and her body twitches and jerks in agony, I know she is feeling every bit of torture the transition is forcing her to endure.

The only sounds in the room are her laboured breathing. Cora is frozen beside me, staring down at her sister. I pay her no mind, still undecided how I feel about her and the things she has done. If she truly still cares for Raya – like I hope she does – then I can look past everything that has happened. I know how manipulative and psychotic my brother is, and she was naïve and vulnerable. He took advantage of her – that part is clear as day – but I have yet to see whether her intentions with Raya are pure or not.

My darling bonded.

Writhing in pain, her skin grows paler by the second as sweat beads across her beautiful face. The transition from human to vampire isn't a kind one. Some have not been able to stand the pain, but she can, and she will. She is strong. Much stronger than her petite frame and gentle eyes let on.

Running my fingers down her arm, I try my best to soothe her, knowing nothing I can do will help much, but I can't sit beside her and do *nothing*.

'You really care for her,' Cora whispers. I look up as her eyes dart from me, to her sister, and back again. 'You love her.'

'I do.'

When she sighs, it sounds heavy with sadness. 'You're nothing like your brother.'

When I don't bother with a reply she continues, 'I was so scared, you know. When I heard Raya was looking for me, and with a vampire at that. Then finding out she is *bonded* to that vampire who is also related to Kian. I was sick with worry for her, my baby sister.' A hiccup escapes her, and she swallows, clearing her throat. 'I hope you're a good guy, Hunter. She deserves nothing less.'

'I will worship the ground she walks on,' I say firmly.

Cora's lips part as she blinks at me. Slowly, she nods, and I can see the resolution of belief in her eyes.

'Good.'

Casting a look over to Alex, who's lifeless eyes stare back at me, I heave a sigh, resting back onto my free hand.

'She won't forgive you for that,' I say, jutting my chin toward the dead body in the room. 'He was her best friend.'

'There was no choice when it was down to her or him.'

'I understand that, but it won't change the fact that it will destroy her. He only came on this trip for her. She will wear this guilt for the rest of her life.'

'I killed him, not her.'

'And yet the blood will be on her hands,' I reply. 'In her mind, at least.'

Cora's eyes narrow. It's clear she doesn't like that I'm talking to her as if I know Raya better than she does. I would never claim to know her better, but I certainly know a different side of her that Cora has never met.

The consistent thudding of Raya's heart, a tune that plays as constant background music in my mind, stops with a booming silence that echoes around inside my head. I sit up and lean over her, scanning her features, looking for any sign of movement.

Her lips part as she chokes on a gasp.

My breath catches in my throat.

Her eyes snap open and I stare into beautiful, black eyes.

'*Legata una*,' I whisper, tenderly caressing her face, assessing her quickly, looking for any signs that something has gone wrong.

'Hunter.' Her voice is barely above a whisper. 'I feel different.'

'You are different.' Leaning down, I kiss her lips, tasting blood.

Staring up at me, looking a little dazed, she lets out a sharp breath.

'I turned. Didn't I?' she whispers, reaching for her throat, touching the once-crushed windpipe, now completely healed.

'Yes,' I say, nodding. 'You're like me now.'

'Like you.' She smiles. 'And with you. Forever.'

'Forever,' I promise.

34

THE PREDATOR

MY STRONG HAND CURLS around Kian's arm as I viciously yank him toward me.

Kian uses the momentum to his advantage, spinning towards me before he slams his open palm into my chest. The unexpected force sends me hurtling backwards, falling onto the ground in a heap. I'm completely winded for a moment as I struggle to get to my feet, knowing I have to be as quick as possible to keep up with him but he's already running.

'No!' I roar, the deep, loudness of my voice rattling the air as I take off toward him. 'Face me like a fucking man!'

Kian's dry cackle drifts back to me, and my anger intensifies at the sound. I have never met someone as remorseless as this creature. So cold, and empty. A hollow shell of a person, any remnants of his humanity long gone. Assuming he had any to start with. Darting forward as fast I can, I land in front of him, my fangs protruding and ready. I thrust my hand forward, in an attempt to drive it into his chest, but he flattens me before I can touch him.

'I will kill you,' I spit, growling as his dark sneer inches closer to me. 'I will not rest until you're a corpse in the ground.'

Kian smirks, and it sends a shiver inching down my spine. Never have I seen such a predatory and gleefully cruel expression on another man's face. He makes a dismissive, guttural sound, like I'm nothing but an inconvenience to him.

Whipping out a knife, he plunges it into the side of my neck. I don't hesitate as I bring my knee up, slamming into him, and knocking him off me. I claw at the ground trying to get to him, but he is on his feet faster than I can comprehend.

'This dance has been fun, but I don't have time for this,' he tells me, and has the audacity to finger salute me. 'We shall meet again, Dante. Bring your A-Game, or don't fucking bother.'

And just like that, he is gone.

35

RAYA

The Survivor

IT'S HARD TO PROCESS the strange numbness that spreads through my body like cool water flowing over cracked riverbeds. It was such a contrast after spending what felt like an eon writhing and twisting in pain. Blackness consumed me entirely, and I wonder how many minutes, hours, or possibly days had passed while the pain engulfed me. A pain like no other. All consuming. A pain that one simply could not survive. And yet . . . here I am. Feeling stronger and better than ever.

I hear everything, even though the room around me is deadly silent. Every movement, every breath, the wind outside, the rustling leaves on trees, low conversations, car engines rumbling, tires spinning over loose gravel on the road . . . it's endless.

My skin, which had felt hotter than the sun during the transition, now feels like cool water on a humid day. Light, free, smooth. Lifting my hands, I stare at them as though seeing them for the first time. It's so surreal – everything looks the same, but different.

'Are you okay to stand?' Hunter asks, his voice just as comforting as it always has been, though now I hear the subtle variations in his tone and the way his breath hitches in the back of his throat. Deep and soothing, like it was designed just for my ears.

Cora shifts her weight from one foot to the other, capturing my attention. She offers me a wan smile.

Turning so that my eyes meet Hunter's, I nod once. I've barely thought of getting to my feet before I'm suddenly standing. I sway for a moment with the rush, my mouth agape at the speed I just moved at. It was one thing to see Hunter and the others move that fast, but quite another to do it myself.

Hunter chuckles, steadying me. 'The speed is something you need to get used to.'

While his touch no longer feels like a flame flickering against my skin, I can still feel the intensity of the chemistry between us. Though I can't tell if we are still bonded, the connection between us doesn't feel the same as it once did, but my heart still sings at his proximity and having him close makes me breathe easier.

He gives my hand a reassuring squeeze and with a nod, I look around. My senses are sharper. Heightened. Like nothing I could have imagined. A coppery smell burns its way through me, making my throat gnaw in hunger.

Blood.

Snapping my head around, locating the source, the all-consuming hunger is suddenly overshadowed with a harrowing realisation.

'No!' I sob, rushing toward Alex and collapsing on my knees. My hands flit fervently over his pale, unbreathing body. My scream echoes around the room as I cry over him, reaching for his limp arms, before grabbing him by the shoulders and shaking him. 'No, no, no!'

Tears run down my face as I wail, and though I'm no longer human, I feel my heart cleave in half at the sight before me.

My best friend.

Dead.

'What happened?' I gasp through harsh breaths. 'Who did this?' I scream, my throat feeling raw as I do.

A distinct, palpable silence meets me. Twisting, I turn to face Hunter and Cora, my fangs bursting out from my gums painfully and harshly as a low whine pours out from my body. Hunter offers me a sad, withdrawn look, which he then directs to his feet. When my eyes turn to Cora, I see the truth of what happened all over her face. I inhale sharply and it hurts, as though an icy blade is embedded in my heart.

'It was you,' I whisper.

'I didn't have a choice,' she says, her eyes filling with tears as she stares at me pleadingly.

'There is always a choice.'

Cora doesn't attempt to wipe the tears away as her expression changes to one of indifference.

'Fine,' she whispers, eyes swiftly turning to meet mine. 'I chose you. I chose my sister over her friend.'

The anger whooshes out of me and I crumble to the floor. The burning sensation rips through me once more and I glance down, seeing the blood on my hands.

'Easy,' Hunter says, approaching me cautiously. 'It's okay. Let me help you wash it off.'

My fangs ache. The desire for blood courses through me until it is all I can think about. Hunter guides me to my feet and directs me to the sink where he bathes my hands. I'm hypnotised by the red swirling with the water before disappearing down the sink. My chest is heaving as I struggle for some semblance of control.

I will *not* touch him. Not Alex.

'I will look after Alex, you don't need to worry,' Hunter murmurs. 'I'll make sure everything is done right.'

Numbly, I nod, barely processing his words, my mind buzzing with blood hunger and everything that is happening. It all feels like too much.

As though sensing my struggle, Hunter places his hand on my arm, and I notice his skin doesn't have the same coldness to it that it usually does. His skin feels smooth, like silk, and a totally normal temperature. I suppose we are the same now in basically every way.

Without needing to look up, I hear Cora as she enters the room and hovers against the wall. Again, I'm amazed at the extent of my new abilities. Turning the tap off, I pivot around to face my sister. She's looking like she has no idea what to do or how to act right now, and to be honest, I have no idea either. Her dark eyes – now once again the exact same as mine – survey me, like she is seeing me for the first time. I guess in many ways, she is.

I feel like I can't stand still and I move to walk back into the other room. There is absolutely no lag in movement or effort in anything I do. I'm smooth and fluid, like a well-oiled machine. Momentarily distracted, I turn a few times, inspecting my skin as the light and shadows move across it.

'We need to go,' Hunter's voice is soft. Startled, I look at him, his bare chest gleams under the florescent light of the kitchen as his shirt is more ripped than not, dangling off of him in ragged strips. 'We aren't safe here.'

'I can't leave him,' I whisper, as I exit the kitchen and hurry back to Alex's side, disgusted that I allowed myself to become distracted by my transition when he gave his life for it.

'He can't come with us,' Cora says.

Slowly, I swing my eyes to her, narrowing them into slits. She steps back, holding her hands out.

'I'm just saying what he is thinking, Raya.'

Hunter moves around me, toward Alex, lifting him, and throwing his body over his shoulder. My stomach twists at the sight of Alex – lifeless – hanging limply and bobbing in a completely inhuman way with each of Hunter's steps.

'Come on, *legata una*,' Hunter murmurs, grazing his finger over my hair, his touch as tender and light as a feather's caress. 'Let's go.'

As much as I wanted to sleep the day away in bed grieving the loss of Alex, the severe ache in my throat forces me from the room I had been cooped up in for hours.

Cora left to go get supplies but hasn't returned. I don't think she will be back for a while, after the way things are between us. Tense and awkward. I need time to process everything.

After all the time I spent trying to find her, now that I have, I sort of feel lost. It's bizarre. I guess I lived in a state of denial that she didn't really choose this life, but now that I know she did . . .

A huge part of me is angry. So angry, I feel the blood boil inside me. And then the other part of me feels helplessly sorry for her and what she has been through. There are so many emotions tangled within me right now, my emotions are heightened, and I feel like a total mess.

With everything else happening to my body, I can't handle trying to sort out my feelings toward her right now. I need to work out how to function, and I also need a distraction, because every time I close my eyes I see Alex's lifeless eyes and it breaks my heart again and again.

The pain. It's too much.

My head hurts.

My heart hurts.

Everything fucking *hurts*.

I shake it off, deciding to deal with all of this later.

Wandering into the living room of the small Airbnb we secured last minute in a small town I had never heard of, Hunter is seated on the lounge, a book in his hand. Snapping it shut, he leaves it forgotten on the coffee table as he moves toward me, his hand reaching out, offering me the comfort I am so desperately seeking. I take his hand and lean into him, burying my face into his chest. His arms wrap around me, tight and secure, the promise of safety spreading through my body.

'What are you feeling?' he asks, stroking my hair.

'Everything,' I whisper. 'It's . . . a lot.'

'It is,' he agrees, threading his fingers through the dark strands of my hair, running them softly through the ends. 'I'm sorry it all happened this way.'

With a sigh, I lean back and reach up, kissing the corner of his mouth.

'I'm so glad nothing happened to you.'

Pressing his forehead to mine, he places his hands either side of my face. 'Are you okay?' he asks.

'I'm not sure. Yes and no.'

'How are you feeling, in regard to the change?'

'Deliriously hungry,' I confess. 'And sick at the thought of that.'

He nods, and I know he understands completely. 'Yeah. That's how I felt, too. But then you taste the blood and it overrides everything.'

'I don't want to hurt anyone,' I murmur, shaking my head. 'I *can't* hurt anyone.'

'You won't. I won't let you, I promise. I've got you.'

Releasing me, he strides to the kitchen, and withdraws a blood bag from the fridge. My fangs snap out with a distinct *pop* as the smell overwhelms me. Passing it to me, he lets me open it. I glance up at him and he gives me an encouraging nod. Raising it to my lips, I take a long sip. The flavour is intense as it fills my mouth. Sweet, delicious, and warm, soothing the fierce ache instantly.

'Oh my God,' I moan, the blood trickling down my chin as I savour the taste. 'This is incredible.'

Hunter grins. 'Yeah. It is.'

'How much can I have?'

Lightly, Hunter sweeps my hair back, his thumb trailing down the side of my face. 'Take it all, love.'

Taking greedy gulps of blood, our eyes stay locked on each other as a tingle of desire shoots through me.

I savour the last drop from the bag and smear the blood across my finger. Hunter leans forward, his tongue dragging across my skin. I shiver as a surge of electricity shoots through me.

A part of me was scared we would lose the bond if I turned. That we may realise that our feelings for each other weren't truly genuine. But here, right now, I can say with absolute certainty that what Hunter and I have is pure and completely untamed.

I love him with every fibre of my being.

Gently placing my hands either side of his face, I stare into his eyes, eyes that perfectly match my own now.

'I love you,' I whisper. 'I love you so much, it hurts.'

He smiles his warm, beautiful smile. 'I love you, *legata una*. More than anything in this world. Beyond Heaven – or Hell. I'd turn a million times over if it meant meeting you,' he whispers, kissing me tenderly. 'If it meant becoming *us*.'

Hunter wraps his hand around the back of my neck as he drags me closer to him. He runs his tongue over my lips, taking the last remnants of blood, before he dives toward my mouth.

We crash toward the wall, the paintings clattering to the hardwood floor. I groan, tearing the remnants of his shirt from him, baring his chest to me. My hands roam wildly over his hard muscles. Hunter lifts me up and I wrap my legs around his waist as he leaves feverish kisses down my neck. His fangs slide into my neck as he bites me and a ripple of desire washes over me in surprised delight at the feeling.

Sliding my hands down his neck, my own fangs drop, as I bite into the soft part of skin between his shoulder and neck. Our collective moans fill the room as we both drink from each other while shamelessly grinding our bodies together.

When we both pull back, he takes my face between his hands and kisses me harder than he ever has. A possessive, toe-curling kiss that sends waves of yearning through me. Energy crackles through my entire body in a way I have never experienced before.

Considering the fact I'm not meant to tell hot from cold, I still can't deny the fiery burn that spreads outwards from everywhere his mouth and hands touch.

My hands squeeze and caress every hard line of his body, exploring the way he feels – so familiar yet unfamiliar at the same time with my new heightened senses.

I crave him. All of him.

'I love you, Raya.' His voice is rough and deep, making me shiver and squirm in his hold.

My gaze hooks onto his and I swallow, feeling breathless and overwhelmed with the fact that he still affects me so much, even though I do not breathe like a human anymore, and my heart no longer beats. He makes it feel like it does.

'I love you more.'

'Impossible,' he whispers, his hand travelling down my side. He pushes the fabric of my skirt up, his thumb making invisible patterns on my pelvic bone. Without warning, Hunter gives an expert flick of his hand, and my underwear shreds off me. I gasp as he thrusts first one finger and then another inside me, making me moan and whimper his name as his fingers curl, reaching the exact spot I need them to.

Liquid fire shoots through every limb as I grind against his hand. His other hand reaches around, slapping my bare ass cheek with a distinct *smack*, making me gasp with surprise. Shockwaves of pleasure flow through me.

'Me and you. Forever.' His eyes bore into mine with unparalleled promise.

'Forever.'

My hands glide greedily over his torso before landing on the bulge of his biceps. Desire swells in every part of my body, a new hunger emerging.

I'm finally strong. I can be the one in charge.

Smirking a little, I curl my fingers, caging his face in my hand as I yank his mouth to mine in a punishing kiss that makes him growl.

I release his face and slam my palms against his chest, sending him sprawling onto his back. He lets out a sound of surprise at my strength. I don't give him the chance to second guess it as I straddle him, pinning his arms above his head. He smiles at me. The kind of smile that has my insides melting.

My *God*, he still makes me feel insane.

'Thank you,' I whisper, leaning down and brushing my lips against his. 'For saving me.'

Resting his hands on my hips, his grip on them tightens deliciously. 'You're the one who saved me, *legata una*.'

Raising my hips, and in one quick tug, I yank his pants down his thighs. My fangs lengthen a little painfully at the sight of his arousal.

'Take it, *legata una*,' he murmurs, scraping his nails down my bare thighs, the pressure drawing blood, increasing the ache in my core. 'Take every inch and claim me as I have claimed you.'

Dragging my nails down his chest, he hisses as I draw blood. I hold his gaze as I slowly sink onto his long, hard length, and groan at the feel of him stretching me. He releases another rough growl, his eyes closing briefly as I seat him deep inside of me.

Grinding against him, I rock and rotate my hips in a slow, sensual way that has him panting and writhing beneath me. His hands spring forward from their pinned position, ripping my shirt in two in his eagerness to grope my breasts.

Hunter lifts himself upwards and takes a nipple between his lips sucking it as I roll my hips faster.

'Fuck,' he says through gritted teeth, planting one hand beside our bodies on the floor, meanwhile using the other to grip my hip as he thrusts upward, hitting me so powerfully in the spot I needed that I let out a scream of pleasure, unable to stop myself.

Our bodies clash together as we fight for dominance. Me slamming him down and pinning his arms as he fights my hold, thrusting into me brutally.

'Submit to me,' I snap, slamming him hard into the ground.

'You've had your fun, *legata una*.' He smirks, his dark hair falling messily onto his forehead as those black eyes glint up at me under the dim lights. 'Now I'm going to remind you who you belong to.'

With his hand wrapped around my throat, he lifts me off of him, choking me at the same time he slams back inside me before my back even hits the ground. I cry out in pain – and wicked delight – as he mercilessly drills into me. The sound of our skin slapping fills the room followed by the echoes of our cries of passion.

'Mine,' I snarl, throwing him sideways, so that I am once more riding him. He chuckles, deep and throaty, loving this game we are playing just as much as I am. 'You don't like not being in control, huh?'

Smirking, he shrugs. 'Maybe. But you sure look sexy trying to take it from me.'

He spins me so fast I feel dizzy and flips me so that I'm on my knees. His hand slaps my bare ass again and I groan at the feel of it. He plunges inside me at the same time his hand wraps around my hair, yanking my head back.

'Fuck.' I am delirious, and breathless, and so damn *close* to breaking, even though I am desperate to overpower him and win. '*Hunter.*'

'Yes, love?'

Ugh. I can hear the smirk in his voice.

'You're an asshole.'

His laugh is rough and laced with desire as he pulls back harder, pins and needles spreading over my scalp.

'Yeah. But I'm your asshole.'

With one more slap, he reaches around the front of me, his fingers dancing over my clit, crumbling the last of my resolve. The orgasm detonates inside me and I choke on a sob as the feeling is just too damn much.

With a guttural groan, Hunter spills inside of me.

We both collapse onto the ground, feeling depleted, even though we are meant to have infinite strength since we both just fed. The energy flowing between us is something I can barely describe. The intensity . . . The power . . .

Rolling to my side, he drags me close, curling his arm around me, kissing my forehead.

'Wow,' I mutter, carving a line from his face, down his neck, placing my hand over where his heart should be beating, if he were still human. 'That's even better than I thought it could possibly be.'

'It's never felt like that,' he murmurs. 'You're made for me, *legata una.*'

Smiling, I kiss his lips tenderly, snuggling into his chest.

I don't want this moment to end. Everything else is a mess.

I want to stay like this – just me and Hunter – forever.

36

THE PREDATOR

FUCK.

He got away.

Again.

I can't believe it. I finally found him. *Spoke* to him. Felt his bones snap beneath my grasp, which I had dreamed about for months.

Years.

I finally had him, only for him to evade me yet again.

Not only did Kian not remember me – or what he did to my family – he didn't care.

Anger surges through me and my fist flies out, slamming into the wall beside it. It splinters, cracking straight down the middle. A lady yelps in alarm, clutching her bag to her chest as she runs away, fearfully glancing over her shoulder at me, but I turn my back to her. I curse myself for forgetting that I am in public.

I have tracked him endlessly, and so far haven't had any luck. It feels like I've started all over again.

I should let it go. Give it up, but I can't.

Kian is still alive.

My revenge plan is not over yet. I will find him, even if it takes me an eternity.

Because his death is *mine.*

37

HUNTER

The Protector

MY HANDS CAN'T STOP touching her. They slide and skim over her bare body as I trail kisses down her chest, over her breasts, and across her stomach.

Her small, petite hands slide over my shoulders and down my back, digging her nails into me. Hissing, I arch my back, getting off on the pain as I sink my teeth into her hip. Her legs wrap around me, pressing against my shoulderblades, drawing me closer to her.

When I finish drinking, I trail my tongue back up her body, before I kiss her hard, forcing her to taste her own blood. She moans, digging her nails in harder. It's enough to drive me crazy and I slide inside her in one, quick thrust.

We haven't stopped. I've lost count of how many times we have done this. Over and over, we claim each other. Sometimes it's sweet and soft like this, other times it's hard and passionate. I've fucked her over every surface of our room and the living room and it isn't even night yet.

Her fangs plunge into my neck and I thrust harder into her, biting her once more so that we blood share at the same time, intensifying the scorching heat between us.

'Fucking hell,' I curse, rotating my hips and hitting into her harder. 'I can't get enough of this. Of you.'

'Me either,' she replies with a content sigh. 'I'm so in love with you, Hunter.'

Kissing the side of her head, I increase my pace and she lifts her hips, meeting me thrust for thrust. Every time we release, it's at the same time. I've never experienced anything like it. I don't know if it's a bonded thing, or if we are really just that in tune with each other's feelings.

I pull out of her and roll onto my back.

'How is none of this enough?' she whispers, her hands finding mine, stroking me, making me feel hot and bothered for her again, even though it hasn't even been half a minute since I was inside her.

'The lust and attraction we felt for each other was already insurmountable and that is only heightened now.'

'Good God,' she mutters.

'I'm not complaining,' I say, as her fingers close around my length, pumping lazily up and down.

'Me either, but we won't be alone for much longer, and it will kill me not to touch you.'

Rolling over, I shuffle down until my head is between her thighs, dragging my tongue along her centre. She sighs blissfully at my touch, sliding her fingers through my hair.

'Jesus Christ!' Cora's voice snaps impatiently from the other side of the front door. 'I have been waiting *hours* for you two animals to stop attacking each other. Enough is enough!'

Raya lets out a shocked gasp, yanking my head up so harshly my neck cracks.

'Ow,' I complain, rubbing it. 'You're strong now, remember?'

'Oops.' She giggles. 'Sorry.'

Moving my head down once more, I press my tongue into her and her eyes widen.

'Hunter!' she hisses.

'Hunter, I swear to God!' Cora's voice booms on the other side of the wall. 'I'm going to beat your ass in a minute!'

Chuckling, I lean back, wiping the back of my hand across my mouth. Raya is a blur of motion as she dresses before toppling over and landing in my lap. I steady her, shaking my head.

'Slow down, hot stuff,' I say, bracing her in my hands. Her long, dark hair flows down her back. Her eyes are intense, silver-black, in a pattern I've never seen before. She says mine are the same, which makes me assume it must be bond related.

At first, her eyes were the same as every other vampire. But after we slept together again as vampires, our eyes morphed into something between the bonded-human eyes and vampire ones, which means people will be able to see the direct link we have to one another. I don't know if that is a good or bad thing.

'Hunter! Put some pants on!' Raya exclaims, slapping my chest.

'Yes ma'am.'

As I yank my pants back on – with reluctance – Cora steps inside, her silver eyes shooting daggers at me.

'Honestly,' she snaps. 'Do you not have any impulse control?'

'Nope,' I say.

Shaking her head. 'I did *not* need to hear any of that.'

Cora and Raya both glance at each other and then just as quickly look away.

The two are scarily similar in appearance. Both the same height, and build, with the same hair colour. The birthmark on Cora's face is a small difference that could easily be overlooked, which may be why Raya has the purple streak in her hair, to define *something* about her own appearance.

Raya sighs, which brings a sobering feeling to the room. Moving into the kitchen, I make up some drinks from the supplies Cora brought and place the glasses down onto the table. Sitting down, Raya drops into the seat beside me, and Cora into the one across from us.

My muscles are tense as I glance between them. This has been building up. Raya has been avoiding Cora – she is unsure how to be around her, after everything – which is definitely understandable.

It's difficult to know what is right and wrong in this situation, when the lines are blurred this much. I get why Cora did what she did. More than anyone ever could.

Despite everything, I want the two to salvage their relationship. They've both survived and endured so much. They need each other now more than ever, but it's not as easy as that.

'So,' Raya begins, leaning forward and closing her hands around the glass, spinning it in a slow circle, not meeting Cora's eyes. She mentioned to me that every time she looks at Cora, she thinks of Alex. The hurt in her eyes when she speaks of him is like a physical blow to my chest. I ache to ease her pain, but I don't know how to. It's not as easy as it was when she was human. 'How did this happen?'

Cora downs the drink in one sip, placing the glass hard back down onto the table before pushing it toward me.

'We are going to need more of this.'

Hearing Cora talk about how she first met Kian makes my blood boil. The age and vulnerability of this girl in front of me – and what my brother is like – is a deadly combination. I'm surprised she is still alive to tell the tale.

'So, you sought him out?' Raya questions, her forehead crumpling adorably as she frowns, looking at her sister with equal parts interest and confusion.

'Yeah. I know. I'm stupid.' She takes a long swig of the bourbon, not even wincing with the taste. Wordlessly, she holds out her glass and I pour more into it. 'I met him on a night out. I was drunk and having fun. He was so bloody hot.' She laughs, shaking her head. 'A walking fucking red flag.' She flashes her teeth at Raya who offers a hesitant smile in return. 'But red is my favourite colour.'

My gaze darts between the two of them, not really understanding the inside joke, but not caring enough to ask them to elaborate.

'He took me down this random alley. We . . .' she trails off, waving her hand in front of her. 'Hooked up. It was totally mindblowing.' She directs her gaze to Raya, who is still staring down at the table. 'I became addicted to the high. A human having sex with a vampire is . . . well . . . you understand.'

'So, you slept together and he didn't hurt you?' I question when Raya doesn't look like she is going to reply.

'Oh, he fed on me,' she replies with a curt nod. 'I think he would have tried to kill me, if a group of drunk party-goers didn't stumble into us.'

'You knew he fed on you?' I ask.

'He never compelled me to forget.'

Releasing a heavy sigh, it's my turn to take a long sip. I'm sure there is a long list of women my brother has done that to. It's a part of his game.

'He wanted you to find out what he was.'

'Exactly. He knew the effect he had on me. My weakness of wanting to escape my life drew me to him. And him to me, too. He knew he could offer me a way out, and I was desperate enough to take it without understanding the fineprint.' She lets out a humourless laugh. 'It's so ridiculous to think about now.'

'What was the offer?'

'He would turn me if I sold myself to him for ten years.'

Wincing, all three of us take a drink. Raya says nothing, and

I can feel the pain coursing through her body at hearing this. Her sister traded her soul to the devil.

Placing a hand on her thigh, I give her a reassuring squeeze.

'I never knew what that would entail, obviously,' she continues, hanging her head in her hands as she rubs her fingers over her eyes.

'I don't know how you two are brothers,' Raya says earnestly, glancing at me. 'Sure, there are similarities in your appearance, but your souls can't be more different. Like day and night.'

Nodding, I tap my fingers against the glass. 'I agree.'

'Explain the car accident to me,' Raya says, and I can feel how tense she is. I tenderly squeeze her thigh once more, trying to offer her comfort.

'Well, Kian loves the dramatics,' Cora says. 'He wanted to stage something 'chaotic'. He told me the sacrifice didn't have to be anyone I know. Just another human being to balance the scales.'

'Right,' Raya says slowly, and I can see she's trying not to look as repulsed as she feels, but she's failing.

'I didn't know how to leave my old life behind. So we staged a car accident. It was perfect. A stranger would die so that I could turn, and you and mum would mourn my death and move on.'

'But he killed her,' I say. 'Your mother. Instead of the other driver.'

Burying her face into her hands, Cora nods. 'The moment I saw him take her life, I knew that I had made a grave mistake. He killed her, turned me, and then went to kill Raya, to really cement the fear into me, but he never got to complete the kill because there were witnesses, one being an on-duty police officer.'

The silence is loud. I don't know what to say. Glancing at Raya, I see a tear slip down her cheek. Leaning over, I collect it on my fingertip. She sighs, looking down at her hands.

'And then I was bound to him,' Cora whispers. 'The psycho that murdered our mother in cold blood.' She sniffles, wiping her cheeks. 'I know that sacrificing a stranger was awful enough, but in my head, I didn't know them. It wouldn't affect me, or my family. I was so fucking selfish and naïve.'

I run my hands roughly down my face, absorbing all of this information.

'I don't forgive you for the decisions you made,' Raya says thickly, her voice firm. She breathes a heavy exhale, tucking her hand behind her ear. 'I . . . can't forgive you for what you did to Mum. To Alex.'

There's a beat of silence. And then another. Swallowing, I drag my thumb back and forth across Raya's skin, as if that would somehow help take away some of her pain.

Cora leans back in her seat, blinking, looking void of emotion. Like she is tapped out of energy, and needs to be recharged. I'd feel much the same, if I had been through what she has.

'I chose to save you,' Cora says, lifting her chin. 'You don't have to forgive me for that, but when it comes down to it, it's what I will always do.'

'He didn't deserve to die for me!' Raya shrieks, slamming her hand down onto the table. It shakes violently under the impact, and the wine glasses topple over. As one rolls off the table, I swiftly reach for it, grabbing it just before it connects with the floor.

'He may not have deserved to die Raya, but neither did you. I made that choice, and I'm going to live with that guilt forever.' She remains exactly where she is, her face pale, her eyes pained but unflinching.

Drawing in a shaky breath, Raya nods stiffly. 'I know why you did it. You love me as much as I love you. But he was there for me when nobody else was.' Finally, she meets her sister's eyes. 'He was there for me when you weren't.'

Cora's face crumples. The air feels heavy in the room. Suffocating, and thick with tension.

Raya's emotions slam into me with a severity that makes me inhale sharply. Placing a hand on her back, I focus on drawing out that dark energy. Her shoulders sag as I take away her pain. Not nearly enough of it, but as much as I am able to. It's the best I've been able to do since she turned.

The pain is written all over her face. The relief and joy of being reunited with her sister. The person she loves endlessly, and has devoted her life to finding. But she also feels hurt, betrayed, and furious with the choices her sister has made.

I can't hate Cora. I really can't. Because she saved Raya. It's something that I would have done. The bond would have forced that. Cora simply beat me to it. If she hadn't, I have no idea how I could have lived with the guilt – or how I would ever convince Raya to forgive me.

Raya releases a heavy breath, tears streaking down her cheeks. I look away, not able to bear seeing her in so much pain when I can't take it from her.

'We can't bring Mum or Alex back,' Raya says after a moment, sniffling. 'But we still have each other. So, that's something.'

Leaning forward, Cora clasps her hands with her sister's. Raya pulls her hand back, and Cora's eyes fill with tears.

'I'm so sorry, Raya,' she whispers. 'I love you so much. I'll never forgive myself for causing you so much pain. But I couldn't watch you die either. You're my little sister.'

Smiling sadly, Raya nods, not able to meet her gaze.

'I know.'

38

RAYA

The Survivor

I'M GOING CRAZY.

Laying here, I'm alone in this apartment, and yet I swear I hear the ghosts of them. The sounds of the front door opening, their soft footsteps as they enter. Hell, I swear the scent of my sister's perfume lingers in the air. I know it's all in my head. Some sort of PTSD or survivor's guilt from the accident.

Staring up at the ceiling, I watch the rusted fan slowly spin. My eyes are sore and puffy. I thought I would have run out of tears by now but somehow, they keep on coming.

'Raya,' a voice murmurs.

Great. Now I'm hearing voices. I can't help but smile. God, I miss them.

'Raya,' the voice says again.

Turning my head, my eyes land on my sister. As beautiful as always. More so, if that's possible.

'I really am going crazy,' I whisper. 'Now I'm even seeing you.'

Cora moves toward me, and sits down on the bed. She touches her hand to mine and I jerk away. That felt way too real.

'You are suspicious of the car accident,' she says, touching her fingertips to my cheek. Her usual emerald eyes are a fierce silver as she stares down at me, ensnaring me into this odd, calm-like state.

'You will grieve, but our mother's and my death will not destroy you. It will make you stronger. You are determined to find out what happened to me. It doesn't make any sense to you.'

Slowly, I nod, completely agreeing with her. 'No sense at all.'

'You will go through my things. You will find my journals. You will read them, and you will do research about the things that you discover in the journals. You will be brave and strong, and you will not give up looking for me. No matter what happens.'

'Yes.' I nod. 'I will not give up.'

'You will wear this ring. You will never take it off unless I say so.' Pulling a black band out of her pocket, she grabs my hand, sliding it down my finger with ease. 'I love you.' Leaning down, she kisses my forehead. 'You won't remember that I was here, and that we had this conversation, but you will do everything I have told you to do. Do you understand?'

'Yes,' I murmur. 'I understand.'

It's night-time now. Opening my eyes, I rub them as I peer around the room. I feel cool metal against my eyelid, and as I pull back my hands, I stare at the ring on my finger. I can't remember where I got this. I know Cora gave it to me, but I don't remember when.

Maybe I really am crazy.

I wake with a gasp and sit upright. Hunter rolls over, pushing himself up on his elbow. The pale moonlight slithers through the blind, showing a snippet of his handsome face as he looks at me with concern.

'What's wrong?' he asks.

'I just . . . had a dream.' Glancing down at my hand, I realise that my ring is no longer there. I hadn't even noticed. 'Only . . . it felt more like a memory, only I don't recall it happening.'

'A memory?'

'Cora came back to me after she was turned,' I whisper, shock coursing through me as the memory plays on a loop inside my head.

'Huh?' Hunter's brow crinkles in confusion.

I rehash my dream while Hunter listens carefully, his eyebrows inching higher. 'I think she compelled me to forget it, but for some reason, I now remember it.' I finish.

'I didn't know that was possible,' Hunter says. 'It must have something to do with you turning.'

I exhale loudly and lay back onto the mattress. 'She wanted me to find her. Cora never wanted to leave me, not really.'

'Yeah,' Hunter says softly, tracing his hand down my arm. 'She loves you. Very much.'

Swallowing, I nod.

Hunter drags me closer to him, resting his forehead into my shoulder. Closing my eyes, I try to relax, but I know I won't be sleeping for the rest of the night.

Dropping soundlessly to the ground, I straighten, a wide smile on my face.

'Pretty cool, huh?' Hunter offers me a crooked grin as he lands beside me, enjoying just how much fun I'm having zooming through the woods and leaping off tree branches.

'Totally awesome.' I laugh, raking my fingers through my windblown hair.

We have been practising running and jumping for the past few hours. This feels like another perk of vampirism that I can't seem to get enough of.

'Your attitude on being a vampire makes no sense to me,' I confess, turning to face him. 'You seemed so miserable when we first met. You hated yourself, and what you were.'

Chewing his lip, he nods. 'Yeah. I did. But it's different now. I have you. I'm seeing things in a new light.'

Smiling, I lean up and kiss him. 'I'm glad we have each other.'

'Me too,' he says, hugging me to him for a moment before stepping back.

No matter how fast I run, or how high I climb, I never fatigue. Being a vampire is totally badass.

When we first ventured outside, it was overwhelming. I could now smell *everything*; scents that I never knew existed before. Somehow, I learnt to deal with the onslaught on my senses relatively quickly.

From all the zooming around, and other . . . activities between Hunter and myself . . . the thirst has returned stronger than ever. Shaking my head, I try to ignore the ache by launching myself up onto a branch overhead. Hunter follows closely as we climb, jump, and swing between the trees. My laughter echoes around me as we glide effortlessly through the air, startling birds and other wildlife.

The laughter falls away when I'm distracted by the sound of soft footfalls approaching. My head snaps around toward the direction of the sound – and then the smell comes.

Blood.

It's pumping through her veins as she jogs.

Before I realise what I'm doing, I take off through the trees, tracking down the source below. As she crosses my path, I jump from the branch and land right in front of her. The girl screeches, rearing back in fright, before tripping over her own feet. Her air pods fall from her ears and she winces, gingerly touching the graze on her leg.

'Where the fuck did you come from?' the girl yelps, glaring up at me.

I barely hear her – I'm mesmerised by the pulsating vein in her neck. Without a second thought, I lunge at the girl, and push her back against the grass as I plunge my fangs into her neck. She screams, slapping her hands against my arms, but I feel nothing.

'Easy.' Hunter's warm, soft voice is in my ear as he crouches down beside us. 'Gentle, *legata una*, you're hurting her.'

Touching my shoulder, I feel his calmness wash over me, and I soften my grip on her, pulling back so that my fangs aren't so deep. Her blood is hot and delightful as I swallow it down, feeling a little high on the feeling of feeding straight from the source.

'That's it,' Hunter encourages, rubbing circles across my back. 'In a few seconds, I need you to stop.'

Savouring the last taste, it takes all the willpower I can muster to retract my fangs. It's a test of self-control I'm determined to pass as I reel back. The feral craving inside of me urges me to continue, but now that I have pulled away, my mind is clearing and I feel more in control.

The girl's heartbeat hammers inside her chest as she breathlessly stares up at the sky, looking stunned. Licking my lips, I lean back, gazing up to Hunter.

'I want you to have a taste,' I say.

He raises his eyebrows in surprise. 'What?'

Swallowing, I glance at the girl, and back up to him. 'I want you to see how good she tastes.'

Hunter's eyes darken, his fangs snapping out. 'You're sure?' he questions, drawing his brows together.

'Yes.' I nod, pushing her towards him.

Nodding, he reaches for her arm. Desire crashes through me as I watch him bite into her, his beautiful dark eyes locked on mine as he does. My own fangs snap back out, and I step toward the girl.

Moving in, I bite into her neck, as we feed at the same time.

Since I only just fed, it is much easier to pull back this time. Licking my lips, I step away from her, curiously watching her face as she gazes past me, looking blissfully unaware of what is happening to her right now.

'You will need to give her some of your blood,' Hunter says, wiping the back of his hand across his mouth. 'We took more than we should have since we both drank at the same time.'

Guilt churns within my stomach at the realisation. As though sensing my distress, Hunter places a hand on my shoulder.

'She will be totally fine. Most vampires take too much. I like to only take as much as is necessary, and nothing more.'

Nicking my thumb on the pointy part of my fang, I hold my thumb over her parted lips. She drinks from me for a few seconds. Pulling my hand back, I stare down at the girl, then up to Hunter.

'Now we make her forget?' I ask.

'Who the hell are you crazy people?' she exclaims, the vampire blood running through her system, healing her and restoring her clarity. She turns on her heel to run, but I am in front of her before she can take a step.

My eyes stare hard into hers. 'Forget this ever happened. You went for a long run. Go home now.'

The command in my voice comes naturally, as easy as breathing was when I was human. The girl's expression slackens for a moment and I worry I've done it wrong. Suddenly, she smiles at me, nodding slowly, and starts jogging away from us.

'Did that work?' I ask in disbelief.

'Yup,' Hunter replies.

'That was so easy!'

'It's not easy for everyone, *legata una*, you're just a natural.'

Beaming at his praise, I snuggle up to his side. He wraps his arm around my shoulders, drawing me closer to him.

I reach for his pants. He stops, looking back at me.

'Raya . . .' he says. 'I think you might be experiencing a high right now.'

'I don't care.'

'Raya . . .' he warns again, but makes no effort to stop me from pushing him up against a tree, while unbuckling his pants. I slide them down his legs with a flick of my wrist. His lips part, and he looks so damn sexy with his dark hair pushed back, his eyes a sparkling silver-black, his fangs on display.

'I want you so bad,' I whisper. 'It's all I can think about.'

Reaching up, I grab him by the back of the neck and pull him towards me, pressing a hard kiss to his mouth before I spin him around, and push him onto his back. He grins mischievously at me as I yank his briefs down, releasing his erection. Circling my fingers around him, I start moving my hand.

I move my mouth to his tip, running my tongue over him. He groans, hips bucking. I move my mouth down his length, taking him as far down my throat as I can. Electricity crackles down my spine as I bob my head up and down, feeling him grow stronger and harder beneath me.

When his hips jerk, I move faster, my tongue sliding and slipping across him with vampire speed. In only a few moments, he spills hot across my tongue and I lap it up greedily, swallowing every bit.

Hunter's eyes are wild, his breaths coming out in short, sharp bursts. 'Holy shit,' he breathes. 'That was . . . incredible.'

Smiling, I move up his body and steal a kiss from him, sucking on his lower lip, tasting the last remaining droplets of the girl's blood. He groans into the kiss, his hand curling around the back of my head, holding me in place.

I should feel awful for what I just did. What we are doing *now* immediately after feeding on her. Yet, I don't.

'This has been one hell of a day,' I tell him. 'I love doing life with you.'

'Me too.' He smiles, the one reserved only for me, making me feel giddy with happiness.

'I don't want to go back,' I whisper, looking in the direction of the town where our Airbnb is. 'I don't want to face reality.'

Threading his finger through my hair, he kisses me softly on the temple. 'I know, love. But we have to.' He hesitates for a moment, as if worried about my reaction to what he is about to say. He curls an arm around me. 'We need to make a plan for Alex's funeral.'

Coldness prickles through me at the thought of laying my best friend to rest. My eyes sting with tears and I bury my face into Hunter's chest, wishing that all of this had gone differently.

Hunter has placed Alex's body in a safe place. I haven't asked much about it because I can't think of him cold and dead somewhere. Lifeless, and alone.

The tears come on stronger and a sob wracks my body as I think about him. How young he was, how much more of life he was yet to experience. All of it stolen from him. And it's all my fault.

'It won't always hurt this much,' Hunter whispers. 'I know that doesn't make it any easier. But I promise you, it will eventually hurt a little less, and you will realise that everything is going to be okay.'

Nodding, I wipe my face, unable to form a sentence yet.

'Also . . .' Hunter says, and I lift my gaze to him.

'What else?' I whisper, dreading what else might be coming.

'I want to find Cas,' he says. 'I want answers.' Swallowing, he leans back against the tree behind us, pulling me close. 'I need to know why he did this to me. To us.' He exhales heavily, looking tired. 'I need to find him.'

'Okay.' I nod, understanding completely. I feel much the same, and I didn't even really know the guy.

'Also, my truck is there,' he points out.

'Oh yeah,' I reply, nodding. 'Let's go to his house. Now.'

'Now?' Hunter questions, frowning.

'I can't go back to the Airbnb,' I admit, covering my face as I rub my eyes roughly. 'I need space between me and that place right now. From Cora. From Alex's . . .' I swallow the lump in my throat, unable to finish that sentence. It hurts to say his name. 'I need to get out of here and focus on something else. It won't take us long to get to his house. Then I will organise the funeral, when my head is a little less . . .' I wave my hand to my face. 'Overwhelmed.'

Hunter nods, giving me a small, sad smile. 'Sure, *legata una*. Whatever you want.'

'Okay,' I nod, stepping back and clearing my throat. 'Let's go.'

39

HUNTER

The Protector

TAPPING MY THUMB ON the steering wheel, I look out the window, watching the trees pass in a blur. The sound of Raya's soft, steady breathing makes me glance over at her. She's been asleep for a few hours now, and although we are getting close to Cas's house, I don't want to disturb her.

She has been through so much in the past few weeks and her nightmares are worsening. Even as a vampire, she is still tense, tossing and turning during the night, waking up screaming. It will pass eventually, the longer she is a vampire, but as everything is heightened right now, it is going to get worse before it gets better.

When I turn off the highway and slow the car down, she stirs. Yawning, she rubs her eyes, and looking over at me, she offers me a small, soft smile.

'I didn't mean to fall asleep,' she mumbles, looking adorably sleepy.

'You needed it. Do you feel better?' I ask, moving my hand across to her thigh.

'A little,' she replies, leaning back in the chair and stretching. 'Are we almost there?'

I nod. 'About two minutes away.'

Straightening, her relaxed expression morphs into one more serious. 'Do we have a plan?'

I exhale. 'No. Not really.'

'I don't think we should expect cooperation,' she says, looking out the passenger window. 'Since he is under Kian's thumb, and all.'

My jaw clenches. It makes me sick to my stomach that someone I thought I could rely on, someone that I trusted, could turn his back on me so swiftly, and without a second thought. This is why I hate meeting other vampires. Most of them are two-faced and manipulative. The main thing I need to remember is that they are always looking out for themselves, and only themselves.

Turning onto the street, it seems unusually dark and quiet. I'm certain there's less cars parked out on the street than when we stayed here. Yet there's something else, something I can't put my finger on.

When we pull up out the front, I frown at the house. It's completely dark. Not totally unusual as we can see well regardless if it is night or day, but it seems a little strange not to see any light on at all.

'Ready?' I ask her, reaching out and placing my hand gently on top of hers. She curls her fingers into mine, giving it a squeeze.

'Ready when you are.'

I give her a nod and we exit the car. Deciding to approach this head on, I walk straight to the front door, and knock. When we're greeted with nothing but silence, I glance at Raya, knocking again.

It's unnaturally quiet. If there was any movement in the house, we would hear it.

Bracing myself, I ram my shoulder against the door, stumbling as it bangs open. If it wasn't for my vampire reflexes I would have fallen. Considering vampires tend to attract attention and trouble, I thought the door might have been harder to open. Deadbolted, or something. But it was simply locked, like any normal front door would be.

Raya flicks the light on, and the space around us brightens into focus. We glance around, and she gasps as I stare with my mouth agape.

Everything is gone.

With the dark aesthetic of the house, it seems even darker and colder without any of the art or furniture. Any hint of Cas, or any presence, is long gone. Swallowing, I lean against the wall, exhaling heavily.

'Of course he left.' I sigh.

'I did wonder if he would,' Raya admits, as she slowly walks around the empty room. 'But I thought he might want us to find him. You know, so he could have the chance to explain himself.'

Rubbing my hand down my face, my shoulders slump. 'Me too.'

'Let's check the house for anything he might have left,' she suggests.

'Okay,' I agree.

Splitting up, I shoot upstairs, and make my way down the hallway, checking the spare rooms. Every room is empty, and so vastly bare that there isn't even dust left behind. It's like the place has been scrubbed clean by someone who had just committed murder and bleach-cleaned the crime scene.

'Where are you, Cas?' I mutter, raking a hand through my hair, feeling frustrated and unresolved. I'm not sure what it is I want from him. Answers, of course, but maybe something else. Someone to take my built-up anger on, since I'm not going to go searching for my brother to do so. I don't ever want to see him again, not that I think I'll be that lucky.

'Oh my God,' I hear Raya whisper, and immediately I am at her side, my feet barely touching the ground as I glide down the stairs.

Finding her in the garage, she is staring at the sleek black Porsche that Cas had gifted to Alex. She is silent as she blinks at it, frozen in shock. Moving toward it, I pluck the note that is tucked underneath the wiper.

I did what I had to do to survive.
I'm sorry about Alex and my role in what happened.
Kian was a worse enemy to have than you.
Be well, my friend. May we meet again in another life.
Cas

Swallowing thickly, I stare down at the note, rereading it over and over, his words slowly sinking in. While it doesn't make the sting of betrayal any less potent, I understand his position, and why he did what he did. Doesn't mean I forgive him for it, but I get it. Vampires look out for themselves above all else.

Raya snuggles up to my side, and I plant a soft kiss on her forehead as she leans into me.

'Super shitty of him,' Raya mumbles, sniffling. 'But I get it.'

I make a noise of agreement. 'Yeah.'

Lightly touching her fingertips to the car, she sighs. 'Alex loved this so much.'

'I know,' I reply, recalling his face when he first saw it. 'I wish he got to spend more time in it.'

'Me too.'

'We need to get out of here,' I say to her. 'Others might be looking for Cas, too. It isn't safe here.'

Nodding, she tucks a piece of hair behind her ear. 'I want to take the car.'

Thankfully, I already made plans for the rental we used to get us here, not that it would be a problem regardless. What Raya wants, Raya gets. I'll make sure of that every damn time.

'Okay,' I say. 'You can drive it back, and I'll drive my truck.

I already compelled the guy from the rental store to come get the car tonight.'

'That was smart.' Raya's lips twitch. 'You're very kind and thoughtful, you know. Most people would just abandon the car and not think twice about it.'

'Well.' I shrug. 'I didn't want anyone to get in trouble over it.'

She offers me a watery smile. 'I love you.'

'I love you, too.'

Standing on her tip-toes, she presses her mouth to mine briefly before she goes around to the side of the car. As expected, it is unlocked, and the keys are sitting in the centre console.

'Be safe, *legata una*,' I say. 'I'm going to wait around until the guy shows. To make sure he's safe. I'll meet you back at the Airbnb.'

She flinches at the mention of it, and I wince. I know it's hard for her. Trying to process Alex's death and everything else that is going on with Cora. It's a lot for one person to handle, and I wish there was something more I could do to help.

'I'll wait with you,' she says, and I know she is dreading going back there and facing all the things she left behind.

'He shouldn't be too far away,' I say, tapping my phone to check the time.

Silence stretches between us, and I worry Raya might get consumed by her thoughts.

'What do you want to do, Raya?' I ask her. 'What's next for us?'

'I want to meet your family,' she says, turning to face me, smiling. 'I want to visit where you were born in Italy.'

Collecting her hand in mine, I bring it to my mouth, and kiss her knuckles. 'I will take you.'

'Really?' she asks. 'I thought you said vampires don't do well at airports.'

'It's tricky, with the long flight and no feeding situation,' I explain. 'But I will get us a private plane, love.'

Her smile widens. 'That's literally insane.'

'We can do anything,' I tell her.

Raya has been through more trauma and heartbreak than one should have in a lifetime. I want to make her happy. Spoil her in every way possible.

Headlights swing across the porch and a car pulls up. The man I compelled exits the car, and walks directly to our rental. The driver who dropped him off cruises down the street, and the worker follows after in the rental shortly after.

'After you,' I say, getting to my feet, and pulling her with me.

When she has reversed out onto the road, I double check the garage door is locked. Raya idles at the edge of the driveway, waiting for me as I go to my truck.

I'm barely seated, when my phone rings. Answering it, I hear Raya's soft breath through my speakers.

'Hi,' she says.

'Everything okay?' I ask.

'I just . . . don't want to be alone. On the drive back.'

Smiling, I nod, meeting her eyes in the dim lighting across the road as she waits for me to pull out behind her.

'I'll always be here,' I promise. 'Always with you. No matter what.'

40

HUNTER

The Protector

IT HAS BEEN A WEEK since we got back from the short trip to Cas's house, and today is the day we are laying Alex to rest. A day that has been simultaneously anticipated and dreaded.

Raya has been in two minds all week. A part of her is not ready to let him go. She doesn't want to accept the fact that he is gone and not coming back, meanwhile, the other half of her understands she needs to let him go and move on with her life. Of course she will never forget him and will cherish every moment they shared together, but either way, it isn't easy saying goodbye, and trying to get on with life almost feels like . . . defeat. In a way.

Paradise Bay. A place I'd never heard of, but one that held a special place in Alex's heart. I visited his family and compelled them so that they are not fretting, or wondering what has happened to him. Not that they seemed to be in touch, or very close at all. Raya seems to be breathing a little easier either way, knowing they are at peace.

Waves crash into the cliffedge of the cliff I stand on. I peer over the side, down at the jagged rocks below. I shift, making sure the umbrella I'm holding is keeping Raya covered. It is an unusually bright and sunny day. This is what this place is apparently known for – it's perfect weather year-round. Or so the tourist websites say, anyway.

Alex wanted to be cremated and have his ashes spread over a beautiful place that people can stop by to remember him at. So, that's what we are doing.

Paradise Bay is a charming, small coastal town with golden-sand beaches and turquoise water that makes me crave to disappear into the water for a while.

'Farewell, Alex,' she says softly, gripping the urn like her life depends on it. 'My best friend. My family. I love you, and I miss you.' Sniffling, the tears pool her eyes, drowning out the darkness for a moment. 'I hope you're happy, wherever you are.'

Chewing on her lower lip, she gazes out at the water, tears streaming down her cheeks. When she grows silent, I look down at the urn.

'Goodbye, *Protettore*. Although we may not have gotten along for the most part, I always appreciated you, and what you did for Raya.' Inhaling, I place a hand on the urn. 'Rest easy.'

'*Protettore*,' Raya murmurs. 'What does that mean?'

'Protector,' I say, pushing the sleeves of my shirt up to my elbows. 'He protected you, and was there for you when you needed it most.'

Inhaling sharply, she sobs. Gently, I pry the urn from her hand, kissing her tenderly as I do.

'Are you ready?' I ask.

Nodding, she unscrews the lid. We spend the next few minutes silently scattering the ashes. The only sounds are the crashing waves and the birds chirping in the trees. It truly is a beautiful, peaceful place.

The sound of a stick snapping has us both whirling to look behind us. Cora hovers under a tree, seeking its protection from the harsh sun. Raya freezes beside me, and I feel the tension crackle in the air.

'What are *you* doing here?' Raya seethes through clenched teeth, visibly shaking in anger as she glowers at her sister.

Cora is silent for a moment, fiddling with her fingers as she glances at me, before looking back at Raya.

'I wanted to pay respect . . . to Alex . . .' she trails off, swallowing, looking pale, and weary. Dark circles line her under eyes, and her expression blank. Considering vampires are meant to have smooth, unblemished skin, she must be feeling extreme exhaustion to look like this. I feel for her. I really do.

'You are the reason he is dead!' Raya shrieks, her voice breaking with a sob, and her knees buckle. I swiftly reach for her, managing to keep her upright as I juggle to hold the urn, the umbrella, and her bag all resting on one arm.

'Easy,' I murmur, trying to soothe Raya. I can feel her emotions roar inside her, threatening to unleash and detonate all of us. The fierce fury washes over me with such a force that I stagger. An angry scowl mars Raya's normally kind, relaxed face. 'She didn't mean anything by it. You know this, Raya. You're just overwhelmed.'

'Don't tell me how I'm feeling,' she snaps, her eyes darting to mine for a moment and I jerk back a little in surprise, as if she slapped me in the face. My jaw flexes. The instant regret flashes across her face but she yanks the urn from my hands and stalks away from us, her dark hair billowing behind her in the breeze.

'At least take this,' I say, quickly handing her the umbrella, my heart tearing at the agony in her eyes.

'Thank you,' she mutters, grabbing it and covering herself.

The urge to go after her fills me so intensely that I take a step toward her, but I force myself to stop, and let her cool off.

It only takes a few seconds for the itch and burn of the direct sunlight to spread across my skin. I hastily step into the shadow of the tree, joining Cora. She stares out at the water, her lips spread into a thin line.

'I can't do anything right,' she says flatly.

Sighing, I drop to the ground and after a moment of hesitation, Cora joins me. Throwing her head back, she rests it against the tree, looking up at the leaves. Drawing her knees to her chest, she flings her arms over her knees.

'I understand what you're going through. I really do,' I say. 'But she is going through a lot, too. This isn't easy on either of you.'

'I'm sorry for what I did to Alex, but it was necessary.'

'I get it,' I murmur softly.

'She doesn't.'

'She does. She just feels guilty, and blames herself. It's going to take time.'

Cora flicks a glance at me as she bangs her head softly back against the tree, chewing her lip. 'She hates me.'

'No, she doesn't.'

'She does,' she insists, and this time, her voice cracks. My stomach tightens at the pain and sadness deep in her voice.

None of this should have happened. They didn't deserve this fate.

'Cora,' I say, turning to face her. 'Raya loves you, she just is trying to work out how to go forward, after everything that has happened. You need to be patient. You may not have known Alex, but he meant a lot to her. He was her family when she had no one. You must understand that this is a serious loss for her, and obviously . . .' I swallow, and she faces me, eyes red-rimmed as they narrow, waiting for me to continue. 'She is still mourning the loss of your mother and the loss of you in her life.'

'I know. I am well aware of what I have done to her. Yet, no matter how much I try to make it better, I only make it worse.'

Deciding not to reply, I look forward, exhaling heavily.

'It'll all work out,' I say eventually.

'Yeah,' she mutters, wiping the tears from her cheeks.

When my phone vibrates against my leg, I quickly reach for it, wondering if it is Raya. My insides curl when I read Lucy's name on the screen. The texts and calls from Theo have died off. I've been meaning to reach out to him, to sort things out, but it's been a pretty crazy time. Guilt stabs at me. I should always make time for him.

After a moment, I answer.

'Hunter!' Instantly, I register the fear and panic in Lucy's voice, and I sit bolt upright in alarm. 'I need your help.'

'What's wrong?' I ask, clambering to my feet, my heart lurching into my throat at the thought of something happening to Theo. A million thoughts whirl inside my mind, recalling our last conversation, and how we ended things.

'You need to come back to Red Thorne,' she says urgently, hardly audible as she cries. 'Right now.'

'What's happened?' I demand.

'We need to find him.' She hiccups, barely getting the words out. 'They've taken Theo,' she whispers. 'They're going to kill him.'

41

RAYA

The Survivor

WHEN I WISHED FOR a distraction to take my mind off of everything, *this* wasn't what I had in mind.

Hunter, Cora, and myself are on our way back to Red Thorne. Since leaving, I honestly haven't thought much about the place. It was never the town I was overly interested in. It was the answers I was hoping to find there to lead me to Cora. Now that I've found her, I don't exactly know how I feel about the place.

It truly terrified me when I first arrived there. Now I've become the very thing I was afraid of.

My eyes drift toward the rear-view mirror, and I stare at Cora. She is looking out the window, arms folded across her chest, jaw tight. I hardly recognise her. She isn't the sister I grew up with. She's a shell of herself. Cold, empty, and haunted. Nothing like the warm, loving sister that I looked up to, and leaned on for support so many times.

She was basically the one who raised me, since our mum was always working, trying to keep food on the table, and our rent paid. I suppose that's why I felt so immensely lost when she was gone. I didn't know how to live without her. Now, everything is screwed up. Beyond anything I could have imagined.

I switch my gaze to Hunter. I've never seen him look so tense, so troubled. I know there are a lot of things on his mind. All of us have a lot on our minds.

'I don't get it,' Cora says after about an hour of silence.

Yanking out my earbud, I flick a glance up to the rear-view mirror, to see she is still staring vacantly out the window.

'Get what?' I ask, the tension between the two of us thick and heavy.

'Why didn't Theo leave town, if he knew people were after him?' she questions, referring back to the conversation Hunter had with us earlier, briefing us both about the situation that Theo has himself in. 'It doesn't make sense.'

'That's what I thought, too,' Hunter murmurs in agreement. 'It doesn't add up. He's hiding something, but I don't know what.'

'He basically asked for it,' she continues, shaking her head.

'I can say the same about you,' I mutter, but since everybody in this car has perfect hearing, it doesn't exactly go unnoticed.

Cora lets out a sigh, but says nothing. Placing my headphones back in, I lean my forehead against the glass and close my eyes, hoping we aren't about to walk into yet another shit show, but I know in my heart that we are.

Hunter and I have gone over a lot of training, in a short amount of time. I'm still getting used to the vampire way of life, but I feel like I've gotten a good grasp on things, rather quickly. I'm feeling confident I can hold my own in whatever we are about to get ourselves into.

The moment we cross the line into Red Thorne, it seems like the temperature drops five degrees. Not that I exactly *feel* hot, or cold, anymore. It just has an eerie feel about it, even when I am now one of the creatures of the night that people whisper about.

When we drive past the small apartment Alex and I had lived in together, acidic bile rises in my throat. My eyes burn and I close them, trying to hold back the painful ache in my chest. I still can't comprehend the fact that Alex is *gone*.

My eyes snap open at the feel of Hunter's hand on my thigh, and as I turn to face him, he gives me a soft, tender smile. As always, he knows exactly what to do to make me feel better. Placing my hand over his, I squeeze it, and turn to gaze back out the window.

The more I think about what awaits us, the more my nerves intensify. I might be stronger, and much better off now, but I know better than anyone that things can go wrong *very* quickly.

I could not live with myself if anyone else died.

'Raya.'

A shiver rolls down my spine. The sound of my name on his lips, in his rich, deep voice, does things to me. Looking back at Hunter, he is looking at me, his eyes filled with concern.

'Are you ready for this?' Hunter asks, in his cool, calm, and collected tone that has my shoulders unwinding.

'As ready as I can be.'

It doesn't take long to reach Hunter's house. I pause, staring out the windshield. Well-manicured lawn, white picket fence, and gorgeous burnt-orange bricks. It looks totally normal. You'd never suspect that multiple vampires took up residence here. It would be a perfect suburban home for a family.

'This house is so . . . normal?' I question, my eyes sliding to his. 'I expected a house that looks like Cas's.'

Hunter flinches at the mention of his friend. Arching a brow, he lifts an eyebrow. 'We aren't exactly going to have a banner over the front door saying "Vampires Live Here" now are we?'

'Guess not,' I say with a weak smile as I exit the car.

Hunter, Cora, and I exchange a weighted glance before we trail toward the door. It swings open before we reach it. A woman I don't recognise stands there with kohl-rimmed, blood-shot eyes.

She is gorgeous, with her raven black hair, and legs that are almost longer than my entire body.

'Hunter,' she chokes out before launching at him. She wraps her arms tightly around him, and he awkwardly pats her shoulder.

'Lucy,' Hunter says.

She steps back, wiping her eyes. Turning, she stares at me. Offering her a tentative smile, I stay where I am, unsure what to make of her expression. I can't tell if she is curious about me, or hates me. Probably a mixture of both.

'This is Raya,' Hunter says, touching my arm tenderly. 'She is one of us now.'

Lucy's eyes quickly assess me, moving quickly as they travel up from my shoes, over my body, and to my face. Not changing her expression, she gives a quick nod. 'I see that.'

'And I'm Cora,' Cora says, giving her an obvious once-over, as Lucy just did to me. 'Her sister.'

Lucy briefly glances at her. 'Pleasure.' Her tone indicates it is anything but. 'Come in.'

We follow her inside, and my eyes roam everywhere. It's a little darker and edgier inside, not matching the exterior at all. Long maroon curtains cover the floor to ceiling windows, blocking out any natural light. Tall arch ways lead us to the high-ceiling living room. A fire softly glows, casting the room in a golden glow.

'Tell us what happened,' Hunter says, getting straight to the point.

Lucy draws in a deep breath, as if trying to collect herself for a moment. Running her tongue across her lower lip, she tosses her hair over her shoulders, turning to face us. 'We had just gotten back from a night out. I hadn't even taken my shoes off yet, and these two vampires came straight through the front door. Literally opened it, walked inside, and knocked Theo out. They didn't even look at me.' She shakes her head, her voice trembling. 'I tried to attack them, but they stabbed me.' She scowls, glancing down at her thigh, but there isn't anything but smooth, unscarred skin, since it would have healed quickly. 'They have him. Those vampires that have been terrorising the town.'

'You said he's still in Red Thorne,' Hunter says, looking extremely calm right now, considering the information he's just been given. He is definitely the person to lead the team through a crisis, nothing ever phases him. Well, unless the bond interferes. 'How do you know that? They could have taken him anywhere.'

Lucy stills for a moment, then shakes her head. 'No, he's here.'

'How do you know?' Hunter frowns.

'Theo can't leave Red Thorne.'

I look at Hunter, but he is still staring at Lucy, looking puzzled. Folding his arms across that deliciously muscled chest, he tilts his head.

'*Can't* leave?'

'No,' Lucy murmurs, eyes nervously glancing at Cora for a moment, who straightens under Lucy's gaze, looking over at me in confusion. 'He can't.'

'Can't leave, or won't leave?' Cora demands.

'Can't!' Lucy snaps in irritation. 'Kian compelled him to stay here, and he was meant to keep you here.' She steps closer to Hunter. 'That's why he was so distraught when you left, Hunter. He was being controlled.'

'What?' I exclaim, as Hunter blinks in silent shock. 'How can that be? Theo is a vampire. Compulsion doesn't work on us.'

'Kian turned him,' Lucy explains, looking frustrated that we aren't understanding this quicker. 'He has power over him because of this. I never knew it was possible, but it's true. When a vampire makes another vampire, the "maker" has a certain level of persuasion when it comes to the vamp they created. Theo cannot leave Red Thorne unless Kian tells him to.'

'That makes no sense,' Hunter argues, shaking his head. 'If that were true, then Theo should have been able to stop me since he turned me.'

'Don't you wonder why you never left, even though you were so desperate to?' Lucy questions, giving him a pointed look. 'You always wanted to get away from here, but you never left. Not until the bond overpowered it. Because Theo had persuasion over you. That's why Theo was so desperate to try and convince you to stay without force, because he knew if he tried to physically stop you, it would only make you suspicious, and wouldn't work anyway.'

I feel the mix of confusion and shock swirl deep in Hunter as he collapses onto the lounge, mouth hanging open. The way Cora looks, I can tell she has experienced this compulsion first hand. My heart aches for her, and I realise I really have no idea what she has been through.

'Fuck,' Hunter mutters, looking pained. 'I feel like a dick.'

'Well, yeah, you were.' Lucy huffs.

I take a step toward her, and she flinches, actually looking a little weary.

'Woah,' Cora breathes. 'Your eyes just did this weird demonic thing, Raya.'

Stopping, I shake myself, not really understanding what just happened. All I know is that I felt an irrational amount of anger towards Lucy for saying that to Hunter.

'Raya,' Hunter says with calm authority, and I instantly step down, returning to his side. Lucy eyes us with fascination.

'Now that everyone is caught up, we really need to make a plan,' Lucy continues, planting her hands on her hips. 'The longer we leave this, the worse it will be.'

'You're saying he is in Red Thorne,' Hunter says, rubbing his fingers across his chin. 'Do you have any idea where?'

Lucy nods. 'There is a house a little out of the main part of town. I've heard rumours that a new group of vamps hold parties out there a lot. I've been trying to get an invite, but any of the humans that know anything about it end up dead soon after.'

I bristle, feeling unnaturally cold as I listen to her words, understanding very well that these rogue vampires are *extremely* dangerous.

'You think he is there?' Hunter questions.

Again, she nods. 'Yeah. It makes sense. There is always someone there to watch over the place, lots of bodies as a distraction, and far enough out of town that people won't accidentally stumble across it.'

'Yeah, okay,' Hunter agrees, seeming to realise she has done her homework on the group, and their location. 'We will try there, then.'

'Their parties are exclusive. Invite-only,' she says. 'But, I have been tracking a vampire who is in charge of recruiting humans. I think we can fool him into inviting us. Compulsion won't work obviously but I think we could charm him into inviting us. What do you think?'

Cora shrugs. 'People are stupid. I think that's a solid plan.'

Sighing, I exchange a heavy glance with Hunter. I don't really like the sound of this. Any part of it. Though I understand the importance of rescuing Theo. He is Hunter's best friend. As much as they have had their differences recently, I know he means the world to him. And if he means a lot to Hunter, he means a lot to me, too.

We spend the next half an hour organising who will do what, and by when. At the end of it, we have a plan. I can't say it's a good plan, but it's a plan nonetheless.

As we part ways to get ready, my heart plunges into my stomach at the thought that one of us might not make it out alive tonight.

*

As I lean over the pool table, my shirt rises, causing my skin to brush against the rough baize material.

Hunter's intoxicating scent washes over me as he presses my back to his chest. His long arms snake around me, steadying the pool cue with his hands over mine. He swiftly hits the ball into the socket, his breath fanning my ear as he tilts his head toward me, grazing his teeth along my earlobe. Desire sizzles through me, making me wish we weren't on a mission right now and surrounded by others.

'I do know how to play pool, you know,' I say with a teasing smile, even though I'm certainly not complaining about his proximity right now.

'I just wanted an excuse to touch you,' he murmurs, and even though I'm not meant to have any changes to my body temperature, I'm positive I'm flushed right now. Pushing himself back, I twist to face him.

Every time we meet eyes, I fall in love with him a little bit more.

I tune in to Cora's low, sultry voice as she leans in close to one of the vampires who is our target of the night. There's two of them. Lucy says they often come here first and scout for humans to take back to the house. She is outside, surveying the premise, while we find a way to be invited.

'A party?' I hear her ask, and sneak a glance to see her tossing her dark hair over her shoulder. It shimmers under the light, and the guy's eyes are focused on her mouth as she smiles at him.

'Yeah. You want to come?' he asks her, and I want to roll my eyes at how easily Cora has always gotten male attention. I'm sure it's only worse now that her natural beauty is heightened by her immortality.

'I would love to,' she replies, her voice silken. 'Can I bring friends?'

'Depends,' the guy answers after a beat. 'It's an invite-only kind of thing. Who are your friends?'

Hunter moves away from me, melting into the crowd of humans on the dance floor. I calmly stroll towards a guy with a similar height and build to Hunter. Placing a hand on his arm, I brush around him.

'Hey,' the guy grins down at me.

'Hey,' I say.

'My sister,' Cora says, and even though she is at the other end of the room, her voice is as clear as if she is standing right next to me. 'And her new . . . friend,' she says, and the way she says it implies that the boy in front of me is my meal for the night. 'We are just looking for people to party with who have similar . . . tastes.'

'Well,' the guy says, and I hate the way I can hear the smirk in his voice. 'My party sounds like the place for you girls, then.'

'Perfect,' Cora replies smoothly. 'When does it start?'

'I was thinking about heading there soon, but the party is already underway.'

'In regards to the humans,' Cora says, leaning in close. 'Do I need to bring my own, or are there plenty to go around?'

My skin crawls at her words. She is a little *too* good at playing the part. The guy grins, obviously loving how forward Cora is. That kind of vampire is who they obviously want around.

'I'll share with you,' he promises, winking. I resist the urge to roll my eyes at how desperate he is.

'Even better,' she purrs.

He prattles off the address, and I meet eyes with Hunter, who does a subtle nod, telling me he heard it, too.

'Come outside for a smoke?' the boy in front of me asks, and I sort of forgot for a moment that he was there.

'Sure.'

Cora sidles up to me and we both follow the guy outside. We calmly leave him when he starts talking to a friend of his who is already out there. My skin prickles, and I feel Lucy's eyes on me, even though I can't see her.

Hunter drives Cora and I to the location the man gave us, and Lucy is tracking us there on foot, but with her speed, she would easily be able to keep up with the pace of the car. We didn't want to risk anyone seeing her get out of the car when we arrive in case they recognise her.

When we arrive, there's a vampire at the door, and his eyes narrow as we pile out of the car. Hunter keeps his head low, and his shoulders hunched, trying to appear as unthreatening as possible, although with his height and broad shoulders, it's near impossible. The vampire's eyes are trained on him as we approach.

The bass thumps loudly from within the house, causing it to vibrate in time with the beat. The deafening level of the music is almost painful with my sensitive hearing. Drawing in a deep breath, I focus, tuning the music out, and after a moment, it isn't so loud inside my head, allowing me to think clearly again.

'Hi!' Cora smiles and waves at the vampire, whose eyes are raking over her appreciatively.

'Cora, is it?' the man asks, obviously having expected us.

'The one and only.' She smiles sweetly.

After a quick assessment, it appears he is the only one guarding the door, which means our plan is ready to go ahead.

At a speed quicker than should be possible, Hunter and Cora advance on the vampire in what looks like a choreographed dance. Hunter is behind him, twisting his neck, while Cora plunges a stake straight into his heart. The vampire is inexperienced and appears inebriated. He never saw it coming.

My hand flies to my chest and I clench my teeth, looking away. For a while now, I've wanted to become a vampire, to be able to protect myself, and equal out the power-play between Hunter and I. I *wanted* this life. This power. But I can't stomach seeing someone murdered right in front of me, even if they would have killed me at the first chance they got.

Hunter disappears with the body at the same time Lucy appears, her perfect hair looking windblown. She flicks it over her shoulder.

'Nice,' she compliments, nodding at Cora.

'That seemed almost too easy,' Cora replies, shifting nervously as her eyes dart around.

Hunter appears back at the doorstep. He touches a hand to my shoulder, and the rising panic soon dissipates, as if he absorbed it straight out of me.

'*Legata una,*' he murmurs, I turn to face him, and I would be blushing right now at his words spoken in front of the others, if I could blush. 'You good?'

'Yes,' I whisper.

Assessing me quickly, he nods after a moment. 'Let us know if we can follow. Stay quiet, stay smart.' He brings two fingers up to his temple, tapping it. 'Stay sharp.'

I nod. Cora and I exchange a quick glance before she walks inside with me hot on her heels. It is so dark in here, I have to squint, but thankfully my vampire eyesight focuses quickly, making everything clear once more. Neon lights dart haphazardly across the room. Stale cigarette and flavoured vape scents clog the air, overwhelming my senses. Shoving the sensory overload to the back of my mind, I do my best to level myself out, trying my best to stay on task.

The house is packed with people. More human than not. My stomach twists when I recognise some faces from the few classes I attended. They probably have no idea the danger they are in right now.

My insides freeze over when I see a girl who used to sit in the row in front of me, draped over the lap of a man who has his fangs in her neck. Swallowing, I look away, battling with my own fierce, rising hunger, mixed with the disgust I feel towards the man. It's confusing to think and feel one way, only to also feel the opposite at the same time. I'm starting to understand why Hunter struggled with so much inner turmoil when we first met.

Hunter and Lucy enter behind us, as quiet and deadly as if walking on thin ice, and one minor movement could cause it to crack.

I can sense a few vampires strolling through the room, but they're all in a blood and alcohol haze; light headed and dazed. None of them spare us a glance as we walk in, but perhaps they're confident of the vampire guard at the front to patrol any unwanted guests.

A door to the right opens, one I didn't realise was there, and a vampire strolls out, his knuckles coated in blood. He swipes a beer straight from a human's hand without a second glance at him as he beelines to the centre of the room. He reaches for a blonde girl and pulls her to his chest.

By the time I look back, Lucy has slipped through the door and disappeared down the staircase. Hunter sighs, and briefly meets my gaze, before shifting to Cora's. He nods, and then follows her.

After confirming no one is paying any attention to us, we head down the stairs too. It's still loud and musky down here, but not as bad as upstairs. The room is dusty, and filled with broken, old furniture. In the middle of the room, suspended from the ceiling, is Theo. I recognise him from the pictures Hunter showed us earlier, when he was telling us about him. His wrists are bound by chains, and there is so much blood I can barely make out his face. I only recognise that ashy blond hair from the time I briefly met him on campus, when he was talking to Hunter that day I borrowed his pen.

'Baby!' Lucy exclaims, rushing toward him.

She barely makes it a few steps before four vampires step out from the shadows, one by one. I'm instantly wired, bracing myself as they flank Theo. I'm kicking myself that I didn't sense their presence as soon as we entered the room, but from the look of surprise on Hunter's and Cora's faces, I wasn't the only one.

I feel a shiver along the back of my neck as they fix their black eyes on me, and it's then that I realise that they were waiting for us. They knew we were coming.

'Hunter.' One of the men smiles, stepping forward. He is taller than the others, with messy, salt and pepper coloured hair, and black, lifeless eyes. Two fangs appear, and he holds his arms out in a welcoming pose, as if he has invited us over for tea. 'I've been a patient man waiting for you to come find us. You sure took your sweet-ass time.'

I glance at Hunter from the corner of my eye, and see the muscles of his jaw twitch as he stares at the vampires. His eyes linger on one of the men to the side, and I wonder if he recognises him. 'Who are you?' Hunter asks, although I'm sure he already knows who he is.

'Adrian Black.' The man smiles, tilting his head to the side as his eyes appraise Hunter slowly, looking darker than midnight sky under these dim lights. 'You may have heard of me.'

Hunter's chin jerks in a sharp nod. 'You're the one responsible for the dead bodies around town.'

Adrian offers a lazy shrug. 'The newbies had to have some practice, and a little fun.'

Hunter scoffs. 'Yeah. Right.'

'You see,' Adrian continues, stepping forward once more, placing his hands behind his back. 'Your friend here crossed me. And no one gets away with that.'

My eyes dart to Hunter, who stares unblinkingly back at Adrian, not giving anything away, his expression cold. He'd told me about Theo and about the woman Theo had fed on and left for dead. Theo didn't know at the time, but she belonged to a dangerous vampire. Adrian, to be more specific.

'What do you want?' Hunter asks, his voice firm, and a little frosty. A tone I have very rarely heard come from my bonded one's mouth.

'We want Theo,' he says matter-of-factly. 'And we don't want trouble from you.'

'That's never going to happen,' Hunter deadpans.

'Exactly.' The man nods in agreement. 'That's why I wanted you to come. So we can,' Adrian's lips twist into a wry smile, and he looks over to one of his men, as if they are having a silent conversation. 'Dispose of you.'

'Why not just kill Theo?' Cora interjects, raising an eyebrow, and having the audacity to cock her hip. 'Why are you keeping him here like your own, little pet? You knew we'd come for him. Why risk your own lives, keeping him alive?'

'I enjoy torturing the man who killed my girl,' Adrian snarls, stepping forward, looking as though he really doesn't appreciate Cora's two cents. 'And I cannot kill Theo because his maker is a vampire I don't dare to go up against.'

Hunter exhales. 'Kian. Of course.' His eyes glance to Cora. 'It always comes back to Kian.'

'Kian didn't make you?' Cora questions, turning to face Hunter, as if there aren't four malicious looking vampires sizing us up less than a few metres away.

Hunter shakes his head. 'Theo did.'

Slowly, Cora nods, looking surprisingly calm given that four vampires are inching closer to us with our deaths on their mind.

'So, you can't kill me, then.' Cora smiles, but as usual, it's cold and empty, not hosting any of the warmth it once had. 'Since he's my maker, too.'

'Maybe not,' one of the other vampires says, his shoulders broad enough that they're almost double the width of mine. 'But we can still hurt you.'

Cora's smile widens. 'Try it. I've been trained by the best psycho in town.'

'Cute,' Adrian replies mockingly. 'But having a smart mouth won't get you a head start around here.'

He lunges toward her, the other three on his heels. I duck, sliding across the floor on my knees. While the others fight, I swipe at the ankle restraints holding Theo and manage to break one of his legs free, before one of the vampires yanks me back by the shoulder. Turning, I kick him straight in the chest, launching him across the room.

I dive back towards Theo and unbolt the other shackle just as quickly. Next, I move up to his wrists, when my hair is pulled, snapping my head back so violently, I momentarily black out. Within seconds, I blink back awake, my neck aching, and as I look up, I see Hunter stake the man straight in the eye. Blood spurts over Hunter's face as he drives it so deeply that the sharp end appears through the back of the vampire's skull.

'Touch her again, and I'll chop your body into bits and feed it to you,' he snarls, and in that moment, I don't recognise him. I feel I might empty my stomach on the floor, but the adrenaline coursing through me pushes away the nausea, and I remind myself that this is not the time to freak out.

Leaping to my feet, I dart around them, and continue unchaining Theo. Groggily, his eyes blink open, and he peers at me.

'Bonded blood bag,' he chokes out, the corner of his mouth lifting. 'I have to say, I'm surprised to see you.'

'Thanks for such a warm welcome.' I huff, yanking him free with a grunt of effort, since the chains were harder to unlatch than I initially thought.

He drops to the ground like a bag of lead, too weak to even stand.

When a vampire runs at me, I duck and weave out of his way, realising that Lucy is no longer in the room. All three of us are fighting the three vampires that are here, with the one Hunter stabbed now dead, another stake deep in his chest – though I don't know who did that.

Grunting, I take a hit from a vampire that jars me to the core, and I stumble back a step.

'What's wrong with your eyes?' the vampire hisses at me, squinting, trying to get a closer look.

Taking advantage of his momentary distraction, I let him approach, waiting until we are only inches apart before I slam my forehead into his. He reels back, landing on his ass, his eyes wide as he grasps his shattered nose. I can't help but give him a satisfied smirk. As much as it hurt, it also felt really fucking good. For the first time in my life, I'm able to truly protect and depend on myself.

'Fucking bitch!' he hisses. Before I can retaliate, a blur of motion darts past me, and I almost shoot silver straight at Lucy as she whips around me, dragging a human with her. She throws the human at an almost unconscious Theo.

Turning to the vampire who is now advancing on me, Lucy hurls herself at him, knocking him to the ground.

'Stake him!' she demands, pinning his arms down.

Numbly, I yank the stake out of the dead vampire, the plastic handle smooth in my hand. Swiftly, I drop to one knee and slam the stake straight into his heart. My eyes never leave his as I watch the light fade within them before his head slumps to the side.

The door above the stairs bangs open, and another five or so vampires fly down the stairs, flooding the room.

'Oh, *shit*,' Lucy mutters, and she's off racing towards them head-first.

'Don't worry,' a voice whispers in my ear, and I yelp, turning to see Theo smirking down at me. Pretty silver eyes blink through the blood and grime that streak his face. He looks nothing like the almost-dead person he was a minute ago. 'We can take them.'

Fangs lengthening, he takes off, and I scream when he swings an axe – God knows where he even got that from – and beheads the blond, broad-shoulder vampire. The blood sprays across my face, and I stagger back, feeling repulsed and sickened at the sight before me. It truly is a bloodbath.

An arm wraps around me, dragging me backward and down onto the ground as the vampire behind me tries to snap my neck. This one I don't recognise, he must be one of the new-comers from upstairs.

Ramming my elbow into his side, I hear a satisfying crunch as his ribs crack. He loosens his hold just long enough for me to spin on my heel, and thrust the other stake I had stashed straight into his heart. A garbled noise escapes him as blood bubbles from his parted lips and he collapses to the floor.

A shriek to my left alerts me to another vampire lunging at me. Another one from upstairs. A wild afro of dark curls block my line of sight as he slams me hard against the wall. I jerk my head out of his grasp, and am distracted for a moment when I see two vampires advancing on Hunter.

Cora materialises, her eyes filled with rage as she hurtles towards the vampire pinning me. Before she can strike, he reaches out and grabs her by the throat, and in one swift motion, snaps her neck. I scream as she drops to the ground. Her dark hair spills across the floor, her dead eyes staring through me.

I try to get to her, but the vampire pins me once more, trying to get his hands around my neck to do the same thing to me. I make the mistake of grabbing his arms, and the vampire's lips twist into a sneer as he lunges at my exposed neck like a rabid wolf, tearing through my skin. Everything slows for a minute as he takes a long drink from me, and my eyes dim in and out of focus as I observe everyone around me.

Lucy, is being held down on the ground by a vampire with stunning ruby red hair, and murderous eyes that look darker than the depths of hell. Lucy grits her teeth, shoving with all her might. She turns her head, shouting for Theo.

Hunter grunts as two vampires slam into him from either side. Theo's chest heaves as his eyes bounce between the two as though unable to decide who needs his help the most.

After a moment, he runs to Hunter's side. His hand curls around the back of one of the vampire's necks, and he tugs it back so hard, the vampire's spine dislodges.

Snarling, the vampire gripping me reels back, slamming a fist into the side of my head.

The vampire pauses, blinking at me, as if only just truly seeing me. 'Your eyes . . .' he trails off, studying me intently. 'What the hell is wrong with your eyes?'

That's when I strike.

Flattening him onto his back, I drive the stake through his chest. He gasps as he claws at my hands, and I press harder against the blade, watching the blood squirt over my hands and pooling across the fabric of his shirt.

Wiping my hands madly across my skirt, I realise that was my last stake.

Theo and Hunter are swinging and grunting as they wrestle with the two vampires who seem to grow angrier by the second. When Lucy screams, I take off towards her, knocking the red-headed vampire off of her. Kicking my leg out, I slam my heel into her nose, which shatters on impact. Lucy gets to her knees, lifting her arms over her head before she slams the dagger down over and over again. I wince, shielding my face as best I can from the onslaught of blood. Lucy goes way beyond piercing the vampire's heart.

We stare at each other breathlessly, and she brushes her hair out of her eyes before we look over at the two boys as they continue their fight.

'He chose to go help Hunter,' Lucy whispers, face hardening. 'He always chooses Hunter over me.'

My heart sinks at the pain in her eyes.

'Hunter had two on one,' I try to justify. 'I don't think it was about *who*, rather than *how many*.'

Lucy lets out a scoff. 'No, he chose Hunter. After everything I have done for him . . .' Running a tongue over her teeth, she shakes her head, standing.

Theo and Hunter are quick to kill the last two vampires. The sudden silence left in the wake of our fighting is beyond eerie. Suddenly my legs start shaking and I lean heavily against the wall, trying to keep upright. Blood runs into my eyes, and when I close them, images of all the horrific things I just witnessed flash through my mind.

Forcing myself to move, I stumble toward Cora, falling to my knees. I roll her onto her back. She groans, rubbing her neck.

'Fucking stupid mother fucker,' she hisses, sitting upright, while glowering down at the dead vampire next to her. 'I'd kill you ten times over if you weren't already dead.'

Reaching for her, I yank her toward me, throwing my arms around her. I sob into her shoulder. Her shoulders tense, but after a second, she hugs me back. She runs her hand down the back of my head like she used to when I was little.

'It's okay,' she murmurs, and for the first time since she's been back, I let myself enjoy the comforting presence of her. 'It's done now. It's all done now.'

I feel Hunter before I see him. His presence wraps around me like a warm blanket, even though he isn't even touching me. He gently helps me to my feet.

'*Legata una*,' he murmurs, and I step back, taking a shaky breath. Those gorgeous eyes stare down at me, the mirror-image of my own, and the exact comfort and warmth I need right now. He opens his arms and I fall into them, pressing my cheek to his hard chest. He wraps his arms tightly around me, holding me to him.

His familiar scent makes it easier to breathe, and slowly, I detach from him. Staring around the room, I watch as everyone slowly assembles together, all looking like we just walked through a warzone.

'Well,' Theo says, planting his hands on his hips. 'Thanks for coming for me. Glad none of you died.' He grins, revealing two rows of shiny, white teeth amongst the blood and dirt that is covering every inch of him. 'Job well done, team.'

Cora breathes a laugh, shaking her head. 'Yeah, thanks.'

'Theo,' he says, throwing his hand out to her, letting it hover between them. 'How do you do?'

She stares down at it for a moment. 'Cora.'

'And who exactly are you, Cora?' Theo asks. 'Where do you fit in,' he continues, waving a lethargic hand in mine and Hunter's direction, 'with these guys?'

'I'm her sister,' Cora replies. 'And if I ever hear you call her a bonded blood bag again, I'll skin you and wear you like a coat.'

Theo's grin widens. 'Feisty. I like it.'

'Fuck. You.' A voice trembles, and we turn to see Lucy glaring at Theo. His face falls, crumpling in concern. She turns her back on us and flees the room faster than my eyes can barely keep up with.

Theo looks baffled as his eyes linger on the stairs for a moment. 'What the hell is her problem? Thought she would be happy to see me.'

'You chose to save Hunter over her,' I say. 'And probably because you just spoke to everyone here except her, and she was the one who rallied us together to rescue you.' I shrug. 'Just a wild guess.'

Theo has the audacity to roll his eyes, as if Lucy being upset is a major inconvenience for him right now.

'Why is she upset? We should be partying!' he protests, and I can't help but shake my head at him, my heart breaking for Lucy.

Cora pats Hunter on the shoulder. 'Great friends you have.'

'Hey!' Theo exclaims, looking offended.

'Let's get the fuck out of here,' Cora says, wiping her bloodied hands on her soiled dress. 'I'm starving.'

I mumble in agreement as she strides towards the stairs, although I'm unsure I could stomach anything after what just happened. As I place my foot on the bottom step, I look over my shoulder at the dead bodies scattered gruesomely across the dirty, cement floor.

'Raya.' Cora's voice is sharp as she stares down at me. 'Let's go.'

With a sigh, I walk up the stairs, trying my best to leave it all behind me.

42

HUNTER

The Protector

IT'S BEEN A FEW WEEKS since we returned to Red Thorne, and I can finally say that I enjoy the place. It's been different since I've been back. I know it's me. *I'm* what is different. It just seems . . . better. Less lonely, less cold, less isolated. And it's all because of the girl in front of me.

'You know what the best thing about drawing you is?' Raya asks, those hauntingly beautiful eyes peering at me over the edge of the paper, her sketchpad placed in front of her. It's a relatively warm day for Red Thorne, but still no sunlight peeks through the dark clouds.

Glancing over at her, I offer her a lazy smile. 'My perfect looks?'

She rolls her eyes. 'That, of course, but not what I meant.'

'What is the best thing?' I ask.

'You sit perfectly still. Makes it much easier to get your position right.' She sits back, and the seat groans a little. 'I'm done.'

Swinging my legs over the bench, I lean forward. 'Can I see?'

She flips the sketchpad. She is so damn talented. Every stroke is precise and clear, capturing this moment so well it looks a little unreal. She beams at me, sensing my approval.

'You're incredible,' I tell her.

'Thanks.'

Placing it down beside her, she stretches, crossing her ankles. 'So, can I know now?'

'Ah, yes,' I say, pushing to my feet. I've been dangling a secret over her head for the entire day now. Dropping into the space beside her, I pull out an envelope, handing it to her.

'What is this?' she frowns, narrowing her eyes at me.

I shrug. 'Open it.'

Eyebrows drawing together, she gently opens the envelope, and slides the letter out. The frown deepens as her eyes quickly scan over the page. Her mouth opens and closes several times before she looks at me.

'What is this . . .' she whispers, too scared to assume the letter is what she thinks it is.

Grinning, I nod. 'It's an acceptance letter.'

'I didn't apply for anything . . .' she trails off, eyes widening. 'An acceptance letter to what?'

'That art school you always wanted to go to. In London.'

Her jaw almost hits the floor. 'What – how – ?'

'The submission period had closed, but I managed to sneak your entry in.' I say. 'Other than a little nudge on my behalf, you got in purely from your talent. No tricks, no persuasion. All *you*. It's yours. If you want it.'

Her eyes close for a moment as she gathers herself. Blinking at me with teary eyes, she gives me a watery smile. 'I love you.'

'I love you,' I say softly. 'You're happy?'

'Too happy for words,' she whispers, and I lean forward, swiping my thumb across her cheek, collecting the tear sliding down it. 'When does the program start?'

'Not until early next year. I thought we could travel for a while. Start in Italy, visit my family, and then go from there. Wherever you want to go. And then we can move to London before your classes start.' I lean back, resting on my elbow. 'If that sounds like something you're interested in.'

Although Cora and Raya's relationship is on the mend, there's still a lot of progress to go, and the thing the both of them need right now is space, but neither wants to make the first move. Their bickering has returned, and I worry it may escalate into something toxic if something isn't done about it.

'This is a dream,' Raya says, shaking her head. 'It's too good to be true.'

'It's not a dream, *legata una*. Anything you want, is yours. All you have to do is ask.'

'Everything I want is right here.' She smiles, touching my face with her small, gentle hands. 'I just wish Alex was here, too.'

Moving my lips to her hand, I kiss her.

'He's here. He'll always be here.' I lean forward, placing a hand on her chest. 'Always with you. No matter what.'

The tears flow easily down her cheeks now and she nods. 'Yes. He is.'

Wrapping my arm around her shoulders, I draw her close to me.

'So,' she says after a moment, sniffling. 'When do we go?'

'I'm ready when you are.'

Theo is throwing us a 'going away' party. The house is filled with people I've never met. Some I recognise from classes, but mostly they're people I've never seen before. Which isn't a surprise. That's Theo's style. He likes numbers. The higher the better, he always says.

'You know, I'm surprised you're not throwing more of a fit,' I say to Theo when he wanders over to me, slinging an arm around my shoulder. The top few buttons of his shirt are unbuttoned and his hair is tousled. Since he just came from his room and two human girls followed shortly after, I can only imagine what he's been doing while I was out getting supplies.

Lucy left him. I wasn't surprised. Their relationship has been a whirlwind of toxicity from start to finish. He's not taking it well, not that he would ever admit it to anyone. He can't even admit it to himself how much it hurt him.

'I'll miss you, but I'm happy for you. You were miserable here, and I know the power Kian has over me won't work if I protest you staying. You're better off gone.' He smiles, and for once, he's taking our conversation seriously. 'I just wish I wasn't stuck here.'

I don't want to leave him again, but he has assured me it's the right thing to do.

'I wish I could track Kian down and convince him to lift this compulsion off of you.' I exhale, shaking my head, feeling helpless and frustrated. 'It's not fair, binding you to this town, and for what? No fucking valid reason, that's for sure.'

'Well, you know your brother, he loves to have control over everything.' Theo takes a long swig of his beer. 'He probably has some fucked up plan for me. Something he wants me to do for him.'

Briefly, I wonder if Dante has had any success finding my brother, and acting out his revenge plans. My heart aches for him, and his loss.

'How do we know Dante didn't get him?' I ask, spinning to face my best friend. 'Have you tried to leave?'

'I test it every night, brother.' Theo sighs. 'He's alive. I'd know if he was dead.'

I nod. 'One can only hope.'

'Anyway,' Theo says, finishing his drink and tossing it in the bin beside him. 'Don't stress about me. I'll be fine.'

'Hey,' I say, lowering my voice, and leaning in a little, hoping the loud music drowns out this part of our conversation, if anyone happens to be listening in. 'I actually have a favour to ask you.'

'Anything,' Theo says, looking at me curiously.

'Will you look out for Cora? She's planning to stay around, and since you're here . . .' I shrug. 'I'd appreciate it.'

Theo looks over at Cora, who is doing a body shot off a shirtless guy on our dining room table. He raises his eyebrows.

'Er . . .' He clears his throat, looking a mixture between amused, a little reluctant, and also impressed. 'Sure. I guess. Can't exactly leave town to do anything better anyway.'

I nod at him. 'Thank you.'

Leaning back against the wall, I survey the growing crowd. My eyes locate Raya. She throws her head back and laughs at something one of the other revellers say, and my heart feels full at the sight of her smile. She will be grieving and dealing with everything that has happened for a long time, but she is strong, and will get through it. Like she once told me, she's got this.

'It's nice seeing you happy, man,' Theo says, nudging me. 'I can't remember seeing you happy. It's been . . . well . . . years.'

'I've struggled a lot,' I admit. 'And I'm sorry that I took my moods out on you when you just needed your best friend.'

'I wasn't very considerate, or understanding of what you were going through,' Theo says, and I turn to him in shock. He has never been honest with me like this. Or at least, not since we turned, and our lives changed so much. 'I'm sorry.'

'I'm sorry, too.'

'I'm not jumping with joy that you are replacing me, but if I had to be replaced, she isn't the *worst* choice,' Theo says, his lips spreading into a thin line. 'She would die for you. I like that.'

I snort. 'How could I replace you, Theo?'

Theo smirks, lifting another beer to his lips. 'Exactly. No one can compare.'

I laugh. 'Totally.'

Theo reaches for one of the bottles in the bucket of ice near us, and silently hands me one. I take it, twisting off the cap, and take a long sip. The beer is cold and crisp, and I take long, greedy gulps.

'How are you doing?' I ask. 'With Lucy gone.'

'It's done,' he says dismissively, not meeting my eyes. 'Time to move on.'

'Right.'

Ignoring me, Theo pushes off the wall. 'I'm going to mingle.'

'Who are these people?' I ask, arching a brow.

'Don't know.' Theo shrugs. 'Don't care.'

He weaves through the bodies and pauses when he sees a girl dressed in a fiery red dress dancing. He smirks down at her, and I shake my head.

I'm alone for barely a minute before Cora strides up to me, shoving a shot glass in my hand. She smacks her glass into mine.

'Cheers,' she mutters, and throws it back.

I mimic her and then place the empty glass down onto the table. When I look back up, she is squinting at me.

'Can I help you?' I question.

'You look after her,' she demands, pointing a finger at me.

'You know I will,' I say flatly, noticing that she is swaying slightly.

'I mean it, Hunter.'

'So do I.'

She blows out a breath, moving to my side, and sagging back against the wall.

'You okay?' I ask, knowing that's a stupid question when she clearly isn't, but much like Theo, she would rather pretend nothing is wrong, rather than face the problem head on.

'Yup,' she says, rolling her lips into her mouth, and brushing the dark strands of her hair out of her eyes.

'Are you okay with Raya going?' I ask.

'Yes.' She nods. 'It will be good for her. She deserves it.' Running a tongue across her teeth, her eyes flick to mine. 'You make her happy, and that's what is most important.'

'Are you still planning to stay here?'

'Yeah. I don't care much for where I live. I like it here. I want to get my head back on straight. Get a job, or go back to study. Or both. Just try to live as normal of a life as I can. That's all I want right now.'

'I think that's the mistake most vampires make. They think they are beyond all the mundane day-to-day stuff. But life gets boring when you don't do things to keep you busy.'

'Yeah,' she says. 'That makes sense. The years just keep on coming when you're a vampire. I can see how life could get dull if you get everything you want all the time.'

'Exactly.'

I watch as Cora gazes over towards Raya and I see a little bit of her frostiness melt away.

'Do you think we will ever go back to how things were before?' Cora asks, folding her arms across her chest. 'Between Raya and I?'

'Maybe not, but I think you will resolve things in time,' I reply honestly. 'And time is something we have.'

'I hope so,' she murmurs softly, chewing her lip.

The front door swings open, and a prickle of awareness rolls down my spine. I stiffen, snapping my head up to see Dante step inside. He's dressed in a casual T-shirt and faded jeans, his long hair pulled into a low bun.

'What the hell is he doing here?' Cora hisses, instinctively stepping closer to me.

Dante's eyes search through the bodies and land on mine. He stills for a moment, and then nods, raising his hands in a peace-like gesture. Unhurriedly, he strolls toward me, and Theo and Raya flock to our sides instantaneously, sensing his arrival, too.

'Evening,' Dante greets us, his voice deep, rumbling from somewhere in his chest. 'I don't mean to intrude.'

'Hi, Dante.' Raya smiles kindly at him. 'How are you?'

'Been better.' He smiles tightly. 'I just wanted to let you know that Kian got away. I've lost all trace of him, yet again.' He throws a hand through his hair, looking weary. 'Wish I had better news.'

'I'm sorry,' I say to him. 'I know how important this was to you.'

Looking down at his feet, he nods. 'I'm hoping that if any of you hear anything about his whereabouts, that you might contact me?'

'Of course,' I say.

Dante looks relieved. Pulling out his phone, he hands it over to me, and I program mine and Raya's numbers into it before passing it around the group for everyone to do the same.

'Thanks,' he says, shoving it back into his pocket. 'That's all, I guess.'

'Stay,' Cora suggests. 'Have a drink. You look like you could use one.'

Dante looks surprised at this.

'A friend of Hunter's is a friend of mine,' Theo says, clapping Dante on the back like they have been buddies for years. 'Stay as long as you'd like.'

'Thank you.' Dante bows his head.

Cora and Theo disappear into the crowd while Raya and I pull up a chair at the table. Dante drops into the one beside me, resting back into it.

Raya pulls out a beer, passing one to Dante, and then one to me. Simultaneously, we crack it open. Dante tilts his drink toward me, and I clink mine with his.

'To new beginnings,' I say.

'Cheers to that,' he murmurs, and silently, we all take a sip.

43

RAYA

The Survivor

THE DOOR CLICKS SOFTLY shut behind us. Hunter and I have been living in Theo's house with him and Cora for the past few weeks. I couldn't bear to go back to the apartment Alex and I shared. It was too soon, and I didn't want to deal with that. Besides, I like having the company of the others, especially since we are leaving and won't see them for a while.

Wandering into the garage, I place a hand on Alex's car. Sighing heavily, I lean forward, pressing my lips to it.

'I love you,' I whisper, my heart feeling full and heavy as I think about Alex's face lighting up when he saw the car for the first time. 'I miss you every day.'

'It's just a car, dude.'

I jerk my head up at the sound of Theo's voice, and frown at him. He grins, that shit-eating, teasing grin he always has on his face.

'Kidding, Ray Ray. I'll keep good care of it.'

'Don't call me that,' I mutter, making a repulsed face at the stupid nickname he insists on calling me.

Shaking my head, I turn to leave, but take one more moment to look back at it. Smiling sadly, I follow Theo out to the front of the house, each step feeling like I'm walking through mud.

Hunter is carrying our luggage towards the car, piling it into the back. Cora and I said our goodbyes this morning. It was an emotional one. I still don't know how I feel about leaving her here. I did offer for her to come with us, but she said she wants time to herself to figure things out. Hunter assured me Theo will be looking out for her, so I feel better about that. I think. Dante has been in and out the past few weeks as well, and I feel better knowing he is keeping an eye on the pair of them, too. He doesn't have ill intentions towards anyone, except Kian, and that is totally justifiable.

Theo throws his arms around Hunter in a tight embrace, and holds him for a long few seconds.

'I love you,' Theo says – a little aggressively – and plants his hands on Hunter's shoulders. 'Be safe. Call when you can. And send me postcards from every country you go to.'

Hunter smiles. 'I will.'

Turning to me, he offers me a small smile. 'You too, Ray Ray. Be safe, and have fun.' I step into his arms as he gives me a brief hug. 'Don't do anything I wouldn't do.'

Hunter snorts at that, and I grin. 'Sure thing.'

'Farewell friends!' Theo cries out dramatically.

Rolling our eyes affectionately, we climb into the car. Hunter starts the engine, and I settle back into the seat, feeling nervous. I've never travelled overseas before. This is a whole new adventure for me, but I can't be more excited about it. I'm ready for this.

'We're really doing this?' I say.

Hunter reaches over, taking my hand in his. He brings it to his lips, leaving a tender kiss on my knuckles.

'We sure are. Are you ready?'

'Absolutely.'

As we cruise through town, I let myself recall the moments I shared with Alex, and my heart bleeds at the thought of him. I miss him terribly, and I wish he was here for this, doing this with us. I can almost hear his voice from the back seat, making sarcastic remarks and it makes me smile.

We drive past the sign on the edge of town Alex and I saw when we first arrived, and I peer out at it.

'*Welcome to Red Thorne. A town you will never want to leave!*'

Ironic, since that is exactly what we are doing.

It's hard to imagine any of this playing out the way it did. Not long ago, it was Alex and I arriving here on the dingy train in the middle of the night. It now feels like a lifetime has passed.

Leaning my head back, I squeeze Hunter's hand.

Ever since my family was gone, I've been so lost, like I had a hole in my heart that never quite healed. A part of me that was broken, and incomplete.

Now, with my sister back, and Hunter by my side, I truly and whole-heartedly feel put together again.

I can't wait to see what the next chapter holds for us.

EPILOGUE

CORA

I'M EXHAUSTED BY THE TIME I walk through the front door. Tossing my keys onto the bench, I kick off my shoes, and head straight to the bathroom for a shower.

When I told myself to keep busy, I didn't realise how much I had actually crammed in my schedule. Classes from nine to three and then working a shift at the diner from four until ten.

I wanted to feel human again, and I am definitely feeling that right now.

Shedding my clothes, I turn my music on, step into the cubicle, and sigh as the hot water runs over my muscles, easing the tension out of the knots that had built through the day. It streaks through my hair and I tip my head back, running my fingers through it. Since I have trouble sleeping, the fatigue weighing me down makes me weaker than I should be. I'm also going too long without blood. Some sort of fucked up self-punishment, I guess.

The first few weeks after Raya left were hard. I felt so lost. Theo and I wandered around that big house aimlessly, both of us not quite sure what to do. So we drank, we fed, we blacked out together a few times. Bonding, some might say. But I decided I didn't want that for myself anymore. So, I moved out to my own little house with a lawn, garden, and even a small backyard and patio. I like it. It's plenty of space for me, and I like being on my own. It's peaceful.

Wrapping my fluffy robe around me, I shuffle toward my bed and faceplant into it, not even bothering to turn my music off. It's always playing. Probably too loudly, but I don't care. It numbs my thoughts, and that's what I need. I need the lyrics, and the beat to keep out the nightmares that plague me at night. Thinking of all those times Kian forced me to do cruel, awful things . . . I shudder at the thought, and push it deep into the back of my mind, into a box I don't plan on opening any time soon. Or ever.

The sound of the garbage truck collecting the bins startles me awake, which means I've slept way later than normal, since they come unusually late in this town. I had been running on empty all week, and it has caught up with me. My wet hair clings to me, and my robe has come loose, meaning my breasts are on full display, and I didn't even close my windows last night. Wincing, I roll off the mattress and pad towards the window, pulling the drapes shut. I yawn, rubbing my eyes.

Dressing into my workout clothes, I pull my hair into a ponytail, and step out onto the porch. It's a dark, gloomy day as usual. It's Friday, which means there should be something from Raya in the mail. It's sweet how they send old fashioned letters and postcards. They send something to me and Theo every week. Sometimes it's gifts and sometimes it's souvenirs from wherever they have recently travelled to. It's something I look forward to every week.

Eagerly, I open my letterbox, seeing something sticking out of it.

Grinning, I rip it open, and read over the postcard. This one is from Paris. Reading over my sister's familiar, neat scrawl, I lean my hip on the letterbox as I read about their latest adventures. I bring it to my chest and hold it there for a moment, the ache of missing her burning deep inside me. I'm happy that she is happy, but I miss her terribly.

Frowning, I notice another letter sitting inside. Pulling it out, I flip over the envelope, but it doesn't have anything written on it. I tear it open and inch the piece of paper out.

I haven't forgotten about you.
You still owe me nine years.
I'll be coming to collect.
See you soon, Cora.

The blood drains from my face as I read it over and over.

Swallowing thickly, I quietly close the lid of the letterbox and walk stiffly back into my house, my skin prickling uneasily. A shiver runs down my spine. My mind races as I slip inside, closing the door behind me, unable to shake the feeling that someone is watching me.

Kian.

THANK YOU

THANK YOU SO MUCH for reading *Die For You*. I really hope you enjoyed Raya and Hunter's story. I love writing romance novels, and always loved reading about vampires, so I thought why not combine both and create my own!

I loved immersing myself in this world and I hope you enjoyed reading it as much as I enjoyed writing it.

Thank you!

ACKNOWLEDGMENTS

FIRST AND FOREMOST, I'd like to thank the readers – thank you from the bottom of my heart for picking up this book and embracing Raya and Hunter's story. Thank you for your love, support, encouragement, and reviews. I will be forever grateful for your support.

I have always loved romance books, especially vampire romance books (I totally never grew out of it), and when I had this idea come to me in a dream, I knew I had to do something with it. I remember sitting around a table with some of the girls from my book club as I told them about the dream, and then the ideas snowballed from there. It was definitely nerve-racking in the beginning since I have never written anything like this before, but I had so much fun doing it!

Thank you to my friends, family, and partner, who have dealt with endless questions, ideas, and offering me much appreciated feedback.

A massive, massive thank you to my beautiful BETA readers – Becka, Libby, Lexi, Sydni, and Haley. This book wouldn't be where it is today without you and I appreciate you forever for all your feedback, advice, and everything else you have done for me.

A huge thank you to Genicious – the person who always answers all my questions and has been one of the most supportive friends I have ever had. Thank you for helping me with all my questions, formatting, and teaching me your ways. I am forever grateful!

My amazing friends who have given me feedback and crucial advice that has helped shape me as a writer and has motivated me to be where I am today – thank you Kenadee, Jess, SJ, and Jordan.

My editor, Liz Butcher for her incredible help. To BooksnMoods and Ashley Marie, my cover designers, for their amazing work. To Jordan Lynde, an amazing friend and supporter of mine, who did a final proofread for me.

To all the bloggers, reviewers, and BookTok accounts that have gone above and beyond to show their support. I can't ever tell you thank you enough.

Thank you!

ABOUT THE AUTHOR

LAUREN JACKSON lives in a small coastal town in Australia. Her hobby of writing stories developed into a passion when she discovered the website Wattpad at fourteen. Since 2012, she has garnered thousands of followers and millions of views on her stories, which helped her grow and develop her love for writing. She lives close to the beach with her partner and little dog, Ace. Lauren loves to write sweet, steamy romances, and is always writing a new book.

Stay tuned for more!

LET'S BE SOCIAL!

IF YOU'D LIKE TO keep up to date with me, please follow me on social media!

Instagram: @laurenjacksonauthorr
TikTok: @laurenjacksonauthorr
Website: laurenjacksonauthor.com
Goodreads: goodreads.com/user/show/18315357-lauren

Can you ever really
run from your past
or change your destiny?

MEANT
to be

LAUREN JACKSON
AUSTRALIA'S OWN ROMANCE WRITING SENSATION

MEANT TO BE

A steamy new adult romance perfect for fans of Ana Huang, Lucy Score, Tessa Bailey and Monica Murphy.

Josie Mayor fled Fern Grove after a scandal that rocked the town, turning her back on her friends and family. She disappeared with no contact, no forwarding address and abandoned the only life she knew.

Now she's back and has to confront what she left behind. When Josie runs into her ex-boyfriend, Nick, and Harley, the boy who stole her heart, she is faced with the pain and heartache of a past she's desperate to forget. Josie must make a choice in doing what's best for her, or risk repeating history once more.

Read on for an extract of *Meant To Be*

1

JOSIE

FERN GROVE. A PLACE I longed to escape. A place I wish I had never come back to.

I pull my car over near the *Welcome to Fern Grove* sign and spray my windows with windshield wiper fluid. The dust smears across them, making it harder to see out than before. Giving up, I continue on my way.

Peering out of the non-smudged section, I pass the sugar mill, the old petrol station, and the café that my mother used to take me to every Sunday morning. Everything looks the same. I follow the familiar route – one I couldn't forget, no matter how hard I tried – ending up at a long gravel road.

Dad's rust-spotted truck is parked where it always is, my mum's SUV and my brother's Subaru beside it. Sam's car is the only one to have changed in the four years I've been gone. He wrapped his last one around a telegraph pole – or so I read on Facebook.

It's only a moment after I cut the engine that humid air fills the car, causing my shirt to feel damp. I exhale, staring at the old, peeling house. If I'd taken a picture the day I left, not one thing in that picture would be different in the one I'd take now.

I really hate that.

My reflection in the side mirror catches my attention as I step outside the car. I flinch at the sight of it. I don't recognise myself. The roundness I used to get teased about at school is gone, replaced with a sharp jawline and gaunt cheeks.

Birds cry from the trees, and I hear Mum's radio blaring as I approach the front screen door, hanging on its final hinges, already partially open. I look at the gap between the door and the porch, thinking it would be far too easy for snakes to enter. Many times, I woke up to find one slithering across our lounge room floor or hiding in my bookshelves.

I knock once, then twice, before entering. The weathered floorboards groan under my weight. There was once a time I had memorised which ones squeaked and which didn't, in my attempts to sneak out uncaught . . .

I barely take a breath as I tiptoe down the stairs, dancing over the floorboards as I reach the front door. Slowly, I swing it open. The warm night air washes over my skin before strong arms wrap around me, dragging me close.

He smells like cigarettes and whisky. Two scents a teenage boy shouldn't smell like, but it's a scent that's become familiar to me. A comforting smell that lingers on my hoodies and stains my pillow after we spend hours together.

'Did you wear that for me?' he asks.

A shiver rolls down my spine. My eyes dart down to the spaghetti-strap white dress that hugs my waist and shows off my legs. 'Yes,' I whisper.

His lips curve. He leans in close, his breath warm against my earlobe. 'Good.'

The smell of baked goods guides me to the kitchen, and I mentally shake off the memories that are threatening to take over. I eye the walls, the faded wallpaper, the hanging photo frames. Everything feels too familiar, too small, too cluttered.

I pause. It looks like one thing has changed after all. My photographs on the walls. They're gone. I trail my finger down one of the dusty frames, seeing my mum, dad, and brother smiling back at me. My finger drifts to the empty spot beside them, where I should have been.

Sweat drips down the side of my face and I wipe it away. The heat is almost unbearable. I begged for years for air-conditioning or even ceiling fans. I glance to the ceilings, seeing nothing but accumulated dust and cobwebs.

Mum is humming under her breath, bent at the knees, inspecting something inside the oven. She slams the door shut and spins on her heels.

Our eyes lock.

The glass of water in her hand slips, shattering on the floor. 'Josephine,' she whispers. She blinks. Her eyes dart over me.

I'm much thinner than I used to be. My skin washed out, hair flat on my shoulders.

Mum creeps closer to me as if scared to make any sudden movements. 'Is this real?'

My eyes feel watery as I nod.

Her gaze roams my face, focusing on my black eye. 'Oh, honey,' she whispers. 'You're okay. You're safe now.'

I fall into her arms and cry all the tears I've held in for so long.

2

HARLEY

THE HAMMER SLAMS ONE, two, three times before the nail is all the way in. The sun is unrelenting as it beats down on my back. I drag the back of my hand over my forehead and stand, my legs protesting from being in one position too long.

'Kid,' my supervisor George roars over the sound of whirring machinery. 'Take a break.'

Kid. I've worked for his construction company for almost four years, only a few months shy of finishing my apprenticeship. I work the longest hours, carry the most weight, and climb the highest cranes. And he still calls me *kid*.

Cupping my hand in a half-moon shape over my eyes, my gaze settles on a familiar ute parked in the lot. My father's car. He must be inside the break room. Exhaling, I shake my head and throw a sloppy wave towards George, indicating I'm not taking a break.

'Suit yourself!' he shouts, shaking his head before disappearing inside.

My throat screams for water, but I'd rather pass out from dehydration than be in close proximity to my father. It's been hard enough earning respect from these guys just from sharing his last name, let alone if they overheard the way he speaks to me.

It's not like they don't know. Everyone knows. But I'd rather not have one of our fights happen with a front-row audience.

Turning my back to the shed they've established as the break room, I continue working. Sweat drips into my eyes, and the sting makes me wince. I rub them heavily and sigh deeply through my nose. I glance down at my watch.

Only six hours to go.

An hour-and-a-half after my shift has ended, the sun is slowly sinking into the horizon.

Slinging my arms over the handles of my bike, I turn the lighter over in my fingers, watching the glint off the gunmetal-grey shell. I strike my thumb against it and light the end of my cigarette. Settling it between my teeth, I suck in a deep breath and tilt my head back, letting the smoke pour from my lips and fade into the breeze.

My phone beeps. Brennon, most likely. My best friend of fourteen years, roommate of three.

Brennon: Drinks tonight?

Pushing my hand through my hair, I let my head hang forward. I should want to do this. Be social. Interact. But everything is so *dull* here. The people. This place. Everything that is Fern Grove. Nothing interests me anymore.

It's time to move on. But to where? To do what?

A few more months, a voice whispers. Your apprenticeship is almost finished. Just hang in there a little longer.

I've been telling myself this for two years now. After a few too many beers and a breakdown yesterday, I packed my bags. They're stuffed inside my closet, hiding from Brennon's prying eyes. I'm so close to walking away from this place. I just don't have anywhere to go.

I shove my phone back in my pocket. Brennon's lack of work ethic frustrates the hell out of me. He's grown up in the safety net of wealth. He's never had to work to survive, and it shows.

Every muscle in my body hurts. Working 6 am to 4 pm in construction, and then 6 pm to 10 pm at the pub makes my body ache like it never has before. On days like this, it doesn't seem worth it. But it is. The more financially independent I am, the sooner I can get the hell out of here. And never come back.

The bike rumbles to life, and I ride directly to work. Shrugging out of my leather jacket, I swing it over a chair in the break room before grabbing my key tag. I swipe the tag over the sensor and punch in my code.

'Evening,' Graham, the owner of the bar, greets me. Crow's feet wrinkles sit at the corners of his eyes and his beard has grown longer and scruffier in the past six months than I've ever seen before.

'Hey,' I reply.

He looks tired as he passes me, clapping me on the shoulder before going out the back to clock off. My eyes settle on the bar, near empty except for a couple of locals in the pokies room.

The pub is small and run-down, but that goes for basically all places in this town. It doesn't make much sense to renovate when the town doesn't get any tourists.

Robotically, I wipe down the tables, restock the fridges, and empty the dishwasher. When no more people have entered in the last hour, I rest against the bar and pull out my phone. I search for rooms to rent, making the radius a minimum of four hours from here. My thumb slides over the screen as I scroll, and I feel deflated when I see the prices of rentals.

Fern Grove is affordable, and I halve the rent with Brennon, but when I move on my own, it will all be on me. As daunting as it is, it's a goal I'm committed to achieving. I can't stand to be here any longer and I'm willing to make just about any sacrifice to get out. My loyalty to Brennon has been a big reason for me staying, but honestly, it's not enough anymore.

The bell dings, indicating the arrival of customers, and I glance up to see Nick. Sighing, I slide my phone into my back pocket and move towards the register. Even after all these years, Nick and I have never comfortably met eyes.

My gaze dips over his neat button-up shirt and beige slacks. I don't really have a valid reason for hating him, but I do.

'Your usual?' I ask.

'Yeah.'

Curling my hand around the schooner glass, I place it under the tap and hold it. I push it across the counter. He slides his card into the machine – which doesn't have payWave because Graham refuses to modernise, even in the most basic form – and it takes several moments to flash approval. Without a word, Nick slinks over to the table furthest from the bar, where his father is already seated.

My gaze drifts towards the wet floor sign, and I'm half tempted to race past it, so I fall and bang my head hard enough to enter a coma for a few days. Or a year.

Discover a
new favourite

Visit **penguin.com.au/readmore**